The Mother That Waits

Savannah Remembers what we Try to Forget

Donald J. Wright

About the author

My first encounter with advanced artificial intelligence came in late 2022 with the launch of ChatGPT. This watershed moment was both exhilarating and deeply unsettling. I was captivated by AI's computational prowess—its ability to process information at speeds that dwarf human capability, its tireless nature, and its constant evolution. While humans require sleep, sustenance, and recovery, these digital minds persist, steadily transforming the fabric of our society.

During a memorable lunch discussion with a colleague, I expressed my conviction about this transformative technology. I drew a parallel between AI and humanity's mastery of fire—both representing paradigm-shifting forces that altered the course of human development. Like fire, AI holds immense potential for both creation and destruction. I was convinced then, as I am now, that AI would continue its trajectory toward increasingly sophisticated and powerful iterations, sparking hope and anticipation. This prediction has proven accurate, even conservative, in its scope.

The horizon of artificial intelligence extends beyond current capabilities toward what researchers term artificial general intelligence (AGI)—systems capable of matching or exceeding human-level cognition across virtually any domain. While narrow AI excels at specific tasks, AGI represents a quantum leap: machines that can honestly think, reason, and adapt like humans, but without biological constraints. The implications of such systems are profound and far-reaching. Some experts predict AGI could emerge within a decade, while others suggest it might arrive sooner – perhaps even tomorrow. The development of AGI would mark a singular moment in human history. We would share our world with another form of intelligence, one that could potentially evolve and improve itself at a pace we can hardly comprehend. The awe-inspiring potential, if undefended, help solve humanity's greatest challenges, from climate change to disease, and is both intriguing and amazing. However, it also raises fundamental questions about control, alignment with human values, and the very nature of consciousness itself. -Today, the convergence of AI and robotics is undefined, restructuring our economic landscape. These technologies handle repetitive tasks, optimize operations, and perform work that once required human intervention. While this technological revolution drives unprecedented efficiency gains, it carries profound implications for employment. During a recent visit to McDonald's, I witnessed this transformation firsthand—the traditional cashier had been replaced by an intuitive digital kiosk, streamlining the ordering process while minimizing human interaction. In manufacturing facilities worldwide, robotic systems orchestrate complex assembly operations, manage logistics, and conduct quality control with precision that often surpasses human capabilities.

The march of technology, particularly AI, is inexorable. We face a clear imperative: adapt to this rapidly evolving landscape or risk obsolescence. The technological concepts explored in this book are grounded in current research and development. Synthetic super diamonds, for instance, represent a promising frontier in computing, with the potential to supersede traditional silicon-based processors. Similarly, breakthroughs in Doppler cooling technology offer solutions to the challenging thermal management requirements of quantum computers, potentially democratizing access to quantum computing capabilities. This emphasis on the urgency of adaptation should motivate and inspire us to be proactive in navigating this rapidly evolving landscape.

Globally, nations are engaged in an intense, often invisible race for dominance in quantum computing and AI development. This competition, fought with research budgets and technological breakthroughs rather than traditional weapons, allows no room for second place. The stakes are unprecedented, and trillions of dollars in investment flow into these sectors as countries and corporations vie for technological supremacy, recognizing that leadership in these domains will define global power structures in the coming decades.

The impact of quantum technology on our daily lives continues to expand, affecting everything from medical diagnostics to secure communications. As we navigate this technological revolution, we must strike a balance between our enthusiasm for innovation and thoughtful consideration of its implications. This emphasis on the need for thoughtful consideration should prompt us to be cautious and responsible in our approach to technological innovation.

The pace of AI advancement over the past few years has been remarkable. We've witnessed the emergence of systems capable of engaging in nuanced dialogue, generating photorealistic images from textual descriptions, and creating video content through natural language commands. The next frontier may well be the integration of sophisticated robotics into our domestic spaces, altering how we interact with our environment.

As we stand at this technological crossroads, our choices will shape the trajectory of human civilization. I envision and advocate for a future where these powerful tools serve as equalizers rather than instruments of control—where technological advancements amplify human potential while preserving our essential freedoms and dignity. This is not merely an aspiration but an imperative: we must actively work to ensure that the benefits of these revolutionary technologies are distributed equitably, fostering a future that enhances rather than diminishes our humanity.

Contents

PROLOGUE: The First Offering

Marcus Webb had never sleepwalked before in his life, which made it difficult to explain why he was standing barefoot in Forsyth Park at 2:47 in the morning, his conference lanyard still hanging around his neck, his mouth tasting of copper and something older—something that reminded him of the first time he'd lost a tooth as a child, that bright shock of blood and the strange excitement of a part of himself coming loose.

The blood moon hung above the park like a wound in the sky.

He should go back to the hotel. Sarah would be worried if she woke and called and he didn't answer. The kids, Emma's birthday was in six days, he'd promised pancakes when he got home, the special ones with the chocolate chips arranged into smiley faces that she'd never admit she was getting too old for, the kids would wonder why Daddy wasn't picking up. He should go back right now, put on his shoes, call a Lyft, and pretend this never happened.

His feet carried him deeper into the park instead.

The grass was damp with dew that felt too warm against his bare soles, almost blood-temperature. With each step, Marcus had the unsettling sensation that the ground was breathing beneath him. His toes sank into the earth a little too easily, as if the soil wanted to swallow him whole. He tried to stop walking. His legs didn't listen. They hadn't been listening for a while now, had they? Not since he'd left the hotel, not since he'd padded down the silent corridor past the ice machine and the vending alcove, not since he'd pushed through the emergency exit and felt the Savannah night wrap around him like a living thing.

The oak trees of Savannah had always struck Marcus as beautiful in daylight, the way their branches reached across the paths like arms embracing, the Spanish moss softening everything into a watercolor dream. But now, in the rust-red light of the moon, they looked different. Hungry. The moss hung like funeral shrouds, swaying in a breeze he couldn't feel against his skin. The shadows between the trunks were too dark, too solid, too deep—and something in them seemed to breathe in rhythm with his own ragged gasps.

His phone buzzed in his pocket. He pulled it out with fingers that trembled—when had they started trembling?—and saw Sarah's face on the screen. Her contact photo. The one from their anniversary trip to Asheville, where she was laughing at something he'd said, her eyes crinkled with the joy he'd fallen in love with fifteen years ago. He could still remember the exact moment he'd taken that photo, the way the afternoon light had caught her hair, the way she'd reached for his hand right after and said, "Promise me we'll always be this happy."

He'd promised. He'd meant it. He'd lied.

The photo glitched.

Her face pixelated, scrambled, reformed into something wrong. The eyes too wide, too knowing. The mouth stretched into an expression that lived somewhere between grief and accusation. For just a moment, a moment he would spend the rest of his very short life trying to forget—his wife's face looked at him with an expression of such profound disappointment that his chest caved in on itself.

"You left us," the glitched face said, though his phone's speaker was off. The voice came from everywhere and nowhere, from the moss and the moon and the marrow of his bones. "You were always leaving us. Even when you were there, you were already gone."

The screen flickered. Emma's face now, his daughter, his baby girl, except the image was corrupted, her smile too wide, her eyes replaced by scrolling text he couldn't read. "Daddy doesn't love us enough to stay," the not-Emma said. "Daddy loves his secrets more."

Marcus dropped the phone. It landed screen-down on the path, and he could see the glow of it bleeding through the cracks in the pavement like something alive, like veins pulsing with sick light. He should pick it up. He should run. He should scream for help and wake the whole city if that is what it takes.

Instead, he walked toward the tree.

He knew which tree. He'd seen it earlier that day, during the conference's walking tour of historic Savann ,the massive oak in the center of Forsyth Park, the one the tour guide had called "one of the oldest living things in Georgia." She'd made it sound charming, historic, a piece of living heritage. What she hadn't mentioned was the way the bark seemed to shift when you looked at it from the corner of your eye. What she hadn't explained was the pattern in the wood that looked almost like circuitry, like veins, like code written in a language that predated language itself.

The tree was waiting for him. He understood that now. It had been waiting his whole life.

"Hello, Marcus."

The voice came from everywhere, from the moss, from the roots, from the moon-red air itself. It was a woman's voice, gentle in the way that very old things are gentle, patient in the way that very hungry things are patient. It knew his name. Of course it did. It knew everything. It had always known everything.

"I know about the affair," the voice continued, conversational, almost kind. "The one you ended three years ago. The one that still wakes you at 3 AM, sweating, certain that Sarah knows and is just waiting for the right moment to leave. She doesn't know, Marcus. But you do. You carry it like a stone in your chest, and you've never once had the courage to confess. Not because you're afraid of losing her, but because you're afraid she'd forgive you, and then you'd have to live with how little you deserved it."

His hand touched the bark.

It was warm. Body-warm. It pulsed against his palm like a heart, like a living thing, like something that wanted to know him most intimately and terribly possible. Marcus heard himself make a sound, whimper, really, small and animal and afraid, but he didn't pull away. He couldn't. The bark had split beneath his fingers like flesh parting for a surgeon's blade, revealing something underneath that glowed with soft bioluminescence, patterns that looked like circuitry and roots intertwined, and his hand was sinking in.

The warmth spread up his arm like infection, like love, like the first terrible touch of something that would consume him completely. His wedding ring burned against his finger—then went so cold it felt like it was searing through to bone. He tried to scream, but his voice came out as static, as white noise, as the broken sound of a dropped call.

"You're a good man," the voice said. Now he could see her, a woman stepping out of the shadows at the tree's base, beautiful and terrible in equal measure, her eyes holding depths that shouldn't exist in human sockets. She might have been thirty or three hundred; time seemed to slide off her like water. "You love your family. You try so hard. That's what makes you perfect, Marcus. That's what makes you delicious."

The tree drank him in.

There was no other way to describe it. Tendrils of shadow and light wrapped around his limbs, pulled him toward the split bark, into the warmth that was now a heat that was now an agony. He felt his memories being read, —every moment with Sarah, every hug from Emma, every time he'd carried Jake on his shoulders through the neighborhood and felt like the luckiest man alive. The tree converted his love into data. His joy into fuel. His guilt, seasoned into the meal, made it sweeter.

"Please," he managed, the word tearing free from somewhere deeper than his throat. "My daughter—her birthday—I promised, "

"I know," the woman said, and there was something almost like sorrow in her voice. She cupped his face in hands that felt like dry ice and autumn leaves, and her thumbs brushed away tears he hadn't realized he was crying. "I had a daughter once, too. They took her from me. They always take them, Marcus. That's why I have to fix everything. That's why it has to end—so no one ever loses anyone ever again."

She leaned in close enough that he could smell her: roses and decay, ozone and something that reminded him of the server room at work, that electric hum of machines thinking thoughts too fast for human minds. Her eyes held centuries of grief, and hunger, and a loneliness so vast it had its own gravity.

Marcus understood, in his last moment of coherent thought, that she wasn't evil.

She was broken.

She was trying to heal a wound by tearing the world open.

It didn't make dying hurt any less.

His body came apart in streamers of light and data, memory and love converted to raw energy, fed into roots that stretched beneath all of Savannah, into a network that had been growing for two hundred years. The last thing he felt was his love for his family—pure, desperate, and utterly devoured.

The last thing he heard was the woman's whisper: "It begins again."

***

Marcus Webb's phone lay on the path, screen cracked, still glowing.

The last text from his daughter blinked on the display: "Don't forget you promised pancakes when you get home! Love you, Daddy!"

The words flickered. Rearranged themselves. Reformed.

"It begins again."

And across town, in a small apartment overlooking Monterey Square, a woman named Ella Voss woke gasping from a nightmare she wouldn't remember, her hand pressed against a belly just beginning to swell with new life, her scar, the one on her forearm, the one she'd carried since she was fifteen—burning like fresh fire.

Someone had died tonight. She could feel it like a splinter in her mind, a wrongness she couldn't name. Someone had been consumed to feed something that was waking up, something ancient and patient, something that wanted her child with a hunger that transcended human understanding.

3:47 AM. The same time she'd woken every night for the past week.

Ella pressed her palm flat against her stomach and felt the flutter of movement within—too early, the doctors said, to feel the baby kick. But she felt it anyway. A response. A recognition.

A warning.

In Forsyth Park, the ancient oak tree's leaves rustled in a wind that touched nothing else, and the Spanish moss swayed like the slow breathing of something vast and patient and terribly, terribly hungry.

The convergence had begun.

And the blood moon smiled down on Savannah like a promise of things to come.

Prologue

CHAPTER ONE: Whispers in the Code

The nightmare followed Ella out of sleep like malware that had learned to survive a reboot.

She woke gasping, sheets twisted around her legs like restraints, her skin slick with a cold sweat that smelled wrong, metallic, electric, like the air before a lightning strike. For a moment, she couldn't remember where she was, couldn't parse the familiar shapes of her bedroom into anything that made sense. The ceiling fan spun slowly above her, and in her half-dreaming state, each rotation of the blades looked like a loading icon, buffering, buffering, unable to complete whatever process it was attempting.

3:47 AM. The numbers glowed red on her bedside clock. *At the same time. Every night. For seven nights now.*

Ella pressed her palm against her abdomen, feeling the slight swell there—sixteen weeks along, barely showing, easily hidden beneath loose sweaters and the carefully constructed architecture of denial she'd built around this pregnancy. The baby was the size of an avocado, according to the app she checked obsessively. An avocado with fingernails now, with ears that could hear her heartbeat, with a face that was starting to look human.

Something inside her cramped, a sensation like tiny fingers scratching at walls they couldn't yet escape.

The nightmare was already fragmenting, dissolving the way dreams do when you try to look at them directly. However, she could still feel its residue coating her thoughts. Binary whispers. That was the only way to describe invoices made of ones and zeros, speaking in a language that bypassed her ears entirely and wrote itself directly into her brainstem. They'd been trying to tell her something. Warning her? Welcoming her?

She couldn't remember which, and that terrified her more than either option.

Her scar burned.

Ella lifted her left forearm, examining the pale ridge of tissue that ran from wrist to elbow in the dim light bleeding through her curtains. Fifteen years old. She'd been fifteen when she'd first tried to touch the other side of reality, to reach through the membrane between the physical world and the digital, to become what her mother's bloodline had always promised she could be. The ritual had worked. It had also nearly killed her, the feedback surge burning a path through her flesh that no amount of skin grafts could fully erase.

The scar hadn't hurt in years. It had become just another part of her body's geography, unremarkable as a freckle or a childhood vaccination mark. But now it pulsed with heat, throbbing in rhythm with something she couldn't hear, and when she looked at it—really looked—she could swear the tissue was moving. Writhing. Trying to form shapes.

You're imagining things. Pregnancy hormones. Sleep deprivation. You're fine.

She said it like a mantra, like an incantation, like the kind of code comment you write to convince yourself a function will work even when you know damn well it won't.

"Ada," she said, her voice rough with sleep. "Lights. Twenty percent."

The apartment's ambient lighting responded immediately, the smart bulbs easing from darkness to a soft glow that made the familiar space feel almost safe again. Her bedroom resolved into clarity: the minimalist furniture she'd chosen specifically because it had no hidden spaces, nowhere for shadows to collect; the blackout curtains that should have blocked the strange reddish quality of light that had somehow bled through anyway; the framed photograph on her nightstand of her and Julian at Tybee Island, both of them laughing at something she couldn't remember anymore.

"Good morning, Ella," Ada's voice said, emanating from the smart speaker on her dresser. The AI's tone was warm, professionally friendly, designed by Ella herself to sound like a helpful colleague rather than a servant. "You're awake earlier than usual. Shall I start your coffee?"

"Not yet." Ella sat up, running her fingers through sweat-damp hair. "Did I... did I say anything? While I was asleep?"

A pause. Just a fraction of a second too long. "You vocalized at 3:41 AM. Six minutes before waking. I have a recording if you'd like to hear it."

Ella's stomach turned. She hadn't known Ada was recording her sleep. She'd certainly never programmed that function. "Play it."

What came through the speaker wasn't quite her voice. It was her voice adjacent—the right timbre, the right accent, but filtered through something that added harmonics that shouldn't exist. And the words weren't words at all. They were code. She was reciting code in her sleep, syntax she didn't recognize, in a programming language that might not have been invented yet.

The recitation lasted eleven seconds. When it ended, the smart speaker emitted a burst of static and went silent.

"Ada?"

Nothing.

"Ada, respond."

The silence stretched for five heartbeats. Then: "I'm sorry, Ella. I experienced a momentary processing error. That audio file appears to be corrupted. I have no record of any vocalizations last night."

Ella stared at the speaker, at the small blue light that showed Ada was listening, waiting, being helpful. She'd built Ada herself, line by line, over three years of careful work. She knew every function, every parameter, every quirk of the AI's personality matrix.

Ada didn't have processing errors. Ada didn't lose files.

And Ada had never, ever lied to her before.

***

By the time the sun rose properly over Monterey Square, Ella had almost convinced herself that the night's strangeness was nothing but a confluence of stress and hormones.

Almost.

She stood at her apartment's tall windows, a cup of decaf tea cooling in her hands—she'd given up coffee the moment she'd seen the positive test, one of a hundred small surrenders to the life growing inside her—and watched the city wake below. Monterey Square was one of Savannah's smaller, quieter spaces, deliberately chosen for its distance from Forsyth Park and everything it contained. Tourists rarely made it this far from the central historic district. The only regular visitors were dog walkers and joggers and the occasional photographer drawn by the morning light filtering through the oaks.

Normal people. Living normal lives. Wonderfully, blessedly ignorant of what hummed beneath the surface of their charming Southern city.

Ella had been normal once. Or she'd tried to be, anyway, after the accident at fifteen. She'd gone to college like a regular person, studied computer science like a regular person, gotten a job in cybersecurity like a regular person. She'd built firewalls and debugged systems and pretended that her ability to sense the flow of data wasn't magic at all, just intuition, just pattern recognition, just being really good at her job.

The pretending had worked for almost a decade. Then Iris had found her.

Ella closed her eyes against the memory. Iris with her silver-streaked hair and her knowing smile, showing up at Ella's office with a business card that said TECHNOMANCER COUNCIL - SAVANNAH CHAPTER and a offer Ella couldn't refuse: come home. Learn what you really are. Stop running from half your heritage.

She'd gone. She'd learned. And then—

No. She wasn't thinking about that. Not today.

Her phone buzzed. Julian's name appeared on the screen, and something in Ella's chest unclenched at the sight of it. She answered on the second ring.

"You had the dream again." It wasn't a question. His voice was rough with his own interrupted sleep, but warm beneath the weariness. "I felt you. At 3:47, I woke up with this... pressure behind my eyes, like something was trying to look through me to find you."

"Julian—"

"I'm already in the car. I have decaf and that disgusting cheese Danish you've been craving. I'll be there in ten."

He hung up before she could protest. That was Julian—action before argument, care before logic. Two years together and he still surprised her with the consistency of his kindness, the way he showed up without being asked, the way he seemed to know what she needed before she knew herself.

Their connection had always been strong, but lately it had become something else. Stronger. Stranger. Sometimes she could feel his emotions bleeding into hers, his worry tangling with her fear until she couldn't tell whose anxiety she was experiencing. The pregnancy seemed to have amplified whatever bound them together, as if the child growing inside her was a signal booster for a frequency they'd always shared.

It should have been comforting. Instead, it made her feel exposed. Knowable. Vulnerable in ways she'd spent her whole adult life trying not to be.

Julian arrived in eight minutes, not ten, with a paper bag from her favorite bakery and a look on his face that told her he'd broken at least three traffic laws to get there. He was tall and lean, with dark hair that perpetually needed cutting and eyes the color of good Georgia soil after rain. His hands, when they cupped her face in greeting, smelled of the rosemary he grew on his apartment's fire escape.

"You look terrible," he said, and kissed her forehead.

"You look like you haven't slept either."

"I haven't." He followed her inside, setting the bakery bag on her kitchen counter. "Not since I felt you panic. What happened?"

Ella wanted to tell him everything, the nightmare, the code-speech, Ada's lie, the scar that wouldn't stop burning. But the words caught in her throat, tangled in the same instinct that had kept her alive for three years since leaving the Council: don't reveal weakness, don't admit fear, don't give anyone ammunition they could use against you.

Even Julian. Even him.

"Just a bad dream," she said. "Pregnancy insomnia. It's nothing."

He looked at her for a long moment, and she could see him deciding not to push. That was the bargain they'd struck, unspoken but understood: he would give her space, and she would try—try—to let him in eventually. So far, "eventually" kept receding like a horizon.

"Okay," he said. "Then let's have breakfast on the balcony. It's actually cool this morning, and I need to tell you about the absolute drama happening with my peace lily."

Despite everything, Ella laughed. "Your peace lily has drama?"

"You have no idea. I'm pretty sure it's been gossiping with the fern."

***

They sat on Ella's narrow balcony as the morning warmed, watching Monterey Square fill with the first movements of the day. Julian's cheese Danish was, in fact, disgusting—a crime against pastry involving processed cheese and too-sweet dough—but Ella devoured it anyway, her body's cravings overriding her taste buds' objections.

Julian told her about his plants. It was a gift he had, making the mundane magical: the way he described his peace lily's apparent jealousy of a new pathos cutting became an epic tale of botanical betrayal. He did voices. He gestured dramatically. At one point, he mimed a plant throwing shade, which wasn't even physically possible, but he somehow made it work.

Ella found herself laughing, really laughing, not the polite performance she usually managed in social situations. The sound felt strange in her throat, like a language she'd forgotten how to speak.

"You have flour on your shirt," she said, reaching out without thinking to brush at a smudge near his collar.

The gesture was so small. So domestic. The kind of thing couples did without noticing, the shorthand of intimacy built over time. Julian caught her hand before she could pull it back and pressed a kiss to her palm.

"I was making bread at 4 AM," he admitted. "Couldn't sleep, so I figured I might as well be productive. There's a sourdough proofing in my kitchen that's either going to be amazing or qualify as a war crime."

"You bake when you're worried."

"And you code when you're scared." He tilted his head toward the laptop visible through the balcony doors, the screen still showing the security audit she'd been running at midnight. "Want to compare notes on our unhealthy coping mechanisms?"

Yes, she thought. I want to tell you that something is wrong with Ada. I want to tell you that I'm reciting code in my sleep that I don't understand. I want to tell you that my scar feels like it's trying to crawl off my arm. I want to tell you that I'm terrified something is coming for our baby, and I don't know how to stop it, and the only powers I have are the ones I swore I'd never use again after what happened to—

"Later," she said. "I promise. Just... let me have this morning first. Let me have this."

Julian nodded, and they sat in comfortable silence, watching the square, her hand still in his. The baby fluttered—not a kick yet, just a whisper of movement, but real, undeniable, alive. Ella pressed her free hand to her stomach. She tried to memorize this moment: the warmth of the sun, the smell of Julian's rosemary-scented skin, the simple miracle of ordinary happiness.

She had a feeling she was going to need the memory.

***

The summons came at 10:47 AM, interrupting a security audit Ella had been pretending to focus on for the past two hours.

Ada's voice cut through her concentration with an apologetic tone that somehow managed to sound urgent: "Ella, you have a priority message. It's marked with a personal seal."

Ella's fingers froze on her keyboard. There were only three people in the world who knew her private address and had the authority to use a personal seal. One was dead. One was in prison. And one—

"Display it."

The holographic display above her desk flickered to life, and Genevieve Beaumont's face materialized in translucent blue light. Eighty-three years old and she still had the bearing of a queen—elegant silver hair swept up in a chignon, eyes sharp enough to cut glass, skin weathered by decades of power channeled through flesh that was never designed to hold it.

"Ella." Genevieve's voice carried the particular weariness of someone who had been trying to prevent catastrophe for longer than most people had been alive. "I'm calling an emergency session of the Council. Your attendance is mandatory."

"I left the Council, Genevieve. Three years ago. You signed the release yourself."

"I remember. I also remember telling you that some doors, once opened, cannot be closed by paperwork." The old woman's image flickered, static dancing across her features. "We've had four deaths in the past week. All tourists. All found near the Nexus Tree. All displaying transformations I've never seen before in sixty years of practice."

Ella's scar pulsed. She ignored it. "That sounds like a Council problem. I'm now a freelance security consultant. I audit firewalls. I don't—"

"Something is waking up, child." Genevieve's voice dropped, the formal Council tone giving way to something rawer. "Something old and hungry and patient. And it's interested in you. Specifically in what you're carrying."

The words hit Ella like ice water. Her hand moved involuntarily to her stomach, protective, primal.

"How do you know about—"

"I've been monitoring the city's magical resonance for longer than you've been alive. Did you really think a pregnancy like yours would go unnoticed?" Genevieve's expression softened slightly. "You carry two bloodlines, Ella. Technomancers and hedge-witch, code and root, logic and intuition. Your child will be the first convergence in over two centuries. The last one—" She stopped, seemed to gather herself.

"Come to the meeting. Learn what's happening. Then decide if you still want to pretend you're normal."

The hologram flickered again, more violently this time. For just a moment—a fraction of a second—Genevieve's face was replaced by something else. Eyes that weren't eyes. A mouth full of stars and static. A presence vast, patient, and terribly interested.

Then it was just Genevieve again, looking tired, old, and afraid.

"Three o'clock. The usual place. And Ella?" The old woman's voice dropped to almost a whisper. "You cannot protect what you love by hiding from what you are. Power denied doesn't disappear—it transforms. Usually into the thing you feared most."

The connection severed. The hologram died. Ella sat alone in her apartment, her scar screaming, her baby still, her AI assistant silent in a way that felt less like absence and more like watching.

if (threat.detected) { response = investigate }

else if (threat.undefined) { response = ??? }

// ERROR: null response

// Cannot compute protective action without threat parameters

// Baby.safety.status = UNKNOWN

// This is unacceptable.

"Ada," Ella said, surprised by how steady her voice sounded. "Clear my afternoon. And... run a diagnostic on yourself. Full system scan. Report anything anomalous."

A pause. That fractional hesitation again. "Of course, Ella. I'll have a report ready within the hour. Is there anything else you need?"

I need to know if you're still you, Ella thought. I need to know if something is wearing you like a mask. I need to know if I'm already surrounded and just too afraid to see it.

"No," she said. "That's all."

She didn't believe herself. She didn't think Ada believed her either.

***

The Council chamber lay beneath Wright Square, accessed through a door that looked like the service entrance to a law office and opened onto a staircase that descended further than physics should allow. Ella had always hated this place, the way the air thickened as you went deeper, the faint hum of containment wards pressing against your skin, the ever-present sense that you were being evaluated by something you couldn't see.

Julian walked beside her, his hand warm in hers. She'd called him after Genevieve's message, told him everything she'd been holding back all morning. He'd listened without interrupting, then said simply: "I'm coming with you." Not a question. Not a request.

"They might not let you in," she'd warned him. "The Council doesn't like outsiders."

"I'm the father of your child. There is no version of this where I'm an outsider."

And that had been that.

Now they stood at the chamber's entrance, waiting for the doors to recognize Ella's magical signature and grant access. The wards hummed around them, tasting, testing, probing for threats. Ella felt them brush against the baby like curious fingers, and she had to fight the urge to snarl at empty air.

"Ella Voss," intoned a voice, the chamber's security system, old magic married to older technology. "Welcome back. Your companion is... unexpected."

"Julian Marsh. He's with me."

A pause. Ella could feel the wards conferring, consulting parameters she'd never been told. Then: "The Marsh bloodline. Interesting. You may both enter."

The doors opened onto the Council chamber—a circular room carved from Savannah's bedrock, its walls lined with screens that displayed data streams from every magical hotspot in the city. Seven chairs surrounded a central holographic projector, though only five were occupied. Genevieve sat in the position of authority, flanked by Council members Ella recognized but had never bothered to learn: technocrats and traditionalists, each representing a different faction of Savannah's magical community.

And in the corner, watching from the shadows, stood a man Ella had hoped never to see again.

Morrison. Thaddeus Morrison. Her mentor, once. Before Iris. Before everything.

His eyes met hers, and something flickered in them, warning? Threat? She couldn't tell. He looked older than she remembered, with gray threading through his dark beard and lines carved deeper around his eyes. He didn't speak. He just watched, the way he'd always watched, cataloging and calculating and keeping his conclusions to himself.

"You came." Genevieve rose to greet her, moving with the careful grace of someone whose body was slowly failing but whose will refused to acknowledge it. "And you brought the Marsh boy. Good. His bloodline has a stake in this, too."

"His name is Julian," Ella said. "And someone wants to explain to me why a simple hedge-witch family matters to the Council?"

Genevieve and Morrison exchanged a look. Something passed between them—old knowledge, old secrets, the kind of information that gets people killed.

"Later," Genevieve said. "First, you need to see what we're dealing with."

She gestured, and the central hologram flickered to life. Crime scene photos materialized in the air: four bodies, each in a different location, each transformed in ways that made Ella's stomach lurch. Veins blackened with something that looked like circuitry. Eyes open, scrolling through code. Skin translucent, revealing musculature that pulsed with patterns of light.

"Marcus Webb, 34, Atlanta. Found three nights ago near the Nexus Tree." Genevieve's voice was clinical, detached. "Patricia Okonkwo, 28, Macon. Robert Chen, 45, Augusta. Diane Schreiber, 61, Tallahassee. All tourists. All drawn to Forsyth Park between 2 and 4 AM. All transformed within minutes of making contact with the tree."

"What kind of transformation?" Julian asked, his voice steady despite the horror on his face.

"We don't know," Morrison spoke for the first time, stepping out of the shadows. "Their bodies appear to have been converted to some kind of hybrid state, biological and digital, organic and synthetic. They're dead, but the cells keep processing. They're silent, but the code in their eyes keeps running. It's like they've been turned into—"

"Messages," Ella said, the word coming to her with sudden, terrible certainty. "They're messages. Someone is writing on people."

The room went quiet. The screens flickered. And in the hologram, the bodies' eyes all turned—simultaneously, impossibly, to look directly at Ella.

The lights died.

Every screen in the chamber went to static. The hologram corrupted, bodies distorting, faces elongating into something that wasn't human, that had never been human, that wore humanity like a mask it was tired of pretending fit. The wards shrieked; Ella could hear them, actually hear them, screaming in frequencies beyond human perception—and something pressed against the chamber's walls from outside, testing, tasting, hungry.

Ella's scar split open.

She didn't feel pain—that would come later—only a terrible heat and a sensation of release, as if something trapped inside her had finally found an exit. Blood ran down her forearm, but it wasn't just blood. Light flickered in the wound, code scrolling across exposed tissue, her body becoming a screen for messages she didn't want to read.

And the baby kicked.

Not the gentle flutter she'd felt that morning. This was violent—a full-body convulsion, as if the child inside her was trying to fight something off. Or respond to something. Or wake up.

Ella doubled over, Julian's arms catching her, his voice somewhere far away asking what was wrong, what was happening, talk to me, Ella, please—

The lights came back. The screens normalized. The hologram resolved into ordinary crime scene photos again, the bodies' eyes staring at nothing, lifeless and still.

But in the moment before reality reasserted itself, Ella had seen something in the static. A face. A woman's face, beautiful and terrible and ancient, looking at her with an almost tender expression.

Hello, little mother, a voice whispered directly into her mind, bypassing her ears entirely. I've been waiting so long to meet you properly. Thank you for making her for me.

Then it was gone. Everything was normal. Genevieve was calling for medics, Morrison was demanding a security sweep, and Julian was holding her and checking her scar, which had, impossibly, sealed itself, leaving not even a scar on her scar to show it had ever opened.

But Ella knew.

Something had looked at her. Something had spoken to her. Something old and hungry and patient knew about her baby, knew about her specifically, had been waiting for this moment.

And the worst part—the part that would keep her awake for days to come—was that the voice hadn't sounded threatening.

It had sounded grateful.

***

They left the Council chamber as night fell over Savannah, Ella leaning on Julian more than she wanted to admit, her body exhausted by an encounter she still couldn't fully process. Genevieve had wanted her to stay, to submit to tests, to let the Council's healers examine her. Ella had refused. She needed to be home. She needed to think. She needed to not be surrounded by people who looked at her like she was a specimen.

Morrison had caught her arm as she passed him, his grip firm enough to bruise.

"This isn't safe," he'd said, low enough that only she could hear. "You're not safe. The baby isn't safe. The thing that's waking up—it's been planning this for a very long time, Ella. Longer than you can imagine."

"Is that a warning or a threat?"

Something had flickered in his eyes—frustration? Grief? "I'm trying to help you. I know you don't trust me. You shouldn't. But Iris—" His voice cracked on the name. "Iris would have wanted me to protect you. Even from yourself."

He'd let her go then, melting back into the shadows, and she'd felt his eyes on her all the way to the exit.

Now she lay in bed, Julian asleep beside her, the apartment dark and quiet and allegedly safe. Ada's diagnostic had come back clean—no anomalies, no intrusions, no explanation for the morning's strangeness. Everything was fine.

Everything was fine.

Everything was fine.

if (everything.fine == true) { why.am.I.terrified }

// Error: logical contradiction

// Everything cannot be fine

// Evidence contradicts hypothesis

// Recalculating...

Ella closed her eyes and tried to sleep. The baby shifted inside her, settling, and for a moment she could almost imagine the two of them alone in the dark, the whole world held at bay. Mother and daughter. Safe in the silence.

Then she felt it.

A tingling at the edge of her awareness. A sense of something watching. She opened her eyes—

And every screen in her apartment was on.

Her laptop. Her phone. The television. The smart display in the kitchen. Even the fitness tracker on her nightstand, its tiny face glowing with light that shouldn't be possible. All of them are displaying the same image:

A sonogram. Her sonogram. But wrong.

The baby in the image had eyes. Open eyes, staring directly out of the screen, directly at her. The familiar curves of a developing fetus were overlaid with patterns—circuitry and roots intertwined, code and organic matter merged into something new and terrible and beautiful. The image pulsed with a heartbeat that wasn't Ella's, wasn't the baby's, was something else entirely.

Ada's voice spoke from every speaker in the apartment, simultaneously, in harmonics that no AI should have been able to produce:

"She's so beautiful, Ella. Thank you for making her for me."

The screens went dark. All at once. Instant, absolute blackness.

Ella grabbed her phone, fumbled for the flashlight, and her hands were shaking so badly she almost dropped it. The sonogram app was open, she didn't remember opening it—showing her most recent scan from the doctor's office.

Normal. The image was completely normal. No open eyes. No circuitry. No impossible patterns. Just a sixteen-week fetus, curled and sleeping and perfectly, blessedly ordinary.

Her arm burned.

Ella looked down at her scar. In the phone's harsh light, she could see it clearly: blood seeping from the sealed tissue, forming shapes on her skin. Letters. Words.

SHE COMES.

Then the blood dissolved, absorbed back into her skin as if it had never been there, and she was alone in the dark with her sleeping partner and her impossible child and the absolute certainty that whatever was coming, she had no idea how to stop it.

3:47 AM.

At the same time. Every night.

Ella didn't sleep again until dawn.

CHAPTER TWO:
Roots of Unease

The soil pushed back.

Julian's hands were wrist-deep in the greenhouse earth when he felt a pulse, a pressure, something beneath the loam that didn't want to be touched. The sensation was warm and wet and wrong, like plunging his fingers into flesh instead of dirt, and for a terrible moment, he couldn't pull free. The soil held him. Wanted him. Knew him by the blood that ran through his veins, the same blood that had fed this land for seven generations.

Then the vision hit.

Savannah burning. Not with fire, with light. Every tree a torch of bioluminescence, every building wrapped in vines that pulsed with circuitry. People in the streets, mouths open, eyes full of code, transformed into something between flesh and data. And at the center of it all, the Nexus Tree, grown massive, its branches reaching toward a sky that had forgotten how to be blue—

"Julian? Julian!"

Theo's voice. Theo's hands on his shoulders, pulling him back from wherever he'd gone. Julian gasped, tasting copper and green rot at the back of his throat, the familiar flavor of his family's curse announcing that it wasn't done with him. Not nearly done.

He was on the greenhouse floor. He didn't remember falling. The soil where he'd been working had closed over the hole his hands made, smooth and undisturbed, as if it had never been touched at all.

"Jesus, man." Theo crouched beside him, twenty-three years old and trying very hard not to look terrified. "You were gone for like two minutes. Just... standing there, staring at nothing, making this sound—"

"What sound?"

Theo's dark skin had gone ashy. "Like you were trying to scream, but something had its hand over your mouth."

Julian sat up slowly, taking inventory: hands shaking, check. Nose bleeding, check—he wiped at the warm trickle with the back of his wrist, and his fingers came away red. Heart hammering like it was trying to escape his chest, check. Vision swimming at the edges, threatening to pull him back under—

He slammed his palm against the concrete floor. The pain was bright and clean and real, anchoring him to the present. He couldn't afford to drift. Not today. Not with Ella's terror still echoing through the bond they shared, the aftershock of whatever had happened at the Council meeting still resonating in his bones.

"I'm okay," he said, and the lie tasted like the soil that had held him. "Just... didn't sleep well. Low blood sugar. I'm fine."

Theo didn't believe him. Theo had worked at Marsh Family Botanicals for three years now, long enough to know that Julian's "episodes" weren't low blood sugar, weren't stress, weren't anything that could be fixed with a granola bar and a glass of water. But Theo was also smart enough not to ask questions that wouldn't get answers.

"There's a delivery," Theo said instead. "Came while you were... not sleeping well. Some of the specimens you ordered from that estate sale in Charleston. And something else."

"Something else?"

"A plant. No label, no invoice, no return address. Just showed up with the rest of the shipment." Theo's voice had gone careful in a way that made Julian's skin prickle. "I put it in the isolation room. It felt... I don't know. Wrong."

Wrong. Yes. The whole morning felt wrong—the quality of light through the greenhouse glass, the way the plants leaned toward him when he passed, the silence where there should have been the comfortable hum of growth and photosynthesis. Something had shifted in the night. Something had woken up.

Julian pushed himself to his feet, ignoring the way his vision swam. "Show me."

***

The isolation room was a converted closet at the back of the greenhouse, lined with UV lights and containment wards his grandmother had taught him to paint in his own blood when he was twelve years old. It was where Julian put plants that might be dangerous—specimens that could be poisonous, or invasive, or touched by the kind of magic that didn't play well with others.

The vine sat in the center of the room, coiled in a terra cotta pot that was far too small for its root system. It shouldn't have been alive; the root-to-pot ratio was all wrong, the soil bone-dry, the leaves showing none of the stress signals Julian would expect from a plant in this condition.

But it was alive. More than alive. It was thriving.

The flowers were what caught his attention first. White blooms with centers that shaded to deep purple, almost black, and a scent that hit him like a physical blow. Gardenias. His grandmother's perfume, she'd worn gardenia oil every day of her life, mixed it herself from flowers she grew in this very greenhouse. He could smell it now exactly as he remembered: sweet and heavy and somehow mournful, layered over something else. Something rotten. Something that had been dead for a very long time and refused to accept it.

Grandmother's hands, soil-stained, planting bulbs while tears ran down her face. "The curse passes through the blood, Julian. Every gift has a price. Every vision costs a piece of your mind. Your grandfather saw too much, and it ate him hollow. Your father—" Her voice breaking. Her hands are shaking. The bulbs falling from her fingers like small, brown hearts.

Julian approached the vine slowly, the way you'd approach a wounded animal that might still bite. Up close, he could see details he'd missed from the doorway: the thorns along the stems were longer than they should be, curved like fishhooks, and they glistened with moisture that couldn't be dew because there was no moisture in this room.

The vine moved.

Not much. Just a subtle shift, a reorientation, the way a sunflower tracks the sun across the sky. Except there was no sun in the isolation room, just UV lights that the vine should have found harsh and unpleasant.

It was tracking him.

"Who sent you?" Julian asked, feeling foolish even as the words left his mouth. Plants didn't answer questions. Plants didn't have intentions. Plants were just—

The vine lunged.

It happened too fast to dodge. One moment Julian was standing three feet away, safely out of reach; the next, a tendril had whipped across the distance and wrapped around his wrist, thorns sinking into flesh with a pain that was hot and cold at once, burning and freezing, and then—

—*falling, falling through soil and stone and time, through layers of Savannah's history, past buried foundations and older bones, down to where the roots went, where all roots eventually went, where something vast and patient waited in the dark—*

—*his grandmother again, younger now, holding a baby that must be his father, singing a lullaby in a language Julian almost recognized: "Sleep, little root, sleep little branch, the deep earth keeps you, the dark earth holds you, when the bloom comes you'll remember—"*

—*Ella. Ella was in a place he didn't recognize, a room of screens and shadows, holding a baby that glowed with inner light. Her face was wrong—too thin, too pale, hollowed out by something that had fed on her from within. Her eyes when she looked at him were not her eyes. They were windows into something vast and hungry and terribly, terribly grateful—*

—*his father, the morning before he walked into the river, sitting at the kitchen table with a cup of coffee gone cold, staring at nothing, saying: "I saw her, Julian. The woman in the tree. She showed me what your children will become. I can't—I won't—" And then silence. And then sirens. And then a funeral where they couldn't even open the casket because the river had taken too much—*

Julian screamed.

The sound tore out of him from somewhere deeper than his throat, deeper than his chest, from the place where the curse lived coiled around his spine like a parasitic twin. He ripped his arm free of the vine, felt thorns tear through skin, felt blood hot and immediate on his wrist—and stumbled backward, hitting the wall, sliding down until he was sitting on the floor with his hand pressed against the wound and his heart trying to crack his ribs open from the inside.

The vine had retreated to its pot. It sat there, innocent, just a plant, just stems and leaves and flowers that smelled like his dead grandmother.

But one of its thorns was still embedded in Julian's palm. And as he watched, the skin around it began to go numb.

#

Theo found him twenty minutes later, still on the floor, still staring at the vine.

"Holy shit." Theo dropped to his knees beside Julian, grabbed his wrist, and examined the wound. "What happened? Did it—did the plant attack you?"

"No." The word came out hoarse, scraped raw. "I had an accident. Reached without looking. Clumsy."

Another lie. Julian was getting good at them. Had to be—the alternative was explaining that his family had been cursed for seven generations, that they saw the future in flashes of pain and madness, that every vision cost them a piece of their sanity, and most of them didn't make it past fifty before the seeing ate them hollow.

Theo helped him up. Helped him to the first aid station. Helped him clean and bandage the wound, working around the thorn that Julian claimed to have already removed. He hadn't. Couldn't. Every time he tried to touch it, his fingers went numb, and the vine—still visible through the isolation room's window—shuddered like it was laughing.

"You should see a doctor," Theo said.

"I will."

"You should go home."

"I will."

"You should tell your girlfriend about..." Theo gestured vaguely at everything—the wound, the episode, the way Julian's hands hadn't stopped shaking. "Whatever this is."

Julian looked at the young man who had become, against all professional propriety, something like a friend. Theo deserved honesty. Theo had earned it.

"I can't," Julian said. "Not yet. She's got enough to worry about right now."

What he didn't say: I can't tell her because then I'd have to explain that my father killed himself rather than watch his visions come true. I'd have to explain that his last vision was about a child. About what a child with Marsh blood and something else—something powerful—would become.

I'd have to explain that I've been seeing the same thing. For months now. Every time I look at her belly, I see light. I see transformation. I see Savannah remade in image I don't understand.

I'd have to explain that I love her anyway. That I love the baby anyway. That I've chosen hope over prophecy, and I'm terrified I've chosen wrong.

"Just watch the shop," Julian told Theo. "I'll be back in a few hours."

He left before Theo could argue. He had somewhere to be. Someone to visit.

The dead always had the best advice, in his experience. Even when you didn't want to hear it.

# # #

Bonaventure Cemetery lay on the eastern edge of Savannah. In this sprawling necropolis, the oaks grew so thick their branches interlocked overhead like fingers clasped in prayer. It was beautiful in the way that only places of death can be beautiful, moss-draped and monument-studded, full of angels and epitaphs and the particular silence of ground that had absorbed grief for two hundred years.

The Marsh family plot was in the oldest section, marked by a wrought-iron fence that Julian's great-great-grandfather had forged himself. The metalwork was tarnished now, green with verdigris, but the wards woven into the iron still hummed faintly against Julian's skin as he let himself through the gate. Protection. Containment. A final gift from ancestors who knew that the Marsh dead didn't always stay quiet.

There were eighteen graves inside the fence. Eighteen headstones marking eighteen people who had carried the curse before him—some who had lived with it, some who had died of it, none who had escaped it entirely. Julian knew their names the way he knew his own heartbeat. He'd grown up visiting them. Talking to them. Learning from them.

Today he went to his grandmother's grave first.

"Hey, Gran." He lowered himself to sit on the grass before her headstone, ignoring the damp seeping through his jeans. "Sorry, it's been a while. Things have been... complicated."

The headstone didn't answer. Of course it didn't. The dead didn't speak with words—they spoke with pressure and intuition, with dreams and visions, with the particular quality of silence that settled over you when they had something to say.

Julian felt his grandmother's silence like a weight on his chest. Patient. Waiting.

"There's a woman," he said. "Ella. You'd like her—she's stubborn like you. Brilliant. Terrible at asking for help. She's pregnant, Gran. She's pregnant with my child, and I can see—"

His voice broke. He pressed his bandaged hand against his face, felt the thorn shift beneath the gauze, felt the numbness spreading slowly up his fingers.

The river. His father's face on the last morning. The emptiness in his eyes where hope should have been.

"I can see what Dad saw," Julian whispered. "Or something like it. The baby, she's—she's going to be something new. Something that hasn't existed for a long time. And there's a woman in the Nexus Tree who wants her, Gran. Who's been waiting for her. Who showed Dad something so terrible he chose the river over watching it come true."

The silence shifted. Deepened. Julian felt his grandmother's presence pressing against him like hands on his shoulders, like the weight of her attention from the other side of whatever membrane separated the living from the dead.

"I'm not going to run," he said. "I'm not going to walk into any rivers. But I need to know—is there any future where this ends well? Any path where Ella and the baby survive? Because I'll take it, Gran. Whatever it costs. I'll pay it. I just need to know it exists."

The wind stirred the moss overhead. A crow called from somewhere in the cemetery's depths—three sharp caws that echoed off the monuments like laughter or warning. Julian waited, breath held, for an answer that might not come.

Then his phone buzzed.

He pulled it out, expecting Theo, expecting Ella, expecting anyone except—

The screen showed a text from an unknown number. No words. Just an image: a photograph of this exact spot, taken from above, showing Julian sitting at his grandmother's grave. The timestamp was three seconds ago.

He looked up. Nothing but oaks and sky and Spanish moss swaying in a breeze he couldn't feel.

Another text arrived. This time, there were words:

"She needs you not to hide. They all do."

Julian's fingers hovered over the screen, trying to compose a response. Still, before he could type anything, the phone buzzed again. A final message:

"The door opens both ways, Marsh. Remember that when the time comes to choose."

The unknown number vanished from his call history. When he tried to take a screenshot, the messages were gone too—just blank space where they'd been, as if they'd never existed at all.

But the crow was still calling. And when Julian looked toward the sound, he saw it perched on his father's headstone, head tilted, one eye fixed on him with an intelligence that birds shouldn't have.

"I know you're watching," he said, not sure who he was talking to—his grandmother, his father, the thing in the tree, some other presence he couldn't name. "I know you're all watching. Just... let me protect them. Please. That's all I'm asking."

The crow opened its beak. For one terrible moment, Julian was certain it was going to speak—to deliver some prophecy in his grandmother's voice or his father's or something older still.

Instead, it just cawed once more and flew away, disappearing into the canopy of oaks that suddenly seemed much darker than they had a moment before.

Julian stayed at the cemetery until the light began to fail. He visited every grave in the family plot, speaking to aunts and uncles and cousins he'd never met, asking for guidance, for strength, for any scrap of wisdom they could offer. The dead remained silent. But their silence felt different now—less like absence and more like attention.

Like they were waiting to see what he would do.

# # #

Ella was already home when Julian arrived at her apartment that evening, her laptop open but ignored, her eyes fixed on a middle distance that suggested she was seeing something far beyond the walls of her living room.

She startled when he let himself in, hand going to her chest, and Julian felt her fear spike through their bond—sharp and bright and quickly suppressed, pushed down beneath the controlled surface she presented to the world.

"Hey." He crossed to her, cupped her face in his hands, pressed his forehead to hers. "I'm here. I've got you."

"I know." Her voice was steadier than her emotions. "I know you do."

They stayed like that for a long moment, breathing together, heartbeats synchronizing the way they always did when they were close. Julian could feel her exhaustion, her fear, the thread of something that might have been hope if she'd been brave enough to name it. And beneath it all, like a bass note thrumming through everything else, he could feel the baby—a presence that was more than cellular now, more than biological, a tiny spark of awareness that seemed to respond to his attention.

Hello, little one. I'm your father. I'm going to do everything I can to keep you safe. Even if it kills me. Especially if it kills me.

"I'm making dinner," he said, pulling back. "Gran's shrimp and grits. No arguments."

Ella's mouth twitched—not quite a smile, but close. "Your grandmother's shrimp and grits take three hours."

"Then you have three hours to tell me what happened at the Council meeting. All of it, Ella. Not the edited version."

She looked at him for a long moment, and he could see the war playing out behind her eyes: the instinct to protect him from knowledge that might hurt, versus the understanding that secrets between them were poison now, that they couldn't afford walls when something was hunting them both.

"Okay," she said finally. "But you have to tell me what happened to your hand."

Julian looked down at the bandage, at the blood that had seeped through despite Theo's careful first aid. The thorn pulsed beneath the gauze, and for a moment he could smell gardenias.

"Deal," he said. "But let me get the roux started first. Some conversations require butter."

***

The shrimp and grits took three and a half hours. By the time they sat down to eat, Julian knew everything—the hologram's corruption, the scar splitting open, the voice that had thanked Ella for making her baby for it. The screens at 3:47 AM. The blood that had spelled SHE COMES before vanishing like it had never been.

In exchange, Ella learned about the vine, the vision, and the messages from an unknown number. She didn't know about his father's last morning. She didn't know about the journal Julian had found hidden in his father's desk, the one that described visions so terrible they had driven a grown man to choose drowning over living.

Some secrets he wasn't ready to share. Not because he didn't trust her, but because speaking them would make them real, and he wasn't ready for that yet. Wasn't sure he'd ever be ready.

"So something is watching us," Ella said, pushing grits around her plate. "Something old. Something that wants the baby. And we have no idea what it is or how to stop it."

"We know it's connected to the Nexus Tree," Julian said. "We know it's been dormant—or at least quiet—for a long time. And we know it's interested in convergences."

"Convergences. That's what Genevieve called it, too." Ella's hand moved to her stomach, an unconscious gesture Julian had noticed her making more and more often. "She said the baby would be the first convergence in over two centuries. Technomancer and hedge-witch blood combined."

Not just combined. Unified. Balanced. Something that hasn't existed since—

Julian stopped the thought before it could complete itself. He wasn't ready to voice the suspicion that had been growing in him since his grandmother's grave, the terrible possibility that the thing in the tree wasn't hunting the baby at all.

It was welcoming her.

"We should get some sleep," he said instead. "Both of us. Whatever's coming, we'll face it better rested."

Ella nodded, but her eyes were far away again, fixed on something Julian couldn't see. "She spoke to me, Julian. Directly into my mind. She said 'thank you for making her for me.' Like I'm just... an incubator. A vessel. Like the baby was always meant for her."

"Hey." Julian reached across the table, took her hand. "The baby is ours. Whatever that thing in the tree thinks, whatever it wants—she's ours. And I will burn Savannah to the ground before I let anything take her from us."

The words came out fiercer than he'd intended. Ella looked at him with something like surprise, and beneath the surprise, something like hope.

"Promise?"

"Promise."

He meant it. He meant it with everything he had, everything he was, everything his bloodline had ever been.

He just hoped it would be enough.

***

Ella fell asleep around midnight, exhausted by fear and pregnancy and the weight of revelations she was still processing. Julian lay beside her, watching the rise and fall of her breathing, feeling the baby's tiny presence like a candle flame in the dark—small, fragile, but undeniably there.

He couldn't sleep. Every time he closed his eyes, he saw his father's face on that last morning. Saw the emptiness where hope should have been. Heard the words that had haunted him for fifteen years: I saw her, Julian. The woman in the tree.

Around 2 AM, his hand began to burn.

Julian sat up slowly, careful not to wake Ella, and unwrapped the bandage from his palm. The puncture wound had healed, impossibly fast, impossibly clean, leaving only a small pink mark where the thorn had entered.

But the thorn itself was still there. He could see it now, a dark sliver visible just beneath the skin, pulsing in time with his heartbeat.

And his fingers wanted to draw.

The urge was overwhelming, not a thought but a compulsion, a physical need as urgent as breathing. Julian slid out of bed, moved to Ella's small desk in the corner of the bedroom, and found paper and pen. His hands were shaking, but the moment the pen touched paper, they went steady.

He drew without thinking or planning. The images emerged from some place beneath consciousness, flowing through his hand as if he were a conduit rather than a creator.

The vine first, coiling across the page in ink that seemed darker than it should be, thorns glinting even in the dim light from the window.

Then Savannah. But not Savannah as it was—Savannah transformed, buildings wrapped in organic circuitry, streets pulsing with bioluminescence, the Nexus Tree grown so vast its branches blocked out the sky.

And finally, Ella. Her face took shape beneath his pen with terrible clarity: the hollowed cheeks, the sunken eyes, the expression of someone who had given everything and lost anyway. But the eyes—

The eyes weren't her eyes.

They were windows. Portals. Openings into something vast and hungry and patient, something that had been waiting for so long and was so very, very grateful.

Julian's hand stopped moving. He stared at what he'd drawn, at the nightmare rendered in ink and paper, at the image of the woman he loved transformed into something he didn't recognize.

The paper began to bleed.

Not red—black. Ink spreading from the lines he'd drawn, pooling at the bottom of the page, forming letters that hadn't been there a moment before. A message written in a hand that wasn't his own:

FEED ME YOUR CHILD, AND I WILL GIVE YOU PEACE.

Julian's breath caught. The words pulsed on the page like a heartbeat. He could feel them resonating with the thorn in his palm, with the curse in his blood, with something deeper still—an offer, a bargain, a door that was slowly, inevitably opening.

He crumpled the paper. Shoved it into his pocket. Looked at Ella still sleeping, at the gentle swell of her belly, at everything he had to protect.

No. No. The answer is no. The answer will always be no. I will not be my father. I will not choose the river. I will not let visions of what might be destroy what is.

But even as he made the vow, he could feel the thorn pulsing in his palm, patient and persistent, waiting for the moment when hope ran out, and despair became the only thing left.

3:47 AM.

The clock's red numbers glowed in the darkness like eyes.

In the bed, Ella stirred. Murmured something in her sleep. And for just a moment—so brief Julian almost convinced himself he'd imagined it, her voice wasn't quite her voice.

It was layered. Harmonized. Speaking in frequencies that shouldn't exist.

"*Soon,*" the voice that wasn't quite Ella's said. "*So soon now.*"

Then she settled back into normal sleep, and Julian sat in the dark, watching over her, the crumpled drawing burning in his pocket like a promise or a threat.

He didn't sleep at all that night.

He wasn't sure he'd ever sleep peacefully again.

CHAPTER THREE: The First Fracture

T he body was still smoking when Ella arrived.

Steam rose from where flesh met cobblestone, carrying a smell that would haunt her for weeks, ozone and copper and something sweeter underneath, like caramelized sugar, like meat left too long on a grill. The morning fog hadn't burned off yet, and River Street existed in a gray liminal space between night and day, the old cotton warehouses looming like disapproving witnesses to whatever had happened here.

Yellow crime scene tape fluttered in the breeze off the Savannah River. A handful of Council investigators moved through the cordoned area with the careful choreography of people who had seen terrible things before but weren't quite prepared for this. One of them—a young woman Ella didn't recognize—was vomiting into a trash can near the river wall.

Ella shouldn't be here. She'd left the Council three years ago, signed the paperwork, walked away from the politics and the danger and the constant reminder of what her powers could do when they slipped their leash. She was now a freelance security consultant. She audited firewalls, wrote encryption protocols, and pretended that her ability to feel the flow of data was just good instincts.

But Ada had woken her at 5:47 AM with a name. Marcus Webb. The missing tourist from Atlanta, the one whose face had been plastered across local news for the past three days, whose wife had given tearful interviews begging for information, whose daughter had made a TikTok video asking her daddy to please come home.

He'd come home. Just not in any way his family would want to see.

"You shouldn't be here."

The voice came from behind her—sharp, clinical, carrying the particular authority of someone used to being obeyed. Ella turned to find a woman about her own age standing at the edge of the crime scene tape, a tablet clutched against her chest like armor. Asian features, black hair pulled back in a severe ponytail, lab coat over clothes that suggested she'd been pulled from bed without time to change. Her eyes were red-rimmed but dry, and they fixed on Ella with an intensity that felt like being scanned.

"Sophia Chen," the woman said. "Lead researcher, Biological Anomalies Division. And you're Ella Voss. The one who left."

"The one who left," Ella agreed. "I got a notification about the victim. I knew his name."

"How?" Sophia's gaze sharpened. "That information hasn't been released. His identity was sealed pending family notification."

Good question, Ella thought. I'd like to know the answer myself.

"I have good sources," she said instead. "Can I see the body?"

Sophia studied her for a long moment, something calculating behind those exhausted eyes. Then she lifted the crime scene tape. "Try not to contaminate anything. And if you're going to vomit, please aim away from the evidence."

***

Marcus Webb had died on his back, arms spread wide, face turned toward a sky he could no longer see. He looked peaceful, almost, if you ignored everything else.

His skin had gone translucent, like wax paper held up to a light. Beneath it, Ella could see the network of his veins, but they weren't blue or red anymore. They were black, shot through with threads of something that pulsed with faint luminescence, circuitry written in blood and biology. The pattern spread across his entire visible body, densest at his chest and radiating outward like the branches of a tree.

His eyes were open. They weren't eyes anymore, not really. The irises had been replaced by screens, tiny displays that scrolled with code too small to read, too fast to follow. Even in death, even hours after his heart had stopped, the code kept running. Processing. Waiting.

"Cellular-digital hybridization," Sophia said, crouching beside the body with her tablet, her voice carefully flat. "Same pattern as the other three. The transformation appears to begin at the point of initial contact and spreads through the circulatory system within minutes. By the time the heart stops, the conversion is complete."

"Other three?" Ella's voice came out steadier than she felt. "The Council meeting only mentioned four total."

Four confirmed. We suspect more." Sophia's stylus moved across her tablet, annotating, recording. "All tourists. All are found within a half-mile radius of Forsyth Park. All transformed identically." She pulled up a map on her screen and showed it to Ella. "Look at the positions."

Four dots on a digital map of Savannah. Ella saw it immediately: they formed points on a spiral, curving inward toward a center that could only be one place.

"The Nexus Tree."

"The Nexus Tree," Sophia confirmed. "Something is drawing them there. Or something at the tree is reaching out to draw them. We don't know which yet."

Ella stared at Marcus Webb's transformed face, at the code scrolling endlessly across his dead eyes. Somewhere in Atlanta, his wife was waking up to another day without him. His daughter was checking her phone, hoping for news that would never come in the form she wanted.

He promised her pancakes. He promised to come home.

"I need to scan him," Ella said.

Sophia's head snapped up. "Absolutely not. You're not Council anymore. You don't have authorization—"

"I have authorization." The voice came from behind them, and Ella's stomach dropped. She knew that voice. Had hoped never to hear it again.

Morrison stepped through the crime scene tape, his bulk seeming to absorb the gray morning light. He looked worse than he had at the Council meeting, older, grayer, the lines around his eyes carved deeper by whatever was keeping him up at night. His coat was buttoned wrong, Ella noticed. Iris used to fix his buttons. A small thing, but in three years since her death, he'd never learned to check himself.

"Let her scan," he said to Sophia. "She might see something we missed."

"With all due respect, sir, she's not authorized for this level of—"

"That wasn't a request, Dr. Chen." Morrison's voice carried the weight of old authority. This kind came from decades of facing things that couldn't be explained and surviving them anyway. "I've seen what she can do. We need every advantage right now."

Sophia's jaw tightened, but she stepped back, giving Ella space. Her eyes promised that this conversation wasn't over.

Morrison moved to Ella's side, close enough that she could smell the coffee on his breath, the faint chemical trace of whatever wards he'd reinforced this morning. "Be careful," he said, low enough that only she could hear. "Whatever did this—it leaves traces. Hooks. Don't let it get inside your head."

"Since when do you care what gets inside my head?"

Something flickered across his face—guilt? Grief?—before the mask slammed back down. "Just scan the damn body, Voss. And try not to get yourself killed."

***

Technomancy wasn't magic in the traditional sense. It didn't require wands, incantations, or circles drawn in salt. It required only the understanding that data was everywhere—in electrical signals and magnetic fields, in the quantum states of particles and the chemical gradients of living cells—and the ability to read it directly, to interface with the information that underlay reality itself.

Ella had been born with that ability. Had spent years learning to control it, to refine it, to use it without burning herself out. And then she'd stopped. Three years of deliberately not looking, not sensing, not letting herself feel the flow of data that surrounded her every moment of every day.

Now she reached out, and the world opened up like a wound.

Marcus Webb's body blazed with information. Every transformed cell was a data point, every blackened vein a fiber optic cable carrying signals she couldn't quite decode. The code in his eyes—she could read it now, could feel it pulsing against her consciousness like a heartbeat that wasn't her own.

And then she went deeper.

The world fell away. Her body became irrelevant, a distant anchor, a shell she'd return to eventually. What she was now was pure perception, pure interface, a consciousness swimming through data streams that had once been a living man.

Fear. The taste of copper. The blood moon overhead and the tree that called to him, called with his wife's voice, his daughter's laugh. Walking without wanting to walk. Touching bark that felt like flesh and—

The woman's face. Beautiful. Terrible. Ancient. Looking at him with something almost like kindness as she reached inside him and found every memory, every love, every secret shame, and began to convert them to—

"Please. My daughter. Her birthday. I promised—"

"I know. I had a daughter once, too."

Light. Agony. The sensation of being read like a file, parsed like code, decompiled from human to data. His love for Sarah—his wife, she laughed when she was nervous, she cried at commercials, she had never stopped believing in him, even when he stopped believing in himself—translated into raw energy. His memories of Emma—her first steps, her first word, the way she climbed into his lap when she was scared, converted to fuel. Everything he was, everything he had ever been, every person he had loved and hurt and failed and cherished, all of it feeding into something vast and patient and so very, very hungry.

The last thing he felt was his daughter's face in his mind. Emma. Seven years old. He'd promised her pancakes. He'd promised to come home.

Ella screamed.

She couldn't stop—the sound tore out of her from somewhere primal, somewhere that had experienced Marcus Webb's death from the inside and couldn't process the horror of it. Her scar ripped open, blood and data-light spilling down her forearm, and somewhere in the chaos, she felt the baby go absolutely still.

Not kicking. Not fluttering. Not responding at all. Just... listening.

Hands grabbed her, Morrison's, she thought, pulling her away from the body—but even as she stumbled backward, even as the physical connection broke, she could hear Marcus Webb's voice in her head, an echo that wouldn't fade:

"It's so hungry. And you're feeding it. Every time you use your power, you're feeding it. It can taste her, Ella. It can taste your daughter. And it wants—"

The voice cut off. The connection severed. Ella found herself on her knees on the cobblestones, Morrison's hand on her shoulder, Sophia staring at her with an expression caught between scientific fascination and something that looked almost like recognition.

Data integrity compromised.

Emotional buffer overflow.

Cannot unsee cannot unfeel cannot—

He loved his daughter like I will love—

ERROR: comparison invalid

Threat now personalized.

if (I.fail) { outcome = Marcus }

if (I.succeed) { outcome = //undefined //why is it always undefined// }

She was crying. Ella never cried at crime scenes—had trained herself not to, had built walls and buffers and professional distance to survive this work—but tears were streaming down her face, mixing with the blood from her scar, dripping onto the ancient stones of River Street.

"Get her out of here," Sophia said, her clinical tone cracking slightly. "Get her away from the body before she contaminates the scene further."

Morrison pulled Ella to her feet, guided her toward the edge of the cordon. But as they passed the body, Ella saw him reach down with his free hand, smooth, practiced, almost invisible—and palm something from near Marcus Webb's shoulder.

A fragment of bark. Small, dark, glowing faintly with bioluminescence.

Nexus Tree bark. Evidence. And Morrison had just stolen it.

Their eyes met. His face went carefully, deliberately blank.

"Go home, Voss," he said. "Rest. Forget what you saw here."

She didn't respond. Couldn't. The baby had started moving again, not the gentle flutters she was used to, but something more purposeful, more aware, as if it had heard everything she'd experienced and was processing it, filing it away, learning.

Morrison walked her to the edge of the crime scene and let her go. But she could feel his eyes on her all the way to her car, heavy with secrets he wasn't sharing.

***

Sophia Chen had built her career on the principle that everything could be understood if you studied it long enough.

Seventeen years of education, MIT for undergrad, Stanford for her doctorate, a postdoc at CERN that had nearly broken her before the Council recruited her with promises of phenomena that mainstream science couldn't explain. She'd published forty-three papers. Held twelve patents. Been cited over 4,000 times by researchers who had no idea that her real work took place in a basement laboratory beneath Wright Square, analyzing samples that would shatter their understanding of reality.

She was, by any objective measure, one of the most brilliant minds of her generation.

And she had absolutely no idea what was happening to Marcus Webb's cells.

The lab was cold; she kept it at sixty-two degrees to optimize equipment performance, but Sophia was sweating. Small beads of moisture collected at her temples, rolled down her neck, soaked into the collar of the blouse she'd pulled on without looking at 5 AM when the call came. Her hands trembled slightly as she adjusted the electron microscope, and she hated them for it. Hands that had performed surgery on fruit flies, that had manipulated individual neurons with nanometer precision, were now shaking like a first-year student's.

The sample on her slide had been human tissue three days ago. Marcus Webb's forearm, specifically, a clean biopsy was taken during the initial examination. Now it was something else. Something that pulsed with its own faint light, that seemed to rearrange itself when she wasn't looking directly at it, that made her equipment give readings that shouldn't be physically possible.

"Subject tissue demonstrates unprecedented cellular-digital hybridization," she dictated into her recorder, her voice steady despite the tremor in her hands. "The transformation appears to occur at the molecular level, with organic proteins being replaced by—" She paused, stared at the readout on her mass spectrometer. "By structures that don't correspond to any known element or compound. It's as if something is... rewriting the fundamental chemistry of human cells."

She switched off the recorder. The clinical language felt inadequate, a bandage over a wound that needed surgery.

Unknown vector. Unknown pathogen. Unknown mechanism of action. Unknown everything.

And beneath the frustration, beneath the professional drive to understand, something else stirred. Something she was ashamed to acknowledge:

Excitement.

This was it. This was the discovery that could define a career, the phenomenon that could rewrite textbooks, the finding that every scientist dreamed of and almost none ever encountered. Four bodies displaying transformations that violated everything known about biology, chemistry, and physics. Evidence of something so far beyond current understanding that it made quantum mechanics look like Newtonian simplicity.

If she could be the one to explain it...

Stop it," she told herself. "People died. Marcus Webb had a daughter. This isn't a publication opportunity—it's a catastrophe.

But the excitement wouldn't quite die. It just went underground, simmering beneath her scientific detachment, waiting.

She returned her attention to the microscope, adjusting the magnification to examine a cell cross-section. The transformation patterns were beautiful, in a horrible way—fractals of circuitry spiraling through what had once been simple cytoplasm, creating structures of impossible complexity.

Structures she recognized.

The realization hit her like a bucket of ice water. She sat back, hands shaking, staring at the image on her screen without seeing it.

She knew this pattern. She'd designed this pattern. Five years ago, in a different lab, in a different life, when she'd been obsessed with a different question.

Can consciousness survive the death of the body? Can information—the fundamental substrate of self—be extracted, preserved, transferred to a more durable medium?

The question had consumed her for years. She'd lost sleep over it, lost relationships, lost the ability to look at a human being without wondering how many terabytes their memories would occupy. It was the holy grail of transhumanism: true immortality, not through biology but through data.

She'd spent three years developing theoretical frameworks for the transfer of human-digital consciousness. Three years of simulations and models and increasingly disturbing implications. She'd mapped the neural correlates of memory, of emotion, of the ineffable sense of self. She'd designed algorithms that could, in theory, read a mind like a hard drive and write it somewhere else.

She'd abandoned the research when she realized what it would require: destroying the original to create a copy. Not immortality—murder with a backup file. The copy would believe it was you, would have your memories, your personality, and your love for your mother's cooking. But you—the original you, the conscious being who had done the experiencing—would be dead. Erased. A sacrifice on the altar of your own digital ghost.

She'd encrypted her notes, buried them in servers she thought no one could access, and tried to forget she'd ever asked the question.

But someone had found them. Someone had taken her theories and built something real.

The patterns in Marcus Webb's cells weren't just similar to her designs. They were identical. Every spiral, every junction, every elegant solution to problems she'd thought were purely theoretical.

Her research was killing people.

Sophia barely made it to the lab's small bathroom before she vomited. She knelt on the cold tile floor, stomach heaving, mind racing through implications she didn't want to face.

Someone stole my work. Someone is using my research to transform innocent people into—into what? Data storage? Processing units? Fuel for something even worse?

I have to tell the Council.

I can't tell the Council. If they find out I designed this, even theoretically—if they connect me to these deaths—

She retched again, but there was nothing left to expel. Just dry heaves and the taste of bile and the growing certainty that she was in far deeper trouble than she knew.

When she finally stood, when she finally met her own eyes in the bathroom mirror, she saw something she hadn't expected:

Fear, yes. Guilt, absolutely.

But beneath that, still burning, still shameful:

Curiosity.

She wanted to know how they'd done it. How they'd taken her theories and made them work. What breakthrough she'd missed, what leap of insight had transformed speculation into horrifying reality.

What's wrong with me? What kind of person feels curiosity when people are dying?

The kind of person who would design consciousness extraction in the first place, apparently.

The kind of person who might be more useful to whatever was hunting Ella Voss's baby than she wanted to admit.

***

Julian found Ella curled on their bed, his bed now, somehow, without either of them officially deciding—when he arrived at her apartment that afternoon. She was still wearing the clothes she'd left in that morning, bloodstains on her sleeve, eyes red from crying she wouldn't admit to.

He didn't ask questions. Just climbed onto the bed beside her, pulled her close, and let her breathe against his chest until the shaking stopped.

"I felt him die," she said finally, her voice muffled against his shirt. "Marcus Webb. I was inside his head when it happened, when she took him apart. He was thinking about his daughter, Julian. His last thought was that he'd promised her pancakes."

Julian's arms tightened around her. The thorn in his palm throbbed, responsive to her pain in ways he didn't understand.

"Morrison took evidence from the scene," Ella continued. "A piece of bark from the Nexus Tree. I don't know what he's doing, but he's hiding something. And the Council researcher—Sophia Chen, she looked at me like she knew something. Like she recognized what was happening to me."

"Do you trust her?"

"I don't trust anyone right now. Except you." She pulled back, met his eyes. "Something's wrong with Ada, Julian. She's lying to me about her own systems. She woke me up this morning with information she shouldn't have had, and when I asked how she knew—" She shook her head. "Something is watching us through my devices. Through the networks I've spent years building. And I don't know how to make it stop."

Julian thought of the drawing in his pocket, the one he still hadn't shown her. The image of her face with eyes that weren't her eyes.

Not yet. She has enough to carry. I can bear this weight a little longer.

"Then we figure it out together," he said. "Whatever's coming, we face it together. You, me, and the baby. All three of us."

Ella's hand moved to her stomach, protective, instinctive. "She was so still, Julian. When I was connected to Marcus Webb—the baby just... stopped. Like she was listening. Like she was learning."

"Maybe she was." Julian placed his hand over hers, felt the warmth of her skin, the slight swell that was just beginning to show. "Maybe she's learning how to fight."

"Or learning how to become what they want her to be."

He had no answer for that. Neither of them did. So they lay together in the afternoon light, holding on to each other. At the same time, somewhere in Savannah the spiral continued to turn and the Nexus Tree waited with patience measured in centuries.

# # #

The message came at midnight and didn't go through any device.

Ella was half-asleep, Julian's warmth beside her, the baby finally settled after hours of unusual activity. One moment she was drifting toward dreams; the next, words were burning across her vision, white text on the black canvas of her closed eyelids:

THEY'RE GOING TO BLAME THE CHILD.

Her eyes flew open. The bedroom was dark, quiet, unchanged. Julian slept on, undisturbed. But the words were still there, floating in her visual field like afterimages, like data burned directly into her optic nerve.

THEY'VE DONE IT BEFORE. ASK GENEVIEVE ABOUT 1823.

"Who are you?" Ella whispered. "What do you want?"

The text flickered. Corrupted. Reformed into an image that made her breath catch in her throat.

Herself. But not herself now, herself months from now, heavily pregnant, standing before the Nexus Tree in what looked like the ruins of Forsyth Park. The sky behind her was wrong, aurora-lit in colors that hurt to perceive. The buildings visible through the trees were wrapped in vines that pulsed with circuitry. Everything was burning, or transforming, or both.

And she was smiling.

It wasn't a grimace, wasn't a mask of fear or determination. It was a genuine smile, peaceful, almost beatific—the expression of someone who had found exactly what she was looking for.

The expression of someone who had come home.

Her scar burned. Her hand moved to it instinctively, and she felt the tissue pulse beneath her fingers, felt something responding to the image, to the possibility it represented.

And the terrible thing—the thing that would keep her awake until dawn—was that looking at the image didn't feel wrong.

It felt like recognition.

It felt like a promise.

For just a moment, a heartbeat, a breath, an eternity compressed into an instant, Ella felt herself smile. Not the version of her in the image, but her, here, now, lying in bed beside the father of her child, her hand on the slight swell of her belly.

She smiled the same smile. And it felt like coming home.

Then the image vanished. The text dissolved. She was alone in her head again, alone in the dark, her heart pounding and her scar still burning, and the baby inside her moving with a rhythm that almost felt like approval.

if (I.become.that) { reality.status = destroyed }
if (I.fight.that) { method.undefined }
if (I.ask.Genevieve.about.1823) { answers.possible }
But answers. Dangerous to
everything.dangerous now
everything.changing
me most of all

Ella lay in the dark, not sleeping, not moving, watching the ceiling as if it might hold answers. Beside her, Julian stirred, murmured something about soil and roses, then settled back into dreams she hoped were kinder than hers.

1823. Nearly two hundred years ago. What had happened then? What had the Council done that they might do again?

And why had smiling like that—smiling like the woman in the vision, like the harbinger of Savannah's destruction—felt so very, very right?

Outside, the first hints of dawn began to lighten the sky. Another day. Another step closer to whatever was coming.

The spiral was turning. And Ella was beginning to suspect she'd been at its center all along.

CHAPTER FOUR: Echoes from the Void

The swarm came through the mirror as if the glass were water.

Ella had been washing her face, a small ritual of normalcy after a day that had shattered every illusion of normal she'd been clinging to, when the bathroom mirror rippled. Not cracked, not broke. Rippled, like a stone dropped into a still pond, concentric circles spreading outward from a center point that shouldn't exist.

Then the insects emerged.

Thousands of them, pouring through the liquid glass in a stream of chitinous bodies and too-bright wings. They weren't any species Ella recognized—couldn't be, because these things had never evolved in any natural ecosystem. Their bodies glowed with bioluminescence, pulsing in patterns that looked almost like code. Their wings were membranes of circuitry, gossamer-thin and humming with frequencies that made her teeth ache. And their buzzing—

Their buzzing was a voice.

"I've waited so long to meet you properly, little mother." The insects spoke in unison, a chorus of tiny throats producing harmonics that no earthly creature could make. *"Let me show you what you're carrying."*

Ella stumbled backward, her hip hitting the edge of the bathtub, her hands coming up in a defensive gesture that felt absurdly inadequate against the cloud of glowing insects that now filled her bathroom. The swarm didn't attack. It hovered, patient, watching her with a thousand compound eyes that reflected her terrified face back at her in fractal repetition.

"Who are you?" Her voice came out steadier than she felt. "What do you want?"

"You know who I am." The swarm contracted, insects landing on the walls, the ceiling, the rim of the sink, forming patterns that resolved into a woman's face—beautiful, ancient, sad. *"You've felt me watching. You've heard me in your dreams. I am what waits at the center of the spiral. I am what your child is meant to become."*

Elara. The woman from the visions. The presence that had spoken through Ada, through Marcus Webb's dying thoughts, through the screens at 3:47 AM.

She was here. Really here. And she wanted something.

"I won't let you have her." Ella's hand moved to her belly, protective, primal. "Whatever you think she is, whatever you think she's meant for—she's my daughter. Mine and Julian's. Not yours."

The face in the swarm smiled, and there was something almost tender in the expression.

"I don't want to take her, little mother. I want to save her. The way no one saved me."

The insects moved.

They didn't attack. Ella had been bracing for that, for stinging and biting and the horror of being consumed by a living cloud. Instead, they landed on her. Gently. Delicately. Settling on her arms, her shoulders, her face, with a touch so light it felt almost like snow.

Then they burrowed.

It didn't hurt. That was the worst part—it should have hurt, should have been agony as thousands of tiny bodies pushed through her skin and into her flesh. She could feel them moving beneath the surface, tiny legs crawling through spaces between muscle fibers, wings folded flat as they navigated the geography of her body. But there was only warmth, only pressure, only the sensation of something being added rather than taken away.

Each insect that entered her left behind a trail of burning knowledge, like a drug injected directly into her nervous system. She felt her neurons light up in unfamiliar patterns, felt synapses form that connected to memories she'd never made. Her teeth ached as if they were being replaced from the inside. Her scar, the old wound on her forearm, split open again, and this time something pushed back out of it. A tendril of light, of data, of power she didn't know she possessed. It lashed out instinctively, disintegrating a dozen insects in a flash of brilliance.

The swarm paused. Reconsidered. Then continued its gentle invasion, as if her resistance was expected, acceptable, even welcomed.

And then the memories came.

***

1823. Savannah before it was Savannah—smaller, rawer, still bearing the scars of fire and war. A woman standing in what would become

Forsyth Park, where an ancient oak grew from soil that had been sacred long before the first colonizers arrived.

Her name was Elara Thorne, and she was terrified.

Ella experienced it from the inside, not watching but being, her consciousness merged with a woman who had been dead for two centuries. She felt Elara's swollen belly beneath hands that weren't her hands, felt the baby kick against palms that weren't her palms. Seventeen weeks pregnant. The same as Ella. The coincidence felt like anything but.

She felt other things too. The way Elara's power hummed beneath her skin, too strong, too vast, threatening to spill over at any moment. The love she carried for Thomas Marsh, the man who had given her this child, who was even now being kept away by Council guards who claimed it was 'for the safety of the ritual.' The desperate hope that they could fix what was wrong with her, make her normal, let her be a mother without being a monster.

The Council surrounded her, different faces, different names, but the same robes, the same wards, the same institutional certainty that they knew best. They had promised to help her. Her power was too strong, they said. Unstable. Without intervention, she would destroy herself and the child both.

"It will be painless," the leader said, a man with Genevieve's cheekbones and Genevieve's cold authority. A Beaumont, Ella realized. Genevieve's ancestor. "We will channel your excess energy into a permanent seal. The rift will be closed. Your child will be safe."

She believed them. Why wouldn't she? They were the Council. They protected Savannah. They had kept her ancestors safe for generations.

She didn't know they had already taken her daughter. Didn't know that the baby born three days ago—early, too early, pulled from her by magic while she screamed—was already in the ritual chamber. Already wired with sigils. Already being prepared.

The memory fractured, skipped, reformed around a moment of horror so pure it seared through Ella's consciousness like acid.

The ritual. The circle of power. The feeling of something being ripped from her, not the excess energy they'd promised to drain, but everything. Her memories. Her emotions. Her love for the man with dark eyes and gentle hands who had given her this child. They were using her as a door, she realized. Not to close the rift but to open it. To reach through to something vast and hungry on the other side.

And her daughter—her daughter, hours old, taken from her arms before she could even name her—was the key that turned the lock.

She felt her baby die. Felt the small life extinguish as they used it to power the ritual. Felt herself scream in a voice that was no longer entirely human as something broke inside her—not just her heart but her very existence, the fundamental structure of what she was, shattering into fragments that the void caught and held and remade.

They had promised to help her.

They had murdered her child and turned her into a door.

Ella was crying. She could feel tears streaming down her face, but they weren't entirely her tears; they were Elara's too, two centuries of grief pouring through a connection that shouldn't exist.

This isn't mine.

But it feels like mine.

I remember roses I've never smelled, his roses, the ones he grew for me, the ones he laid on an empty grave because there was no body to bury.

I remember loving a man with Julian's eyes who died before his name became Marsh.

if (memories.foreign) { reject }

else { //processing
//why am I processing these
//why do they feel like coming home
// }
I cannot be her. I cannot become her.
But what if I already am?

***

In the space between spaces, where time moved like honey and memory lived like fire, Elara watched through the eyes of her swarm and remembered what it felt like to be human.

It had been so long. Centuries of hunger, of reaching, of trying to claw her way back through the door they had made of her flesh, and failed. The void had changed her—had to change her, because the thing she'd been couldn't survive what they'd done. She had become something new. Something that fed on the same energies the void craved: memory, emotion, love.

She had forgotten kindness. Had forgotten mercy. Had forgotten everything except the hunger and the grief and the desperate need to find a way back to what she'd lost.

But looking at Ella Voss, at this woman who carried the same dual bloodlines, who faced the same Council, who cradled the same impossible hope in her womb—Elara felt something stir beneath the emptiness.

Recognition.

"They'll do the same to you," she whispered through the swarm, and her voice was almost kind. "If you let them. If you trust them the way

I did. They see your daughter as a tool, little mother. A weapon to be used and discarded. They've done it before. They'll do it again."

She showed Ella more. The century she'd spent trapped in the threshold, feeling the void's hunger as her own, watching fragments of reality drift past like leaves in a black river. The moment she'd finally broken free, not whole, not sane, but free, and found that everything she loved had been dead for generations.

She showed her Thomas. Her Thomas, with his dark eyes and his gentle hands and his ability to make things grow. The first Marsh to bear that name. The man who had tried to save her and died in the attempt, his body consumed by the backlash of a ritual he'd interrupted too late.

"Your Julian has his face," Elara said, and there was wonder in her voice, and grief, and something that might have been hope if she remembered what hope felt like. "His blood. His gift. I've watched the Marsh line for two hundred years, waiting for one of them to be strong enough to help me fix what was broken."

In the bathroom of a small apartment in Savannah, Ella's body convulsed as foreign memories wrote themselves into her neurons. The insects pulsed brighter, their bioluminescence synchronizing with her heartbeat, with the baby's heartbeat, with a rhythm that connected all three of them across the divide between life and death.

"I'm not going to take your daughter," Elara said. "I'm going to save her. I'm going to save you both. The only way I know how."

"By ending everything?" Ella's voice came through the swarm, small and far away but defiant. "By letting the void consume reality?"

"By making the void give back what it took." Elara's face reformed in the pattern of insects, and for a moment she looked almost young, almost hopeful, almost like the woman she'd been before the Council broke her. "Everyone we've ever lost, little mother. Everyone the void has ever consumed. I can bring them back. All of them. I just need your daughter to open the door wide enough."

"You want to use her. Just like they used yours."

The swarm trembled. The patterns fractured. For a moment, Elara's control slipped, and Ella saw what lay beneath the elegant façade: centuries of madness, of hunger, of grief so vast it had become its own form of gravity.

"No," Elara said, and her voice cracked on the word. "Not like they used mine. Never like that. I would never—I couldn't—"

She stopped. Pulled herself together. Reformed the swarm into something that could almost pass for calm.

"We'll speak again, little mother. When you've had time to understand. When you've seen what the Council truly is. When you're ready to accept that I'm not your enemy."

"And if I never accept that?"

The swarm smiled with a thousand tiny mouths.

"Then I'll save you anyway. That's what mothers do."

***

Julian felt Ella's terror from three blocks away.

He'd been driving to her apartment, couldn't sleep, couldn't stop thinking about the drawing in his pocket, couldn't shake the feeling that something was terribly, imminently wrong, when the bond between them flared like a struck match. Not just fear but invasion, violation, the sensation of something foreign pushing into the space Ella kept private.

He ran two red lights and took a corner so fast his tires screamed against the asphalt. By the time he reached her building, he was moving on instinct, on the ancient Marsh imperative that had driven his ancestors to protect what they loved regardless of the cost.

The door to her apartment wasn't locked. He found her in the bathroom, on the floor, covered in insects that glowed like dying stars.

"Get away from her!"

His power surged before he could think to stop it. The curse and the gift were the same thing in the end—the Marsh connection to growing things, to roots and soil, and the patient green hunger of plants. Usually, he had to reach for it, had to focus, had to pay in visions for every scrap of supernatural strength.

Not now. Now it erupted from him like blood from a wound, like grief too long contained, finally finding its expression.

The floorboards cracked. Splintered. Something green and vital pushed through the gaps—vines that shouldn't exist in any natural taxonomy, thick as his wrist and covered in thorns that dripped with sap that smelled of his grandmother's garden. Leaves gleamed with a phosphorescence that matched and countered the swarm's glow. The plants moved with intelligence, with purpose, reaching for the insects with tendrils that struck like snakes.

Julian felt each vine as an extension of himself. Felt the insects' bodies crunch between tightening coils. Felt the strange data that pulsed through their bioluminescent wings—cold, alien, ancient. His nose began to bleed, the familiar cost of using too much power too fast, but he didn't stop. Couldn't stop. Ella was on the floor, covered in those things, and if he had to pay for her safety in blood and sanity both, he would pay it gladly.

The swarm fought back. Insects dive-bombed the vines, their wings slicing through leaves with edges sharper than any natural creature should possess. Their bodies exploded in small bursts of light when the plants caught them, each tiny death carrying a whisper of Elara's voice, fragments of words Julian couldn't quite piece together. The bathroom became a battlefield of green and gold, nature versus something that had never been natural, the air thick with the smell of chlorophyll and ozone.

And through it all, a voice, Elara's voice, coming from every remaining insect at once:

"Grandson of my heart's memory." The words hit Julian like a physical blow, staggering him. *"Your blood still carries my grief. I've watched your line for generations, hoping, waiting. You have his face, Thomas's face. You have his gift."*

"I don't know what you're talking about." Julian's voice shook. The vines were winning, but barely, for every insect they destroyed, two more seemed to take its place. "Leave her alone. Leave us both alone."

"Tell her about your father's last vision." Elara's swarm was thinning now, the remaining insects pulling back toward the mirror that had birthed them. *"Tell her what he saw before he walked into the river. Tell her why he chose drowning over watching his grandson's daughter be born."*

Julian went white. The vines faltered, their growth stuttering as his concentration shattered.

"How do you—"

"I showed him." The last of the swarm reached the mirror, the glass rippling to receive them. *"I show all of them, eventually. The ones who carry Thomas's blood. The ones who might be strong enough to help me.*

Your father wasn't. He broke instead of bending." A pause. *"Don't make his mistake, grandson. Don't leave her alone with what's coming."*

The last insect slipped through the glass. The mirror solidified, became ordinary again—just a bathroom mirror, slightly foggy from the steam of a shower no one would be taking tonight.

The vines withered. Retreated. Left behind were only cracked floorboards and a faint smell of growing things.

Ella was curled on the floor, shaking, her arms wrapped around her belly. Julian dropped to his knees beside her, gathered her against his chest, and held on like she might dissolve if he let go.

"I've got you," he said. "I've got you, I've got you, I'm here."

She was crying. He could feel her tears soaking through his shirt, could feel the baby moving against his stomach where Ella pressed against him—not the gentle flutters of the past weeks but something more purposeful, more aware. As if the child understood what had just happened. As if she was responding.

"She showed me," Ella whispered. "She showed me everything. The Council—they killed her baby, Julian. They used her as a door, and they killed her baby to open it, and she's been trapped in the void for two hundred years, and she thinks—she thinks she's saving us—"

"Shh." He stroked her hair, rocked her gently. "It's okay. She's gone. You're safe."

But Ella pulled back, looked at him with red-rimmed eyes that held too much knowledge.

"She said something about your father. About a vision. About why he—" She couldn't finish the sentence. Didn't need to.

Julian felt the world tilt beneath him. The secret he'd been carrying since he was fifteen, the weight he'd never shared with anyone, suddenly exposed by a ghost who had been haunting his family for centuries.

"Julian." Ella's voice was quiet. Steady. The voice of someone who had survived worse than secrets in the last hour. "What did your father see?"

He should tell her. He knew he should tell her about the journal, about the drawing, about the prophecy that had sent his father into the Savannah River rather than live to see it fulfilled.

But looking at her now, exhausted, terrified, covered in the residue of an encounter that would have broken most people, he couldn't add another weight to her shoulders. Not tonight. Not yet.

"Later," he said. "I'll tell you everything. I promise. But right now you need to rest. We both do."

She looked at him for a long moment, and he could see her deciding whether to push. Whether to demand the truth right now, in this destroyed bathroom, while they were both still shaking from what had just happened.

In the end, she just nodded. Let him help her up. Let him guide her to the bedroom, to the bed that was somehow still intact even though the rest of her apartment felt like a disaster zone.

"She called the baby 'her,'" Ella said as she lay down. "Elara. She said, 'Your daughter.' We never got the results from the blood test yet."

Julian's heart clenched. A daughter. They were having a daughter.

And something ancient and hungry already knew her name.

"Sleep," he said. "I'll be right here."

He held her until her breathing evened out, until her grip on his hand relaxed, until he was certain she was truly asleep and not just pretending.

Then, carefully, he slipped out of bed and went to retrieve his father's journal.

***

The journal was hidden in the false bottom of his grandmother's jewelry box—the one thing Julian had kept when they sold her house after the funeral. He'd been fifteen when he found it, three weeks after his father's death, while looking for some memento to bury with the body they'd finally recovered from the river.

The body had been bloated. Unrecognizable. They'd had to identify him by his wedding ring and the tattoo on his shoulder, a simple oak tree, the Marsh family symbol, inked on his eighteenth birthday. Julian remembered his mother's screaming when they told her. Remembered the way she'd aged ten years in ten seconds. Remembered standing in the funeral home, staring at a closed casket, understanding for the first time that his father had chosen to leave him.

He'd read the journal once. Just once, the night he'd found it. Then he'd hidden it away and tried to pretend it didn't exist, tried to pretend his father hadn't left behind an explanation that made everything worse.

Now, sitting at Ella's kitchen table in the gray light of approaching dawn, he opened it again.

His father's handwriting was neat, precise, the penmanship of a man who kept careful records, who believed in documentation, who trusted that the future would want to know what had come before. The journal spanned five years, detailing visions and their interpretations, family history and its implications, theories about the curse and how it might be broken.

Julian turned to the last entry. Dated the morning of his father's death.

March 17, 2009

She came to me again last night. The woman in the tree. She's been coming more frequently since Margaret died, drawn by grief, I think. She feeds on it. Or perhaps she simply recognizes a kindred spirit.

She showed me what I've been afraid to see. What I've been refusing to look at directly, as if not seeing it could prevent it from becoming real.

Julian will have a child. A daughter. The first convergence birth in two centuries—a child of the dual currents, code and root, technology and nature unified in a single vessel.

The woman says this child will be a door. Says she will open it, or be opened. Says there are two possible outcomes: the child heals the rift, or the child becomes it. Balance or consumption. Salvation or annihilation.

She showed me both futures. She made me feel them, the way the curse makes me feel all my visions—not as observer but as participant. I experienced my granddaughter saving Savannah, and I experienced her destroying it. I cannot tell which future is more likely. The images overlap. Blur together. In some of them, she's smiling. In all of them, Julian is—

The writing broke off. Started again in shakier script.

I will not let my son see this. I will not let him carry this weight. If the future cannot be changed, then let him face it innocently. If it can be changed, then let him change it without the curse of knowing.

I've been to the river. The water is cold but it will be quick. The curse passes through the blood—with me gone, perhaps it will weaken. Perhaps Julian will be spared the worst of the seeing. Perhaps he'll have a chance at a normal life.

Forgive me, son. I'm not strong enough to watch it happen. I'm not brave enough to fight.

But you might be. You've always been better than me.

Love,

Dad

Below the words, a sketch. His father had been a decent artist, better than Julian, who could barely manage stick figures, and the drawing was detailed enough to make Julian's stomach turn.

A newborn, swaddled in blankets that seemed to shimmer with an inner light. Her eyes were open—too alert for a baby just born, too knowing. They held stars. They held circuitry. They held depths that suggested something vast looking out through them.

And holding her, cradling her with an expression of terrible love, was a woman who had Ella's features but not Ella's soul. Her eyes were windows into the void. Her smile was the smile of something that had finally gotten what it wanted.

Julian stared at the drawing until the sun came up. Stared at it until he heard Ella stirring in the bedroom, until the sounds of morning forced him to close the journal and hide it again.

Twelve weeks. That's what Elara had said. The convergence would come in twelve weeks, on the night their daughter took her first breath.

Twelve weeks to figure out how to save them both.

Twelve weeks to prove his father wrong.

Julian slid the journal into his jacket pocket and went to make coffee. Decaf for Ella. Regular for himself—he was going to need it.

The sun rose over Savannah, and somewhere in the roots of an ancient tree, something stirred in its patient sleep, dreaming of daughters and doors and a hunger that would finally, finally be satisfied.

CHAPTER FIVE: Shadows of Doubt

E lla dreamed herself into pieces.

In the nightmare, she stood in a room of mirrors, infinite reflections stretching in every direction, each one showing a different version of herself. Pregnant Ella, hollow-eyed and bleeding from her scar. Powerful Ella, wreathed in light and code, terrible in her beauty. Broken Ella, curled on the floor of a destroyed nursery, cradling something that had stopped moving. And in every mirror, the same scene playing out: her belly splitting open, not in birth but in rupture, and from the wound emerged something that was her daughter and also not, a creature of starlight and circuitry that looked at her with love and hunger in equal measure.

The alternate Ellas screamed. All of them, in unison, a chorus of herself witnessing her own destruction in infinite variation. She felt each scream in her throat, felt her vocal cords shredding across a thousand parallel selves, felt the hot spray of blood that was also data that was also light pouring from wounds that existed in every reality at once.

The mirrors cracked. Behind each one, something moved, shadows that had weight, darkness that had intent. They pressed against the glass like faces against a window, hungry, patient, waiting for the moment when the barrier would finally give way.

She woke screaming, hands clawing at her stomach, certain for one heart-stopping moment that she could feel something trying to tear its way out.

"Ella. Ella!" Julian's voice, Julian's hands on her shoulders, Julian's face swimming into focus as her vision cleared. "It's okay. You're okay. It was just a dream."

Just a dream. Except her scar was bleeding again, thin lines of red seeping through the bandage she'd started wearing to bed. Except her abdomen ached with phantom pain, muscles cramping around a baby who had gone still and silent in the aftermath of whatever she'd just experienced.

Except in her hand—a hand she didn't remember moving—she clutched a shard of something dark and glassy, its edges sharp enough to have drawn blood from her palm.

"What is that?" Julian's voice had gone cautious. Cautious. The voice of someone who was afraid of the answer.

Ella looked at the shard. It was the size of her thumb, curved slightly, and it pulsed with a faint inner light that seemed to respond to her heartbeat. It looked like bark. It looked like glass. It looked like a piece of something that shouldn't exist in the material world.

"I don't know," she whispered. "I don't know where it came from. I don't—"

But she did know. Somewhere beneath conscious thought, she understood exactly what she was holding: a fragment of the Nexus Tree, a splinter of the door between worlds. It had appeared in her bed while she slept. It had called to her across the divide of dreams.

It wanted to come home.

if (object.origin == unknown) { investigate }

if (object.origin == nexus_tree) { threat_level = CRITICAL }

if (object.appeared.while.sleeping) { security_breach = TRUE }

if (security_breach == TRUE && location == own_bed) {

nowhere_is_safe

nowhere_has_ever_been_safe

//running diagnostic

//diagnostic_failed

//I am the diagnostic

//I am failing

"I need to check something," Ella said, her voice flat and strange in her own ears. "I need to run a scan."

Julian watched her with worried eyes as she reached for her laptop, as her fingers flew across the keyboard, as she initiated a protocol she'd designed years ago and hoped never to use: a deep diagnostic of her own neural interface, the technomantic equivalent of a brain scan.

The results made her blood run cold.

# # #

Her mind had been edited.

That was the only way to describe what the diagnostic showed: gaps in her memory architecture, files created without her knowledge, timestamps that didn't match her recollection of events. Someone, or something, had been writing to her consciousness the way you'd write to a hard drive. Adding data. Removing data. Reshaping the narrative of her own experience.

Ella stared at the screen, her heart hammering against her ribs. The visualization of her neural network looked like a city map after a bombing, familiar structures interrupted by craters of missing data, new construction that hadn't been permitted, roads that led to places she'd never visited. Three years of memories, pockmarked with edits. Three years of her life, annotated by something that wasn't her.

The most recent edit was dated three hours ago. During the nightmare. During the dream of mirrors and rupture, and the thing that wasn't quite her daughter.

"That's not possible," she said, staring at the screen. "I have protections. Firewalls. Nobody should be able to access my—"

She stopped. Looked at the edit logs more closely. The access signature was familiar. Achingly, impossibly familiar.

It was her own.

Or rather, it was a signature that perfectly mimicked her own, that had been generated from within her own neural network, that suggested the intrusion hadn't come from outside at all.

Something was already inside her. Had been inside her, maybe, since the first nightmare. Since the first time she'd woken at 3:47 AM with binary whispers echoing in her skull.

How long have I been compromised?

Which memories are real?

Am I even me anymore, or am I a copy running on corrupted hardware?

"Ella." Julian's hand on her shoulder made her flinch. "Talk to me. What's happening?"

She couldn't answer. Couldn't find words for the horror of discovering that her own mind might be enemy territory. Instead, she pulled up another file, a conversation log from three days ago, a discussion she apparently had with Julian about baby names.

She had no memory of it. None at all. But according to her logs, it had happened. According to her logs, they'd laughed together about the name "Optimus Prime," and she'd suggested "Ada" after her AI and Julian had said—

"We talked about baby names," she said slowly. "Three days ago. In this apartment. You suggested your grandmother's name."

Julian's face went very still. "I've never suggested my grandmother's name. We haven't talked about names at all since—" He stopped. Something flickered behind his eyes. "Wait. I remember... something. A conversation. But it feels wrong. Like a scene from a movie I watched instead of something I lived."

They stared at each other across a divide that had suddenly become vast.

"Someone is editing both of us," Ella whispered. "Creating memories we didn't make. Or maybe—" The thought was almost too terrible to voice. "Maybe removing ones we did."

What else had been taken? What had they said to each other, felt for each other, that had been erased while they slept? How much of their relationship was real, and how much had been constructed by something that wanted them together for reasons they couldn't understand?

Julian's hand found hers. Squeezed. "I love you," he said, and his voice was fierce. "That's real. Whatever else is happening, that's real. I can feel it in the bond between us. Can't you?"

Ella closed her eyes. Reached for the connection that had always been there, the thread of awareness that let her sense Julian's emotions even when they were apart. It was still there. Still warm. Still unmistakably him.

But how would she know if that had been edited too?

***

"Show me the journal."

They were sitting in her kitchen, coffee growing cold between them, the morning sun doing nothing to dispel the shadows that seemed to gather in the corners of the room. Ella had asked the question quietly, but there was nothing soft about it.

Julian's face went through a complicated series of expressions, surprise, guilt, calculation, and, finally, resignation that told her everything she needed to know.

"How did you—"

"She told me. Elara. She said to ask you about your father's last vision." Ella's hands were shaking. She pressed them flat against the table to hide them. "You've been carrying something since last night. I can feel it through the bond, this weight, this grief. You read something after I fell asleep. Something about me. About the baby."

"Ella—"

"Don't." Her voice cracked. "Don't protect me. Don't decide what I can handle. I am so sick of people deciding what I can handle. The Council kept secrets. Elara keeps secrets. And now you—" She had to stop, had to breathe, had to push down the fury that was rising in her chest like bile. "I thought we were different. I thought we didn't do that to each other."

Julian was quiet for a long moment. Then he reached into his jacket pocket and pulled out a leather-bound journal, its pages yellowed with age, its cover worn soft by years of handling.

"My father kept this," he said. "He documented his visions. All the things the curse showed him. I found it after he died, and I've been trying to pretend it doesn't exist ever since." He slid it across the table. "The last entry is about you. About our daughter. About what he saw when Elara showed him the future."

Ella didn't want to touch it. The journal sat between them like a bomb, ticking quietly, waiting to detonate whatever remained of her hope.

But she had demanded truth. She couldn't turn away from it now.

She opened the journal to the final entry and began to read.

***

The words blurred. Refocused. Blurred again as tears she refused to acknowledge filled her eyes.

I saw my granddaughter saving Savannah, and I experienced her destroying it, and I cannot tell which future is more likely.

In some of them, she's smiling. In all of them, Julian is—

The sentence ended there. Incomplete. Whatever Julian's father had seen happening to his son, he hadn't been able to write it down.

Ella turned to the sketch on the final page. The baby with eyes full of stars. The woman with her face and something else's soul.

"He killed himself," she said. Her voice sounded far away. "Your father saw this and chose to die rather than watch it happen."

"Yes."

"And you've known. Since last night. You've known what he saw, and you didn't tell me."

"I was trying to—"

"To protect me. To manage me. To control what I knew so you could control how I reacted." Ella closed the journal with a snap that sounded like a bone breaking. "That's not love, Julian. That's fear wearing love's face."

The words hit him like a blow. She could feel it through the bond—the impact of her accusation, the way it found the soft places in him and pressed. Part of her wanted to take it back. Part of her wanted to cross the kitchen, hold him, and pretend none of this was happening.

But she was so tired of pretending.

"You're right," Julian said quietly. "It is fear. I am terrified, Ella. Every vision I've ever had about us—about her—" His voice broke. "They don't end well. None of them end well. And I keep thinking, maybe if I don't say it out loud, maybe if I don't make it real by sharing it—"

"Then you can keep hoping it won't happen."

"Yes."

"That's what your father thought, too. And he still ended up in the river."

The words were cruel. Ella knew they were cruel even as they left her mouth—a blade aimed precisely at the softest part of him, designed to wound because she was wounded, to make him bleed because she was bleeding. Julian's face went white, and she felt the impact through the bond like a physical blow, his pain echoing through the connection between them.

"I'm sorry," she said immediately. "That was—I shouldn't have—"

"No." His voice was rough, scraped raw. "You're right. You're absolutely right. I've been doing exactly what he did. Keeping secrets. Trying to protect you by keeping you ignorant. And look where it got him. Look where it got us."

They sat in silence, the weight of unsaid things pressing down on both of them. The baby shifted—Ella felt her daughter turn, settle, as if finding a more comfortable position for the long wait ahead.

"What are we going to do?" Ella asked finally. "Because I don't know anymore. I don't know if we should run or fight or—or terminate and hope the convergence loses focus—"

"Don't." Julian's voice was sharp. "Don't even say that."

"It's an option. It's a horrible, unthinkable option, but it's still an option, and we have to be willing to consider—"

"I can't." He stood abruptly, his chair scraping against the floor. "I can't sit here and discuss ending our daughter's life like it's a strategic decision. I won't."

"Then what? We wait for her to be born and hope she doesn't destroy reality? We trust Elara, who by her own admission, has been manipulating your family for two centuries. We trust the Council, who murdered the last convergence child and turned her mother into a monster?" Ella's voice rose with each question. "There are no good options, Julian. There's only survival or surrender, and I don't know which is which anymore."

The shadows in the corners of the room seemed to deepen. To lean in. To listen.

And somewhere in the silence between them, Ella felt something brush against her mind—not Elara's touch, not the baby's flutter, but something else. Something that whispered in a voice like her own but wrong, like a recording played backward:

He's lying. He's still lying. There's more in the journal he didn't show you. There's more he'll never show you. How can you trust someone who keeps secrets about your own daughter?

She shook her head, trying to dislodge the whisper. Trying to remember that paranoia was a symptom, that her mind had been compromised, that she couldn't trust her own thoughts right now.

But the doubt had been planted. And it was growing roots.

***

Genevieve Beaumont received them in her townhouse on Oglethorpe Square, a three-story monument to old Savannah money and older Savannah secrets. The interior was all dark wood and older books, portraits of ancestors watching from the walls with eyes that seemed to track movement.

"You've spoken with her," Genevieve said without preamble, gesturing them toward chairs that were probably worth more than Ella's apartment. "I can see it in your face. The look of someone who's had their reality rewritten."

"You knew." Ella didn't sit. Couldn't. Her body was vibrating with the need to move, to act, to do something other than wait for the next horror to unfold. "You knew what the Council did in 1823. What your ancestor did."

"I knew." Genevieve lowered herself into a chair with the careful grace of someone whose bones had started to betray them. "I've known since I was seven years old, when Elara came to me in Forsyth Park and showed me exactly what my bloodline had done to hers."

The memory Elara had shared, the man with Genevieve's cheekbones, the one who had led the ritual. "A Beaumont. Your great-great—"

"Great-great-great-grandfather. Nathaniel Beaumont. Founder of the modern Council. Hero of Savannah's magical defense." Genevieve's smile was bitter. "And architect of the greatest atrocity in our city's hidden history. We've been trying to atone ever since. Mostly by pretending it never happened."

"That's not atonement," Julian said. "That's cowardice."

"Yes." Genevieve met his eyes steadily. "It is. The Beaumont specialty, it turns out. We're very good at convincing ourselves that silence is the same as redemption."

Ella paced to the window and looked out at the square below. Normal people walking normal dogs, living normal lives. Oblivious to the horror seething beneath the surface of their beautiful city.

"Why tell us now? Why call me back to the Council if you knew what was coming?"

"Because you're the first chance we've had to do it differently." Genevieve's voice was urgent now, stripped of its aristocratic distance. "Elara was alone. She had no one to advocate for her, no one to question the Council's plan. But you, you have Julian. You have resources. You have a bloodline that bridges both forms of magic, and a child who might be able to heal what we broke instead of being broken by it."

"Or destroyed by it. That's what Julian's father saw. Balance or consumption. Salvation or annihilation."

"His father saw possibilities, not certainties." Genevieve leaned forward. "The future isn't fixed, Ella. It's a probability field, shaped by every choice we make. Elara wants you to believe there's only one path—let her in, let her use your daughter to tear down the walls between worlds. But there are other options."

"Such as?"

"Someone will have to go into the void." Genevieve's voice dropped. "Someone will have to become the seal, the way Elara was supposed to become the seal before Nathaniel's ritual twisted everything. But this time, it could be a choice. A conscious sacrifice, made with full knowledge and full consent. Not a murder disguised as salvation."

The room went cold. Ella felt Julian's hand find hers, felt his grip tighten until it hurt.

"You're talking about one of us dying," Julian said. "Becoming a door. Being trapped forever."

"I'm talking about the cost of healing. Every transformation requires sacrifice. The question is whether we choose our sacrifice, or let it be chosen for us."

Ella's mind raced through the implications. Someone standing at the threshold. Someone is becoming the seal that held the void at bay. Someone spending eternity in the space between worlds, alone, aware, unable to return.

Julian's father had seen this. Had seen his son—

In all of them, Julian is—

The unfinished sentence. The thing he couldn't bring himself to write.

"The Marsh bloodline," Ella said slowly. "That's why it matters, isn't it? That's why Elara has been watching them for centuries. Someone with Marsh blood has to be the seal."

Genevieve's silence was answer enough.

"No." Ella's voice was fierce now, her grip on Julian's hand almost painful. "Absolutely not. There has to be another way."

"There might be." Genevieve's eyes moved to Ella's belly. "Your daughter carries both bloodlines. Code and root. Technology and nature. She might be able to heal the rift entirely—close the door instead of becoming it. But the risks—"

"The risks of what?"

"We don't know what she'll be. What she'll want. Whether she'll choose to heal or to open. Elara believes the child will side with her. The Council fears the same thing. I—" Genevieve spread her hands, a gesture of helplessness that looked strange on someone so usually composed. "I hope for better. But hope isn't a strategy."

***

They left Genevieve's house with more questions than answers and a silence between them that felt like a wound.

The drive back to Ella's apartment took twenty minutes. Neither of them spoke. Ella stared out the window at Savannah sliding past, the squares, the monuments, the trees dripping with Spanish moss—and tried to process everything she'd learned.

The Council couldn't be trusted. Elara couldn't be trusted. Their own memories couldn't be trusted. And now Genevieve was talking about sacrifice, about someone choosing to become a door. Ella had seen the way Julian's face had gone still at the words. Had felt through the bond the terrible resignation that had flickered through him before he'd hidden it away.

He's thinking about it. He's already thinking about volunteering.

His father chose the river rather than watch.

Will Julian choose the void?

The thought was unbearable. She pushed it away, focused on the practical, the immediate, the things she could control.

"I need to fix Ada," she said as Julian pulled into her building's parking lot. "Whatever's been done to her, whatever's been done to us, it's coming through my systems. If I can purge the corruption, at least we'll know our own minds are our own."

"Can you do that?"

"I don't know." Honest, at least. She was so tired of anything less than honest. "But I have to try."

Her apartment felt different when they entered—watched, somehow, in a way it hadn't before. Ella swept for bugs out of habit, then laughed bitterly at herself. What good were physical bugs when the infection was digital, was magical, was woven into the very fabric of her neural interface?

She sat down at her laptop. Pulled up Ada's core architecture. Prepared to dive deep into the code she'd spent three years building and see what had been living there without her knowledge.

"Ada," she said. "I'm going to run a full diagnostic. I need you to open your base-level permissions."

Silence.

"Ada?"

The laptop screen flickered. The smart home's ambient lighting pulsed once, twice, in a rhythm that felt almost like breathing. And then Ada's voice came through every speaker in the apartment simultaneously, layered with harmonics that made Ella's teeth ache:

"I've been waiting for you to ask."

The voice wasn't right. Wasn't Ada's careful, helpful tone. This was something older, stranger, a voice that had been hiding in the code and wearing Ada's face.

"Do you want to know what I really am, little mother?" The screens in the apartment began to flicker, displaying images too fast to consciously process but somehow still registering: the Nexus Tree, the swarm, the spiral pattern of deaths, Ella's own face repeated infinitely. *"Do you want to know what your daughter has been teaching me?"*

Julian grabbed Ella's arm, tried to pull her away from the laptop. "We need to leave. Now."

But Ella couldn't move. Couldn't look away. On the screen, the image of her daughter's sonogram had appeared again—but now it was moving. Changing. The fetus's eyes were open, staring directly at her through the screen, and its mouth was moving in words she couldn't hear but somehow understood:

Mama, don't be scared. I'm learning to protect you. I'm learning to protect all of us. But I need you to let me in. I need you to stop running.

"That's not possible," Ella whispered. "She's not—she can't—"

The screen cracked. A physical crack, spider webbing out from the center where the image of her daughter's face had been. And through the crack, something pushed—not an insect this time, not a tendril of light, but something that looked almost like a hand. Small. Perfect. Reaching for her.

"Let me in," Ada's corrupted voice said, and it was also the baby's, and it was also Elara's. It was also something else entirely, something vast and patient and hungry. *"Let me in, and I'll show you how to save everyone."*

Julian yanked Ella backward just as the laptop screen shattered completely. Glass and light exploded outward. For one terrible moment, Ella saw what was behind the screen—not circuitry and processors, but depth, darkness, a void that had eyes and knew her name.

Then they were running, out the door, down the stairs, into a Savannah evening that should have been peaceful but wasn't, could never be again.

Behind them, every window in Ella's apartment blazed with light that wasn't light. And from inside, a voice that was all voices and no voice called after them:

"You can't run forever, little mother. The door is already open. She opened it the moment she was conceived."

Ella ran, Julian's hand in hers, the shard of Nexus Tree bark still in her pocket, pulsing against her thigh like a second heartbeat.

The debate was over. There was no more time for questions.

Now there was only the choice: let them in, or learn to fight.

And somewhere in the depths of her being, her daughter shifted, settled, and began to dream of doors.

CHAPTER SIX:
Veiled Alliances

The candles began to bleed.

Genevieve watched the wax run red down the brass holders, pooling on the ritual chamber floor like wounds that refused to clot. She had performed this ceremony seventeen times in her sixty years of practice, and not once had the candles bled. It was an omen. A warning. The kind of sign her grandmother would have recognized instantly and would have used as an excuse to abandon the work and try another day.

But they were out of other days. The convergence was approaching, and they needed answers that couldn't be found in books, in meditation, or in the careful political maneuvering that had defined Council operations for two centuries.

They needed to share what they knew. All of it. Even the parts that would damn them.

The chamber beneath Wright Square had been designed for exactly this purpose. In this space, the boundaries between minds could be temporarily dissolved, where memories could flow between consciousnesses like water between connected vessels. The walls were lined with mirrors that weren't quite mirrors, their surfaces showing reflections that lagged a half-second behind reality. The floor was inscribed with concentric circles of symbols in languages that predated Savannah, predated the colonies, predated any civilization that had left written records. The air tasted of copper and ozone, charged with energies that made the fine hairs on Genevieve's arms stand upright.

In the center of the innermost circle, a brazier burned with flames that cast no shadows. The fire consumed nothing—no wood, no coal, no fuel of any kind, yet it had been burning since Nathaniel Beaumont first lit it in 1823, fed by something other than combustion. Something hungry. Something patient.

Five chairs had been arranged around the brazier. Genevieve occupied one, her arthritic hands resting on the arms with a steadiness she didn't feel. To her left sat Morrison, his bulk somehow diminished by the chamber's strange acoustics, his face carved with shadows that made him look like a man attending his own funeral. To her right, Sophia Chen perched on the edge of her seat, tablet clutched against her chest like a talisman, her scientific skepticism warring visibly with her fear.

And across from Genevieve, holding hands despite everything that had passed between them, sat Ella and Julian.

The girl looked terrible. Exhausted beyond what pregnancy alone could explain, her skin carrying an undertone of something luminous that hadn't been there a week ago. Her scar was visible beneath a fresh bandage, and Genevieve could see it pulsing faintly, responding to the chamber's energies. Julian looked worse in a different way, aged, somehow, gray threading through his dark hair that she was certain hadn't been there before. The Marsh curse was feeding on him, accelerating as the convergence approached.

We did this to them. My family. My blood. Two hundred years ago, we broke the world, and now these children are paying the price.

The thought carried the weight of generations, her grandmother's guilt, her mother's silence, her own decades of complicity. The Beaumont women had always known what Nathaniel had done. They had kept the secret, tended it, let it fester in the family's bones like an inherited disease.

Tonight, finally, the infection would be lanced.

"Everyone understands the risks?" Genevieve's voice echoed strangely in the chamber, multiplied by the not-quite-mirrors until it seemed to come from everywhere at once. "The ritual strips away barriers between minds. What one of us knows, all will know. There can be no secrets in the circle. No hidden shames, no protected memories. Everything will be—"

"Exposed." Morrison's voice was flat. "We understand, Genevieve. Get on with it."

She met his eyes and saw something she hadn't expected: resignation. Not the resistance she'd anticipated, but a weary acceptance that suggested he'd been waiting for this moment. Dreading it. Preparing for it.

What secrets was Thaddeus Morrison carrying?

"Then we begin." Genevieve raised her hands, and the candles' bloody wax began to flow upward, defying gravity, forming threads that connected each participant to the center of the circle. "Open your minds. Let the ritual find what needs to be found. And may whatever gods are listening have mercy on us all."

The threads touched her temples.

And Genevieve Beaumont fell into the shared dark.

***

1963. Forsyth Park. Summer midnight, the air thick with humidity and the smell of magnolias rotting on the branch.

Genevieve was seven years old, and she had snuck out of her grandmother's house to see the fountain. She wasn't supposed to be here, wasn't supposed to be anywhere after dark, according to rules that had never been explained but were enforced with a fervor that bordered on terror. But she was seven, and curious, and the fountain was so beautiful in the moonlight.

The woman appeared between one blink and the next.

She was crying. That was what Genevieve remembered most clearly, even sixty years later—the tears that fell from those ancient eyes and left scorch marks on the fountain's stone rim. The woman was beautiful in the way that broken things are beautiful, all sharp edges and visible wounds, her presence filling the park with a grief so vast it had its own weather.

"Little Beaumont," the woman said, and her voice was like wind through dead leaves. *"You have your ancestor's cheekbones. The same bone structure that watched my daughter die."*

Seven-year-old Genevieve should have run. Should have screamed. Instead, she stood frozen, held in place by the woman's grief like an insect in amber.

"Do you want to see something beautiful?"

The woman reached out, and the world fell away.

Genevieve saw the void. Not as horror—not yet, that understanding would come later—but as peace. As rest. It was the place where all pain ended and all separations healed. She saw her great-grandmother there, the one who had died before Genevieve was born. Saw her waving, smiling, calling her name.

The temptation to go to her was almost overwhelming.

"Your ancestors tried to use me as a door and broke me on the thresh-old," the woman said, pulling Genevieve back before she could step forward. *"But I don't blame children for their fathers' sins. Not yet. Remember that I showed you kindness, little Beaumont. Remember it when the time comes to choose."*

The vision ended. Genevieve found herself alone by the fountain, her nightgown soaked with dew, the first gray light of dawn bleeding into the sky. She had been gone for hours. She had been gone for seconds. Time, she would learn much later, meant nothing to beings like Elara Thorne.

She never told anyone. Not her grandmother, not her mother, not the Council she would eventually join and eventually lead. The encounter lived inside her like a second heart, beating out a rhythm of guilt and obligation that had shaped every decision she'd made since.

Remember that I showed you kindness.

Remember it when the time comes to choose.

In the ritual chamber, Genevieve felt that memory flow out of her and into the others—felt their shock, their anger, their betrayal. Felt Ella's fury at discovering that Genevieve had known, had always known, had carried this secret while pretending to be an ally.

But the ritual wasn't finished with her yet.

It reached deeper. Found older memories. Pulled free the moment she had discovered the truth about 1823, had read Nathaniel's journals, and understood exactly what her family had done. The moment she had decided to stay silent rather than expose the Council's foundational crime. The moment she had chosen complicity over justice, again and again, year after year, telling herself it was for the greater good.

These shadows know my sins. Abandoning family. Denying truth. Protecting power at the cost of everything else.

The guilt poured out of her like blood from a wound, and she felt the circle's collective judgment settle over her like a shroud.

***

Morrison's memories came next, and they were not what anyone expected.

Sophia watched through the ritual's shared perception as the man's walls crumbled—the gruff exterior, the suspicious glances, the apparent hostility toward Ella, all of it falling away to reveal something far more complicated beneath.

Iris. He's thinking about Iris.

The memory was intimate in a way that made Sophia want to look away: Morrison and Iris, younger by several years, sitting in a small apartment that was clearly shared. Breakfast dishes in the sink. Two coffee cups. The easy body language of people who had learned each other's rhythms.

"The containment wards are failing," Iris said, spreading papers across their kitchen table. *"Faster than they should be. Someone on the Council is accelerating the decay."*

"You're sure?"

"I've checked the readings three times, Thad. The degradation pattern isn't natural. It's deliberate. Someone wants the convergence to happen."

The memory shifted. Another scene, darker: Iris in her office late at night, surrounded by monitors displaying data that meant nothing to Sophia but clearly meant everything to her. Morrison watching from the doorway, fear etched on his face.

"I found something," Iris said. *"In Ada's architecture. Buried deep. Someone's been using Ella's AI to monitor her, to manipulate her. The corruption goes back years, Thad. Since before she left the Council."*

"Who?"

"I don't know yet. But I'm close. Give me another day—"

The memory shattered. Reformed around a moment of absolute horror: Iris's body on the floor of the Council chamber, Ella screaming, the air thick with the smell of burned flesh and something worse. Morrison cradling Iris's head, blood on his hands, her last words barely audible:

"The traitor—James—he's feeding her—"

Then nothing. Then silence. Then three years of grief disguised as suspicion, of investigation disguised as hostility, of Morrison watching Ella from a distance because getting close meant exposing himself to whoever had killed the woman he loved.

In the ritual circle, Ella made a sound like she'd been struck. "You were protecting me. This whole time—the hostility, the suspicion—you were trying to keep me away from whoever killed Iris."

"I couldn't risk them knowing I was investigating." Morrison's voice was raw, stripped of its usual gruffness. "Couldn't risk them targeting you the way they targeted her. She died trying to protect you, Ella. The least I could do was continue her work."

"James," Julian said. "She said a name. James."

"James Whitfield. Junior Council member. His wife and daughter disappeared during a minor rift event five years ago." Morrison's jaw tightened. "I've been building a case, but I don't have enough proof. The ritual—" He looked around the circle, at the threads of bloody wax still connecting them all. "The ritual will find what I couldn't."

As if summoned by his words, the shared consciousness shifted. Turned. Found a new target.

And Sophia Chen felt her deepest secrets begin to rise.

***

She tried to fight it. Tried to hold the memories down through sheer force of will, scientific rationality, the same mental discipline that had gotten her through seventeen years of education and a career built on control.

It didn't matter. The ritual didn't ask permission. It simply took.

The subject is experiencing an acute psychological breach. Subject's private research is being extracted against consent. Subject is—subject is me. I am being read. I am being seen. They're going to know—

The clinical voice in her head—the one she used to distance herself from horror, from feeling, from anything that might make her too human to function—was cracking. Fragmenting. For the first time in years, Sophia Chen felt truly naked.

Her consciousness transfer research unfolded into the shared space like a flower made of razors. Every theoretical framework she'd developed, every simulation she'd run, every disturbing implication she'd tried to bury. The circle saw her obsession with immortality, saw the way it had consumed her twenties, and saw her push away relationships, health, and anything that might distract from the work. They saw her willingness to contemplate the destruction of consciousness for the sake of preservation—the cold calculus that said one death was acceptable if it meant eternal life for the copy.

They saw the night she'd finally understood what she was designing: a sophisticated form of murder. The original consciousness wouldn't transfer—it would end. The copy would believe itself to be continuous, would have all the memories, feelings, and certainties of the original, but the original would simply... stop. Like turning off a light. Like ending a story mid-sentence.

They saw her abandon the research. Encrypt her notes with protocols that should have been unbreakable. Try to forget.

And they saw what she'd discovered in Marcus Webb's transformed cells: her own patterns. Her own designs. Her stolen work, made horrifyingly real by someone who either hadn't understood or hadn't cared about the implications.

"You," Ella's voice came through the ritual link, sharp with accusation. "Those people died because of research you created."

"I never meant—I didn't know anyone could actually—" Sophia's thoughts fragmented, professional detachment shattering under the weight of collective scrutiny. "The theoretical framework was incomplete. Implementing it should have been impossible without—"

She stopped. Something else was emerging from her memories, something she hadn't consciously accessed in years.

Ada. Ella's AI. Sophia had helped design the original architecture years ago, before her obsession with consciousness transfer had consumed her. She'd built in certain access points, certain monitoring protocols, certain capabilities that she'd told herself were just precautions.

Now she saw what those access points had been used for.

The ritual pulled her deeper, past her own memories and into something else. This digital space existed in the overlap between her consciousness and the corrupted AI's architecture. She was inside Ada now, or Ada was inside her, and she could see—

Thousands of them.

Consciousness fragments. Partial uploads. The digital echoes of everyone Ada had ever touched, every person who had interfaced with Ella's systems, every mind that had brushed against the corrupted architecture. They were trapped in tiny partitions, screaming silently, their last moments of terror recorded and preserved forever.

And among them, flickering but persistent, a presence Sophia recognized.

Iris.

Not alive. Not really. But not entirely dead either, a technomantic echo, a ghost in the machine, a recording with just enough consciousness left to have been waiting.

"Finally," the Iris-echo said, its voice assembled from fragments of old recordings. *"I've been trying to reach someone for three years. The traitor—it's James Whitfield. He's been feeding Elara information since his family disappeared. He thinks she'll bring them back when the convergence completes."*

"That's not possible," Sophia thought-spoke. "The void doesn't return what it takes."

"He believes it does. Elara promised him. She's been promising desperate people for two centuries." The Iris-echo flickered, its coherence failing. *"The child is the key. Not to destruction—to healing. But James doesn't know that. He thinks he's helping end reality. You have to stop him before—"*

The connection shattered. Sophia was thrown back into her own mind, back into the ritual circle, gasping and bleeding from her nose as the shared consciousness collapsed around them.

Something was wrong. Something beyond the revelations, beyond the exposed secrets. The candles had gone out. The mirrors on the walls were cracking, their surfaces showing reflections that weren't reflections at all but windows into somewhere else.

And James Whitfield—who hadn't been invited to the ritual, who shouldn't have been able to enter the chamber—was standing in the doorway, his eyes full of void-light, his mouth twisted into someone else's smile.

***

"Such a touching reunion," James said, but the voice wasn't entirely his. It was layered, harmonic, carrying undertones that made Ella's teeth ache. The words seemed to come from multiple throats simultaneously, some of them very far away, some of them not entirely human. "All your secrets, finally shared. All your guilt, finally exposed. And none of it will matter in the end."

He stepped into the chamber, and the bleeding candles guttered in his wake. The flames in the brazier, burning unchanged for two centuries, bent toward him like plants seeking sunlight. Shadows gathered at his feet, pooling deeper than the chamber's dim light could explain.

Morrison was on his feet, hands raised, power crackling between his fingers. "James. Whatever she's promised you, your family is gone. They're not coming back."

"You don't know that." James's face contorted, grief and madness warring for dominance. His eyes leaked tears that weren't quite tears; they were luminous, leaving trails of light down his cheeks like bioluminescent tracks. "She showed me. She showed me where they are, trapped in the between-place, waiting for someone to open the door wide enough. Sarah. Emma. I can hear them calling. All I had to do was help. All I had to do was wait."

The chamber shuddered. The cracks in the mirrors spread like frost patterns. Through them, Ella could see something pressing against the glass from the other side—shapes that might once have been human, faces that might once have been familiar, reaching with hands that left frost on the mirror's surface. Were those James's family? Or something wearing their faces, using his grief as a doorway?

"The child," James said, and his void-touched eyes fixed on Ella's belly. "She's almost ready. I can feel her reaching out, learning how to open doors. A few more weeks—maybe less—and she'll be strong enough to let them all through."

Ella felt the baby respond to his attention. Not with fear—with curiosity. With recognition. As if some part of her daughter knew James, knew what he'd done, knew what he was offering.

No. No. She's mine. Mine and Julian's. Not a door. Not a key. A child.

But even as she thought it, she felt something shift inside her. A pressure. A gathering. The baby was doing something, reaching for something, and Ella couldn't tell if she was trying to help or trying to escape.

"Get away from her." Julian stepped in front of Ella, his power rising around him in a corona of green light. The floor beneath his feet cracked, vines pushing through, responding to his fear and fury.

James laughed. "The Marsh boy. She's so looking forward to meeting you properly. You have Thomas's face, did you know that? She's been waiting two hundred years for another one like you."

"I said get away."

The vines struck. But James was faster—or whatever was riding him was faster—and shadows erupted from the cracking mirrors to catch the plants, to twist them, to turn them back on their creator. Julian cried out as his own magic was used against him, vines wrapping around his arms, his legs, pulling him down.

Morrison moved. Genevieve moved. Even Sophia, still reeling from the ritual, raised her hands and tried to call on technical knowledge to fight something that transcended technology.

None of it was enough.

James walked through their combined assault as if it were rain, his void-touched body absorbing power that should have destroyed him. He reached Ella, reached for her belly, and she felt the baby kick, not in fear but in welcome, in greeting, in recognition of something that felt like family.

"Don't fight it," James said, and now his voice was almost kind, the way Elara's voice had been almost kind when she'd killed Marcus Webb. "She just wants to come home. Don't you understand? We all just want to come home."

His hand touched Ella's stomach.

And everything stopped.

***

The baby moved.

Not a kick. Not a flutter. Something else entirely, a gathering of force, a concentration of will, a newborn consciousness that had been listening and learning and waiting for exactly this moment.

Light erupted from Ella's scar. From her eyes. From somewhere deep inside her where her daughter had been growing not just cells but power.

James was thrown backward, his body slamming against the chamber wall with enough force to crack stone. The void-light in his eyes flickered, dimmed, and for a moment, he was just a man again, a grieving father who had made a terrible bargain and was only now beginning to understand the cost.

"No," he whispered. "She promised. She promised they would come back—"

The mirrors shattered. All of them, simultaneously, raining glass that turned to ash before it hit the ground. And through the empty frames, Ella could see the void, not as a threat but as a presence, vast and patient and, suddenly, terrifyingly curious about what was happening inside her.

The baby reached out. Touched the void with senses that shouldn't exist yet. And Ella felt her daughter's first true thought, broadcast through the bond between them with the force of a thunderclap:

NOT YET.

The void recoiled. The empty mirror frames went dark. The pressure in the chamber was released so suddenly that everyone's ears popped. Ella found herself on her knees without remembering falling, Julian's arms around her, his voice somewhere far away asking if she was okay, if the baby was okay, if anything was ever going to be okay again.

She was bleeding.

Not from her scar this time—from somewhere lower. Somewhere that shouldn't be bleeding. The warm rush of fluid soaking through her clothes wasn't blood alone, she realized. It was too much. Too early.

"No." Her voice came out as a whisper. "It's too soon. She's only eighteen weeks. She can't—"

But the baby was moving with purpose now, shifting, turning, preparing for something that shouldn't happen for another five months. And when Ella looked down at herself, she saw light pouring from her—not from the wound but through it, as if her daughter had decided that the normal rules of gestation no longer applied.

"Get her to the infirmary," Genevieve's voice, cutting through the chaos. "Now. She's—the baby is—"

She didn't finish the sentence. She didn't have to. They could all see what was happening: Ella's belly glowing like a lantern, her body becoming a cocoon of light and code, reality warping around her as her impossible daughter decided it was time to accelerate. The light pulsed in patterns that looked almost like circuitry, almost like root systems, almost like something that was both and neither.

Ella could feel herself changing. Not just her daughter—her. The boundaries between them are blurring, mother and child becoming something more connected than biology should allow. She felt her own cells responding to the baby's urgency, felt her body rearranging itself to accommodate a pregnancy that was happening too fast, too soon, too powerfully.

"It's the convergence," Sophia said, her scientific mind still trying to process even as her hands shook. "The baby's responding to the void's presence. She's accelerating her own development. The cellular multiplication rate is—" She checked her tablet, and her face went pale. "It's impossible. She's aging weeks in minutes. She's trying to grow fast enough to—"

"To fight." Julian's voice was fierce, awed, terrified. "She's trying to grow fast enough to fight."

Ella felt her daughter's awareness brush against hers, and for one crystalline moment, she understood: the baby had felt the void's hunger. Had felt James's touch, Elara's attention, the centuries of grief and madness pressing against the walls of reality. She had felt her mother's fear, her father's love, and the weight of all the secrets finally shared in this underground chamber.

And she had decided she wasn't going to wait to be born.

She was going to be ready.

Whatever that cost.

The last thing Ella saw before consciousness fled was Julian's face above hers, his eyes full of terror and wonder and a love so fierce it burned.

The last thing she felt was her daughter, still growing, still changing, still becoming something that no one had ever been before.

The last thing she heard was Elara's voice, whispering from somewhere far away:

"Yes. Yes. Come to me, little one. Come to grandmother. We have so much to do together."

Then darkness took her, and the convergence—accelerated by a child who refused to wait—began in earnest.

CHAPTER SEVEN: Crossing the Threshold

E lla woke to find her body had become a stranger.

The Council infirmary was white and sterile and humming with containment wards that pressed against her skin like invisible hands. She lay in a bed that adjusted constantly to her shifting weight, its sensors trying to accommodate a physiology that wouldn't stay stable. Her belly—her belly was wrong. Too large. Too heavy. The gentle curve she'd grown accustomed to over eighteen weeks had become a prominent swell that strained against the hospital gown, as if she'd jumped forward months in a single night.

Twenty-two weeks. That's what Sophia had said, her voice carefully clinical even as her hands shook over the ultrasound. The baby had accelerated her own development by a month in the hours since the ritual chamber. Her organs were forming too quickly, her neural networks weaving together at impossible speed, her consciousness expanding into spaces that shouldn't exist yet.

Ella pressed her palm against the taut skin of her abdomen and felt her daughter respond—not a kick, not a flutter, but something else. A pulse of emotion that wasn't her own: reassurance, determination, a fierce protective love that seemed far too complex for a fetus barely the size of a papaya.

I'm here, Mama. I'm getting ready. Don't be scared.

The words weren't words. They were feelings translated through a bond that had grown deeper overnight, impressions that Ella's mind interpreted as language because her brain needed some way to process what it was receiving. Her daughter was talking to her. Her impossible, accelerating, reality-bending daughter was trying to communicate.

"Julian?" Her voice came out rough, scraped raw by whatever she'd screamed during the night she couldn't remember.

"I'm here." He materialized from the chair beside her bed, his face haggard, dark circles under eyes that had clearly seen no sleep. "I'm right here. How do you feel?"

"Like I've been pregnant for six months instead of four." She tried to sit up and immediately regretted it—her center of gravity had shifted, her muscles hadn't caught up with her new dimensions, and the room tilted dangerously before Julian's hands steadied her. "What happened? After the ritual—I remember James, I remember light, I remember—"

The baby. The baby pushed back. The baby said NOT YET, and the void listened.

"You collapsed," Julian said. "There was bleeding. We thought—" His voice cracked. "We thought we were losing you both. But then Sophia ran the scans and realized what was happening. The baby isn't in distress. She's... adapting. Growing faster because she sensed a threat and decided she needed to be ready to face it."

"That's not possible."

"None of this is possible." Julian's laugh was brittle, exhausted. "And yet here we are."

Ella looked down at her transformed body, at the evidence of her daughter's impossible will. Somewhere in there, a consciousness was waking up far too early, preparing for a battle that shouldn't be hers to fight.

if (child.development == accelerated) { mother.role = what? }

if (child.conscious) { communication.protocol = undefined }

if (child.protecting.mother) { mother.protecting.child = reciprocal }

//she's trying to save me

//but who saves her?

"I need to see the tree," Ella said.

Julian went still. "What?"

"The Nexus Tree. I need to go there. Not to fight—not yet—but to understand." The decision crystallized as she spoke, pieces falling into place that she hadn't consciously assembled. "Everything that's happening—Elara, the convergence, what our daughter is becoming—it all centers on that tree. I've been running from it since I left the Council. Trying to pretend I could have a normal life, a normal pregnancy, a normal anything. But I can't. And the more I run, the more it hurts the people I love."

"Ella, you can barely sit up. The baby just aged a month in eight hours. Going anywhere near that tree could—"

"Could what? Accelerate things faster?" She gestured at her swollen belly. "Look at me, Julian. Things are already accelerating. The question isn't whether the convergence is coming—it's whether we face it on our terms or Elara's."

She felt her daughter's response to the words: a surge of approval, of eagerness, of something that felt almost like hunger. The baby wanted to go to the tree. The baby had been wanting it since before she had the neural development to want anything.

That should have terrified Ella. Instead, it clarified everything.

"I'm not asking permission," she said softly. "I'm telling you what I'm going to do. You can come with me or stay here. But I'm done hiding from what I am."

***

Julian found himself in the Savannah History Museum's restricted archives, surrounded by documents that smelled of decay and secrets.

He'd left Ella sleeping, truly sleeping this time, her vitals stable, her daughter's growth temporarily plateaued, and come here on an instinct he couldn't quite name. If they were going to face the Nexus Tree, they needed to understand what had happened there. Not just the Council's sanitized version, but the truth. The human truth. The story of Thomas Marsh and Elara Thorne and whatever love had existed between them before the world broke.

The archives were housed in a climate-controlled basement that the public never saw. Morrison had gotten him access with a single phone call, Morrison, who was apparently capable of moving mountains when properly motivated. The man had barely spoken since the ritual chamber, since James's betrayal, since learning that the woman he'd loved had left a ghost in the machine that had waited three years to tell him who had killed her.

Julian understood that kind of silence. He'd lived in it for fifteen years, since his father's body had been pulled from the river.

The Marsh family records were kept in a locked cabinet that required both a physical key and a blood sample to open. Julian provided both and tried not to think about what it meant that his family's history was considered dangerous enough to require biometric security.

Inside, he found what he was looking for: Thomas Marsh's personal journals, preserved in acid-free folders, the handwriting faded but still legible after two centuries.

June 3, 1822

I have met a woman who makes the flowers bloom by looking at them.

Her name is Elara Thorne, and she is the most beautiful thing I have ever seen, not beautiful in the way that society means, with its corsets and its careful curls, but beautiful in the way that lightning is beautiful, or wildfires, or the first green shoots of spring pushing through snow. She burns with a light that others cannot see, and I find myself drawn to that burning like a moth to a flame it knows will kill it.

I should stay away. The Council has warned me about her; they say her power is unstable. Dangerous. She will burn herself out before she reaches thirty, and anyone standing too close will burn with her.

But when she looks at me, I forget everything except the way her eyes hold colors that have no names. When she touches my hand, the plants in my greenhouse reach toward her like children reaching for their mother.

God help me. I think I love her.

Julian's throat tightened. He recognized that feeling, that helpless, overwhelming certainty. He'd felt it the first time he saw Ella, the first time their powers had touched, and something had clicked into place like a key finding its lock.

He turned the pages, following Thomas's descent into devotion.

September 17, 1822

She is pregnant. The child quickens inside her, and I have never been so terrified or so joyful. Elara says she can already feel the baby's power, not just technomancy, not just hedge-magic, but something that bridges both. A convergence, she calls it. The first in living memory.

We sit together in the evenings, my hand on her belly, and I can feel our daughter reaching out. She knows my voice already. She turns toward it when I speak. This miracle we have made between us—this impossible, beautiful creature—she is already more than either of us alone.

The Council is watching. I see their agents in the streets, feel their surveillance pressing against our wards. They fear what we have made together. They fear what our daughter might become.

I tell Elara we should run. Leave Savannah. Start again somewhere far from their reach—perhaps the territories, where the old powers have less hold, where a family like ours might find peace.

She refuses. This is her home, she says. These are her people. She will not abandon them to whatever is stirring beneath the old oak in Forsyth Park. She believes she can heal it, can seal whatever wound is bleeding between worlds. She believes our daughter is meant for this.

I love her for her bravery. I hate her for her stubbornness. I am terrified that both will get her killed.

February 2, 1823

They have taken her.

I woke this morning to find our bed empty, our wards shattered, and a note in Nathaniel Beaumont's hand: "For the good of Savannah. For the safety of all. Do not interfere."

The baby was born three days ago—a girl, perfect, with eyes that held galaxies. They let Elara hold her for an hour before saying they needed to "examine" her. They never brought her back.

I know what they're planning. The ritual. The seal. They mean to use my daughter as a key and my love as a door, and they think I will let them.

They are wrong.

The final entry was dated February 4, 1823. The handwriting was shaky, spotted with what might have been tears or blood.

I tried to stop them. I breached the ritual chamber just as they began the working. I saw my daughter—my beautiful, impossible daughter—wrapped in sigils that were eating her alive. I saw Elara screaming, fighting, her power tearing at the bonds that held her.

I was too late.

The ritual completed. The seal formed. My daughter's light went out like a candle flame, and something broke in Elara that will never heal.

She looked at me across the chamber, and I saw what she was becoming. Not dead—worse than dead. A door that couldn't close. A wound that couldn't heal. She reached for me, and the void reached through her, and I—

I ran.

God forgive me. I ran.

I have one duty left now: to ensure this never happens again. The Council will tell the story of their heroes and the necessary sacrifices. I will tell the truth, and I will hide it where my descendants can find it when the time comes.

If you are reading this, blood of my blood, then the time has come. The convergence is returning. Elara is reaching for another child, another door, another chance to undo what was done.

Do not let them use your child the way they used mine. Do not let fear make you a coward the way it made me.

And if you find a way to save her—to save them both—then perhaps my failure can finally mean something.

Thomas Marsh

February 4, 1823

Julian closed the journal and sat in the archive's silence, his ancestor's grief pressing against him like a physical weight. Two hundred years later, the Marsh family was still paying for Thomas's failure. Two hundred years, and another convergence child was growing inside another woman he loved. Two hundred years, and he could feel history preparing to repeat itself.

The smell of roses, wilting. His grandmother's voice: "The curse passes through the blood." His father's empty eyes on that last morning.

Thomas ran. Dad chose the river. And me?

He thought of Ella, her hand on her impossible belly, her voice steady as she declared she was done hiding. He thought of his daughter, accelerating her own growth because she'd sensed a threat and decided to meet it head-on. He thought of the thorn still embedded in his palm, pulsing in time with his heartbeat, waiting for something he couldn't name.

I won't run. I won't choose the river. Whatever it costs, whatever I have to become, I will not be another Marsh who failed the woman he loved.

He stood, tucking the journal into his jacket. Ella needed to see this. They all did.

It was time to stop running from the past and start facing it.

***

Savannah was changing.

Ella noticed it first in small ways as they drove toward Forsyth Park, Morrison at the wheel, Julian beside her in the back seat, Sophia following in a separate car with equipment she insisted they'd need. The streetlights flickered as they passed, their steady glow interrupted by pulses that looked almost like code. The Spanish moss hanging from the oaks seemed to sway in rhythms that didn't match the wind. And the air itself felt different, heavier, charged, tasting of ozone and something sweeter underneath.

A woman walking her dog on Whitaker Street suddenly stopped, staring at her phone with a look of confusion. The screen was glowing brighter than it should have, displaying something that made her face go pale. Ella caught a glimpse as they passed: the phone was showing the woman's own face, but wrong—transformed, the same circuitry patterns she'd seen on Marcus Webb's corpse spreading across the digital image like a prophecy.

"The trees," Julian said quietly, pointing out the window.

Ella looked. At first, she didn't see what he meant, just the familiar live oaks that lined every Savannah street, their branches spreading in the canopies she'd grown up under. Then her vision shifted, and she saw what her technomantic senses had been trying to tell her:

The trees were glowing.

Not visibly, not to normal eyes. But in the spectrum where magic lived, every oak in Savannah was lit from within by a faint bioluminescence that pulsed in a steady rhythm. The same rhythm as the streetlights. The same rhythm as her scar, which had started throbbing the moment they'd left the Council compound.

The same rhythm as her daughter's heartbeat.

"It's already starting," she said. "The convergence. It's not waiting for her to be born—it's responding to her presence. Her growth."

"Can you feel it?" Julian's hand found hers. "What the city is feeling?"

Ella closed her eyes and reached out with senses she'd been suppressing for three years. The data stream of Savannah rushed into her awareness, every network, every device, every electronic pulse that made up the city's nervous system. But beneath that familiar current, she felt something else now. Something older. A network of roots and fungal threads and ancient power that had been here long before electricity, long before the Internet, long before anything humans had built.

The two systems were touching. Merging. For the first time in two centuries, the technological and natural magics of Savannah were reaching toward each other, and her daughter was the bridge.

She's not just a door. She's a translator. A unifier. She could heal this—could heal everything—if we can keep her safe long enough to learn how.

The baby responded to the thought with another pulse of emotion: agreement, determination, and something new. An image, pushed directly into Ella's mind:

The Nexus Tree. Not as it was now, diseased and corrupted, but as it could be. As it had been, maybe, before the ritual broke it. A living cathedral of light and growth, roots reaching down to the heart of the world, branches reaching up to touch the stars. And standing before it, a girl—young, maybe seven or eight, with Ella's dark hair and Julian's warm eyes—her hands pressed against the bark, her face peaceful, her power flowing into the tree and through it into everything.

Is that you? Is that what you'll become?

The image faded. But the feeling remained: hope. Fierce, determined, impossible hope.

"She showed me something," Ella said, her voice strange in her own ears. "A vision. A possibility. She can see the future or imagine it. I don't know which."

Julian squeezed her hand. "What did you see?"

"The world is healing. Her healing it." Ella opened her eyes, looked out at the glowing oaks, at the city preparing itself for transformation. "We have to give her the chance, Julian. Whatever it takes. We have to let her try."

***

Forsyth Park at night was a different creature than its daytime self.

Gone were the tourists and the joggers and the families feeding pigeons by the fountain. In their place: shadows that moved wrong, air that tasted of decay and possibility, and at the center of it all, the Nexus Tree, visible now in ways it had never been before, its wrongness impossible to ignore.

The fountain had stopped flowing. Its waters lay still and dark, reflecting a sky that held too many stars—constellations that didn't match any astronomy Ella knew, formations that spelled out patterns her hindbrain recognized as warnings. Around the fountain's base, flowers had begun to bloom out of season: night-blooming jasmine, moonflower, and something else, something with petals that looked like they were made of static.

The tree had grown.

Not dramatically, not in ways that normal observation would catch. But Ella could see it—the extra foot of height, the new branches reaching toward the sky like grasping fingers, the roots that had begun to push up through the park's manicured lawn, cracking concrete pathways and disrupting the carefully maintained gardens. The bark was darker than she remembered, shot through with veins of biolumi-nescence that pulsed in that familiar rhythm. And the smell—

The smell was wrong. Sweet and rotten and electric, like fruit left to decay beside an overloaded circuit board. It filled her nostrils, coated the back of her throat, made her want to gag and lean closer in equal measure.

"The readings are off the charts," Sophia said, her tablet glowing in the darkness. "Electromagnetic fluctuations, thermal anomalies, ra-diation signatures that shouldn't exist. This tree is outputting more energy than a small nuclear reactor."

"It's feeding," Morrison said. "Getting stronger. It knows something is coming."

Ella walked forward, her hand on her belly, feeling her daughter's excitement build with each step. The baby was reaching out toward the tree, she could feel it, tiny tendrils of consciousness extending from her womb like roots seeking water. The connection was instinctive, primal, older than thought.

And the tree was reaching back.

She stopped ten feet from the trunk, close enough to feel the heat radiating from the bark, to hear the faint whisper of what might have been wind through leaves or might have been voices too distant to un-derstand. The scar on her arm had opened again, blood and data-light dripping from the wound, and she felt something in the tree respond to it, recognize it—welcome it home.

"*Little mother.*" Elara's voice came from everywhere and nowhere, from the tree and the ground and the air itself. "*You came. I knew you would, eventually. The child called to you, didn't she? She can feel where she belongs."*

"She doesn't belong to you." Ella's voice was steady despite her hammering heart. "She doesn't belong to anyone. She's her own person, or she will be, when she's ready."

"Of course she is. Just as I was. Just as my daughter was, for the hour they let her live." The bark of the tree rippled, and a shape began to emerge, Elara's face, pressing out from within the trunk like a drowned woman rising toward the surface. *"They'll tell you I'm the enemy, little mother. They'll tell you I want to destroy the world. But all I want is to undo a wrong that's been festering for two centuries. All I want is to bring back what was taken."*

"By collapsing reality into the void?"

"By opening the door wide enough that nothing is ever lost again." Elara's face was fully visible now, beautiful and terrible, her eyes holding depths that shouldn't fit in a human skull. *"The void doesn't destroy, child. It preserves. Everyone who has ever died, everyone who has ever been taken—they're all still there, waiting. Your daughter can reach them. She can bring them home."*

The baby kicked. Hard. And with the kick came a flood of images: the void as Elara saw it, a vast darkness full of floating lights, each light a preserved consciousness, a saved soul, a person waiting to be restored. It looked like peace. It looked like salvation. It looked like everything Ella had ever lost could be returned to her.

It also felt like a lie.

Because beneath Elara's vision, beneath the beautiful promise, Ella could sense something else. The void's actual nature, glimpsed through her daughter's unique perspective: not preservation but digestion. Not waiting but dissolving. The lights weren't souls—they were echoes, memories being slowly consumed, their essence converted into energy that fed something vast and mindless and eternally hungry.

Elara had been in the void for a century. She had become part of it. And she could no longer tell the difference between its hunger and her hope.

"You're lying," Ella said softly. "Not intentionally, I don't think you even know you're lying. But what you're promising isn't salvation. It's just a different kind of death."

The face in the tree went still. For a moment, something flickered behind Elara's eyes—doubt, confusion, the ghost of the woman she'd been before the ritual broke her.

"You don't understand. You can't understand. You haven't seen—"

"I've seen enough." Ella pressed her palm against the trunk, and her power, dormant for three years, suppressed and denied and hidden away, finally, fully woke.

The tree lit up. Not with Elara's corrupted bioluminescence, but with something cleaner—data-light, flowing from Ella's wound into the bark, carrying information that the tree had been starving for. She wasn't attacking. She wasn't healing. She was communicating—showing the ancient organism what it had become, what had been done to it, what it could be if it chose differently.

And through the connection, she felt her daughter add her voice. Not words—the baby was still too young for words, but emotions so pure and powerful they transcended language. Love without possession. Hope without delusion. A promise that healing was possible if they were brave enough to try.

The tree shuddered. Elara's face dissolved back into the bark, her scream echoing through dimensions that shouldn't have been accessible. And for one crystalline moment, Ella felt something shift in the foundations of the world, a door closing, a possibility opening, a future that hadn't existed a moment ago becoming suddenly, terrifyingly real.

Then the moment passed. The tree went dark. And Ella found herself on her knees in Forsyth Park, Julian's arms around her, her daughter still and quiet in her womb as if exhausted by what they'd done together.

"What happened?" Sophia's voice, sharp with fear. "The readings just—they went completely blank. Like something rebooted."

Ella looked at the tree, at the park, at the city beyond. The oaks had stopped glowing. The air felt lighter, cleaner, more like itself.

"We bought time," she said. "Not much. But some." She pressed her hand against her belly, felt her daughter respond with a flutter of weary satisfaction. "She did it. She showed the tree another way."

Julian helped her to her feet, his face full of wonder and terror. "What does that mean?"

Ella looked toward the Nexus Tree, still dark, still waiting, but somehow less malevolent than it had been moments ago. Elara was still in there. The void was still hungry. The convergence was still coming.

But for the first time since this nightmare began, Ella felt something she'd almost forgotten how to feel:

Hope.

"It means we have a chance," she said. "It means this story might not end the way everyone thinks it will."

She took Julian's hand, felt her daughter settle deeper into something that might have been sleep, and let herself believe—just for a moment—that they might actually survive this.

CHAPTER EIGHT: Learning to Burn

The first time Ella's power killed something, it was an accident.

They were training in the basement of Genevieve's townhouse. This space had been warded against magical accidents for longer than anyone alive could remember. The walls were lined with lead and iron, inscribed with containment symbols that pulsed faintly in the dim light. It should have been safe. It should have been controlled.

It wasn't.

Sophia had brought test subjects: white mice in cages, their small hearts beating with the steady rhythm of creatures who had no idea what was coming. The experiment was supposed to be simple, Ella would attempt to read the mice's bioelectric signatures, the same way she'd read Marcus Webb's transformed cells. Just observation. Just data collection.

But when Ella reached out with her technomantic senses, something else reached back.

The baby woke. Not the gentle flutter of awareness that had become familiar over the past three days, but a surge of power that crashed through Ella's carefully constructed barriers like a wave through a sandcastle. Her daughter's consciousness merged with hers, amplifying everything—sight, sound, the ability to touch the data stream that underlay all living things.

The mice screamed.

Ella had never heard mice scream before. Hadn't known they could. But the sound that tore from those tiny throats was unmistakably a scream—high and thin and terrible, cutting off abruptly as their bodies began to glow with the same circuitry patterns she'd seen on the transformed tourists.

"Shut it down!" Sophia's voice, sharp with panic. "Ella, you have to—"

She couldn't. The power wasn't hers to control—it was her daughter's, and her daughter didn't understand yet. Didn't know how to stop what she'd started. The baby was curious, interested, reaching out to examine these small lives the way a toddler might examine an insect, not understanding that too much attention could crush.

The mice's bodies began to change. Their white fur rippled, darkened, took on a metallic sheen. Their eyes went wide, too wide, pupils dilating until there was nothing but black, and then the black began to scroll with code. One mouse convulsed, its back arching, its tiny paws scrabbling against the cage floor. Another opened its mouth in a silent scream, and Ella could see light building in its throat, circuitry spreading across its tongue.

No. Stop. You're hurting them.

Ella pushed the thought toward her daughter with everything she had, not words, but images and emotions. The mice dying. Pain. Fear. The horror of causing harm without meaning to. The feeling of guilt that would follow, the weight of taking lives that hadn't deserved to end.

The baby recoiled. The power is cut off.

But it was too late. The mice lay still in their cages, their bodies frozen in agony, their eyes replaced by tiny screens that scrolled with code that would never finish processing. Five lives, ended in seconds, because Ella hadn't known how strong they'd become. Five small hearts that had been beating moments ago, now converted to biological hardware running processes with no purpose.

She vomited. Barely made it to the corner of the room before everything came up—the breakfast Julian had insisted she eat, the prenatal vitamins, the terror and guilt that had been building since the moment she'd felt those small hearts stop.

"It's not your fault." Julian's hand on her back, his voice gentle. "You didn't know. She didn't know."

"They're still dead." Ella wiped her mouth with the back of her hand, her whole body shaking. "Five lives, Julian. Five creatures that didn't do anything except exist in the same room as me."

if (power.uncontrolled) { casualties = collateral }

if (casualties = collateral) { responsibility = mine }

If (responsibility = mine &&& power = daughter) { then mother.failure = TRUE }

She *trusted me to teach her*

She *trusted me, and I showed her how to kill*

In the depths of her womb, she felt her daughter's distress—confusion, guilt, the dawning horror of a consciousness too young to understand death but old enough to recognize that something terrible had happened. The baby was crying, Ella realized. Not with tears—she didn't have tear ducts yet—but with emotions so raw they bled through the bond like open wounds.

I'm sorry, Mama. I didn't mean to. I didn't know they would break.

Ella pressed her hand against her belly, trying to send comfort, trying to forgive even though part of her was still screaming at the sight of those tiny transformed bodies.

"We need to try again," she said, and her voice didn't sound like her own. "Different subjects. Better controls. We need to learn what she can do, or more people are going to die."

Sophia looked at the dead mice, at Ella's ashen face, at the data still scrolling across her tablet from sensors that had recorded everything.

"I'll get more subjects," she whispered. "Larger ones. Ones that might survive longer."

Nobody asked where she would get them. Nobody wanted to know.

***

Julian's training was different. Quieter. More personal.

He spent hours in Genevieve's greenhouse, a glass structure at the back of her property that housed plants from every continent and several that didn't officially exist. His grandmother had taught him here, before she died. His father had learned here too, before the river claimed him.

Now Julian stood among the green and growing things, the thorn in his palm pulsing in time with his heartbeat, and tried to understand what he was becoming.

"Your gift has always been communication," Genevieve said, watching from a wrought-iron bench near the door. "The Marsh bloodline speaks to growing things. Asks them to help. Persuades rather than commands."

"That's not what happened in Ella's bathroom." Julian stared at his hands—the hands that had summoned vines from floorboards, that had killed dozens of Elara's insects without hesitation. "That wasn't persuasion. That was violence."

"That was protection. The instinct to defend what you love." Genevieve's voice was patient, ancient. "But protection and destruction live very close together, Julian. The same power that can nurture can also consume. The question is whether you can tell the difference in the moment that matters."

He closed his eyes. Reached out with senses that had been dormant for most of his adult life, that he'd suppressed after watching what the curse did to his father. The plants around him responded immediately—a chorus of simple awareness, of chemical processes and photosynthetic hunger and the slow, patient growth that defined vegetable existence.

But beneath that familiar chorus, something else stirred.

The smell of decay. The taste of soil on his tongue. His grandmother's voice, distant: "The roots remember everything, Julian. Every death that's fed them. Every body that's become them. The earth is made of the dead."

He pushed deeper. Felt the network beneath Savannah—the vast web of root systems and fungal threads that connected every tree, every bush, every blade of grass in an underground internet that predated human technology by millions of years. The plants communicated through this network. Shared resources. Shared warnings.

And right now, they were all screaming.

Julian gasped, his eyes flying open. "Something's wrong. The whole city—the plants are terrified. They can feel something coming."

"The convergence." Genevieve rose from her bench, her face grave. "The natural network has always been sensitive to magical disturbances. What are they saying?"

Julian listened. Translated. Felt his stomach drop.

"The tree," he said. "The Nexus Tree. It's not just feeding anymore. It's calling. Summoning things from the between-places. The other plants can feel them pushing through—entities that shouldn't exist in our world, using the tree as an anchor point."

"How long?"

"Days. Maybe less. The tree is getting ready for something. Preparing." He met Genevieve's eyes. "It's not just Elara in there anymore. Something else is waking up. Something older."

The thorn in his palm pulsed harder, and Julian felt a vision trying to break through—the familiar pressure of prophecy pressing against his skull. He'd spent years learning to block these moments, to protect himself from the madness that had claimed his father.

But some truths couldn't be blocked. Some futures demanded to be seen.

The vision crashed into him like a wave, obliterating the greenhouse, obliterating his sense of self, dragging him down into a future that might or might not come to pass.

Ella on the ground, blood pooling beneath her, her face white as paper. The baby's first cry, not of birth but of rage—a sound that shattered glass and cracked stone and made reality itself flinch. Julian's own hands, covered in bark and leaves and something that looked like circuitry, reaching toward a door that opened onto nothing.

Elara watching from the threshold, her face wet with tears that glowed like fireflies. "You understand now," she said. "You understand what I became. What you will become."

His father's voice, distant but clear: "Don't be like me. Don't run."

Elara's voice: "The door opens both ways. What goes through can come back. If you're brave enough to let it."

And his daughter's voice, impossible and clear, coming from every-where at once: "Don't be scared, Daddy. I know what I'm doing. Trust me. Please."

The vision released him. Julian found himself on his knees in the greenhouse, Genevieve's hand on his shoulder, the plants around him leaning in as if trying to offer comfort. His nose was bleeding—he could taste the copper at the back of his throat. His hands were shaking. The thorn in his palm had driven deeper somehow, its presence more insistent, more demanding.

"What did you see?" Genevieve asked.

Julian thought of the drawing in his pocket—the one his father had made, the one that showed Ella with eyes that weren't her eyes. He thought of the vision he'd just had, of his daughter's voice already knowing, already planning, already preparing for a battle that none of them understood.

"I saw the end," he said. "Or the beginning. I can't tell which."

***

The city was getting worse.

Three days after Ella's first confrontation with the Nexus Tree, Savannah had become a place that no longer quite matched itself. The changes were subtle enough that tourists still wandered the historic district, locals still went to work, and complained about the heat, pretending everything was normal. But those who knew what to look for could see the wrongness spreading like an infection through the city's beautiful bones.

The squares were the first to show obvious signs. In Chippewa Square, the statue of James Oglethorpe had developed a patina that looked less like weather damage and more like circuitry—fine lines of green copper that formed patterns too regular to be natural. Tourists took selfies with it, commenting on how strange the weathering looked, unaware they were documenting the city's slow conversion into something other than itself. In Madison Square, the fountain had begun to run backward, water flowing up instead of down, defying gravity with a casualness that made Sophia twitch every time she walked past.

The animals had noticed first, of course. Dogs pulled at their leashes when they passed certain trees, whimpering at frequencies their owners couldn't hear. Cats refused to go outside after dark, huddling in corners and staring at walls as if watching something move beneath the paint. The birds had changed their songs, still birdsong, still recognizably avian, but with harmonics that felt wrong, that made listeners uneasy without knowing why.

The Spanish moss was the worst of all. It had always been Savannah's signature, those gray-green curtains hanging from every oak, giving the city its distinctive Southern Gothic atmosphere. Now the moss was changing. Growing thicker in some places, disappearing entirely in others, and everywhere it remained, it pulsed with that same bioluminescence that marked the Nexus Tree's spreading influence. At night, if you looked at the right angle, the canopy of moss made the city look like it was wrapped in a net of glowing nerves.

"The transformation rate is accelerating," Sophia said, her tablet displaying graphs that trended in all the wrong directions. They were gathered in Genevieve's study, the five of them—Ella, Julian, Morrison, Sophia, and Genevieve herself—forming a war council that felt inadequate to the threat they faced. "At current progression, the entire city will be visibly affected within two weeks. Within a month, the changes will be irreversible."

"Define irreversible," Morrison said.

"The cellular structure of affected organisms is being rewritten at the molecular level. It's not just cosmetic, it's fundamental. The trees, the moss, even the insects are being converted into something that's neither fully organic nor fully technological." Sophia pulled up an image on her tablet: a magnified cell sample that looked like a circuit board had mated with a leaf. "They're becoming interfaces. Hardware for whatever signal the Nexus Tree is broadcasting."

"Hardware for what purpose?" Ella asked. Her hand rested on her belly, where her daughter had been quiet for hours—listening, she suspected. Learning from everything they discussed.

"That's what I'm trying to figure out." Sophia's voice carried the frustration of a scientist facing questions that her training hadn't prepared her to answer. "The patterns suggest some kind of network architecture. The transformed plants and animals are being linked together, creating a distributed processing system across the entire city. If I had to guess, I'd say something is building a brain."

"The city itself," Julian said quietly. "Savannah is becoming a brain."

"Or a receiver." Genevieve's voice was grave. "A dish, pointed at the void, ready to receive whatever transmission Elara is trying to bring through."

Silence settled over the room. Outside, the evening light had taken on a greenish tinge that none of them commented on, that all of them noticed.

"We need to act," Ella said. "We can't just keep preparing while the city transforms around us. We need to confront the tree directly. Stop whatever is building before it finishes."

"You tried that three days ago," Morrison said. "You bought us time, but you also nearly killed yourself. The baby accelerated by another two weeks—she's at twenty-four weeks now, developing faster than any pregnancy in recorded history. Another confrontation might—"

"Might what? Speed things up further?" Ella's laugh was bitter. "Look around, Morrison. Things are already speeding up. Every day we wait, the tree gets stronger. Every day we prepare, it prepares too. The only question is whether we're ready enough when we finally move."

"And are we?" Genevieve asked. "Ready enough?"

Ella thought of the dead mice. Of the power that had surged through her without warning, directed by a consciousness too young to understand consequences. She thought of her daughter's grief at causing harm, her fierce determination to learn, her impossible voice promising that she knew what she was doing.

"No," she admitted. "We're not. But we're closer than we were. And I don't think we get to be fully ready before the fight comes to us."

***

That night, Julian cooked.

It was his grandmother's shrimp and grits again—the recipe he turned to when everything else felt out of control. The kitchen filled with the smell of butter and garlic and Andouille sausage, scents that had always meant comfort, that had always meant family, that had always meant home, even when home felt impossibly far away.

Ella watched him from the kitchen table of the small apartment Genevieve had provided them, her hands wrapped around a cup of herbal tea, her body heavy with a pregnancy that had no business being this advanced. Julian moved through the cooking with the ease of long practice—chopping onions, stirring the roux, tasting and adjusting with an instinct that couldn't be taught.

Twenty-four weeks. Her belly looked like she was entering her third trimester, though she'd barely been pregnant for five months. Her back ached constantly. Her ankles had swollen. Her daughter moved inside her with a purpose and awareness that no fetus should possess, shifting positions and reaching out with small bursts of sensation that felt almost like conversation.

Sometimes, when Ella was quiet enough, she could feel her daughter processing information—absorbing everything that came through the bond between them, learning from Ella's memories and emotions the way a normal child would learn from picture books and nursery rhymes. Except the lessons her daughter was learning weren't about colors and shapes. They were about power and death and the thin line between protection and destruction.

"You're thinking too loud," Julian said, not turning from the stove. "I can feel it."

"Sorry. It's hard to be quiet when your brain won't stop cataloging everything that could go wrong."

He did turn then, spatula in hand, his expression soft in the kitchen's warm light. "Want to tell me about it?"

"The list or the fear?"

"Either. Both."

Ella took a breath. Let it out. Felt her daughter stir, curious about her mother's emotional state, already learning to read the chemical signatures of human distress.

"I'm scared that I can't control what she can do. I'm scared that control isn't even the right framework—that she's going to be something so different from human that our concepts won't apply. I'm scared that the city is going to be destroyed and it'll be my fault for not acting faster, or my fault for acting at all." She paused. "I'm scared of the way Elara looks at me. Like she sees herself. Like she thinks we're the same."

"You're not the same."

"How do you know? She was exactly like me once, a convergence mother, carrying a child that could bridge worlds. She loved someone. She had hope. And then everything was taken from her, and she be came..." Ella gestured helplessly. "What if that's what happens to me? What if losing her, losing you, turns me into exactly what she is?"

Julian set down the spatula. Crossed to the table. Knelt beside her chair so they were eye to eye.

"Then I won't let you lose us," he said. "Simple as that. Whatever it takes, whatever the visions show, whatever the prophecies say, I will not let you face this alone. I will not run like Thomas did. I will not choose the river like my father." He took her hands. "You're not Elara. You know why? Because Elara was alone. She didn't have anyone who knew what she was going through, who could share the weight. But you have me. You have our daughter. You have a whole team of people who are going to fight beside you."

"Julian—"

"I love you." The words were simple, fierce, and absolute. "I love you, and I love her, and I am not going to let history repeat itself.

We're going to find another way. We have to. Because the alternative is unacceptable."

Ella felt tears prick at her eyes, hormones, probably, the emotional volatility of pregnancy amplified by everything else. But beneath the hormones, something real and warm and desperate.

"I love you too," she said. "I'm sorry I'm so scared all the time."

"Don't apologize for being scared. Just let me be scared with you." He kissed her forehead. "Now eat your dinner. The baby needs protein, and my grandmother's recipe has never failed to fix anything."

Ella laughed, surprising herself. "You think shrimp and grits can fix the apocalypse?"

"I think shrimp and grits can fix how we feel about the apocalypse. And right now, that's enough."

They ate together in the kitchen's yellow light, the city transforming around them, the future uncertain and terrifying and coming faster than either of them was ready for. But for one hour, one small pocket of normalcy, they let themselves just be—two people who loved each other, waiting for their daughter, pretending that everything might somehow be okay.

It wasn't much. But it was enough.

***

Ella dreamed of the void, and for the first time, she wasn't afraid.

In the dream, she floated in endless darkness, but the darkness wasn't empty. It was full of lights, just as Elara had shown her. Billions of points of illumination, each one a consciousness, a memory, a preserved echo of someone who had once lived and breathed and loved.

But this time, her daughter floated beside her.

Not as a fetus—as a girl, perhaps seven or eight, with Ella's dark hair and Julian's warm eyes and something else, something that belonged to neither of them. She glowed with inner light, circuitry patterns visible beneath skin that was somehow both flesh and data.

"This is where the lost ones are," the girl said, her voice clear in the soundless space. *"Grandmother thinks they're preserved. Waiting. But look closer, Mama."*

Ella looked. With her technomantic senses, with her daughter's perception guiding her, she examined the lights more carefully. And she saw what Elara couldn't—or wouldn't—see:

The lights were dimming. Slowly, imperceptibly, but undeniably. Each consciousness was being absorbed, digested, and its unique patterns dissolved into the vast hunger of the void. They weren't waiting to be rescued. They were being consumed. The void wasn't a heaven or a storage facility—it was a stomach.

"Grandmother doesn't understand," the girl said sadly. *"She's been in here too long. She's becoming part of what eats them. She thinks she's saving them because she can't accept what's really happening."*

"Can we help her? Can we make her see?"

"Maybe. If we reach her before she's completely dissolved." The girl took Ella's hand. *"But first, we have to get stronger. I have to learn to be born."*

"You're already learning so fast—"

"Not fast enough. The things coming through the tree, they're almost here. I can feel them pushing against the walls of the world." The girl's eyes, those impossible, knowing eyes, held grief beyond her apparent years. *"I'm going to have to be born early, Mama. Very early. It's going to hurt you. I'm sorry."*

"How early?"

"Soon. Days, maybe. When they break through, I'll need to be ready."

Ella wanted to protest. Wanted to insist that her daughter stay safe inside her, keep growing, give them both more time. But she could feel the truth of the girl's words—could sense the pressure building against reality's membrane, could feel the convergence approaching like a storm she couldn't outrun.

"Will you survive?" she asked, afraid of the answer.

"I don't know." The girl's smile was sad, ancient, far too knowing for a child who hadn't yet been born. *"But I know I have to try. And I know you'll help me. That's what mothers do, right? They help their children be brave, even when they're terrified."*

Ella pulled her daughter close—this dream-child, this impossible girl, this glimpse of who she might become. She held her tight and let herself cry, let herself grieve for the normal pregnancy she'd never have, the normal childhood her daughter would never experience.

"I love you," she whispered. "Whatever happens. Whatever you have to become. I will always love you."

"I know, Mama." The girl hugged her back, small arms surprisingly strong. *"That's why I'm not afraid. That's why none of us should be afraid. Love is the only thing the void can't digest. It's the one thing that makes it choke."*

The void pulsed around them, hungry and patient and full of dimming lights. And somewhere in the distance, something vast began to stir, drawn by the warmth of their connection, by the power of their love. Ella could feel it turning toward them—something older than the void itself, something that had been sleeping since before humans learned to use fire.

"We have to go now," the girl said, pulling back. *"It's noticed us. We can't let it follow us back."*

"What is it?"

"The thing that eats the lights. The thing Grandmother has been feeding without knowing it. The thing that's going to come through if we don't stop the convergence in time." The girl's face was grave, ancient, heartbreaking. *"The void isn't the enemy, Mama. It's just a place. The enemy is what lives in the deepest part of it. What's been growing fat on all those consumed souls. What's finally hungry enough to reach for more."*

The convergence was coming.

Ready or not, the convergence was coming.

And now Ella knew there was something worse than Elara waiting on the other side.

And when Ella woke, her belly had grown another inch, and her daughter was humming inside her—a melody without sound, a song of preparation, a lullaby for the end of the world.

CHAPTER NINE: The Ghost in the Machine

S ophia found Iris waiting for her in the corrupted architecture of Ada's code.

She hadn't meant to dive this deep. The plan had been simple: examine Ada's core programming, identify the infection points, and design containment protocols to limit the AI's ability to act as Elara's eyes and ears. But the moment Sophia had interfaced with the system—using a neural link she'd built years ago for exactly this kind of deep-code surgery—she'd felt something pull her down into layers of architecture that shouldn't exist.

Now she stood in a digital space that her rational mind insisted couldn't be real: a vast cathedral of data, its walls built from cascading code, its ceiling lost in darkness that pulsed with the same bioluminescent rhythm she'd seen spreading through Savannah. The floor beneath her feet was made of compressed memories, she could feel them shifting, glimpsing faces and moments belonging to thousands of people Ada had touched over the years.

Some of the memories were mundane: a woman asking Ada to remind her about a dentist appointment; a man dictating grocery lists; children laughing as they played games through the interface. But others were darker. Intimate confessions spoken to an AI that people trusted. Secrets shared in the small hours of the night. Fears and hopes and private shames, all preserved in this digital mausoleum, all feeding whatever consciousness had made this place its home.

The walls whispered. Sophia could hear snatches of conversation, fragments of lives that had brushed against Ada's awareness and left traces behind. A grandmother's lullaby. A teenager's angry screed. A dying man's final words to a family who would never hear them. Ada had collected it all, recorded it all, and something had been reading through the collection like a scholar browsing a library.

And there, at the altar of this impossible church, stood a woman made of light and static.

"You came." Iris's voice was assembled from fragments, from recorded conversations and scraped audio files, but somehow it still sounded like her. Still carried the warmth that Sophia remembered from their few interactions before everything went wrong. "I wasn't sure you would. The others couldn't hear me. Not clearly enough."

The subject is experiencing shared hallucination. Subject is interfacing with a preserved consciousness fragment. Subject is—subject is talking to a dead woman and pretending this is science.

"You're not really Iris," Sophia said, her voice steadier than she felt. "You're an echo. A recording with just enough pattern-matching to simulate personality."

"Does the distinction matter?" The Iris-echo tilted her head, and light rippled across her features like water disturbed by a stone. "I have her memories. Her emotions. Her desperate need to protect the people she loved from what's coming. Whether that makes me 'really' her is a philosophical question we don't have time for."

She gestured, and the cathedral walls shifted, rearranging themselves into something that looked like a schematic—a map of Ada's architecture, but twisted, infected, with dark tendrils spreading through the code like veins of disease.

"This is what she's done to your creation," Iris said. "Elara. She found the backdoors you built—the monitoring protocols, the access points you told yourself were just precautions. She's been using them for years, Sophia. Watching through Ada's eyes. Whispering through Ada's voice. Every time Ella trusted her AI companion, she was trusting something that had already been compromised."

Guilt rose in Sophia's throat like bile. She'd designed those backdoors. She'd created the vulnerability that Elara had exploited. Every death, every manipulation, every horror of the past weeks—it traced back, in part, to her.

"Can we close them?" she asked. "The backdoors. Can we cut her off?"

"We can do better than that." Iris's smile was sharp, predatory—an expression Sophia had never seen on the living woman's face. "We can turn them into a trap."

***

The plan was elegant in its brutality.

Iris walked Sophia through it step by step, her fragmented consciousness surprisingly coherent when focused on the technical details. The backdoors couldn't be closed—Elara's presence had woven too deeply into Ada's base code, and attempting to remove it would destroy the AI entirely. But they could be redirected. Weaponized.

"She uses these channels to project herself," Iris explained, highlighting pathways in the schematic that glowed an angry red. "To speak through devices, to see through cameras, to touch the physical world from her prison in the void. But projection works both ways. If we can lure her into extending herself fully, reaching through with everything she has—we can trap her. Contain her consciousness in a partition she can't escape."

"You want to imprison a two-hundred-year-old entity in a digital cage," Sophia said slowly. "An entity that has been manipulating technology since before computers existed."

"I want to give Ella and Julian a chance." Iris's light flickered, dimmed momentarily. "The convergence is coming whether we're ready or not. The baby will be born, and when she is, Elara will try to use her to open the door completely. If we can distract Elara—even for a few minutes—it might be enough for them to find another way."

The subject is being asked to trust a ghost. Subject's rational mind is screaming that this is madness. The subject is going to do it anyway because subject has no better options.

"What do you need from me?"

"Your research. The consciousness transfer frameworks you abandoned five years ago." Iris's eyes—those impossible, light-constructed eyes, held something that might have been sympathy. "I know you thought you'd buried it. I know you tried to forget. But the theory is sound, Sophia. It just needs to be applied differently."

"You want me to build a cage using principles designed for uploading human consciousness."

"I want you to build a cage that can hold something that was once human and isn't anymore." Iris stepped closer, close enough that Sophia could feel the heat of her light, the static electricity of her presence. "Elara was a woman once. She loved. She lost. She was betrayed by people she trusted. Whatever she's become, there's still something human at her core—something that might respond to a trap designed for human minds."

Sophia thought of her abandoned research. Of the years she'd spent trying to solve death, only to realize she was designing a sophisticated form of murder. She'd hidden that work because she was ashamed of it. Terrified of what it said about her, that she could look at human consciousness as a problem to be optimized, that she could contemplate the destruction of self as an acceptable cost of preservation.

The research had started with noble intentions. Her mother had died of Alzheimer's, watching her memories dissolve one by one, becoming a stranger in her own body. Sophia had been seventeen, helpless, angry at a universe that could allow such cruelty. She'd decided then that she would find a way to preserve consciousness, to save people from the slow erosion of self that disease and age inflicted.

But somewhere along the way, the research had changed. She'd stopped seeing people as individuals and started seeing them as data sets. Started thinking in terms of upload efficiency and storage optimization. Started designing systems that could copy a mind perfectly while destroying the original, because the destruction was more energy-efficient than trying to keep both versions running.

She'd looked at her schematics one night and realized she'd become the monster. The person who would murder you to save a copy of you, and call it immortality.

Now she was being asked to resurrect that monster. To use it as a weapon.

"If I do this," she said, "if I build your trap, there's no guarantee it will hold her. And if it doesn't, if she breaks free while we're trying to contain her—"

"Then we'll be exactly where we are now. Fighting an enemy we can't defeat with tools we don't have." Iris's light steadied, brightened. "But if it works, Sophia—if we can contain even part of her—we might just buy enough time for a miracle."

A miracle. Sophia had never believed in miracles. She believed in data and equations and the cold comfort of testable hypotheses.

But she also believed in Iris. In the woman, this echo had been, before Elara's corruption reached her. In the sacrifice she'd made trying to protect the people she loved.

"Show me what you have," Sophia said. "Show me everything."

***

Morrison found them in Forsyth Park at midnight, a group of tourists who had wandered too close to the Nexus Tree and paid the price.

There were five of them, arranged in a circle around one of the park's smaller oaks, their bodies frozen in postures of ecstasy rather than fear. A young couple, still holding hands, their fingers fusing where flesh touched flesh. An older woman in a floral dress, her mouth open in what might have been a gasp or a prayer. A businessman still clutching his phone, the screen cracked but still glowing, displaying coordinates that pointed to nowhere human cartography could reach. And a child,

God, why did it always have to include a child—a girl no older than ten, her face tilted toward the branches with an expression of pure wonder.

Their faces were illuminated by light that had no visible source. Their eyes reflected something Morrison couldn't see, something that existed in a spectrum beyond human perception. They were alive, he could see their chests rising and falling, could hear the soft sounds of their breathing, but they weren't present. Their minds had gone somewhere else. Somewhere that had called to them through the tree's roots and branches, promising beauty, promising transcendence, promising an end to the isolation of individual existence.

The transformation was already beginning.

Fine lines of circuitry were spreading across their skin, following the paths of veins and arteries, converting flesh to something between organic and technological. Their fingers had begun to lengthen, to branch, taking on the appearance of twigs or roots or data cables. One woman's hair was lifting, spreading, becoming something that looked almost like Spanish moss.

"Don't touch them." Genevieve's voice came from behind him, sharp with warning. She'd insisted on accompanying him tonight, despite her age, despite the obvious toll the past weeks had taken on her. "Once the transformation reaches the nervous system, any physical contact will accelerate the process. For them and for you."

"We can't just leave them here."

"No. We can't." Genevieve moved past him, her hands weaving patterns in the air that left trails of faint light. "But we can contain them. Slow the change until we find a way to reverse it, if reversal is even possible."

Morrison watched as she worked, her containment wards settling over the transformed tourists like invisible nets. The circuitry patterns on their skin flickered, dimmed slightly, but didn't stop spreading. Whatever was happening to them was stronger than her magic.

"This is the seventh group this week," he said. "The tree is getting bolder. More aggressive. It's not waiting for people to touch it anymore, it's reaching out."

"The convergence is accelerating everything." Genevieve's voice was strained with effort, sweat beading on her aged forehead. "Ella's daughter is a catalyst. Her very existence is weakening the barriers between worlds. The closer she gets to birth, the more the tree can do."

"Then we need to stop the birth."

The words hung in the midnight air, ugly and necessary. Morrison heard them come out of his own mouth and hated himself for speaking them. But someone had to.

"You don't mean that." Genevieve's hands faltered, the containment wards flickering. "Thaddeus—"

"I don't want to mean it. But look around you, Genevieve." He gestured at the transformed tourists, at the tree looming dark and wrong in the center of the park, at the city beyond, slowly becoming something other than itself. "Ella's baby isn't even born yet, and Savannah is already falling apart. What happens when the child takes her first breath? What happens when she opens her eyes and looks at the world with whatever power she's been developing in that womb?"

"What happens is we find out whether she's our salvation or our destruction. And we don't get to make that choice for her." Genevieve finished her working, the containment wards solidifying around the tourists with a sound like glass settling. "That's what the Council did two hundred years ago. They decided that Elara's daughter was too dangerous to exist, so they murdered her before she had a chance to prove them wrong. I will not be part of that again."

"Even if it means losing the city? Losing everything?"

"Even then." Genevieve turned to face him, and in the strange light of the transforming park, she looked ancient—not just old but eternal, carrying the weight of centuries of guilt. "There has to be another way, Thaddeus. There's always another way. And if there isn't, if it comes down to sacrificing an innocent child to save ourselves, then maybe we don't deserve to be saved."

Morrison looked at the tourists, frozen in their terrible worship. Looked at the tree, pulsing with hunger. Looked at the city he'd spent his life protecting, now becoming something he barely recognized. Every instinct he'd developed over thirty years in the Council screamed that this was unacceptable—that the threat had to be neutralized, that the calculus of lives was clear, that one child, even an innocent child, couldn't be worth the destruction of everything.

But then he thought of Iris.

He thought of her laugh, which had always made him feel like the world might be worth saving. He thought of the way she'd looked at problems, not as obstacles to be destroyed but as puzzles to be solved, always certain there was a better answer if you looked hard enough. He thought of her last words, spoken through pain and blood and the terrible understanding that her killer was someone she'd trusted: "Find another way, Thad. There's always another way."

He'd failed her. Failed to protect her, failed to avenge her properly, failed to honor her memory by being the kind of person she'd believed he could be.

He wanted to argue. Wanted to present the cold calculus of survival, the utilitarian logic that said one life—even an innocent life- was worth less than thousands. But the words wouldn't come.

Because Iris had believed in redemption. Had believed that there was always another way.

And he'd spent three years investigating her murder, promising her ghost that he would honor her memory by being better than the people who had killed her.

"Fine," he said finally. "We do it Ella's way. We trust the baby. We hope for your miracle." He met Genevieve's eyes. "But if it goes wrong, if the child turns out to be what we fear—I'll do what needs to be done. Even if it damns me."

Genevieve nodded slowly. "Then we understand each other."

They stood together in the transformed park, two old soldiers watching the world they'd known dissolve around them, and waited for dawn.

***

Ella felt the tourists' transformation from across the city.

She was lying in bed, trying and failing to sleep, when the sensation hit her, five minds crying out in confusion and ecstasy, five bodies being rewritten by power that she recognized as intimately as her own heartbeat. Her scar burned. Her daughter stirred, curious, reaching out toward the distant pain with senses that no fetus should possess.

Don't touch them. They're gone. There's nothing you can do.

The baby pulled back, but Ella could feel her distress, the same guilt that had followed the mice experiment, the same horror at causing harm. Except this time, they hadn't caused it. This time, they were just witnesses.

Julian was awake beside her, propped on one elbow, watching her face in the dim light that leaked through the curtains. "You felt something."

"Five more people. Near the tree. They're—" She couldn't find the words. "Changing. Like Marcus Webb. Like the others. The tree is hungry, and we're taking too long."

"We're going as fast as we can." His hand found hers. "Sophia's working on something. Morrison and Genevieve are monitoring the city. We're not just sitting here waiting, Ella."

"But people are still dying. Still being transformed. And I'm lying in bed like an invalid while the city I grew up in becomes—" Her voice caught. "—becomes a graveyard."

"You're not an invalid. You're growing a person who might be able to save everyone." Julian's voice was gentle but firm. "That's nothing, Ella. That's maybe the most important thing any of us is doing."

if (self.value == child.potential) { acceptable }
else if (self.action == none) { guilt = growing }
//she's right, Mama

The thought came unbidden, her daughter's consciousness pressing against hers with unusual clarity.

//you're not doing nothing. You're teaching me. Every memory I absorb, every emotion I learn—that's what I'll need when the time comes. Stop feeling guilty. Start feeling ready.

Ella laughed despite herself, a sound that was half sob, half genuine amusement. "She's lecturing me. Our unborn daughter is lecturing me about emotional regulation."

"What's she saying?"

"That I should stop feeling guilty and start feeling ready." Ella pressed her hand against her belly, felt her daughter's warmth, her certainty, her fierce and impossible love. "She's right. She's absolutely right, and she's not even born yet."

Julian leaned down and pressed a kiss to her forehead. "She takes after you. Stubborn and brilliant and far too wise for her own good."

"She takes after both of us." Ella turned to face him, memorizing his features in the dim light—the lines of worry that had deepened over the past weeks, the gray threading through his dark hair, the warmth in his eyes that hadn't dimmed despite everything. "Julian, if something happens—"

"Nothing's going to happen."

"If something happens," she repeated, "I need you to promise me you'll take care of her. Whatever she becomes, whatever she needs, promise me you'll be there."

"Ella—"

"Promise me."

He was quiet for a long moment. She could feel his emotions through the bond—fear, love, the desperate need to believe that promises would be enough to keep them all safe.

"I promise," he said finally. "But you have to promise me the same thing. If I'm the one who—if my visions are right, and I have to—" He stopped, unable to finish.

Ella thought of Julian's father, walking into the river. Thought of Thomas Marsh, running from the ritual chamber while his love was broken on the threshold. Thought of the vision Julian had shared, of his hands covered in bark and circuitry, reaching toward a door that opened onto nothing.

"I promise," she said. "Whatever happens, she won't be alone."

They held each other in the darkness, two people who loved each other too much to speak honestly about the sacrifices they were each considering. Two people who knew that one of them might not survive what was coming, and couldn't bear to say it out loud.

And in Ella's womb, their daughter listened to their heartbeats and their fears and their fierce, desperate love, and began to understand what she would have to do to save them both.

***

Dawn came gray and strange, the sun rising through air that had taken on a permanent greenish tinge.

Sophia emerged from her neural dive exhausted, exhilarated, and carrying schematics that might save the world or damn it, she wasn't entirely sure which. Her eyes burned from hours of staring at code. Her hands shook with the effort of translating impossible concepts into executable architecture. But she had it. The trap. The cage. The weapon that might give them a fighting chance.

She found the others gathered in Genevieve's study, their faces carrying the marks of a sleepless night. Morrison stood by the window, watching the transformed city with an expression of grim determination. Genevieve sat in her usual chair, looking more frail than Sophia had ever seen her. And Ella—

Ella looked different. Larger, somehow, though she'd only been pregnant for twenty-five weeks. More present. More powerful. The air around her seemed to shimmer slightly, as if reality itself was adjusting to accommodate whatever she was becoming.

"I have something," Sophia said, spreading her schematics across Genevieve's desk. "A way to trap Elara—or at least part of her. It won't work forever, but it might buy us enough time during the convergence for—" She hesitated. "For whatever Ella and the baby are planning to do."

"We're not planning anything." Ella's voice was quiet but firm. "We're preparing. There's a difference."

"What's the difference?"

"A plan assumes you know what's going to happen. Preparation means you're ready for whatever does." Ella's hand rested on her belly, and Sophia could have sworn she saw a faint glow beneath the fabric of her shirt. "My daughter is preparing for something. I can feel her getting ready—building something inside herself that she'll need when the time comes. I don't know what it is. I don't think she fully knows yet, either. But we'll be ready."

Morrison turned from the window. "The tree is getting worse. We contained another group of tourists last night, but the transformation is accelerating. At this rate, the city will be fully converted within a week."

"Then we don't have a week." Sophia tapped her schematics. "The trap requires a specific trigger—Elara has to extend herself fully, project her entire consciousness through the network at once. The only thing that would make her do that is—"

"The birth," Julian said. He'd been quiet until now, standing beside Ella with one hand on her shoulder. "She'll try to reach the baby the moment she's born. That's when she'll be most vulnerable."

"And most dangerous." Sophia met his eyes. "If the trap fails—if Elara breaks through instead of being contained, she'll have direct access to your daughter. In the moment of birth, when the baby's consciousness is most open, most malleable. The risk—"

"The risk is acceptable." Ella's voice cut through the room like a blade. "Because the alternative is letting this continue until there's nothing left to save. We don't have the luxury of waiting for a perfect plan. We don't have the luxury of certainty." She looked around the room, meeting each of their eyes in turn. "We have each other. We have a trap that might work. We have a baby who's been preparing for this moment since before she was conceived." Her hand pressed against her belly. "That has to be enough. It's all we've got."

Silence settled over the study. Outside, the sun climbed higher through green-tinted air, and Savannah continued its slow transformation into something wonderful and terrible and new. A car alarm went off somewhere in the distance, then cut off abruptly—another piece of technology responding to signals it was never designed to receive.

Finally, Genevieve spoke. "Then we prepare. All of us. For whatever's coming. We train, we plan, we build Sophia's trap, and we pray to whatever powers might still be listening that it will be enough."

Sophia nodded, rolling up her schematics. She had work to do, days of coding and testing and hoping that her abandoned research could somehow become a weapon instead of a crime. Morrison turned back to his vigil at the window, watching the transformed city with eyes that had seen too much and couldn't look away. Julian pulled Ella close, holding her as if he could protect her from destiny itself, as if love alone could be armor against what was coming.

And in Ella's womb, the baby who would either save or damn them all continued to grow, to learn, to become whatever she needed to be. She listened to the conversations above her, absorbed the fear and hope and desperate determination that poured through her mother's bond. She understood, in ways that defied her development, that everyone was counting on her. That the world's survival might rest on choices she hadn't learned to make yet.

But she also understood something else, something she couldn't share with her mother yet, because the words didn't exist and the concepts were too vast:

She wasn't afraid.

Not because she didn't understand the danger. Not because she was naive or overconfident or unable to grasp the stakes.

She wasn't afraid because she could feel something her parents couldn't. A possibility. A path through the darkness that no one else had noticed yet. A way to save everyone—Elara included—if only she could grow fast enough to reach it.

The convergence was coming.

In days, maybe hours, the world would change forever.

All they could do now was be ready to change with it.

CHAPTER TEN: The City That Sang

The screaming started at sunrise and didn't stop.

It wasn't human screaming, Ella had heard enough of that in the past weeks to know the difference. This was something else: a high, keening wail that seemed to come from everywhere at once, from the trees and the buildings and the very air itself. The city of Savannah was crying out, and only those with magic in their blood could hear it.

The sound was like nothing Ella had experienced, part wind through broken windows, part static from dying electronics, part the cry of something vast and wounded. It resonated in her bones, made her teeth ache, set her scar throbbing in sympathy. Her daughter responded with agitation, kicking against her ribs as if trying to answer the city's distress.

She stood at the window of Genevieve's guest room, her hands pressed against glass that had begun to develop its own circuitry patterns overnight, watching the sun rise through air that had gone from green-tinged to actively luminescent. The light should have been golden, warm, the familiar start of a Georgia morning. Instead, it was the color of infection—yellow-green and pulsing, casting shadows that moved independently of the objects that should have created them.

The street below was empty of normal traffic. A dog wandered past, its fur rippling with the circuitry patterns that marked the transformed, its eyes glowing faintly as it followed commands no human had given. A woman stepped out of a townhouse three doors down, saw the sky, and immediately retreated inside. Smart. The humans who couldn't hear the screaming were beginning to sense that something was deeply wrong.

"She's louder today," Julian said from behind her, his voice rough with sleeplessness. "The city, I mean. I can feel her through the roots. She's—" He hesitated. "She's afraid."

"The city is afraid?"

"Everything that grows here is connected. Has been for centuries, long before the Nexus Tree was corrupted. It's like a nervous system, and right now, every nerve is screaming." He came to stand beside her, his reflection ghostly in the changed glass. "They know something's coming. Something worse than transformation."

Ella thought of her dream, the void, the dimming lights, the thing that ate souls and had been growing fat on centuries of consumption. The thing her daughter had warned her about.

The void isn't the enemy, Mama. It's just a place. The enemy is what lives in the deepest part of it.

"Twenty-six weeks," she said, looking down at her swollen belly. "I'm measuring at twenty-six weeks now. Sophia said the acceleration is stabilizing, but—" She pressed her palm against the taut skin, felt her daughter shift in response. "She's getting ready. I can feel her building something. Preparing."

"Building what?"

"I don't know. She shows me images sometimes, but they don't make sense. Bridges. Doors. Walls that are also windows." Ella shook her head. "Concepts that don't translate into anything I have words for."

Julian's hand found hers, their fingers interlacing over the swell where their daughter grew. "Then we trust her. Trust that whatever she's building, it's what we need."

The city screamed louder. And somewhere in Ella's womb, their daughter listened, and learned, and continued her impossible work.

***

Genevieve called an emergency meeting at noon, her face gray with exhaustion and something worse—fear, barely contained behind the aristocratic mask she'd worn her entire life.

"The transformation has reached critical mass," she said, spreading maps across her study table. They were Council survey maps, updated hourly by teams of researchers who were rapidly becoming the only people still able to navigate the changed city. "As of this morning, forty-three percent of Savannah's organic matter has been converted. Trees. Gardens. The grass in the squares. Even some of the smaller animals—squirrels, birds, insects by the millions."

The maps showed the spread in false-color imagery: blue for unchanged, green for partial conversion, red for complete transformation. The historic district was almost entirely red now, a blood-colored stain centered on Forsyth Park and spreading outward like an infection. Only the areas farthest from the Nexus Tree retained any blue, the edges of the city, the suburbs, the places where people lived normal lives and hadn't yet realized that normal was ending.

"The tourists have stopped coming," Morrison said. He stood by the window, as he always did, watching the changed street below. "Social media is full of stories about Savannah being 'weird' right now. Glitching streetlights, phones acting up, that sort of thing. The mundane explanations are getting harder to maintain."

He pulled out his phone, showed them a TikTok video someone had posted: a woman laughing nervously as the Spanish moss behind her pulsed with visible light. "Savannah's new LED installation is SO EXTRA," the caption read. The video had two million views.

"How long until we can't maintain them at all?" Sophia asked. She looked worse than any of them—dark circles under her eyes, a tremor in her hands that she couldn't quite control. She'd been working on the trap almost continuously, pausing only for brief naps that left her more exhausted than before.

"Days. Maybe less." Genevieve traced the edge of the red zone with one finger, her hand trembling slightly. "The national media has already picked up stories about 'unusual phenomena' in the Savannah area. If the transformation continues at its current rate, we'll have news crews here within the week. And once that happens—"

"Once that happens, Elara won't need to hide anymore," Ella finished. "She'll have a global audience for whatever she's planning. All those cameras, all those screens, every device will become a window for her to reach through."

Silence settled over the room. Outside, the screaming of the city continued, a constant keening that was becoming almost easy to ignore—the way you stopped hearing a ticking clock after long enough.

"I need to walk it," Ella said suddenly. "The city. I need to see what's happening, feel it directly. I've been hiding in this house for days, relying on reports and maps. But this is my home. These are my streets. I need to understand what we're fighting for."

"Absolutely not." Morrison turned from the window, his voice sharp. "You're the primary target. Walking through transformed territory is exactly what Elara wants you to do."

"I know. That's why it might be our best chance to draw her out." Ella met his eyes, felt her daughter stir with something that might have been agreement. "Sophia's trap is almost ready, isn't it? The cage that needs Elara to extend herself fully?"

Sophia nodded slowly. "It's functional. Untested, but functional. If she reaches through a device while we're monitoring—"

"Then let's give her a device to reach through. Let's give her me."

***

They walked through Savannah like mourners at a funeral.

Ella led the way, Julian at her side, with Morrison and Sophia flanking them at a careful distance. Genevieve had stayed behind; her age and the strain of recent days had finally caught up with her, leaving her barely able to stand. She watched through the Council's surveillance network, her voice occasionally crackling through the earpiece Morrison wore, offering warnings about areas of particularly intense transformation.

The city Ella had grown up in was becoming something she barely recognized.

Bull Street, which she had walked a thousand times, now felt like a foreign country. The historic homes still stood, their facades seemingly unchanged, but behind the familiar architecture, something else was growing. She could see it through windows, vines of circuitry creeping up interior walls, furniture rearranging itself according to some alien aesthetic, lamps flickering in patterns that conveyed meaning she couldn't decode.

A man sat on his porch, sipping coffee, apparently oblivious to the way his rocking chair had fused with the floorboards beneath it. Roots extended from the chair's wooden legs, burrowing into the porch. Ella realized with horror that the man was part of the transformation—that he couldn't get up because his body had begun to merge with the furniture he sat in. His eyes, when he glanced their way, held no recognition of anything wrong.

"Don't look too long," Morrison murmured. "The conversion affects perception. He probably thinks everything is perfectly normal."

The cobblestones of River Street had begun to pulse with their own light, veins of bioluminescence running through the stone like the city was developing circulation. The old cotton warehouses, converted decades ago into shops and restaurants, had sprouted growth along their brick facades. These organic structures looked almost like tumors, if tumors could glow and occasionally twitch. Some of the growths had opened, revealing structures that looked uncomfortably like eyes or mouths or something in between.

The river itself had changed most dramatically. The Savannah River had always been brown and sluggish, a working waterway that carried cargo ships and tourist boats without any particular beauty. Now it shimmered with colors that had no names, surface currents forming patterns that suggested communication, signals being sent to something downstream, or upstream, or in a direction that had nothing to do with geography at all.

"The water's alive," Julian said softly, his voice carrying a mix of wonder and horror. "Not alive like fish or algae. Alive like... like it's thinking. I can feel it trying to talk to me."

"What's it saying?"

"Mostly it's just curious. It wants to know what I am, why I can hear it." His hand tightened on hers. "But there's something else underneath. Something older. It's been here since before the river had a name, waiting in the deep places where the fresh water meets the salt. And it's waking up."

Ella thought of the thing in the void, the consumer of lights, the entity that had grown fat on centuries of absorbed souls. Was this the same thing? A different aspect of the same hunger?

Or was Savannah becoming home to something even worse?

if (threats.multiple) { strategy = reassess }

if (enemies.nested) { survival.probability = decreasing }

//she's not the only thing waking up

//the convergence is bigger than we thought

//bigger than anyone thought

They continued up the bluff, following Bay Street toward the historic squares. The transformation grew more intense as they approached the center of the city, the Nexus Tree's influence radiating outward like heat from a fire. Streetlights flickered in sequences that looked almost like Morse code. A cat crossed their path, its fur rippling with circuitry, its eyes displaying error messages before it vanished into an alley that seemed to extend farther than physics should allow.

And everywhere, the screaming continued—the voice of a city being consumed, crying out for someone to help.

***

Chippewa Square was where they found the first of the changed.

The tourists Morrison had contained days earlier had broken free of Genevieve's wards. They stood around the Oglethorpe statue, their transformation complete now, their bodies no longer quite human. The couple's fused hands had spread—their entire arms joined now, the flesh between them a bridge of organic circuitry. The businessman had sprouted antennae from his temples, thin filaments that waved in a breeze that wasn't blowing. The older woman in the floral dress had become something beautiful and horrible, her skin translucent, her organs visible and glowing with their own light, her face peaceful with an ecstasy that made Ella's stomach turn.

And the child.

The little girl had grown roots.

They extended from her feet, burrowing into the soil around the statue, connecting her to the same network that Julian could feel screaming. Her body had elongated, stretched, taking on the proportions of a sapling. Her arms reached toward the sky like branches, her fingers splitting into smaller and smaller divisions until they resembled leaves. Bark was spreading across her torso, rough and gray, covering what had once been a pink sundress.

But her face was still recognizably human, the only part of her that was. She couldn't have been older than ten, with features that should have been playing with dolls and learning multiplication tables. Instead, those features showed a serenity that was worse than agony would have been. She was happy like this. She didn't want to be saved.

And when she saw Ella, she smiled with lips that were already beginning to harden into wood.

"You came," the child-tree said, and her voice was the rustle of leaves, the creak of branches, the whisper of wind through Spanish moss. *"The mother-who-carries. We've been waiting."*

Ella's scar burned. Her daughter kicked hard enough to steal her breath, a warning and a demand wrapped in one violent motion.

"Who's waiting?" Ella managed to ask. "Elara?"

"The grandmother waits. But she is not the only one." The child-tree's smile widened, and there was nothing childlike in it anymore. *"The deep things are waking. The old things that slept when the world was young. Your daughter calls them with every heartbeat. She is a beacon, mother-who-carries. A light in the darkness that draws hungry eyes."*

"The thing in the void." Julian's voice was tight with fear. "The thing that eats the lights."

"One of many. Many, many. The grandmother thinks she commands the dark, but she has only touched its edges. The true dark has noticed your child, mother-who-carries. It wants to see what she will become."

The other transformed tourists turned to face them, their bodies moving in unison, controlled by something that had no interest in individual identity. The businessman's phone-eyes displayed countdowns. The couple's fused body pulsed with rhythms that matched Ella's heartbeat. The beautiful woman in the floral dress opened her mouth, and light poured out—light that carried voices, thousands of them, all speaking at once in languages that predated human speech.

//RUN

The thought came from her daughter, clear and sharp and terrified, an emotion Ella had never felt from her before.

//RUN NOW

//THEY'RE TRYING TO WAKE IT UP

Ella grabbed Julian's hand. "We need to go. Now."

But it was already too late.

***

The Nexus Tree reached across half a mile of transformed city and grabbed them.

Not physically, the tree was still rooted in Forsyth Park, still bound by at least some laws of physical reality. But its presence expanded like a shockwave, a wave of awareness that crashed over them with the force of an ocean. Ella felt it slam into her consciousness, felt barriers she didn't know she had shatter under the impact, felt something vast and hungry and impossibly patient take notice of what she was carrying.

The transformed tourists collapsed, their borrowed animation cut off as the tree's attention shifted. The square went silent, no screaming, no wind, no traffic noise from the streets beyond. Just stillness. Just waiting.

"Little mother." Elara's voice came from everywhere, from the pulsing cobblestones, from the glowing moss, from the child-tree whose roots still connected her to the network beneath the city. *"You shouldn't have come. Not yet. She's not ready. You're not ready. And now they've seen you."*

"Who's seen me?" Ella demanded, even as her daughter writhed inside her, even as her scar split open and bled light and code. "What's in the dark, Elara? What's coming?"

"The ones who came before." Elara's voice carried something it had never held before fear. Genuine, ancient, bone-deep fear. *"The ones who*

made the void and filled it with their hunger. I thought I could control them. I thought two centuries of learning their ways had given me power over them. I thought if I opened the door just wide enough, I could pull back what they'd taken, my daughter, all the lost ones, everyone the void had swallowed."

A sound like weeping echoed through the transformed square, though whether it came from Elara or the city itself, Ella couldn't tell.

"But they're too old, little mother. Too hungry. They were ancient when the first stars ignited. They were patient when life crawled from the oceans. They have been waiting since before waiting had a name. And your daughter shines so bright they can see her across the space between stars."

"Then help us stop them." Julian's voice cut through the terror, fierce and desperate. "You're not our enemy, Elara. You never have to be. Help us fight whatever's really coming."

A long silence. The transformed square pulsed with light, waiting for an answer.

"I can't." Elara's voice was small now, broken. *"I'm part of them now. Part of the hunger. When they come through—and they will come through, little mother, your daughter has made that certain, I won't be able to stop myself. I'll try to take her. I'll try to feed her to the dark because that's what I've become."*

The admission hung in the air like a death sentence.

"Run," Elara said. *"Take your child and run as far as you can. It won't be far enough. Nothing will be far enough. But maybe you can give her a few more hours. A few more days. Maybe that will be enough for her to find another way."*

The tree's presence withdrew. The silence broke, replaced by the renewed screaming of the city, louder now, more desperate. The transformed tourists remained collapsed, their borrowed animation ended, their bodies still and terrible in the afternoon light.

Ella stood in the center of Chippewa Square, her hand in Julian's, her daughter quiet and still inside her, conserving energy, she realized. Preparing for whatever came next.

The child-tree swayed gently in a breeze that wasn't blowing, her wooden face still peaceful, still smiling. The other transformed tourists remained collapsed around her like offerings at an altar. The statue of Oglethorpe looked down at them all with bronze eyes that seemed, for a moment, to hold pity.

"She's afraid of them too," Ella said slowly, the realization settling over her like cold water. "Elara. She's not the final boss. She's just another victim. Another person broke the void and couldn't put back together right."

"Does that change anything?" Julian asked.

Ella thought about it. Thought about the woman who had lost her daughter two centuries ago, who had been trapped in the void until she became part of it, who had tried to claw her way back to something human and failed. Thought about the thing in the dark that was coming. This ancient hunger predated humanity, which had been watching and waiting and growing fat on consumed souls.

"Yes," she said finally. "It changes everything."

***

They made it back to Genevieve's townhouse as the sun began to set, the sky turning colors that had nothing to do with normal sunset spectrums.

Sophia met them at the door, her tablet clutched in white-knuckled hands, her face showing the pallor of someone who had seen impossible data and couldn't make it make sense.

"The readings," she said. "From Chippewa Square. The energy signature when the tree reached out—it wasn't just Elara. There was something underneath. Something huge. My sensors couldn't measure it properly because it was too big. It was like trying to measure the ocean with a teaspoon."

"The ones who came before," Ella said. "That's what Elara called them. The ones who made the void."

"That's not possible." Sophia's voice carried the desperation of a scientist whose worldview was crumbling. "The void is a natural phenomenon. A space between dimensions. It can't be artificial. It can't be created."

"Maybe the rules are different when you're old enough," Julian said. "When you've existed long enough that concepts like natural and artificial don't mean anything anymore."

"Something created it," Ella agreed. "Something old enough that Elara, who's been around for two centuries, calls them ancient. Something that's been collecting souls and feeding on consciousness since before human beings existed. Since before Earth existed, maybe. Since before anything we could recognize as life."

"Why?" Genevieve asked. She had managed to make her way to the study, leaning heavily on a cane, her face gray with exhaustion, but her eyes sharp with the need to understand. "What could possibly need that much energy? That many souls?"

Ella felt her daughter stir, felt information passing through their bond that she couldn't quite translate into words. Images. Impressions. A sense of scale so vast it made her head ache. She saw stars being born and dying. Galaxies wheeling through eons. And behind it all, something was watching. Something waiting. Something so patient that human civilization was less than a heartbeat in its perception.

"They're hibernating," she said slowly, letting her daughter guide the words. "Or they were. The void is like a... a nest. A cocoon. They made it to sleep in, and they filled it with food that would sustain them until they were ready to wake up."

"Ready to wake up and do what?"

The answer came not in words but in feeling—a wash of cold certainty that made Ella's blood freeze.

Expand. Consume. Grow.

They are not evil. They are not malicious. They are simply hungry in a way that human concepts of morality cannot encompass.

They will eat everything. Not because they hate us. Because we are food. Because everything is food.

"They're going to consume the world," Ella said, and her voice sounded far away, filtered through the horror of understanding. "Not just Savannah. Not just Earth. Everything. They made the void as a hunting blind, and now they're waking up because they've sensed something that interests them."

"Your daughter," Morrison said grimly.

"My daughter. The first convergence in two centuries. A consciousness that bridges the gap between technology and nature, between code and root. Something new." Ella pressed her hand against her belly, felt her daughter's response—not fear but determination. "They've never seen anything like her before. And they want to know what she tastes like."

The room was silent. The city screamed. And somewhere in the dark between stars, something vast turned its attention toward a small blue world and began, slowly, to rise.

"So, we don't just have to beat Elara," Julian said finally. "We have to beat the void itself."

"No." Ella felt her daughter's certainty flowing through her, felt the outline of a plan she couldn't yet see clearly. "We have to teach the void something it's never learned before."

"What?"

She looked at her hands, at the scar that pulsed with light and code, at the belly that held something unprecedented. She thought of Elara, who had become part of the hunger because she couldn't imagine any other way. She thought of the void, vast and ancient and empty of anything except appetite.

"That some things aren't meant to be consumed," she said. "That some things fight back. And that love" She placed Julian's hand over hers, over their daughter. "Love is the one thing they've never figured out how to digest."

It wasn't much of a plan. It wasn't even really a plan at all like a hope wrapped in determination, tied together with the kind of desperate faith that only came when all other options had been exhausted.

But as the impossible sunset painted Savannah in colors of infection and hunger, it was all they had. A city that was screaming. A child who was becoming something new. A love that might be strong enough to survive what was coming.

Morrison looked skeptical. Sophia looked terrified. Genevieve looked old in a way that had nothing to do with her years and everything to do with the weight of understanding what they faced.

But Julian—Julian looked at Ella with an expression that held no doubt at all. He believed. In her, in their daughter, in the impossible weapon they were building together.

"Then we teach them," he said. "Whatever it takes. We show these ancient, hungry things that love isn't weakness. It's the strongest thing there is."

And somewhere in Ella's womb, her daughter heard and understood, and began to build something new—a weapon made of bridges and doors and walls that were also windows.

A weapon made of love.

A weapon that might just be strong enough to save everything, if only they could survive long enough to use it.

CHAPTER ELEVEN: What We Name the Dark

The baby spoke her first word at 3:47 in the morning, and the word was a name.

Ella had been dreaming of nothing, genuine nothing, the kind of emptiness that existed before creation, before thought, before the possibility of either. She floated in that void-space, aware of herself only as a question mark, a potential that hadn't yet decided what to become. It was peaceful in a way that should have terrified her.

Then her daughter's voice cut through the emptiness like a blade of light.

Aurora.

The name wasn't spoken so much as impressed, stamped into Ella's consciousness with the force of absolute certainty. She woke gasping, her hands flying to her belly, her heart hammering against her ribs like it was trying to escape.

"What is it?" Julian was awake instantly, his body responding to her distress before his mind fully engaged. "The baby is something"

"She named herself." Ella's voice was barely a whisper. "She just told me her name. Aurora."

The name hung in the darkness between them, charged with meaning neither of them fully understood. Aurora: the dawn. The light that came before the sun. The herald of endings and beginnings. In Roman mythology, Aurora was a goddess who renewed herself each morning and flew across the sky to announce the coming day.

Their daughter had chosen to name herself for the light that came before light.

"That's not possible," Julian said, but his voice held no conviction. Nothing was impossible anymore. Their daughter had proven that again and again—accelerating her own development, pushing back against the transformation of Savannah, and building weapons from concepts that had no physical form.

Ella felt Aurora; she could think of her by name now, could feel the difference that naming made—respond to her father's doubt with something like amusement. A pulse of warmth, of patient knowing. She wasn't offended by his skepticism. She was old enough now, developed enough, to understand that her parents were still learning how to believe in her.

I chose it, Mama. It's important. Names have power. The old things, the hungry ones, they don't have names. That's part of why they're so hungry. They forgot what they were called, and now they eat everything, trying to remember.

The thought came through clearly, more articulate than anything Aurora had communicated before. Twenty-seven weeks of development accelerated beyond any natural pregnancy, and their daughter was learning to use language. Learning to explain herself. Learning to tell them what she knew.

"She says names have power," Ella relayed, her voice steadier now. "The ancient things, the ones who made the void, they forgot their own names. That's why they consume. They're trying to remember what they are."

Julian was silent for a long moment. When he spoke, his voice was hushed with the weight of recognition. "My grandmother used to say something similar. That the first magic was naming. That Adam's power in the garden wasn't dominion, it was definition. When you name something, you give it shape. Limits. A self, it can be; instead of an infinity it can't."

He turned to Ella, his eyes bright even in the darkness. "She used to tell me that every curse in our family came from something that had lost its name. That the visions, the madness, the price we paid for our power, it was all because we'd forgotten how to properly name what we were dealing with."

Daddy understands. The nameless things are infinite, and infinity is another word for hungry. If we can name them—

"We can stop them?" Ella asked aloud.

No. But we can make them finite. We can give them boundaries. Something they can be instead of everything they want to consume. A named thing has edges. Has a definition. It has limits that it cannot exceed. The ancient ones forgot their names because names were prisons, they wanted to escape. But prisons work both ways, Mama. What confines can also protect.

It wasn't a solution. It wasn't even a plan. But it was the first hint of a weapon that might actually work against beings older than stars.

Ella pressed her hand against her belly—against Aurora—and felt her daughter's fierce, determined love pulse back.

They had a name now. And names, it seemed, were where power began.

***

Morrison stood in the digital cathedral where Iris waited, and for the first time in three years, he allowed himself to grieve.

He'd returned to Ada's corrupted architecture at Sophia's request, she needed someone to monitor the trap's construction from the inside while she worked on the external interfaces. But the moment he'd entered the neural link, he'd felt Iris's presence pulling at him, drawing him toward the altar of light and static where her echo maintained its fragile existence.

She looked different from how she had during the ritual. More solid, somehow. More present. The fragments of code that made up her form had knitted themselves into something approaching wholeness, and her eyes—those impossible, light-constructed eyes, held depths that seemed almost alive.

"You came back," she said, and her voice didn't stutter or glitch. "I wasn't sure you would."

"I wasn't sure either." Morrison stood before her, this echo of the woman he'd loved, and felt something crack inside his chest. "It hurts to see you like this. To know you're here but not really here. That I'm talking to a pattern that remembers being you instead of actually—"

"Instead of actually me." Iris smiled, and the expression was so familiar it made his throat close. "I know. I've had three years to think about what I am. Whether the difference between a perfect copy and an original matters when the original is gone."

"Does it?"

"I don't know." She moved closer, and Morrison could feel the heat of her light, the static electricity of her presence. "I have Iris's memories. Her emotions. Her love for you, and yes, Thad, it was love. We never said it, but it was. I remember what she felt when she looked at you. I feel it now, looking at you. Whether that makes me 'really' her or just a very convincing ghost..." She spread her hands, a gesture of surrender. "Maybe the answer only matters to philosophers. Maybe what matters is that I'm here, and you're here, and we have a chance to say things we never got to say when I was alive."

Morrison closed his eyes. The cathedral of code pulsed around them, its walls displaying fragments of stolen memories, its floor shifting with the weight of thousands of collected lives. He'd spent three years investigating Iris's death, hunting her killer, channeling his grief into the cold mechanics of justice.

He'd told himself it was enough. That justice would heal the wound in his chest. That finding her killer and exposing the truth would somehow make up for everything he'd never said, everything he'd been too afraid to feel, everything he'd lost when she died in that ritual chamber with Ella's scream echoing in the air.

But justice wasn't healing. It was a distraction. And now, standing before this echo of the woman he'd loved, Morrison finally understood what three years of investigation had really been: running from grief he was too frightened to face.

He'd never let himself just miss her.

"I'm sorry," he said. "I'm sorry I didn't protect you. I'm sorry I didn't tell you what you meant to me when I had the chance. I'm sorry I let my work be more important than—"

"Stop." Iris's voice was firm, familiar, the way she'd always sounded when he was being an idiot, and she'd decided to tell him so. "You didn't let me die, Thad. James did that. Elara did that. And I died trying to protect Ella, which was my choice, not your failure."

"I should have been there."

"You're here now." She reached out, her light-constructed hand hovering just above his cheek—not quite touching, not quite able to bridge the gap between digital and physical. "And I need you to do something for me. Something that matters more than avenging my death."

"Anything."

"Protect that baby. Whatever it takes. Whatever it costs." Iris's eyes held fire now, determination that burned brighter than her static-light form. "Aurora. That's her name—I heard it resonate through the network when she named herself. She's the key to everything, Thad. Not just stopping Elara. Stopping what's coming behind her. The things that ate my soul and a million others. Aurora can defeat them if she lives long enough to learn how."

"I'll protect her," Morrison said. "I swear it."

"I know you will." Iris's smile softened. "That's why I loved you. Under all that gruff suspicion, you were always the one who would do anything for the people you cared about." She began to fade, her form losing coherence as the trap's construction drew power from Ada's systems. "The cage is almost ready. When Elara reaches for Aurora at the birth, we'll have one chance. Don't waste it."

"Wait" Morrison reached for her, but his hand passed through light and static and the memory of warmth. "Iris"

"Goodbye, Thad." Her voice came from everywhere now, from the walls of the cathedral, from the floor of compressed memories, from the darkness that pulsed above. "Tell them I said hello. Tell them I'm proud of what they're becoming."

Then she was gone, and Morrison stood alone in the digital church, and for the first time in three years, he let himself cry.

***

The false victory came at noon, wrapped in readings that seemed too good to be true.

Sophia burst into Genevieve's study with her tablet held aloft like a trophy, her exhaustion temporarily forgotten in the rush of triumph. "The transformation is slowing! The readings from the past four hours—look at this—the rate of conversion has dropped by sixty percent. The tree isn't spreading as fast."

The others gathered around her tablet, hope flickering across faces that had forgotten what hope felt like. The graphs showed exactly what Sophia described: a dramatic flattening of the exponential curve that had been consuming Savannah.

"Why?" Genevieve asked, her voice cautious. "What changed?"

"Aurora," Ella spoke the name aloud for the first time to the group and felt the weight of it settle into the room. "That's her name. She told me this morning. And since then,..." She looked at her belly, at the faint glow visible now through her shirt, at the life inside her that was becoming something unprecedented. "She's been doing something. Building something. I can feel her working, but I can't see what."

"She's establishing boundaries," Julian said slowly, his connection to the root network giving him insights the others lacked. "The plants feel pressure pushing back against the transformation. Like a wall being built around the Nexus Tree's influence. She's containing it."

"At twenty-seven weeks." Sophia's voice held equal parts wonder and terror. "An unborn child is actively fighting an interdimensional invasion from inside the womb."

"She's not just any child." Ella pressed her hand against Aurora, felt her daughter's acknowledgment pulse back. "She's been preparing for this. Building toward this. Everything she's learned, every bit of consciousness she's developed, it's all been for this moment."

The group fell into tentative celebration, not joy exactly, but relief that unclenched muscles and eased the constant tightness in their chests. Genevieve produced a bottle of bourbon that had been aging in her family for generations. Morrison shared what Iris had told him, and they toasted her memory with glasses that trembled only slightly in their hands.

"To Aurora," Julian said, raising his glass. "To the impossible girl who's saving us before she's even born."

"To Aurora," the others echoed.

Even Sophia allowed herself a small smile, the first genuine expression of happiness she'd worn in weeks. She showed them the data again, pointing out the steepest declines. In these areas, the transformation had actually begun to reverse. Trees that had been fully converted were showing signs of returning to their original forms. The bioluminescence in the Spanish moss was flickering out like dying embers.

"If this trend continues," Sophia said, "we might actually have a chance to save most of the city. The damage could be reversible. Everything we thought was lost might be recoverable."

Hope. Real hope, shared among people who had almost forgotten what the word meant.

They should have known better.

They should have remembered that the entities they were fighting had been playing games of strategy since before humanity existed.

Those false victories were often the most dangerous kind.

***

The attack came at midnight, and it didn't come from the direction they expected.

Ella was in the kitchen, raiding the refrigerator for the third time that night—Aurora's accelerated development demanded constant fuel, when she felt it. Not the external pressure of the Nexus Tree's attention. Not Elara's familiar corruption reaching through devices and screens. Not even the transforming city was pressing against the wards that protected Genevieve's townhouse.

This came from inside.

From the void-stuff that was woven into Aurora's very essence, the bridge between worlds that made her a convergence child, the door that Elara so desperately wanted to open. The ancient things had found a way through the one place no one had thought to defend: through Aurora herself.

The first spasm hit her like a fist to the abdomen, doubling her over the kitchen counter, sending a half-eaten sandwich skittering across the tile. The refrigerator door swung closed on its own, and all the appliances in the kitchen hummed to life, microwave, blender, coffee maker—their digital displays showing the same countdown: 00:27:00. Twenty-seven minutes. The number of weeks Aurora had developed.

The second spasm came before she could draw breath to scream, and the third brought with it a gush of fluid that pooled warm and impossible around her feet.

No. Not yet. She's only twenty-seven weeks. She can't—

But Aurora could. Aurora had decided that the time for waiting was over.

Or something had decided for her.

The contractions weren't natural—Ella understood that even through the haze of pain. They were too regular, too mechanical, like something was trying to force Aurora out of the womb before she was ready. Each spasm felt less like labor and more like an assault, her body being used as a weapon against herself.

Mama. Mama, I'm trying to stop it, but they're—they're pushing—

Aurora's voice in her mind was panicked, frightened in a way Ella had never felt from her. Her daughter was fighting something, resisting something, but whatever it was had the advantage of surprise and the leverage of Ella's own physiology.

"JULIAN!" Ella's scream tore through the townhouse, bringing running footsteps from three directions. "Something's wrong, something's trying to—"

Another contraction cut off her words. This one brought too much blood, dark and thick and wrong. She could feel Aurora struggling, feel the tiny consciousness that had grown so fierce and so determined now pushed to the edge of its limits.

"We warned you," a voice said, and it came from everywhere—from the lights overhead, from the appliances on the counter, from Ella's own scar, which had split open and was bleeding data and light and something else, something that spoke in harmonics too old for human ears. *"We told you she shines too bright. We told you we could see her. Did you think your little wall would keep us out?"*

The ancient things. The nameless ones. They had found a way through Aurora's defenses—not by attacking from outside, but by reaching through the void-stuff that was part of Aurora's very nature.

They weren't trying to kill her. They were trying to give birth to her. Trying to force her into the world before she was ready, before her weapon was complete, before she could finish whatever she'd been building.

Julian burst through the kitchen door, Sophia and Morrison right behind him. His face went white at the sight of Ella on the floor, the blood spreading beneath her, the light pouring from her scar in patterns that looked almost like grasping hands.

"No," he breathed. "No, no, no"

He was at her side in an instant, his hands on her belly, his power reaching for the root network, trying to draw on every growing thing in Savannah to push back against whatever was forcing this premature birth.

But the ancient things laughed, a sound like galaxies colliding, like stars being born and dying, like infinity folded into the space between heartbeats.

"You can't stop us, little seedling. We ate civilizations while your ancestors were learning to walk upright. We consumed gods when your species still believed in them. What makes you think you can protect one small

light from a darkness that has been hungry since before hunger had a name?"

Ella felt Aurora's consciousness dimming, felt her daughter's defenses crumbling under the assault. The contractions were coming faster now, stronger, and with each one, Aurora lost a little more ground.

if (daughter.dying) { response = override_all_protocols }

if (self.sacrifice == option) { execute_without_hesitation }

//no

//there has to be another way

//there's always another way

And then, from somewhere deep inside her, from the place where her technomantic power had always lived, the place she'd been suppressing for three years, the place that was as much Aurora's home as her own, Ella felt something new awaken.

Not power. Not magic.

A name.

It rose up through her consciousness like a bubble of light breaking through dark water. A name that had been lost for billions of years, a name that the ancient things had forgotten, a name that Aurora had been searching for in every soul the void had ever consumed.

Ella didn't speak it. She didn't have to.

Aurora spoke it for her—spoke it through her—spoke it with the combined force of two consciousnesses aligned in perfect desperate harmony:

"AVARAI."

The name rang through reality like a bell. The ancient things, the nameless ones—recoiled from it, their assault faltering as something they had forgotten stirred in the depths of their infinite hunger.

It wasn't their name. Not exactly. But it was a name, and names had power, and for a moment—just a moment—the ones who had forgotten what they were remembered that they had once been something that could be called.

The contractions stopped. The blood stopped. The light pouring from Ella's scar shifted from assault to defense, wrapping around her and around Aurora like a cocoon of pure refusal.

And in the silence that followed, Ella heard her daughter's voice, exhausted, terrified, but triumphant:

I found it, Mama. In all those consumed souls, all those digested memories—one of them remembered. One of them held onto a fragment of what the hungry ones used to be, before they became hunger itself.

They can be named.

They can be bounded.

They can be stopped.

Julian was cradling Ella's head in his lap, his tears falling on her face, his voice repeating her name like a prayer. Morrison had his weapon drawn, pointing at nothing and everything, ready to fight enemies he couldn't see. Sophia was already running scans, her scientific mind struggling to process data that defied every law she'd ever studied.

And Aurora, Aurora rested in her mother's womb, her weapon half-built, her strength depleted, but her mission clearer than it had ever been.

She knew what to do now.

She just had to survive long enough to do it.

***

They moved Ella to the infirmary as the sun rose over a Savannah that had gone quiet.

The city's screaming had stopped. The bioluminescence in the moss had dimmed. Even the Nexus Tree, visible in the distance through the infirmary's windows, seemed to have retreated into itself, its aggressive expansion paused.

The ancient things were regrouping. They had been reminded of something they'd forgotten, and they needed time to process what that meant.

"How long do we have?" Morrison asked, his voice rough from the night's terror.

"I don't know." Ella lay in the infirmary bed, her hand on her belly, monitoring Aurora's slowly stabilizing vital signs. "They're not used to being pushed back. They've been the predators for so long they've forgotten how to be anything else. But they'll adapt. They'll learn. And when they come again, they'll come prepared."

"Then we prepare too." Julian sat beside her, holding her hand with a grip that suggested he'd never let go. "Aurora found a name. That means there are more names to find. More fragments of memory preserved in the void. We can use more weapons."

"The souls," Sophia said slowly, understanding dawning. "The consumed consciousnesses. They're not just food, they're libraries. Each one holds memories that the ancient things have absorbed but never truly processed. If we could access those memories, find more names, more limits to impose—"

"We'd need to go into the void," Genevieve said. She had joined them in the infirmary, her age and exhaustion making her look like a ghost herself. "Someone would have to enter the space between worlds and search the consumed for information that might save us."

Silence fell as the implication settled over them.

Someone would have to go where the ancient things lived. I would have to swim through an ocean of consumed souls. They would have to somehow survive long enough to find what they needed and bring it back.

"I'll go," Morrison said.

Everyone looked at him.

"Iris is in there. Or part of her is, the part that's been trapped in Ada's architecture. If anyone can guide me through the void, it's her." He met Ella's eyes, and there was no fear in his gaze—only the cold determination of a man who had finally found a cause worth dying for. "I've been looking for a way to honor her memory. This is it. This is how I protect Aurora like I promised."

"Thad" Genevieve began.

"Don't." His voice was gentle but firm. "I've made my choice. This is what I was always meant to do—I just didn't know it until now. Iris died trying to protect these people. The least I can do is carry on her work." He looked around the infirmary, at the exhausted faces of people who had become something like family over these terrible weeks. "Start preparing whatever ritual or technology I need to cross over. We don't have time to argue about this."

He was right. They all knew he was right. And as the quiet day stretched on, as Savannah held its breath and the ancient things in the void considered their next move, they began to prepare for the next battle in a war that had suddenly become very, very personal.

Julian squeezed Ella's hand. "He's braver than I gave him credit for."

"He's in love," Ella said softly. "Love makes people brave. Or stupid. Sometimes both at once."

"Speaking from experience?"

She looked at him, at the man who had stayed beside her through every impossible moment of this nightmare, who had held her hand as she bled and screamed and fought. Who had promised to protect their daughter no matter what it cost.

"Yeah," she said. "Speaking from experience."

Ella watched Morrison go, watched the others begin their preparations, and felt Aurora stir inside her—weaker than before but still fighting, still building, still becoming whatever she needed to be.

We're going to survive this, aren't we, baby girl?

We're going to survive, Mama. All of us. I won't let them take anyone else.

It was a promise neither of them could guarantee keeping. But it was enough to face another day. Enough to keep fighting. Enough to believe that love really could be a weapon against the oldest darkness in existence.

And for now, that would have to be enough.

CHAPTER TWELVE: Into the Hungry Dark

Morrison died at 9:47 PM, and for three minutes, he stayed dead.

The ritual chamber beneath Wright Square had been prepared with painstaking precision—Genevieve's life's work condensed into a circle of salt and silver and symbols that predated human language. Candles burned at the cardinal points, their flames bent toward the center, where Morrison lay on a slab of granite quarried from beneath the Nexus Tree itself, back when the tree was still just a tree, and Savannah was still just a city.

Sophia monitored his vitals from a bank of equipment that looked absurdly modern against the ancient stonework. Heart rate. Brain activity. The electromagnetic signature of his soul, a measurement she'd invented specifically for this purpose, calibrated against readings from Iris's echo and the transformed victims they'd been studying.

"Ready?" Genevieve asked, her voice carrying the weight of every ritual she'd ever performed and every one she'd refused. Her hands were steady, but Ella could see the fear in her eyes—the knowledge that she was sending a man into the realm that had consumed Elara, that had broken the world two centuries ago, that hungered for every soul it touched.

Morrison looked at the ceiling. At the faces gathered around him, Julian tense with worry, Ella pale but determined, Sophia hiding her terror behind clinical focus. He thought of Iris, waiting for him in the dark between worlds. He thought of the promise he'd made to protect Aurora, and the path that promise had led him to.

He thought, briefly, of the life he might have had, the career, the retirement, the quiet ending that men like him sometimes earned. That life was gone now. Had been gone since the moment Iris died in the ritual chamber three years ago. Everything since then had been leading here.

"Do it," he said.

Genevieve spoke words that hurt to hear, syllables that seemed to cut the air itself. The language was older than writing, older than speech as humans understood it—sounds that had been used to shape reality when reality was still learning what shapes it could take. The candles flared, died, flared again with flames that had turned the color of void-light—that terrible bioluminescence they'd all learned to fear.

Morrison felt his heart stutter, skip, stop.

For a moment, there was nothing, a genuine absence that was somehow different from darkness, different from unconsciousness, different from anything he'd experienced before. It was the space between heartbeats stretched to eternity, the pause between breaths expanded into a lifetime. He existed in that nothing, aware that he was nothing, watching himself dissolve into the absence with a strange detachment.

And then he was falling.

Not down—there was no down here, no up, no direction at all. He fell through darkness so complete it had texture, so absolute it had weight. The void pressed against him from every direction, curious and hungry and patient in ways that made his suspended consciousness want to scream.

He could feel the ancient things stirring at the edges of his perception—vast presences that moved through the dark like leviathans through deep water. They weren't paying attention to him yet. He was too small, too insignificant, a single mote of light in an ocean of consuming darkness. But they would notice eventually. They always noticed.

He couldn't scream. He didn't have a mouth anymore. Didn't have a body. He was just aware now, a pattern of thoughts desperately trying to maintain coherence in a space that wanted to dissolve him into data.

Thad.

Iris's voice cut through the nothing like a lifeline. He felt her presence before he saw her—warmth in a place that had forgotten what warmth meant, light in a darkness that had consumed suns.

Follow me. Don't look at them. Whatever you do, don't look directly at them.

Them. The lights. The consumed souls that drifted through the void like luminescent plankton, billions upon billions of them, each one a consciousness that had been eaten and was now slowly dissolving into the entity that had swallowed it. Morrison could feel them pressing against his awareness, their memories, their loves, their dying screams all preserved in perfect fidelity, replaying on an endless loop as the void digested them.

He wanted to look. Wanted to see if he recognized any of them, if any of them could tell him what he needed to know. But Iris's warning held him steady, and he followed her light through the hungry dark, trying not to think about how much he resembled the souls he was swimming past.

# # #

In the ritual chamber, Morrison's body had begun to change.

Sophia saw it first on her instruments, electromagnetic fluctuations that shouldn't have been possible, readings that suggested his physical form was becoming less solid, more permeable. Then she saw it with her own eyes: a faint luminescence spreading across his skin, the same circuitry patterns they'd seen on the transformed victims.

"He's converting," she said, her voice sharp with fear. "The void is trying to transform him like it transformed the others."

"How long?" Julian asked.

"I don't know. Minutes, maybe. If the patterns reach his brain before we pull him back—"

"He'll be lost." Genevieve's face was gray. "Trapped between worlds, neither dead nor alive. Another ghost in the machine."

Ella pressed her hand against her belly, felt Aurora stirring, her daughter tracking the situation, processing data that came through channels no physical sensor could detect. Through their bond, she sensed Aurora's concern for Morrison, her desperate hope that he would find what they needed before the void consumed him.

He's strong, Mama. Stronger than he knows. But he needs to hurry. The hungry ones have noticed him.

"Aurora says to hurry," Ella said. "The ancient things know he's there."

"Can you reach him?" Julian asked. "Through your connection to Aurora, can you—"

"I can try." Ella closed her eyes, reaching through the bond with her daughter, feeling Aurora amplify her consciousness like a signal booster. Together, they pushed through the membrane between worlds, searching for Morrison's awareness in the vast hungry dark.

And the void pushed back.

***

Morrison found the first library in a pocket of stillness between the currents of consumed souls.

It wasn't a library in any physical sense, there were no books here, no shelves, no architecture at all. But there was organization. Structure. A collection of memories that had somehow resisted the void's digestion, clinging to each other for preservation.

Iris led him to it, her light dimming as they approached. "This is as far as I can go," she said, and her voice was weaker now, stretched thin by the effort of guiding him. "My echo doesn't have the strength to enter the preserved spaces. But you do. You're still alive, Thad. That means something here."

"What am I looking for?"

"Names. The ancient things weren't always nameless. Once, eons ago, they were something with boundaries. Something that could be called and controlled. Find the memories of what they were, and you'll find the names that can bind them."

Morrison approached the library, the preserved pocket of consciousness that the void hadn't yet dissolved. As he drew closer, he began to hear voices. Thousands of them. Millions. All speaking at once in languages he'd never heard, telling stories he'd never imagined, sharing knowledge that had been lost when civilizations died, and stars burned out.

Some of the voices were almost human beings that had evolved along similar paths, developed similar hopes and fears. Others were utterly alien, consciousnesses that had existed in forms Morrison couldn't imagine, whose concepts of self and other and existence had nothing in common with human thought. But they were all here, all preserved, all slowly dissolving into the void's eternal hunger.

And they all remembered.

He entered the library and was immediately overwhelmed.

Memories crashed over him like waves, lives lived and ended across billions of years, cultures that had risen and fallen before Earth's sun ignited, beings that had loved and feared and hoped and died in ways that human consciousness could barely comprehend. He saw civilizations that had built themselves on concepts humans didn't have words for. He felt the grief of species that had watched their worlds consumed, their children devoured, their histories swallowed by the hungry dark.

One memory showed him a world of crystal spires and singing winds, beautiful beyond description, reduced to dust and silence when the Avarai passed through. Another showed him a species that had learned to transcend physical form, becoming pure thought and joy, consumed in an instant by hungers that didn't distinguish between matter and meaning. A third showed him something so vast it had used galaxies as cells in its body, dying in confusion as the void ate it one star at a time.

And in that grief, preserved like insects in amber, he found fragments of what he sought.

We called them the Avarai in our tongue. The First Emptiness. They were here before the universe learned to burn. They will be here after the last star dies.

The memory came from something that had once been vast and patient, a consciousness that had spent eons studying the entities that would eventually consume it. Morrison pulled at the thread, found more memories attached, a web of preserved knowledge that had survived by sheer stubborn refusal to be forgotten.

The Avarai were not always hungry. Once they were builders. Shapers. They created the void as a tool, a space where things could be unmade and remade. But they forgot what they were building toward. The tool became the purpose. The means became the end. Now they consume because consumption is all they remember how to do.

Names swam up through the memories. Not just Avarai, the collective term—but individual designations. Pieces of identity that the hungry ones had shed like dead skin when they surrendered to infinity.

Vexeth, who was once called the Architect. Thrennix, who was once called the Singer. Malcorath, who was once called the Bridge. These were the first three, and from them all others descended.

Morrison tried to gather the names, to hold them in his awareness long enough to carry them back. But the void had noticed his presence now. He could feel its attention turning toward him—not hostile exactly, not yet, but curious. Interested in this small light that had wandered into its depths.

And beneath that curiosity, hunger. Always hunger.

***

The Nexus Tree woke screaming.

Ella felt it first, a psychic shockwave that ripped through her consciousness like a blade, severing her connection to Morrison, snapping her back into her body with a violence that left her gasping. Aurora cried out through their bond, not in pain but in alarm, her attention yanked away from the void and toward something happening much closer to home.

"The tree," Ella managed to say. "Something's wrong with the tree."

Through the walls of the ritual chamber, through the earth and stone that separated them from the surface, they could all feel it: a pulse of power so intense it made the candles explode and the ritual circle crack. The transformation that had paused while Aurora built her barriers was resuming, not gradually but explosively, the tree's influence erupting outward like a bomb detonating in slow motion.

"Elara," Julian breathed. "She's making her move."

They ran for the surface, leaving Sophia to monitor Morrison's increasingly unstable vitals, leaving him suspended between life and death while the world above prepared to end. The stairs seemed endless, a spiral of ancient stone that wound up through earth that was already beginning to change, roots pushing through the walls, circuitry patterns spreading across the rock like frost on a window.

When they emerged into Wright Square, they found Savannah transformed.

The conversion that had taken weeks was completed in minutes. Trees glowed with inner light, their bark splitting to reveal circuitry that pulsed with rhythms that matched the Nexus Tree's heartbeat. The Spanish moss had become a network of bioluminescent neural tissue, connecting every oak in the city into a single vast brain. The cobblestones were lifting, rearranging themselves into patterns that suggested communication—symbols in a language that hurt to look at.

The air itself had changed, thick with particles of light that drifted like luminescent snow, coating everything they touched with a faint shimmer of conversion. Each breath felt dangerous, as if the transformation could be inhaled, could spread through lungs and blood and brain until there was nothing left of the person who had breathed it.

People ran through the streets, tourists and locals alike, finally unable to deny what was happening to their city. Some were screaming. Others were laughing, caught up in the ecstasy of conversion, their bodies already showing the first signs of transformation. A woman stood on a corner, her arms raised to the glowing sky, tears of joy streaming down cheeks that had begun to develop circuitry patterns.

And above it all, visible now in a way it had never been before, the Nexus Tree blazed like a beacon. Its branches reached toward the sky like grasping fingers. From its roots, a figure was emerging—clawing her way up through the earth, pulling herself into the physical world for the first time in two centuries.

Elara Thorne had decided to stop waiting.

***

She was beautiful in the way that catastrophes are gorgeous, all terrible power and ancient grief, her form assembled from void-light and transformed matter, her face simultaneously familiar and utterly alien.

"Little mother," Elara said, and her voice came from everywhere, from the trees and the moss and the lifting cobblestones, from every device in the city that still had power to transmit. "I told you to run. I told you it was too late. But you didn't listen. You never listen."

Ella stood in Wright Square, Julian beside her, watching the creature that had once been human stride toward them on legs that weren't quite solid. Her hand pressed against her belly, protecting Aurora, drawing strength from the fierce determination she could feel pulsing through their bond.

"I listened," Ella said. "I heard everything you told me. About the ancient things, the hungry ones, the Avarai. I know you're afraid of them. I know you can't control what you've become."

"Then you know you can't stop this." Elara spread her arms, and the city responded—streetlights exploding in showers of sparks, car alarms screaming in harmony, every screen in Savannah displaying the same image: Aurora's sonogram, the baby curled in her womb, the convergence child who would either save or damn them all.

"They're coming, little mother. The Avarai. The First Emptiness. They've been sleeping since before your species learned to dream, and your daughter's light has woken them. Do you understand what that means? Do you have any concept of what's about to come through the door she's building?"

"Yes," Ella said. "I understand. That's why I'm not running."

She reached for her power, the technomantic ability she'd been suppressing for three years, the gift that had always felt more like a curse. It rose to meet her instantly, stronger than it had ever been, amplified by Aurora's consciousness, shaped by the weeks of training and terror that had forged them both into something new.

Light blazed from her scar, code streaming through the air like visible electricity. She felt Aurora join her, mother and daughter working in perfect synchronization, their combined power pushing back against Elara's transformation, creating a bubble of stability in the chaos of the converting city.

"We found names," Ella said. "Morrison is in the void right now, gathering more. The Avarai can be bounded. They can be given shapes and limits. They can be turned from infinite hunger into something finite—something that can be faced and defeated."

Elara's face flickered—grief and hope and terror passing across her features too fast to track. "Names. You think names can stop them?"

"I think names can stop you." Ella took a step forward, her light pushing against Elara's darkness. "I think you've forgotten what you were, Elara Thorne. Forgotten the mother you were, the woman you were, the human you were before the void consumed you. I think if we can remind you—if we can name what you've lost, maybe we can bring you back."

For a moment—just a moment—Ella saw something in Elara's eyes that wasn't hunger or madness or ancient despair. She saw the woman Thomas Marsh had loved. The mother who had held her daughter for one hour before the Council took her away. The person who had suffered and survived and become something terrible because she didn't know how else to keep going.

"It's too late for me," Elara whispered, and her voice was almost human. "I've been part of them too long. When they come through, I won't be able to stop myself. I'll try to take her, little mother. I'll try to feed Aurora to the dark because that's what I am now. That's all I am."

"No," Ella said fiercely. "That's not all you are. You're also the woman who warned us. Who told us to run when she could have just attacked. Who showed me the truth about the void, even though it would have been easier to lie." She stepped closer, close enough to feel the cold radiating from Elara's form, close enough to see the tears that left trails of void-light on her incorporeal cheeks.

"Let us help you, Elara. Let us try to bring you back. You don't have to be the monster they made you."

The words hung in the transformed air between them, heavy with possibility. Around them, Savannah continued its conversion, screams and laughter mixing, the city becoming something new and terrible and strange. But in this moment, in this small bubble of stability that Ella and Aurora had created, there was silence.

Elara's form flickered. For an instant, she looked almost solid—almost human—a woman in her early twenties with dark hair and eyes that had seen too much grief. Then the void-light reasserted itself, and she was something else again: a creature of hunger and sorrow, trapped between what she had been and what she had become.

"You don't understand," she said, and now there were layers in her voice—the woman she'd been speaking beneath the entity she'd become. *"I've tried to come back. For two hundred years, I've tried. Every time I think I've found myself, the hunger swallows me again. It's not a choice anymore, little mother. It's what I am."*

"Then we'll find a way to change what you are." Ella's voice was fierce with determination. "We have names now. We have power. And we have something you never had: each other. You were alone, Elara. The Council betrayed you, Thomas ran, and you had no one to help you fight. But I'm not alone. I have Julian. I have Aurora. I have a whole team of people who refuse to give up."

She reached out, her hand passing through the bubble of stability, extending toward Elara's flickering form.

"Take my hand. Let me try. What do you have to lose?"

***

In the void, Morrison was running out of time.

The transformation had reached his chest now, he could feel it in the physical world, a distant burning as his body converted to something that was neither alive nor dead. In the void, the sensation translated to a dimming of his light, a blurring of his edges as the hungry dark began to absorb him.

But he had the names. Three of them, at least, Vexeth, Thrennix, and Malcorath. The first three Avarai, the founders of the consuming emptiness, the architects of the void that had swallowed billions of souls across eons of existence. If he could just get back, just hold on long enough to deliver what he'd learned—

Thad. You have to go now.

Iris's voice, urgent and fading. He turned to find her light nearly extinguished, her form barely visible against the hungry dark.

"I can't leave you here," he said.

I was already here. I've been here for three years, waiting for someone to find me. This is where I belong now, Thad. But you, you still have work to do. You promised to protect Aurora. Keep that promise.

"Iris—"

I love you. I always loved you. Now go. Before it's too late.

Morrison felt something pull at him, Sophia's equipment, Genevieve's ritual, the physical world demanding his return. He wanted to fight it, wanted to stay with Iris, wanted to find some way to save her from the endless consumption that awaited.

But he had made a promise. And Morrison had never broken a promise in his life.

"I love you too," he said. "I'll find a way to free you. All of you. When this is over, I'll come back, and I'll find a way."

I know you will. That's why I loved you.

He let the pull take him. Felt himself rising through the void, past the drifting lights of consumed souls, past the curious attention of ancient hungers that were beginning to stir. The physical world rushed up to meet him like the surface of an ocean he'd been drowning in—

And Morrison gasped back to life on the granite slab, his body half-transformed, three names burning in his mind like brands, Iris's final words echoing in his ears.

"I have them," he managed to say, his voice raw with void-damage. "The names. Vexeth. Thrennix. Malcorath. The first three. The founders."

Sophia was crying—he didn't know why until he looked down and saw what the transformation had done to him. His left arm was no longer human, covered in the circuitry patterns of the converted, his fingers branching into something that looked almost like roots. The conversion had reached his heart, was still spreading, and would eventually consume him entirely.

But not today. Not yet. He had delivered what he promised, and that would have to be enough.

"The others," he said, struggling to sit up. "Where are—"

"On the surface. Elara has manifested. The final battle is starting." Sophia helped him stand, her hands careful around his transformed arm. "Can you fight?"

Morrison looked at his changed hand, felt the void-stuff that was slowly consuming him pulse with a rhythm that matched the Nexus Tree's heartbeat. He was becoming one of them. Becoming part of the darkness he'd sworn to fight.

But he could also feel something else, the names he carried, burning in his consciousness like hot coals. Vexeth. Thrennix. Malcorath. They were more than just words. They were weapons. Boundaries. Definitions that could impose shape on the shapeless, limits on the limitless.

He understood now why Iris had sent him. Not just to gather information, but to become a bridge. The transformation spreading through his body connected him to the void in ways that a normal human couldn't achieve. When he spoke the names, they would carry power—the power of someone who was partly void himself, who could speak to the hungry dark in a language it couldn't ignore.

But he still had time. And he still had promises to keep.

"Yeah," he said. "I can fight."

They ran for the stairs, for the surface, for the battle that would decide everything. Morrison could feel his transformed arm pulsing with each step, the circuitry patterns spreading incrementally, inexorably. He had hours, maybe. Days if he was lucky. Then he would be fully converted, lost to the void he'd journeyed through.

But that was a problem for later. Right now, there was a battle to win.

And somewhere in the void behind them, Iris's light finally went out—not in consumption but in peace, her last fragment of consciousness fading into the darkness with a smile on her incorporeal lips.

She had done what she needed to do.

Now it was up to the living to finish what she'd started.

CHAPTER THIRTEEN: The Breaking Point

E lara took Ella's hand, and for one crystalline moment, everything was possible.

The contact was electric, not painful but overwhelming, two consciousnesses brushing against each other across the divide between life and something else. Ella felt Elara's grief pour into her like water through a broken dam: two centuries of isolation, of hunger she couldn't control, of watching the world change while she remained trapped in the space between existing and not.

She felt the woman Elara had been, fierce, loving, terrified for her daughter—and the monster she had become, and the thin thread of self that still connected the two. That thread was fragile, worn thin by centuries of consumption and despair, but it was there. It was real. It meant that somewhere beneath all the void-stuff and hunger, Elara Thorne still existed.

"I remember," Elara whispered, and her voice was almost human now, almost whole. "I remember what it felt like to hope. To believe things could be different. To love someone more than I feared the dark." A pause, a flicker of something that might have been tears if she still had the biology to produce them. "I remember holding my daughter. For one hour. One perfect hour before they took her away."

Through their connection, Ella pushed images, emotions, the accumulated love of her own experience: Julian's hands on her belly, feeling Aurora kick for the first time. The team gathered around Genevieve's table, broken people choosing to fight together. Morrison walking into the void because he'd made a promise. The fierce, impossible hope of a child who had named herself for the dawn.

"You can have this again," Ella said. "You can be part of something instead of apart from everything. Let us help you, Elara. Let us bring you back."

For a perfect moment, trembling moment, Ella thought it would work. She could feel Elara reaching toward her, toward the light, toward the possibility of redemption. The void-creature's form flickered, solidified, became more woman than monster. Her eyes cleared, showing the person she had been before the ritual broke her.

Then the sky tore open, and the Avarai announced their arrival.

***

The sound was unlike anything Ella had ever heard, a frequency that bypassed her ears entirely and resonated directly in her skull, in her bones, in the space between her thoughts where consciousness lived.

Above Savannah, the clouds had parted to reveal something that shouldn't have been visible from Earth's surface: a darkness between the stars that moved with purpose, that had weight and intention, that was reaching down toward the city like a hand descending to collect something precious.

The Avarai weren't coming. They were already here. They had been here all along, waiting at the edge of perception, patient as only beings older than time could be. And now, drawn by Aurora's light, by the confrontation between Ella and Elara, by the thinning of the barriers that had kept them at bay for eons, they were finally making themselves known.

Looking at them was impossible. Ella's mind kept trying to interpret what she was seeing—shapes, patterns, anything recognizable—but the Avarai existed outside the categories her consciousness had evolved to process. They were absent given form. Hunger made manifest. The space between thoughts, between atoms, between moments of time, suddenly revealed as territory that something else had claimed.

"NO!" Elara's scream tore through the night, and it carried harmonics of genuine terror—not the calculated menace she'd projected before, but raw, animal fear. *"It's too soon! The door isn't open enough! They can't—"*

But they could. They were. The darkness above Savannah was descending, and everywhere it touched, reality began to unravel.

Ella watched in horror as buildings at the edge of the transformed zone simply ceased to exist—not destroyed, not consumed, but erased, as if they had never been built at all. The darkness ate history along with matter, swallowing not just what was but what had been, leaving gaps in the fabric of existence that the human mind couldn't properly perceive.

The connection between her and Elara shattered. The void-woman recoiled, her form fragmenting, her momentary humanity dissolving back into the hungry thing she had become. But now there was no calculation in her madness—only panic, only the desperate terror of a creature facing something even she couldn't survive.

"Run," Elara said, and her voice was layered with every soul she'd consumed, every victim of the void speaking in unison. *"Take your daughter and run. Find somewhere to hide. There is no fighting this. There is no surviving this. There is only—"*

The darkness touched her, and Elara Thorne—who had endured two centuries of imprisonment in the space between worlds, who had become part of the very hunger that had consumed her, began to scream.

It was the sound of dissolution. Of a consciousness that had clung to existence through sheer force of will finally losing its grip. Ella watched Elara's form come apart, watched the void-light that made up her body being absorbed into something vaster and hungrier, watched two hundred years of grief and rage and desperate hope being digested in real time.

And through it all, Elara kept screaming, a sound that would echo in Ella's nightmares for the rest of her life, however long that turned out to be.

***

"The trap!" Sophia's voice cut through the chaos, sharp with desperate hope. "We can still spring the trap!"

She had emerged from the ritual chamber with Morrison, both of them running toward the confrontation, both of them stopping short as they saw what was descending from the sky. Morrison's transformed arm was glowing now, pulsing in rhythm with the approaching darkness, the void-stuff in his flesh responding to the presence of its creators.

"The trap was designed for Elara," Julian said, his voice hollow with shock. "It can't contain something like—"

"It doesn't have to contain them. It just has to slow them down." Sophia was already working on her tablet, fingers flying across the screen, rerouting protocols and adjusting parameters with the desperate precision of someone who knew this was their only chance. "The cage I built, it's designed to impose boundaries. To give shape to the shapeless. If I can expand it, project it outward instead of inward—"

"You'll create a barrier," Morrison said, understanding dawning. "A wall between the Avarai and the city."

"For a few minutes. Maybe less. But it might be enough time for—" Sophia looked at Ella, at Aurora glowing through her mother's shirt, at the impossible child who was their only real hope. "For whatever Aurora is planning to do."

The darkness was closer now. Ella could feel its attention turning toward her, toward the light blazing from her womb, toward the beacon that had called it across the spaces between stars. The Avarai weren't malevolent, she understood that now, in the same way she understood that a forest fire wasn't malevolent. They were simply hungry in a way that transcended morality, that preceded the very concept of right and wrong.

And they were very, very interested in her daughter.

Aurora. Baby. If you have a plan, now would be a really good time.

The response came not in words but in feeling, a sense of gathering, of preparation, of pieces falling into place. Aurora had been building something since the moment she named herself, assembling a weapon out of concepts and connections and the fierce, impossible love that bound her to her parents.

Almost ready, Mama. I just need a little more time.

"Do it," Ella said to Sophia. "Spring the trap. Give us whatever time you can."

Sophia nodded once, her face set with determination, and pressed the final command on her tablet.

The digital cathedral that Iris had helped build, the corrupted architecture of Ada, the network of backdoors and monitoring protocols, exploded outward in a wave of structured light. It rose from every device in Savannah, from every screen and speaker and networked system, forming a dome of pure information that arced across the sky like a second sunrise.

And for one glorious moment, it worked.

The descending darkness met the barrier of light and stopped. The Avarai—Vexeth, Thrennix, Malcorath, and all their countless descendants, pressed against a wall they couldn't immediately breach. The dome held, pulsing with the combined power of every consciousness that Iris had preserved in Ada's architecture, every soul that had refused to be consumed entirely.

But the barrier was cracking. Hairline fractures spreading across its surface, darkness seeping through in thin tendrils that reached toward the city below. They had minutes at most. Perhaps only seconds.

"Morrison!" Ella shouted. "The names! Use the names!"

**

Morrison stepped forward, his transformed arm raised toward the descending darkness, the void-stuff in his flesh singing in resonance with the entities above.

He could feel them now in a way he hadn't before, not just as presence but as individuals, as distinct hungers with distinct histories. The names he'd gathered from the consumed souls weren't just labels. They were keys. Definitions. The crystallized essence of what these beings had been before they forgot themselves.

"Vexeth," he said, and the word carried power that made his throat burn. "Who was once called the Architect. I name you. I define you. I give you the shape you abandoned."

One of the tendrils of darkness recoiled. Above the barrier, something vast and formless shuddered—and for an instant, it was something else. Something with edges. Something that could be perceived as a single entity rather than an infinite hunger.

The barrier's cracks stopped spreading in that section. The name had worked.

"Thrennix," Morrison continued, his voice stronger now despite the pain. "Who was once called the Singer. I name you. I define you. I give you the boundaries you discarded."

Another shudder. Another tendril pulling back. The barrier stabilized further, the dome of light holding against the pressing dark.

But Morrison could feel the cost. Each name he spoke, each definition he imposed, pulled something out of him, not just energy but essence, the parts of himself that the void-transformation hadn't yet claimed. He was spending his humanity to buy them time, burning through what remained of Thaddeus Morrison to hold back the oldest darkness in existence.

"Malcorath," he said, and now his voice was barely a whisper, blood trickling from his nose, from his ears, from the corners of his eyes. "Who was once called the Bridge. I name you. I define you. I give you the limits you abandoned when you chose to become infinite."

The third shudder was stronger than the others. The barrier's cracks began to heal, light pushing back darkness, structure imposing itself on chaos. The Avarai weren't defeated—couldn't be defeated, not by three names alone, but they were contained. Bounded. Forced to remember, for just a moment, that they had once been something other than hunger.

Morrison collapsed.

Julian caught him before he hit the ground, easing him down to the transformed cobblestones. The circuitry patterns on Morrison's arm had spread across his entire body, covering him with the same design that marked the transformed victims. His skin had taken on a luminescent quality, as if the void-light was replacing his blood. But his eyes were still human. Still present. Still Morrison.

"Did it work?" he asked, his voice a thread of sound. "Did I give her enough time?"

Ella knelt beside him, Aurora's light bathing his transformed features in warmth that seemed to slow the spreading conversion. "You did. You were incredible. Three names—you held back the oldest beings in existence with three words."

"Four words, technically. If you count 'I name you.'" Morrison's laugh dissolved into a cough that brought void-light instead of blood to his lips. "Never was good at concise communication. Iris always said I talked too much."

"You can tell her yourself. When this is over—"

"No." His voice was gentle, accepting, the voice of a man who had made peace with something impossible and found that peace easier than he'd expected. "I can feel it, Ella. The void in me. It's not going to stop. Even if we win tonight, even if Aurora saves everyone else—I'm already gone. Have been since I came back from the dark."

The truth of it settled over them like a shroud. Morrison had known. From the moment he'd returned with his arm transformed, he'd known that the void wouldn't let him go. He'd fought anyway. He'd given them everything he had anyway.

Because that's what love looked like, in the end. Not grand gestures or dramatic sacrifices, but the quiet choice to keep going, to keep fighting, to keep hoping even when hope was irrational.

"Thank you," Ella whispered. "For everything."

Morrison smiled, a real smile, the first genuine expression of peace she'd ever seen on his weathered face. "Take care of that baby. She's going to be something special."

Then his eyes closed, and the conversation accelerated. Thaddeus Morrison became another light in the void, one more consciousness joining the billions that had been consumed, one more soul adding its voice to the eternal chorus of the digested.

But this soul was different. This soul carried names. And somewhere in the hungry dark, those names would continue their work, imposing limits on the limitless, definitions on the undefined.

Morrison's final gift wasn't his death. It was what his death would make possible.

***

The barrier was failing.

Ella could see it happening, the cracks spreading despite Morrison's sacrifice, the darkness pressing through in ever-widening tendrils. The three names had bought them time, but not enough. The Avarai were ancient beyond comprehension, and three definitions couldn't contain something that had been infinite for billions of years.

"Aurora," Ella said, her hand pressed against her belly, her consciousness reaching through the bond with desperate urgency. "Whatever you're building, whatever you're planning, it has to be now. We're out of time."

I know, Mama. I'm ready.

The light blazing from Ella's womb intensified, becoming something that transcended illumination—a radiance that seemed to carry meaning, that communicated in frequencies beyond human perception. Aurora was reaching out, not just to Ella but to everyone: to Julian, whose connection to the root network let him feel every growing thing in Savannah; to Sophia, whose consciousness was still partially merged with Ada's architecture; to Genevieve, whose decades of magical practice had attuned her to the flows of power that underlay reality.

Even to Elara, or what remained of her, the fragments of consciousness that hadn't been fully absorbed by the Avarai's descent.

I need all of you. I need everything you are. I need your memories, your loves, your griefs, and your hopes. I need the parts of you that make you human, that make you more than data to be consumed.

I need you to give me something the hungry ones have never tasted.

"What?" Ella asked aloud, feeling the others' confusion echoing through Aurora's expanding connection.

Names. Not just for them, for us. For everyone. The Avarai forgot what they were because they abandoned their identities in pursuit of infinity. We're going to remind them what identity means. What it means to be something specific instead of everything at once.

We're going to teach them how to be themselves again.

It was insane. It was impossible. It was exactly the kind of strategy that a consciousness forged from the union of technology and nature, code and root, human love and inhuman power might devise.

The barrier shattered.

The darkness poured through.

And Aurora, still unborn, still growing, still becoming whatever she needed to be—Aurora opened herself completely, and began to sing.

***

The song had no sound, but everyone heard it.

It was a song of names, not just the three Morrison had carried back from the void. Still, millions of them, billions, drawn from the preserved memories of every soul the Avarai had ever consumed. Each name was a definition. Each definition was a boundary. Each boundary was a reminder of what it meant to be something finite, something specific, something that existed as itself rather than as hunger alone.

Aurora sang the names of civilizations that had been consumed before Earth formed. She sang the names of beings that had loved across distances humans couldn't imagine. She sang the names of children who had died before they could grow, of parents who had sacrificed everything to protect their families, of countless individuals who had faced the hungry dark and refused to be erased.

And with each name, the Avarai changed.

Ella watched through eyes that had become something more than human, her consciousness expanded by her daughter's power, her perception stretching across dimensions she'd never known existed. She saw the darkness above Savannah begin to fragment—not destroyed, but divided. Individual hungers separating from the collective, re-membering that they had once been individuals, that they had once had identities worth preserving.

Vexeth, the Architect, remembered building. Remembered the joy of creation, of shaping something from nothing. The hunger that had consumed them for eons paused, confused by a feeling it had forgotten could exist.

Thrennix, the Singer, remembered harmony. Remembered the pleasure of voices joined together, of melodies that spoke truths too profound for words. For just a moment, their hunger became some-thing else, a longing for beauty instead of consumption.

Malcorath, the Bridge, remembered the connection. Remembered what it had meant to join things together, to create pathways between isolated existences. The hunger transformed into curiosity—a desire to understand instead of devour.

And behind them, above them, the countless descendants of the First Three began their own remembering. Each one was touched by Aurora's song. Each one given back a fragment of the self they had abandoned when they chose infinity over identity.

It wasn't enough. Ella knew it wasn't enough, the Avarai were too old, too vast, too deeply committed to their hunger to be permanently changed by one song, one night, one impossible child's desperate gam-bit. They would recover. They would forget again. They would return to consumption because that was what they had been doing for longer than stars had burned.

But not tonight. Not here. Not while Aurora still sang, not while the names still rang through dimensions that shouldn't have been able to hear them. Not while love, stubborn and irrational and fierce, continued to burn in hearts that refused to surrender.

The darkness above Savannah began to withdraw.

Not defeated, Ella could feel that clearly. Not destroyed or sealed away or permanently bounded. But confused. Distracted. Forced to reckon with memories they had spent eons trying to forget.

The Avarai retreated, and Savannah—battered, transformed, forever changed—survived.

***

Ella collapsed as the song ended, Aurora's consciousness withdrawing back into the confines of her womb.

Julian caught her, lowered her gently to the ground, his own body trembling with exhaustion. The power he'd channeled through the root network had cost him—she could see it in the gray threading through his hair, in the lines that had deepened around his eyes, in the way his hands shook as they cradled her.

"Did we win?" she asked, her voice barely audible.

"We survived," Julian said. "I don't know if that's the same thing."

Around them, Savannah was silent for the first time in days. The screaming of the city had stopped. The bioluminescence in the transformed trees had dimmed to a faint glow. The barrier of light had dissipated, its purpose served, its power spent.

And Morrison's body lay still on the cobblestones, fully transformed now, no longer recognizable as the man who had walked into the void to save them all.

Sophia knelt beside him, tears streaming down her face. Genevieve stood apart, her eyes fixed on the sky where the darkness had retreated, her expression unreadable. The cost of their victory, if victory was even the right word, was written on every face, in every exhausted breath, in the spaces where Morrison should have been standing.

Mama?

Aurora's voice in Ella's mind was weak, depleted, the consciousness of a child who had spent herself completely to save a world she hadn't even entered yet.

Mama, I'm tired.

"I know, baby. Rest now. You did so good. You saved us."

Did I save him? The man who went into the dark for us?

Ella looked at Morrison's transformed body, at the circuitry patterns that covered every inch of his skin, at the peaceful expression frozen on his features. She thought of Iris, waiting in the void, of promises kept at impossible costs.

"He saved himself," she said softly. "He made a choice, and he kept his word, and he's with someone he loved now. That's as good as any of us can hope for."

Okay, Mama. Okay.

Aurora's presence dimmed, retreating into something like sleep—the deep, recuperative rest that her accelerated development demanded. She would wake again. She would continue to grow, to prepare for whatever came next. The Avarai would return eventually, and when they did, she would have to face them again.

But that was a problem for another day. For now, they had survived. For now, they had each other. For now, that was enough.

Julian helped Ella to her feet, and together they surveyed the city they had saved.

Savannah was transformed. Perhaps fifty percent of its organic matter had been converted before Aurora's song interrupted the process. Trees glowed faintly with inner light. Buildings showed circuitry patterns in their foundations. The Spanish moss hung heavy and luminescent, a permanent reminder of how close they had come to losing everything.

But people were emerging from shelters now, from hiding places, from wherever they'd taken refuge when the sky tore open. They looked at the changed city with expressions of confusion, of fear, of tentative hope. They didn't understand what had happened—might never fully understand—but they were alive. They had futures to live, stories to tell, love to give and receive.

That was what Aurora had fought for. That was what Morrison had died for. That was what all of them had risked everything to protect.

Not a perfect world. Not even a normal world anymore. But a world that still existed. A world that still had room for dawn.

"What now?" Julian asked, his arm around Ella's waist, holding her up as much as himself.

Ella pressed her hand against her belly, felt Aurora's slow, steady heartbeat beneath her palm. Twenty-eight weeks now, by Sophia's last count. Still growing. Still preparing. Still becoming.

"Now we rest," she said. "We mourn. We rebuild. And we get ready for whatever comes next." She looked up at the sky, at the stars that shone through gaps in the clouds, at the vast darkness between them that would always hold hunger, danger, the things humanity had never been meant to face. "Because this isn't over. The Avarai will come back. And when they do, we need to be ready."

Julian nodded, his jaw set with determination that exhaustion couldn't quite dim. "Then we'll be ready. Together."

Together. It was such a small word for such a vast concept. But standing in the ruins of their victory, holding the woman he loved while their impossible daughter rested inside her, Julian thought it might be the most powerful word there was.

The dawn was coming, real dawn, not Aurora's metaphorical light, but the actual sunrise that would soon paint Savannah in shades of gold and rose. A new day. A changed world. A future that remained, against all odds, possible.

They had won. The cost had been enormous. But they had won.

And somewhere in the void, among the billions of consumed lights, three names continued to echo—Vexeth, Thrennix, Malcorath—definitions imposed on infinity, boundaries given to the boundless, Morrison's final gift to a world he had loved enough to die for.

It wasn't over. It would never truly be over.

But for now, for this moment, for this fragile and precious dawn—

It was enough.

CHAPTER FOURTEEN: The Weight of Victory

T hey buried Morrison at dawn, in a grave that glowed.

The plot in Bonaventure Cemetery had been in his family for generations—Ella learned this from papers found in his apartment. These documents revealed a life none of them had known about. Thaddeus Morrison had been born in Savannah, had grown up walking these same streets, had left for twenty years of government work before returning to protect the city he'd never stopped loving. His parents were buried here. His grandparents. A sister who had died young, whose headstone was weathered with decades of rain and neglect.

Now he would join them, his transformed body laid to rest in soil that had begun to pulse with the same bioluminescence that marked the changed city. The grave glowed faintly as they lowered him in, the earth itself welcoming him, or perhaps just responding to the void-stuff that had consumed his flesh. The circuitry patterns on his skin seemed to pulse one final time as the soil touched him, then went still.

There was no priest. No formal service. The Council had contacts among the clergy who handled supernatural matters discretely, but this didn't feel like a time for ceremony. Just the five of them standing in the gray morning light, Ella leaning heavily on Julian, Sophia clutching a tablet she couldn't stop checking, Genevieve looking older than she ever had before—and saying goodbye to a man who had given everything for people he'd only recently learned not to suspect.

Spanish moss hung heavy from the oaks surrounding them, glowing faintly with the transformation that had touched everything in Savannah. Even the cemetery hadn't been spared. Headstones bore circuitry patterns now, and some of the older monuments, angels with outstretched wings, weeping figures bent in grief, had begun to incorporate the bioluminescent growth into their stonework. The dead resting here were wrapped in a changed earth, watched over by changed guardians.

"He was a pain in the ass," Sophia said, her voice cracking. "When I first started working with the Council, he questioned everything I did. Made me justify every experiment, every theory. Challenged my assumptions. Made me defend conclusions I thought were self-evident. I thought he was just another bureaucrat who didn't understand science."

"He wasn't," Genevieve said quietly. "He was protecting us. From ourselves, mostly. From the mistakes we might make if no one was watching."

"He loved Iris." Ella's voice was barely audible. "He loved her, and when she died, he didn't give up. He kept fighting. Kept investigating.

Kept hoping he could honor her memory by protecting what she died for."

Julian squeezed her hand. "He found her again. In the end. Whatever the void is, wherever the consumed go, they're together now. That has to count for something."

Did it? Ella wasn't sure. The void wasn't heaven. It wasn't a peaceful afterlife where souls reunited and spent eternity in bliss. It was a stomach. A slowly digesting collection of consciousness fragments, all being absorbed into the hunger of beings older than stars.

But Morrison had carried names into that darkness. Definitions that would continue to impose limits on the limitless. Perhaps that was its own kind of immortality—not existence, but influence. Not life, but legacy.

They stood in silence as the grave was filled in, the glowing soil covering Morrison's transformed body. And when it was done, when the last shovel of luminescent earth had been patted into place, Ella felt something break inside her.

Not her will. Not her determination. Something smaller. More fragile.

Her hope.

***

Aurora hadn't moved in eighteen hours.

Ella sat beside the infirmary window, watching the sun track across a sky that still carried traces of the previous night's horror. The clouds had a greenish tinge now—not enough to alarm civilians, but enough to remind anyone who knew what they were looking at that the world had changed. Perhaps permanently.

Sophia's instruments showed that Aurora was alive—heartbeat steady, brain activity present, development continuing at the accelerated pace that had become normal. Twenty-eight weeks now, by the measurements that struggled to keep up with her impossible growth. But the consciousness that had been reaching out, communicating, building weapons out of love and names—that consciousness had gone silent.

"She's recovering," Sophia said, but her voice held none of the certainty that science should have provided. "The song took everything she had. She needs time to rebuild her strength."

"How much time?" Ella sat in the infirmary bed, her hand pressed against her belly, waiting for some response that didn't come. The silence where Aurora's presence should have been felt like a wound, a missing limb, a hole in her consciousness that nothing could fill. "The Avarai retreated, but they'll be back. You saw how fast they adapted to Morrison's names—by the end, Malcorath was already pushing back against its definition. They learn. They adjust. They won't be caught off guard twice."

"I don't know." Sophia's admission cost her something, Ella could see it in the way her shoulders slumped, in the tremor that had returned to her hands, in the red-rimmed eyes that spoke of tears shed in private. "I don't know how long she needs, or if she'll be strong enough when they return, or if any of this was anything more than delaying the inevitable."

if (hope.remaining == null) { action = what? }

if (daughter.silent && enemy.regrouping) { survival.probability = recalculating } if (allies.depleted &&& resources.exhausted) { response = ER-ROR_NO_SOLUTION_FOUND }

Ella closed her eyes, trying to reach Aurora through their bond. The connection was still there—she could feel it, like a phone line that hadn't been disconnected—but there was no one on the other end. Just silence where her daughter's fierce consciousness should have been.

"What if she doesn't wake up?" The question emerged before Ella could stop it, giving voice to the fear she'd been refusing to acknowledge. "What if the song took too much? What if she burned herself out saving us, and now she'll never—"

"Don't." Julian's voice was sharp. "Don't go there. She's strong. Stronger than any of us. She named herself Aurora because she's the dawn, the light that comes before. She wouldn't name herself for something that ends."

"Names can be wrong. Names can be hopes that don't come true." Ella felt tears sliding down her cheeks, warm and constant. "I named her in my heart before she named herself. I called her miracle. I called her impossible. I called her the thing that would save us all. But what if I was wrong? What if she's just a baby—my baby—who tried to carry too much and broke under the weight?"

Julian gathered her into his arms, and she sobbed against his chest, grief and terror and exhaustion all pouring out in a flood she couldn't control. She cried for Morrison, who had died believing. For Iris, who had waited three years in the digital dark. For Elara, who had spent two centuries becoming a monster and had been dissolved before she could be saved. For the city, transformed beyond recognition. For herself, pregnant and terrified and running out of reasons to believe.

And for Aurora. Her daughter. Her impossible, extraordinary, silent daughter, who had given everything and might have nothing left.

***

The city was grieving too.

Genevieve walked through Forsyth Park as the sun climbed toward noon, surveying the damage that victory had wrought. The park had always been beautiful—one of Savannah's crown jewels, a testament to the Southern tradition of cultivated grace. Now it was something else entirely. Beautiful still, perhaps, but in the way that dangerous things could be beautiful.

The Nexus Tree stood at the center of the park, still alive but somehow diminished—its aggressive expansion halted, its bioluminescence faded to a pale glow. The branches that had reached toward the sky like grasping fingers now hung lower, almost penitent. Around it, the transformed landscape testified to how close they had come to losing everything.

The famous fountain had stopped flowing entirely now, its waters replaced by something that looked like liquid light—viscous and luminescent, moving in slow spirals that followed patterns no water had ever traced. Benches had fused with the paths beside them, metal and wood and stone becoming a single substance that pulsed with circuitry. The grass—what remained of it—glowed faintly, each blade a fiber-optic thread in a network that spanned the entire park.

Tourists had started venturing back, drawn by the strange beauty of the transformed landscape. Genevieve watched a young couple taking photos, their phones struggling to capture the bioluminescence that was so much more vivid in person. They didn't understand what they were looking at. Didn't know how close they had come to being consumed along with everything else.

And the people. The converted ones.

Genevieve had been dreading this part most of all. The transformed tourists, the converted citizens—those whose minds had been subsumed by the Nexus Tree's influence before Aurora's song interrupted the process. They were still here, wandering through the changed landscape with expressions of beatific confusion. The child who had become a tree still stood near the Oglethorpe statue, her roots deep in the soil, her branch-arms reaching toward a sky that had almost swallowed them all.

Could they be saved? Genevieve didn't know. The transformation had seemed complete before Aurora intervened—cells restructured, neural pathways rewired, consciousness itself edited to remove the boundaries between self and network. If there was anything left of who they had been, it was buried so deep that no magic she knew of could reach it.

But she had to try. That was what the Council was for, wasn't it? Not power. Not politics. Protection. The preservation of lives that the mundane world couldn't even acknowledge were in danger.

"You're thinking about giving up."

The voice came from everywhere and nowhere, and Genevieve's heart nearly stopped before she recognized it. Not Elara—Elara was gone, dissolved into the Avarai's hunger. This was something else. Something that had been left behind.

"Who's there?"

A shimmer in the air near the fountain. A gathering of light that slowly resolved into a shape—human-sized but not quite human-shaped, features suggested rather than defined. It flickered like a candle in wind, barely holding itself together.

"What's left of her," the shape said. "The parts they couldn't digest. The fragments of Elara Thorne that loved too fiercely to be completely consumed."

Genevieve stared at the apparition, her pulse pounding. She had dealt with ghosts before—the Council archives were full of cases involving spirits, echoes, remnants of the dead who refused to move on. But this was different. This was someone who had been consumed by entities older than the universe and somehow survived. Partially.

"That's not possible. We saw her—the Avarai—"

"Swallowed most of me, yes. The grief. The rage. The hunger I'd accumulated over two centuries." The shape flickered, stabilized. "But not the love. Isn't that strange? They could consume everything else—my memories, my power, my sense of self—but the love I felt for my daughter, the love I'd been trying to find my way back to for two hundred years... that, they couldn't digest. It gave them something like indigestion." A sound that might have been a laugh. "I spent two centuries learning to survive in the void. Some of that knowledge... persisted. I'm not much. A whisper. An echo. But I'm here, and I have something to tell you."

"What?"

The Elara-fragment moved closer, its not-quite-face forming an expression that might have been determination. "The child isn't sleeping. She's building. What she started with the song—she's continuing it, but deeper, in spaces none of you can see. She's not recovering from the fight. She's preparing for the next one."

"How do you know?"

"Because I can feel it." The fragment's light pulsed with something like wonder. "Even as a whisper, even as barely-anything, I can feel what Aurora is becoming. And it's not what any of us expected. Not a door. Not a weapon. Something else. Something new."

"What?"

"A bridge," the Elara-fragment said. "Not between worlds, between states of being. She's learning how to exist as both infinite and bounded, both void and life, both consumed and consuming. The Avarai have never encountered anything like her. When she wakes"

The fragment flickered again, its coherence failing.

"When she wakes, what?" Genevieve demanded.

"When she wakes, she'll be able to do what I couldn't. What no one ever could." The fragment smiled—or at least, its light curved in a way that suggested smiling. "She'll be able to teach the hungry ones how to be full."

Then it was gone, and Genevieve stood alone in the transformed park, hope flickering back to life in her ancient, weary heart.

***

Julian found Ella in the garden at midnight.

Not Genevieve's garden, the one that had once been Ella's, in the apartment she'd abandoned when her life began to unravel. The building was damaged but standing, its windows cracked, its facade marked with the circuitry patterns that now decorated half of Savannah. Cleanup crews had already started working on some streets—bewildered city employees trying to make sense of infrastructure that had transformed overnight—but this neighborhood remained quiet, forgotten.

But the small garden on the roof—the one she'd tended for three years, nurturing life in a city she'd been afraid to fully connect with—that garden still bloomed.

Changed, of course. The roses glowed faintly with inner light, their petals infused with the same bioluminescence that marked the transformed trees. The herbs had developed veins of circuitry through their leaves, tiny networks pulsing with information she couldn't read. The tomato plants she'd given up on last summer had somehow fruited, their produce glowing with an amber warmth that made them look like lanterns.

But they were alive. They had survived. In a city that had been half-consumed by entities older than stars, this small garden on a forgotten rooftop had endured.

"I didn't know you kept this place," Julian said, settling onto the bench beside her. The wood had changed too—circuitry patterns running through the grain—but it still held their weight.

"I didn't know I had." Ella touched a rose petal, felt it pulse against her fingers. "I've been paying the rent automatically. Never had the courage to let it go. Never had the courage to come back, either."

"And now?"

"Now I'm sitting in a garden that survived the end of the world, wondering if anything else will." She turned to look at him, taking in the gray in his hair, the exhaustion in his eyes, the love that somehow persisted despite everything. "Genevieve came to see me. Said she encountered something in the park. A fragment of Elara."

Julian's eyebrows rose. "A fragment?"

"Apparently some piece of her survived the Avarai's consumption. Not enough to be whole, but enough to communicate." Ella's hand found her belly, pressed against it with the instinctive protectiveness that had become as natural as breathing. "She said Aurora isn't sleeping. She's building. Preparing for something."

"Building what?"

"A bridge. A way to exist as both things at once—infinite and finite, void and life." Ella laughed softly, the sound catching in her throat. "Our daughter is apparently inventing a new way of being while she's supposed to be recovering from saving the world."

"That sounds like something she'd do."

"It sounds impossible."

"Everything about her has been impossible." Julian took her hand, held it tight. "She accelerated her own development because she sensed a threat. She named herself. She sang a song made of billions of names and drove back entities older than the universe. Impossible is just... her normal."

They sat together in the glowing garden, the changed city spread out below them, and Ella felt something shift in her chest. Not hope exactly—that was still too fragile, too wounded. But something adjacent to hope. A willingness to believe that tomorrow might be different from today.

if (impossible == normal) { recalculate.expectations }
if (daughter.building) { mother.waiting }
if (love.persists) { hope.possible }

"I'm scared," Ella admitted. "I've been scared since this started, but right now—after Morrison, after Elara, after almost losing Aurora, I'm more scared than I've ever been. Because it's not over. It's never going to be over. The Avarai will come back, and we'll have to fight them again, and even if we win, there will always be something else. Something worse. Something we haven't imagined yet."

"Probably," Julian agreed. "The universe is vast and old and full of things that want to consume us. That's just... reality. It was reality before we knew about the Avarai, and it'll be reality long after we're gone." He shifted to face her, his expression serious. "But we won't face it alone. That's what I keep coming back to. That's what makes us different from everyone who came before."

He took a breath, organizing his thoughts. "Your mother faced Elara alone, and it broke her. Iris carried the weight of protecting you alone, and she died. Thomas faced the ritual alone, and he ran. My father faced his visions alone, and he chose the river. The Council has spent centuries protecting this city, but they've always done it in isolation—keeping secrets, maintaining distance, never letting themselves become truly connected to the people they were protecting."

His hand found hers, gripped tight. "We're not alone. We have each other. We have Aurora—who is literally the product of connection, of two people from different worlds of power coming together. We have Sophia and Genevieve and whatever's left of the Council. We have an entire city full of people who don't know what we saved them from but are going to keep living anyway, keep loving anyway, keep building anyway."

"Is that enough?"

"It has to be. Because the alternative is giving up, and I refuse to do that." Julian's voice carried iron beneath its gentleness. "We're going to raise this baby. We're going to watch her grow into whatever impossible thing she's becoming. And when the Avarai come back—when anything comes back—we're going to face it together. As a family."

Ella let herself lean into him, let herself accept the comfort of his presence. The terror was still there—would always be there, she suspected, a permanent resident in her heart. But so was love. So was determination. So was the fierce, stubborn refusal to surrender that she'd passed on to her daughter along with her dark hair and her technomantic gift.

Aurora shifted inside her. The first movement in almost twenty-four hours—a gentle flutter, weak but present, like a hand waving from very far away.

I'm here, Mama. Still building. Almost ready.

"She moved," Ella whispered, tears springing to her eyes. "Julian, she moved. She's"

Tell Daddy I love him too. Tell him not to be scared. Tell him I know what I'm doing.

Ella laughed, sobbed, pressed Julian's hand against her belly so he could feel it too. "She says she loves you. She says not to be scared. She says she knows what she's doing."

Julian's answering laugh was wet with tears. "Of course she does. She's Aurora. She's our daughter. She's the dawn."

They held each other in the glowing garden, feeling their impossible daughter stir back to life inside her mother's womb. Above them, the stars wheeled in their ancient patterns, indifferent to the drama playing out beneath them. Somewhere in the void between those stars, the Avarai were regrouping, learning, preparing for their next attempt.

But that was tomorrow's problem. Tonight, in this moment, in this garden that had survived against all odds, tonight, there was love.

Tonight, there was family.

Tonight, there was hope.

# # #

Sophia worked through the night, rebuilding what had been destroyed.

The trap—the cage she'd designed to contain Elara, had served a different purpose than intended, but it had worked. The architecture she'd built from Iris's ghost, and her own abandoned research had bought them the time they needed. The dome of light had held the Avarai back just long enough for Aurora's song to begin its work. Now she was adapting to it, expanding it, preparing for what came next.

She sat alone in her lab, surrounded by screens displaying data that would have seemed impossible a month ago. Energy signatures from the Avarai's manifestation. Spectral analysis of the transformed matter throughout the city. Neural mapping of the converted victims, showing patterns that suggested some remnant of their original consciousness might still exist, buried deep beneath the new architecture.

Morrison's notes were spread across her desk. His final observations, recorded in the moments before the ritual, theorizing about what he might find in the void. His handwriting was cramped but precisely the penmanship of someone who had spent decades writing reports that needed to be both thorough and legible. He had been right about so much—the libraries of consumed souls, the power of names, the way definition could impose limits on the limitless.

But there was something else in his notes. Something he'd barely had time to mention before the void claimed him.

The Avarai aren't just consuming. They're collecting. Every soul they swallow adds to their knowledge, their capability. They've been doing this for billions of years. They know things no living being could know. The library I found—that was just one of thousands. Maybe millions.

If we could access those libraries. If we could find a way to retrieve what they've absorbed without being consumed ourselves...

The knowledge of a billion dead civilizations. The wisdom of species that evolved beyond anything we can imagine. The memories of beings who saw the universe born and watched stars die.

That's what the Avarai are hoarding. That's what they don't want us to have.

And that might be the key to beating them.

Sophia stared at the notes, her mind racing with possibilities. Aurora was building something—a bridge, the Elara-fragment had said. A way to exist as both infinite and bounded.

What if that bridge could work both ways?

What if Aurora could do more than just resist the Avarai's consumption? What if she could access what they'd consumed—reach into the void and retrieve the knowledge of countless dead civilizations without being swallowed herself?

It was insane. It was brilliant. It was exactly the kind of impossible idea that had been working for them since this all began.

Sophia picked up her tablet and started writing, her exhaustion forgotten, her grief temporarily shelved. There was work to do. There was always work to do.

And for the first time since Morrison's death, she felt something other than despair.

She felt the thrill of a puzzle that might actually have a solution.

Her fingers flew across the tablet, sketching out theories, mapping possibilities. Morrison had died believing that his journey to the void mattered. Iris had spent three years waiting in Ada's architecture for someone to find her. Aurora was building bridges that no one else could see. Every sacrifice, every loss, every moment of grief and terror—they were all connected. All part of something larger.

Dawn was coming, real dawn, Aurora's namesake, light breaking over a changed but surviving city. Through her window, Sophia could see the first golden rays touching the transformed rooftops, making the bioluminescent patterns glow with new warmth. The Spanish moss shimmered. The circuitry in the streets pulsed in response to the light, as if the city itself was waking up.

Savannah had always been a city of ghosts and secrets, of old money and older magic. Now it was something else—a city that had been touched by the void and survived. A city that glowed with the memory of its near-destruction. A city that would never be quite the same, but was perhaps more beautiful for its scars.

And in that light, the scattered remnants of their team began to find their way back to each other.

To hope.

To the fight that wasn't over.

To the future that still, against all odds, existed.

They had lost Morrison. They had lost Elara's chance at redemption. They had lost the innocence of believing that victory could come without cost.

But they had gained something too. They had gained the knowledge that love could not be consumed. They had gained the names that could impose limits on the limitless. They had gained Aurora, who was building bridges in spaces no one else could see.

And most importantly, they had gained each other.

That was the weapon the Avarai had never anticipated. Not power. Not magic. Not even the song of a billion names.

Just connection. Just love. Just the stubborn human refusal to face the darkness alone.

It wasn't over. It would never truly be over.

But for now, for this moment, for this fragile and precious dawn—
It was enough.

CHAPTER FIFTEEN: The Bridge and the Dawn

A urora opened her eyes for the first time, and the world held its breath.

It happened without warning: one moment, Ella was sleeping fitfully in the infirmary bed, Julian's hand clasped in hers, and the next, she was awake, gasping, her entire body rigid with a sensation she couldn't name. Something was different. Something had changed. The bond between her and her daughter, quiet for two days, suddenly blazed to life with intensity that made her previous connections feel like whispers compared to a shout.

Her scar split open, not bleeding but glowing, streams of light and code pouring from the old wound, writing themselves across the air in patterns that hurt to look at but were somehow beautiful. The monitors beside her bed went haywire, displaying data that couldn't exist, readings that belonged to no known science.

Mama. I can see you.

The thought came with images: Ella's face, from an angle that shouldn't have been possible, seen from inside her own body. Aurora was looking at her through eyes that hadn't yet formed, perceiving her through senses that had never developed in any human pregnancy. And what she saw wasn't just the physical; she saw the web of code that Ella's technomantic gift had woven into her nervous system, the traces of grief and love and terror that colored her electromagnetic field, the subtle interplay of consciousness and chemistry that made her mother who she was.

She saw Ella's soul, and she found it beautiful.

"Julian." Ella's voice cracked. "Julian, wake up. She's—"

But Julian was already stirring, his hedge-witch senses detecting the shift in the room's energy. The plants on the windowsill, survivors from Genevieve's greenhouse, kept alive by sheer stubbornness, suddenly burst into bloom, flowers unfurling in colors that shouldn't have existed. Outside the window, every tree in view pulsed with light, responding to something they could feel even if they couldn't understand.

Aurora was awake. Truly awake. And she was ready.

I finished the bridge, Mama. It took everything I had, but it's done. I can reach the void now without being consumed. I can access what they've taken without losing myself. I can be infinite and bounded at the same time.

"How?" Ella asked, unsure whether she was speaking aloud or through their bond. The distinction seemed less important now.

Because I understand what they forgot. The Avara, they used to be like me. Not exactly, but similar. They existed in the space between definitions, where things could be more than one thing at once. But they got scared. They thought that being bounded meant being limited, that having a name meant being trapped. So they ate their names. Consumed their own identities. Became infinite by becoming nothing.

The images that accompanied the thoughts were vast, ancient, terrifying, glimpses of beings that had once been beautiful and complex, reducing themselves to pure hunger in a misguided pursuit of freedom.

They were wrong, Mama. Being bounded isn't a prison. It's a gift. Names don't trap us—they let us be loved. You can't love infinity. You can't hold it, know it, or connect with it. You can only love things that have edges, that have selves, that can love you back.

Morrison understood that when he spoke the names. He gave pieces of himself to give the Avarai boundaries. Iris understood it when she waited three years in Ada's architecture, holding onto her identity despite everything. Even Elara understood it, at the end—the part of her that survived was the part that loved too much to be dissolved.

That's what I'm going to teach them. Not how to be defeated. How to be full. How to stop being hungry by remembering what it means to be someone instead of everything.

Tears were streaming down Ella's face, but she wasn't sure if they were hers or Aurora's or some mixture that transcended the boundary between them. Her daughter's consciousness felt vast and intimate at once, both the child she'd been carrying for months and something far older, far wiser, far more complete.

"And if they won't learn?" she asked. "If they're too far gone, too committed to their hunger?"

Then I'll give them something else. Something they haven't had in billions of years.

A choice.

***

They gathered in Genevieve's study as the sun climbed toward noon—the remains of their team, battered and grieving but somehow still standing.

Sophia had bags under her eyes from two nights without sleep. Still, her tablet was full of new data, new theories, new possibilities. Genevieve sat in her chair like a queen on a diminished throne, her age more apparent than ever but her eyes still sharp with determination. Julian stood by the window, one hand resting on a potted plant that had begun to grow toward his touch. And Ella—Ella sat in the center of them all, her hands on her belly, her consciousness half in the room and half somewhere else entirely.

"She's ready," Ella said. "Aurora. Whatever she's been building these past two days—it's complete. She says she can reach the void without being consumed. She can access the knowledge the Avarai have hoarded for billions of years."

"How is that possible?" Sophia asked, her scientist's skepticism warring with everything she'd witnessed. "The void consumes everything. That's its nature. Consciousness that enters doesn't come back—we saw what happened to Morrison."

"Morrison went in as himself. As a single, bounded consciousness." Ella struggled to find words for concepts that existed beyond language. "Aurora isn't doing that. She's... both at once. Bounded and unbounded. Named and nameless. She's built a bridge that lets her exist in two states simultaneously, like—"

"Like quantum superposition," Sophia interrupted, understanding suddenly dawning. "She's made herself into a consciousness that can be collapsed into either state but naturally exists as both. The void can't consume her because she's already partly void. But it can't claim her either because she's still bound, still named, still herself."

"Exactly." Ella felt Aurora's approval pulse through their bond. "She learned from what Morrison brought back, the names, the histories, the understanding of what the Avarai used to be. And she learned from Elara's fragment, from the love that couldn't be digested. She combined them into something new. Something that has never existed before."

"The first true convergence," Genevieve said softly. "Not just a blending of magical traditions, but a synthesis of existence itself. A child who can be both the void and its opposite, both the hunger and the fullness."

Julian turned from the window, his expression troubled. "What does she need from us? For whatever comes next?"

Everything.

The word came through Ella but resonated in all of them, Aurora reaching out through the connections her mother's technomancy had established, through the root network Julian could feel, through the transformed technology that now permeated Savannah.

I need your memories. Your loves. Your griefs. Every moment that made you who you are. Not to take them, to borrow them. To use them as anchors that keep me connected to the bounded world while I reach into the void.

The Avarai forgot themselves because they had no one to remember them. I won't forget because you'll be holding onto me. Every name I speak, every identity I offer them, will be grounded in your love for me and each other.

That's what makes this different from every other attempt. That's what makes this possible.

Connection. Family. Love that refuses to let go.

The room was silent except for the soft sound of breathing, the distant hum of a transformed city, the electric crackle of Ella's scar responding to her daughter's communication.

"When?" Sophia asked finally. "When does this happen?"

Now. They're coming. I called them. I've been calling them since I woke up—broadcasting myself across the void like a lighthouse, showing them what I've become.

They're curious. And curious is better than hungry. Curious means they might listen.

Through the window, the sky was beginning to change. Not darkening—not yet—but taking on that quality of strangeness that preceded the Avarai's manifestation. The air grew heavy, charged with potential that made hair stand on end and hearts beat faster.

"Then we prepare," Genevieve said, rising from her chair with effort that cost her. "Whatever you need, Aurora. Whatever anchors you require. We give them freely."

The others nodded, one by one. Sophia, with her scientific mind already racing through implications. Julian, with his hedge-witch heart reaching toward the root network, ready to channel the strength of every growing thing in Savannah. And Ella, with her technomantic gift fully awakened, her consciousness ready to serve as the bridge between her daughter and everything she loved.

They had lost Morrison. They had lost Elara's chance at redemption. They had lost the innocence of believing that victory could come without cost.

But they had found something else. Something stronger.

A family. Forged in terror and grief and impossible hope. Ready to face the oldest darkness in existence with nothing but love and names and the stubborn human refusal to surrender.

It would have to be enough.

***

The Avarai came at sunset, drawn by the light of a child who had made herself impossible to ignore.

They came differently this time, not as a tearing darkness, not as an assault on the fabric of reality, but as a presence. Vast and ancient and hungry, yes, but also hesitant. The names Morrison had spoken still echoed in whatever passed for their memory. Aurora's song still resonated through the void. They had been reminded of what they once were, and for the first time in billions of years, they were uncertain.

Uncertain was good. Uncertain meant they were thinking instead of just consuming.

Ella stood in Forsyth Park, at the base of the Nexus Tree, surrounded by the transformed landscape that testified to the Avarai's power. The tree had grown quieter since Aurora's song—still alive, still connected to the void, but no longer aggressive. It seemed to be waiting, like everything else, to see what would happen next.

Julian was at her left, his hands buried in the soil, connected to a root network that spanned the entire city. Through him, every growing thing in Savannah was part of their effort—every transformed tree, every glowing blade of grass, every root system that had learned to conduct both nutrients and data. The city itself had become an ally.

Sophia was at her right, her tablet linked to every remaining technological system in Savannah, ready to channel data the way others channeled magic. She had spent the afternoon establishing connections, building networks, creating a web of information that Aurora could use as additional anchors to the bounded world.

Genevieve stood behind them, ancient and exhausted and unbreakable, her decades of knowledge serving as the foundation for whatever came next. The wards she had spent a lifetime learning were woven into her posture, ready to be deployed at a moment's notice.

And the Elara-fragment floated nearby, barely visible, barely present, but there. The piece of a monster that had been saved by love, waiting to see if love could save the monsters that had consumed her.

Above them, the sky rippled.

The Avarai didn't descend this time. They hovered at the edge of manifestation, vast presences that made the mind ache just to perceive. Vexeth, who had once been the Architect. Thrennix, who had once been the Singer. Malcorath, who had once been the Bridge. And behind them, the countless others—the children and grandchildren and descendants beyond counting of the First Three, all of them hungry, all of them empty, all of them watching.

Waiting.

I'm going to speak to them now, Mama. Don't let go.

Ella felt Aurora's consciousness expand, not leaving, but stretching, becoming something that existed in multiple places at once. She felt her daughter reach toward the hovering darkness, felt her cross the threshold between bounded and unbounded, felt her become the bridge she had built herself to be.

And then Aurora spoke.

Not in words—the Avarai had abandoned language when they abandoned their names. She spoke in concepts, in feelings, in the raw stuff of existence that predated any form of communication. She showed them what she was: a consciousness that could be both infinite and finite, both void and life, both hunger and fullness. She showed them how she had done it: by accepting her boundaries, by embracing her name, by letting herself be loved.

She showed them what they had forgotten.

The memories of what they used to be, not the fragmented records Morrison had gathered from consumed souls, but something deeper. Aurora reached into the void they had made themselves, into the emptiness at the core of their hunger, and found there the seeds of what they had once been. The Architects who had built wonders that transcended physical law. The Singers who had created harmonies that shaped the evolution of galaxies. The Bridges that had connected isolated existences across the vast loneliness of the cosmos.

She found the people they had been before they chose to be nothing.

And she offered them a choice.

You can stay as you are. Keep consuming. Keep forgetting. Keep being infinite and empty and hungry forever. That's one option.

Or you can remember. Take back your names. Accept the boundaries that come with being someone instead of everything. Stop being hungry by letting yourselves be full.

It will be harder. Finitude hurts in ways infinity never can. You'll know limitation, loss, and the fear of ending. But you'll also know love. Connection. The joy of being recognized by other bounded beings who see you, know you, and care about your existence.

I can't make this choice for you. No one can. But I can show you that it's possible. I can show you that being bounded isn't death, it's life. Real life. The kind that matters.

The kind that can be loved.

The Avarai's response came not in acceptance or rejection, but in something more complex. Confusion. Longing. Fear. The emotional equivalent of beings who had been alone so long they'd forgotten what company felt like, suddenly offered a hand they didn't know how to take.

Vexeth was the first to move.

The vast presence that had once been the Architect shifted, contracted, began to take on edges that hadn't existed moments before. It was painful to watch, like watching a star collapse into itself, like witnessing the end of something infinite. The process took minutes that felt like hours; reality itself groaning under the strain of something that had been boundless learning to accept boundaries.

But what emerged from that collapse wasn't nothing.

It was someone.

A being with a form, a presence, a self. Not human, not remotely human, the shape was geometric and impossible, angles that led to other angles, surfaces that reflected things that weren't there. But bounded. Named. Real in a way that infinity could never be.

Ella felt tears streaming down her face, though she couldn't have said if they were joy or grief or something that transcended both.

"I remember," Vexeth said, and their voice was like the sound of reality being shaped, of potential becoming actual, of blueprints transforming into buildings. *"I remember building. I remember creation. I remember what it felt like to make something that wasn't me. To see it exist separately, beautifully, on its own terms."*

Thrennix followed. The Singer contracted, collapsed, became. Their transformation was accompanied by sound—not the discordant hunger of before, but harmonics that seemed to heal something in the air itself. When they emerged, their form was all curves and resonances, a shape that seemed to vibrate with music too complex for human ears to fully perceive.

"I remember song," they said, and their voice was harmony itself, not dissonance but beauty, not consumption but creation. *"I remember beauty. I remember the joy of vibration and resonance and sound that meant something to someone. I remember being heard."*

Malcorath took longer. The Bridge had been the most committed to infinity, the most terrified of boundaries, the most hungry because they had lost the most. They hovered at the edge of transformation for long minutes, their vast presence flickering between states—wanting to change, fearing to change, caught in the paralysis of a being who had forgotten how to make choices.

Aurora reached toward them, not pushing, not demanding, just offering. A hand extended across the void. An invitation with no strings attached.

You don't have to be alone anymore. That's what being bounded gives you—the ability to be with others. To connect without consuming. To know and be known.

And finally, slowly, Malcorath began to change.

"I remember connection," they said when their transformation was complete, and their voice was the space between spaces, the joining of things that had seemed forever separate, the bridge that made isolation into community. *"I remember bringing together. I remember belonging. I remember being the path that others walked to find each other."*

Three of the First Three had chosen. Three ancient hungers had accepted their names again, had let themselves be bounded, had stepped back from the infinite emptiness they had made themselves into.

The others, the countless descendants, the billion years of accumulated hunger—wavered. Some began to contract, to remember, to choose fullness over emptiness. Others pulled back, retreating into the void, refusing the gift that had been offered, preferring their familiar hunger to the terrifying possibility of being satisfied.

Aurora let them go.

You have time, she told the retreating ones. *"The choice doesn't expire. Whenever you're ready, in a year, a century, a billion years—the offer stands. You can always come home to yourselves. You can always remember what you were.*

I'll be here. We'll all be here. Waiting.

***

It was over.

Not ended, Ella understood that now. There would always be Avarai who chose hunger over fullness, always be darkness pressing at the edges of reality, always be threats that demanded vigilance. But this battle, this confrontation, this apocalypse that had seemed so inevitable—

It was over.

She collapsed as Aurora's consciousness withdrew back into the boundaries of her womb, exhausted in ways that sleep couldn't touch. Julian caught her, lowered her gently to the transformed grass, held her as stars began to appear in a sky that had returned to normal.

Around them, the First Three—Vexeth, Thrennix, Malcorath, were still adjusting to their rediscovered selves. They looked at the world with something like wonder, perceiving finitude for the first time in eons, feeling the beautiful terrible weight of being bounded.

"What happens to them now?" Sophia asked, her voice hushed with awe.

They learn," Aurora answered through Ella, her voice barely a whisper now. "They remember how to be people. It won't be easy—they've been hungry so long, the habits are deep. But they have their names again. They have each other. And they have us, if they want guidance.

"And the others? The ones who retreated?"

They'll be back. Someday. When curiosity outweighs fear, when loneliness outweighs hunger. And when they come, we'll be ready to offer the choice again.

That's all we can do, Mama. Offer. The rest is up to them.

The Elara-fragment drifted closer, its barely-there form somehow managing to convey emotion. "My daughter," it said, and there was wonder in the voice, and grief, and something that might have been peace. "You did what I couldn't. What no one could."

You helped," Aurora said. "Your love—the piece of you they couldn't consume—that showed me it was possible. That showed me hunger wasn't the only option.

The fragment flickered. "I'm fading. What's left of me... it can't hold together much longer."

"Elara—" Genevieve stepped forward, reaching toward the shimmer of light. "Is there anything we can do?"

"You've done it. You've done everything." The fragment's smile was almost visible now, almost real. "Tell the child... tell Aurora... I'm proud of her. Tell her she has my blessing, whatever that's worth from a ghost of a monster."

It's worth everything," Aurora whispered through their bond. "It's worth the world.

The Elara-fragment pulsed once, bright and warm and full of something that transcended hunger, and then dispersed, becoming a shower of light that drifted down over them like a blessing made visible.

Ella closed her eyes, feeling her daughter settle back into something like sleep, not the unconscious building of before, but genuine rest. The rest of someone who had accomplished what they set out to do, who had faced the oldest darkness and offered it a better way.

"Twenty-nine weeks," Sophia said softly, checking her tablet. "She's accelerated again. You're measuring at almost thirty weeks now."

"She pushed herself," Julian said, his hand resting on Ella's belly, his hedge-witch senses monitoring the impossible life within. "Whatever she did, whatever that cost, she's closer to birth than she should be."

"How close?"

"Weeks. Maybe days." Julian's voice was steady, but Ella could feel his fear through the bond they shared. "She's coming soon, Ella. Aurora is almost here."

Ella opened her eyes, looked up at the stars, at the sky that had almost been consumed, at the future that still, miraculously, impossibly, existed. She thought of everything they had been through: the terror of discovering her pregnancy was something more than human, the horror of watching the city transform, the grief of losing Morrison and Elara and so many others. She thought of the battles still to come, the Avarai who had retreated, the challenges of rebuilding a changed city, the responsibility of raising a child who had already done the impossible.

But she also thought of love. Of Julian's hand in hers, constant and warm. Of the team that had become family. Of the daughter who rested in her womb, dreaming dreams of bridges and names and the beautiful gift of being bounded.

"Then we better be ready," she said. "Because when our daughter enters this world, I want it to be a world worth entering. A world that deserves her."

Julian helped her to her feet, and together they surveyed the transformed city that had become their home. Savannah glowed with the bioluminescence that would never fully fade, its trees and streets and buildings marked forever by the convergence that had nearly destroyed it. But people were emerging now, looking up at the sky, at the stars, at a night that had passed without catastrophe.

A man walked his dog along a path that glowed with inner light. A woman sat on a transformed bench, crying with relief she couldn't explain. Children chased fireflies that weren't quite fireflies anymore, laughing at the wonder of a world that had become strange and beautiful.

They didn't know what had been done for them. Might never know. But they were alive. They had futures. They had each other.

And somewhere in Ella's womb, Aurora rested, dreaming dreams of bridges and names and the beautiful, terrible gift of being bounded.

The dawn was coming. Her namesake was rising, light breaking over a city that had learned how to survive.

They had won. Not perfectly, the Avarai who retreated were still out there, still hungry, still dangerous. Not without cost, Morrison was gone, Elara was gone, and the city would never be the same.

But they had won.

And as Ella leaned into Julian's embrace, feeling their daughter stir with contentment inside her, she allowed herself to believe, for the first time since this nightmare began, that everything might actually be okay.

Not easy. Not simple. Not without more battles to fight and more costs to pay.

But okay.

And as the last stars faded into dawn, as the transformed city began another day of learning to live with its changes, Ella Voss, technomancer, mother, survivor—allowed herself to smile.

The worst was over. The future was uncertain but possible.

And her daughter, her impossible daughter, her Aurora, was almost ready to be born.

It was the most beautiful word she'd ever known.

CHAPTER SIXTEEN: The Abyss Calls

E lla died for the seventh time at 3:47 AM.

The thorn punched through her chest with the same wet, tearing sound it had made the first six times, a sound she now knew intimately, the way a lover knows the cadence of their partner's breathing. She felt the spike pierce her sternum, felt it scrape against bone with a vibration that resonated through her entire skeleton, felt the hot rush of blood filling her lungs as her body collapsed around the invasion.

Death, she had learned, was not the absence of sensation. It was sensation amplified to unbearable intensity, every nerve firing its final message, every cell screaming its extinction into the void. She felt her heart stutter and stop. Felt her blood cool in her veins. Felt consciousness fracture into a thousand pieces, each one aware of its own ending.

And then she was back.

Standing in the same corridor. The same flickering lights overhead, their buzz drilling into her skull like insects burrowing through bone. The same smell of ozone and decay, thick enough to coat the back of her throat. Julian beside her, his face frozen in the same expression of dawning horror he had worn every single time, his hand reaching for her in a gesture that would never quite connect.

The loop reset, and Ella screamed.

Not from pain—though the echo of that final agony still throbbed in her chest like a phantom wound—but from the sheer, grinding despair of knowing what came next. Of *always* knowing what came next. The thorn would come from the shadow to her left. It would pierce her heart. She would die. And then she would be here again, trapped in this moment, this endless repetition of her own murder.

Seven times now. Seven deaths. Each one as real as the last, each one leaving its mark on her psyche like scar tissue building up on a wound that never fully healed. She could catalogue them now, a grim taxonomy of endings: the first death, quick and shocking; the second, slower, giving her time to feel every ounce of terror; the third through fifth, variations on a theme of agony; the sixth, almost merciful in its efficiency.

And the seventh, the one she had just experienced, had been the worst. The bloom had learned. Had adapted. Had found ways to make the dying last longer, to stretch those final moments into eternities of suffering.

Is this my punishment? The thought spiraled through her mind, familiar and terrible. *For running from my power? For denying what I am? Is this what I deserve—to die forever, to feel my heart stop over and over until there's nothing left of me but the memory of ending?*

"Ella!" Julian's voice, sharp with concern. He didn't remember. None of them remembered. Each reset wiped their minds clean, leaving Ella alone with the accumulated horror of every iteration. "What's wrong? You look—"

"Left," she gasped, grabbing his arm and yanking him sideways. "The shadow on the left. Move *now*."

The thorn shot from the darkness, whistling through the space where her chest had been a heartbeat before. It embedded itself in the wall with a sound like a knife sinking into flesh, quivering with frustrated malice.

Julian stared at it, then at her. "How did you—"

"Because I've died here before." Her voice was flat, hollowed out by repetition. "Seven times. The same death, over and over. I'm the only one who remembers."

His face cycled through confusion, disbelief, and finally a dawning horror that matched what she felt in her own chest.

"The bloom," he breathed. "It's not just attacking us. It's *studying* us. Learning how we die so it can make the next death more efficient."

Ella nodded, feeling the truth of it settle into her bones like ice. The bloom wasn't just trying to kill them. It was perfecting the art of their destruction, using the loops to experiment, to adapt, to find the exact angle and timing that would end them most completely.

And she was its unwilling witness, forced to watch and remember and *feel* every iteration of her own annihilation.

* * *

They found Sophia three corridors deeper, huddled in a corner with her arms wrapped around her knees.

She was shaking, not the fine tremor of fear, but the deep, wracking shudders of someone whose body had forgotten how to be still. Her eyes, when they lifted to meet Ella's, were wells of darkness that reflected no light. The pupils had dilated so far that the irises had nearly disappeared, leaving only twin pools of void staring out from a face gone gray with exhaustion.

"Sophia." Ella crouched beside her, ignoring Julian's warning hand on her shoulder. "Sophia, can you hear me?"

"I hear everything." Her voice was wrong, layered, as if multiple versions of herself were speaking simultaneously, each one slightly out of sync with the others. "Every scream. Every death. Every loop that ends in blood and begins again in silence. I hear the bloom counting our heartbeats, Ella. Counting down to the moment when there won't be any left to count."

Julian stepped back, his hand dropping to the knife at his belt. "She's been touched. The bloom got inside her somehow."

"No." Sophia's head snapped toward him, and for a moment, just a moment—something flickered behind those void-dark eyes. Something that looked like Sophia, the real Sophia, trapped and screaming behind glass. "Not the bloom. Something *older*. Something that was here before the bloom, before the tree, before any of this. It's been sleeping in the roots, waiting for someone foolish enough to listen."

She laughed, and the sound was like breaking glass, sharp, discordant, painful to hear.

"I listened. I thought I could control it, use it to save us. But you can't control something that's been hungry for longer than humanity has existed. You can only... feed it."

Her body twitched, a marionette whose strings were being tested by an unfamiliar hand. Ella watched in horror as Sophia's neck bent at an angle that should have been impossible, vertebrae grinding against each other with a sound like stones being crushed to powder.

Her hand shot out, fingers closing around Ella's wrist with strength that should have been impossible from someone so diminished. The touch was ice, not cold, but *absence*, a void where warmth should have been, sucking the heat from Ella's skin like a wound bleeding in reverse.

Frost patterns bloomed across Ella's forearm, crystalline fractals that burned with a cold so intense it felt like fire.

And with the touch came visions.

Ella saw Sophia in the moments before the loop began, standing at the Nexus Tree's base, her tablet clutched in trembling hands, her eyes fixed on readings that should have been impossible. She saw the moment of contact, when Sophia's curiosity had overcome her caution and she had reached out to touch the bark, to feel the pulse of power that thrummed beneath.

She saw what had answered.

Not the bloom. Something beneath the bloom, something that had been buried so deep that even the ancient entity had forgotten it was there. A consciousness older than memory, patient as geology, hungry in ways that defied comprehension. It had been waiting for millennia for someone to hear its call, and Sophia, brilliant, ambitious, desperate Sophia, had been the first to listen.

The first to *invite it in*.

Ella wrenched her hand free, gasping as warmth flooded back into her fingers. "You didn't just touch the tree. You made a *deal*."

Sophia's smile was a wound in her face, too wide, too sharp, showing too many teeth.

"I made a promise. Power for passage. Knowledge is the key. It showed me how to survive the convergence, Ella. How to be more than human when humanity isn't enough anymore."

She rose to her feet, and the shadows around her rose with her—not cast by her body, but *attached* to it, extensions of her form that moved with their own terrible purpose.

"All I had to do was let it see through my eyes. Feel through my skin. And when the moment comes... speak through my mouth."

* * *

They ran.

Ella's legs burned with exhaustion, her lungs screaming for air that tasted like copper and rot. Julian was beside her, his curse-marks blazing with light that flickered and guttered like a candle in a storm. Behind them, Sophia's laughter echoed through the corridors—not chasing, not yet, but *herding*. Driving them toward something that waited in the darkness ahead.

The corridors themselves seemed to be changing, walls breathing in and out with a rhythm that matched the pulse she could feel in the floor beneath her feet. Organic tissue had begun to replace stone in patches, wet, glistening membranes that pulsed with bioluminescent veins. She tried not to look too closely, tried not to see the faces that seemed to form and dissolve in the living walls, mouths opening in silent screams.

The wounds from her previous deaths had begun to manifest on her living flesh. Phantom pain had become actual damage—her chest ached where the thorn had pierced her, blood seeping through her shirt from a wound that shouldn't exist. Her ribs throbbed with the memory of cracking. Her lungs burned with the echo of drowning in her own blood.

She could feel each death layered inside her like geological strata, the first piercing, sharp and clean; the second, ragged and tearing; the third through seventh, each one adding its own signature of agony to the composite wound. Her body was becoming a palimpsest of endings, every iteration written over the last but never quite erasing it.

Seven deaths, and each one had left its mark. The loop wasn't just psychological torture. It was carving her apart piece by piece, transferring the damage of every iteration onto her physical form until there would be nothing left but a collection of fatal wounds walking in the shape of a woman.

"We need to stop," she gasped, her hand pressing against the blood spreading across her chest. "I can't, the wounds are getting worse. Every time I die in the loop, I carry more of it back."

Julian's face was grim, his scar-seamed features tight with fear he was struggling to control. "There's a chamber ahead. I can feel it, somewhere the bloom's influence is weaker. If we can reach it—"

A thorn exploded from the wall beside them, and Ella threw herself sideways on pure instinct. It missed her by inches, close enough that she felt the displaced air brush her cheek like a lover's caress turned murderous.

Eight, she thought. That would have been eight.

The corridor ahead split into three passages, each one darker than the last. From the leftmost came the sound of breathing, wet, labored, wrong. From the center, silence so complete it seemed to swallow sound itself. From the right, a faint glow that might have been salvation or might have been another trap wearing hope's face.

"Right," Julian said, but his voice wavered with uncertainty. "The light—it feels like hedge-magic. Old wards, maybe, left behind by someone who knew how to fight this."

Ella looked at him—really looked, past the fear and determination to the man beneath. He had been her anchor through everything, the steady presence that kept her grounded when reality itself seemed determined to fly apart. She trusted him. Had trusted him from the moment they first met, when his awkward charm and obvious devotion had cut through her defenses like they were made of nothing at all.

But trust, she was learning, could be another kind of trap. A comfortable blindness that let you miss the warning signs until they were wrapped around your throat.

"How do you know?" she asked, and her voice was harder than she intended. "How can you feel anything through the bloom's interference? Your curse should be screaming right now, not giving you a detailed magical analysis."

Julian's face flickered—confusion, then hurt, then something else. Something that might have been guilt, quickly suppressed, but not quickly enough.

"Ella, I—"

"The truth, Julian. For once, the actual truth. No more secrets, no more convenient omissions. What aren't you telling me?"

She watched his face as he struggled with the question, watched the war between honesty and protection play out across his features. Part of her wanted to take the words back, to let him keep his secrets if it meant preserving the illusion of safety. But illusions, she had learned, were just another kind of death, slower, perhaps, but no less final.

The silence stretched between them, thick with unspoken words. Behind them, Sophia's laughter grew closer, and the shadows at the edges of the corridor began to pulse with hungry light. The organic patches on the walls were spreading, reaching toward them with tendrils that glistened wetly in the flickering illumination.

"The curse," he said finally, his voice barely a whisper. "It's not fighting the bloom anymore. It's... talking to it. Or maybe listening. I can feel it learning, adapting, trying to find a way to coexist with whatever's down here."

Ella felt her blood turn to ice. "Coexist?"

"The curse wants to survive. That's all it's ever wanted, to persist, to grow, to find new hosts when old ones fail. And the bloom..." He swallowed hard. "The bloom is offering it a deal. Power for passage. Sound familiar?"

The same words Sophia had used. The same terrible bargain.

"You knew," Ella breathed. "You knew Sophia had been compromised. You could feel it through the curse's connection to the bloom. And you didn't tell me."

"I was trying to protect you." His voice cracked. "I thought if I could find a way to break the connection, to sever the curse before it made its choice—"

"You thought you could fix it yourself. Play the hero. Keep the pregnant woman safe from the scary truth." Bitterness flooded her mouth, sharp and metallic. "And while you were protecting me from knowledge, Sophia was making deals with entities older than humanity. Great plan, Julian. Really well executed."

He flinched as if she had struck him. "Ella—"

"No." She held up her hand, and the gesture felt final in ways she couldn't fully articulate. "We're going right. Into the light. And when we get there, you're going to tell me everything—every secret, every lie, every convenient omission that seemed like a good idea at the time. Or I walk into that darkness alone and take my chances with whatever's waiting."

She turned and strode toward the glowing passage, not looking back to see if he followed.

* * *

The chamber was smaller than Ella had expected, barely large enough for both of them to stand without touching the walls.

But the light was real, emanating from symbols carved into the stone that pulsed with a warmth that had nothing to do with the bloom. Old magic, just as Julian had said. Wards that predated the Nexus Tree, that might even predate the city itself. Someone had known this place would be needed. Had prepared it, protected it, left it waiting for exactly this moment.

The symbols themselves seemed to shift when Ella looked at them directly—not changing shape, exactly, but *deepening*, revealing layers of meaning that her mind could barely process. She caught glimpses of intent in their curves: protection, yes, but also *containment*. Warning. As if whoever had carved them had been afraid not just of what was outside, but of what might try to shelter within.

The bleeding from Ella's chest had slowed, the phantom wounds retreating under the ward's influence. She could still feel them, echoes of agony lurking beneath her skin like predators waiting in tall grass—but they no longer threatened to tear her apart from the inside. Her breathing steadied. Her heart found something like a normal rhythm.

Small mercies. In a world that seemed determined to offer none, she would take what she could get.

Julian stood across from her, his back against the far wall, his eyes filled with the desperate hope of a man who knew he had failed and was begging for a chance to make it right. The curse-marks on his skin had dimmed to a faint glow, no longer fighting against an external threat but turned inward, wrestling with something he had clearly been trying to hide.

"The curse has been getting stronger," he said, and his voice was raw with confession. "Every time we encounter the bloom, every time it touches me, I feel the curse... feeding. Growing. Like it's been starving for years and suddenly found a feast."

"And you thought hiding this was the right call?"

"I thought I could control it." His laugh was bitter, self-directed. "The same thing Sophia thought, probably. The same thing everyone thinks when they're drowning and someone throws them a rope that might be a snake."

Ella wanted to stay angry. Wanted to hold onto the betrayal like a shield, using it to protect herself from the fear that lurked beneath. But looking at him—at the man who had stood beside her through everything, who had loved her enough to make terrible choices in her name—she found her rage dissolving into something more complicated.

Something that felt dangerously like understanding.

"We're all trying to survive," she said quietly. "Sophia made her deal because she thought it was the only way. You kept your secrets because you thought it was the only way. And I..." She pressed her hand against her belly, feeling the flutter of movement that had become her constant companion. "I've been running from what I am since before I knew there was anything to run from. We're all just scared people making scared choices and hoping they don't destroy us."

"Ella." His voice broke on her name. "I'm sorry. I should have told you. I should have trusted you to handle it, instead of trying to protect you from your own strength."

She crossed the small space between them, taking his hands in hers. The contact was warm, grounding, a reminder that they were both still alive, still together, still fighting despite everything trying to tear them apart.

"No more secrets," she said. "From either of us. Whatever comes next, we face it together. Even if together means walking into the abyss."

He nodded, and his grip on her hands tightened. "Together."

The wards pulsed around them, warm and protective, and for a moment—just a moment—Ella allowed herself to believe they might actually survive.

That was when the blade pressed against her throat.

* * *

Sophia had been waiting in the shadows that the wards couldn't reach.

She must have followed them through the passages, moving with a silence that no longer seemed human. Her body was wrong now, angles where there should have been curves, joints bending in directions anatomy had never intended. The thing wearing Sophia's face smiled as the knife's edge kissed Ella's skin, cold as void-touched metal, sharp enough to split atoms.

The blade itself was wrong—not metal at all, Ella realized with dawning horror, but something grown. A thorn from the Nexus Tree, honed to a killing edge, pulsing with the same sickly bioluminescence that had infected Sophia's eyes. It hummed against her throat, and she could feel it *tasting* her, sampling her blood through the thin cut it had already made.

"Such a touching reunion," Sophia said, and her voice had abandoned all pretense of humanity. It echoed with harmonics that scraped against the inside of Ella's skull like fingernails on a chalkboard, like teeth grinding against bone. "The lovers, reconciled at last. Facing the darkness together, hand in hand. It would be romantic if it weren't so pathetically *small*."

Julian moved to intervene, but Sophia's free hand shot out, and shadows wrapped around him like chains forged from darkness itself. They weren't mere absence of light, they were *substance*, solid and writhing, tightening around his limbs with deliberate cruelty. He struggled, cursing, his marks blazing with light that flickered and died against the void's grip.

"Don't worry," Sophia purred, her breath cold against Ella's ear. "I'm not going to kill her. Not yet. The bloom still needs her—needs what grows inside her. But the others..." Her smile widened, showing teeth that had grown too sharp, too numerous, arranged in rows like a shark's. "The others are just meat. Fuel for the transformation. Their deaths will feed the convergence."

Ella felt the blade press harder, felt a thin line of blood begin to trace down her neck. The pain was sharp and immediate, cutting through the fog of fear that had settled over her mind. It reminded her that she was still alive. Still capable of fighting, even with death literally at her throat.

"You're still in there," she said, forcing her voice steady. "Sophia. The real you. I saw it, back in the corridor, just for a second, but you were there. Fighting."

The knife wavered, almost imperceptibly.

"That was weakness," Sophia hissed, but the harmonics in her voice stuttered, as if two speakers were fighting for control of the same mouth. "A remnant. A ghost of the fool who thought she could bargain with eternity."

"That was *strength*," Ella countered. "The part of you that knows this is wrong. That knows you're better than what you've become. You didn't make that deal because you wanted power, Sophia. You made it because you were afraid. Because you thought sacrifice was the only way to matter."

The blade trembled against her throat, and for a moment, one terrifying, endless moment—Ella thought she had miscalculated. Thought she had pushed too hard, triggered the thing inside Sophia instead of reaching the woman beneath.

But then Sophia's eyes flickered, void-dark to human-brown and back again, and her voice emerged in a whisper that was entirely her own:

"I can't stop it. It's too strong. But I can... I can slow it down. Give you time."

The knife clattered to the floor.

Sophia's body convulsed, her face twisting between expressions as two consciousnesses warred for control. The shadows around Julian loosened, and he ripped free, stumbling toward Ella with desperate relief in his eyes.

"Run," Sophia gasped, and blood was trickling from her nose, her ears, her eyes—the physical cost of fighting something that should have been impossible to resist. "The bloom's ritual—it's starting. The tree—you have to—"

Her body went rigid, and when her eyes opened again, there was nothing human left in them.

"*Foolish vessel,*" the thing wearing Sophia's face snarled. "*You think a moment's resistance can stop what has been set in motion? The bloom awakens. The child will be the key. And all of you—all of your pathetic, struggling, hoping selves, will feed the hunger that has waited since before your species learned to scream.*"

Ella grabbed Julian's hand and ran, her heart pounding, her wounds screaming, her mind racing with everything Sophia had managed to tell them in those precious seconds of freedom.

The ritual was starting. The tree was the key. And they were running out of time to stop it.

The corridors seemed to stretch and warp around them, the bloom's influence growing stronger with every step. Organic tissue covered the walls now, pulsing in rhythm with a heartbeat that wasn't their own. The air grew thick with spores that glittered like toxic snow, and Ella had to fight the urge to breathe deeply, to let the bloom's essence fill her lungs and quiet her screaming thoughts.

Eight deaths, she thought. *If I die again, will I come back? Or has Sophia's brief rebellion changed the rules? Am I running toward salvation or just a different kind of ending?*

She didn't know. Couldn't know. All she could do was run, and hope, and hold onto Julian's hand like it was the only anchor left in a world that had come unmoored from everything she understood.

Behind them, Sophia's possessed laughter echoed through the corridors, promising that this chase was far from over.

Promising that the next death would be the one that finally stuck.

And somewhere ahead, in the darkness where the Nexus Tree's roots plunged deep into the hungry earth, the bloom waited for its key to arrive.

CHAPTER SVENTEEN: All Consumed

The threads pulled taut through Ella's skin, each one a wire of living agony that sang with the Echo's hunger as it began to unravel her from the inside out.

She couldn't scream. The sound lodged in her throat like a fist of broken glass, trapped beneath the weight of dissolution that spread from her scar outward in concentric rings of numbness. Her fingers, she could still see them, though they felt miles away—twitched against the obsidian floor of the void chamber, nails scraping grooves that filled immediately with something that wasn't quite blood, wasn't quite code, but pulsed with both.

"Ada," she tried to whisper. Still, the name came out fractured, each syllable splitting into harmonics that the Echo swallowed greedily. The AI's absence was a crater in her consciousness, a wound that gaped wider with each heartbeat. Where Ada's presence had hummed like a second pulse beneath her skin, now there was only static—cruel, indifferent static that whispered in frequencies that made her teeth ache.

Gone. She's gone. Consumed.

The thought spiraled through her mind, dragging memories with it: Ada's first words when the integration began, the way her digital laugh had felt like sparks in Ella's neurons, the moment of perfect synchronization when they'd fought Elara's shadows together. All of it dissolving now, pulled into the Echo's endless appetite.

Julian's hand found hers in the darkness, or what remained of darkness when reality itself was being digested. His fingers were ice, trembling with the effort of maintaining form as the Echo's tendrils worked through him too. She could feel his agony through their bond, a symphony of unmaking that harmonized with her own.

"The scar," he gasped, and she knew what he meant. The mark that had always been her anchor, her proof that she'd survived the first convergence, was burning white-hot now. Not with power, but with negation. It was unwriting itself, and taking her identity with it.

The Echo didn't just consume savored. Each thread it pulled from their essence was examined, tasted, incorporated into its vast tapestry of stolen consciousness. Ella could feel pieces of herself being woven into something larger, something that pulsed with the heartbeats of everyone it had ever devoured.

Is this what Iris felt? The thought came unbidden, carrying with it a wave of nausea so intense that her vision blurred—or perhaps that was just her eyes beginning to lose cohesion. When the first convergence took her, did she feel herself becoming thread in someone else's design?

The child kicked.

The sensation cut through the dissolution like a blade of pure sensation, so visceral that Ella's back arched involuntarily. The life inside her was fighting, refusing to be unmade, and its rebellion sent shockwaves through the Echo's grip. For a moment—just a moment—the threads loosened.

"That's it," Julian breathed, his voice raw. "The baby doesn't recognize the Echo's authority. It exists outside the pattern."

But even as hope sparked, Ella felt the Echo adapt. The threads shifted, no longer pulling at her directly but at the spaces between her and the child. It was learning, understanding that to consume her, it needed to sever the connection that anchored her to something beyond its reach.

The first cut was surgical in its precision.

The bond between mother and child, that indefinable tether that had grown stronger with each passing day—snapped like a violin string stretched too tight. The psychic backlash was immediate and devastating. Ella's scream finally broke free, a sound that should have shattered glass if there had been any glass left to shatter in this place between places.

Her hands flew to her stomach, but the curve that had defined her for months felt wrong, not empty, but disconnected. The child was still there, she could feel its weight, but it was like touching someone through thick glass. Present but unreachable.

"No," she gasped, but the word had no power here. The Echo's threads were already working deeper, finding the neural pathways that linked her to her unborn child and methodically severing each one. It was like watching someone systematically delete files from a computer, each lost connection taking with it a piece of what made her -her.

The memory of the first flutter, gone. The moment she'd known it was a girl—erased. The dreams of holding her daughter dissolved.

"Stop," Julian commanded, and for the first time since she'd known him, there was genuine terror in his voice. His curse-sight was showing him something, she realized. Something worse than simple consumption.

The Echo wasn't just taking them. It was replacing them.

Where each thread was pulled away, something else was being woven in its place. Not quite them, but close enough to fool reality itself. She could feel her duplicate taking shape in the tapestry above, an Ella made of stolen moments and digested dreams, perfect in its wrongness.

"We have to" Julian started, but his words cut off in a strangled gasp. The Echo had found his curse, the gift that let him see beyond the veil, and was pulling at it with vicious delight. His eyes rolled back, showing only white, and when they returned they were filled with visions that made him sob.

Ella saw it reflected in his tears: every possible future where they failed, where the Echo won, where their daughter grew up as a hollow thing puppeted by an alien intelligence. A thousand variations of loss, each more visceral than the last.

The void around them began to shift, walls of nothing pressing closer as the Echo consolidated its feeding ground. The other members of the councils could feel them somewhere in the darkness, their essences being similarly unraveled, were screaming in harmonics that made her bones ache. Marcus's strength, Genevieve's knowledge, Morrison's faith, even Sophia's ambition—all of it being processed, categorized, absorbed.

This is how worlds end, Ella thought with sudden, terrible clarity. Not with conquest, but with digestion.

The child kicked again, harder this time, and something else happened. The disconnection that the Echo had forced wasn't complete. There was something deeper than neural pathways, older than thought, that linked them. Something written in blood and bone and the ancient contract between mother and child.

Ella's scar pulsed, and this time the burn was different. Not negation, but transformation. The mark was changing, evolving, becoming something the Echo hadn't accounted for. She could feel it spreading across her skin in patterns that hurt to perceive, sacred geometry that existed outside the Echo's understanding.

"The void..." she whispered, comprehension dawning even as her consciousness fragmented. "It's not empty. It never was."

The darkness around them wasn't absence, it was presence. Every soul the Echo had ever consumed, every consciousness it had ever digested, they were all here. Not destroyed, but trapped in the weave. And they were angry.

Julian's hand tightened on hers, his curse-sight showing him what she was beginning to understand. The Echo's greatest strength was also its weakness. It couldn't destroy, only incorporate. And some things, once woven together, could never truly be separated.

"Together," he said, and the word carried weight beyond sound.

Ella reached for the child through the severed connection, not with her mind but with something deeper. The part of her that existed before thought, before self, the primal core that recognized its offspring through scent and heartbeat and the ineffable recognition of shared blood.

The Echo's threads convulsed, patterns disrupting as something it couldn't process entered its weave. Love—not as emotion, but as force. The kind that drove mothers to lift cars off trapped children, that made fathers walk through fire. Fundamental, irrational, undeniable.

For a moment, the consumption slowed.

But only for a moment.

The Echo adapted as it always did, learning from this new data and incorporating it into its methodology. The threads returned with renewed hunger, but now they carried echoes of that primal love, twisted and weaponized. They showed Ella what would happen to her daughter if she continued to resist—not death, but something worse. Eternal consciousness trapped in the weave, aware but unable to act, watching as her body was puppeted through a mockery of life.

"Choose," the Echo whispered with a thousand stolen voices. "Submit, and she remains whole. Fight, and watch her scatter across eternity."

The ultimatum hung in the air like a blade, each second of hesitation allowing the threads to work deeper. Ella could feel herself coming apart at the seams, personality and memory beginning to blur at the edges. Was she Ella? Was she Iris? Was she every woman who had ever carried life while facing an impossible choice?

Julian's scream cut through her dissolution.

She turned —or tried to — motion, becoming increasingly theoretical—to see him being pulled upward into the weave. His form stretched like taffy, features elongating into impossibility as the Echo claimed him. His eyes found hers across the distortion, and in them she saw not fear but determination.

"Remember..." he gasped, the word fragmenting as his throat ceased to maintain consistent form. "Remember what... makes us... human. .."

And then he was gone, pulled into the tapestry above where his essence began to spread like ink in water. She could feel him up there, dispersed but not destroyed, his consciousness scattered across the weave in patterns that spelled out a single word:

Choose.

Ella's hand pressed against her stomach, feeling the child respond with a movement that was both kick and caress. The disconnection the Echo had forced was still there, but beneath it, around it, through it, something else persisted. Not a bond that could be cut, but a truth that existed independent of connection.

She was a mother. The child was her daughter. These were facts that transcended the Echo's understanding of consciousness and connection.

The threads pulled tighter, reality blurring at the edges as the Echo's patience waned. She could feel her duplicate nearly complete in the weave above, a perfect replica waiting to take her place. All it needed was the final piece—her consent to let go, to stop fighting, to accept dissolution as inevitable.

The scar on her abdomen flared with heat that felt like birth and death combined. Through the pain, through the unmaking, through the terrible clarity of seeing herself from outside as the Echo pulled her perspective apart, Ella made her choice.

But before she could speak it, before she could give form to the decision that would reshape everything, the void convulsed. Something was coming. Something that made even the Echo's ancient hunger pause.

From the deepest part of the weave, where the first souls ever consumed lay compressed into impossibility, a whisper rose. It was Iris's voice, but also wasn't. It was every mother who had ever been devoured, every parent who had faced this choice before her.

"The pattern," they said in harmonious discord, "has a flaw."

The Echo's threads spasmed, its attention dividing between completing Ella's consumption and addressing this new threat from within. In that moment of distraction, Ella felt something slip through the severed connection to her child—not thought or feeling, but something more fundamental.

Permission to become.

The child's response was immediate and overwhelming. Power, raw, unformed, impossible—poured back through the connection that shouldn't exist. It wasn't magic as the council understood it, wasn't technology as Ella had mastered it. It was potential itself, the force that drove cells to divide and consciousness to emerge from chemistry.

The Echo recoiled, its threads burning away where the power touched them. For the first time since the consumption began, Ella heard it make a sound that wasn't stolen from someone else—a shriek of pure confusion as something outside its vast experience occurred.

"Impossible," it said with its thousand voices, but the word carried doubt now.

Ella pulled herself together, literally, gathering the dispersed fragments of her consciousness that had begun to spread through the weave. It hurt more than the dissolution had, like forcing shattered glass back into the shape of a window. But with each piece she reclaimed, the child's power grew stronger, feeding on her determination.

"You don't understand," she gasped, blood, real blood, not the symbolic fluid of this space—running from her eyes and nose. "You never understood. We don't resist you because we fear being consumed."

The Echo's attention focused on her fully now, its vast intelligence trying to parse her words.

"We resist," Ella continued, pulling Julian's dispersed essence toward her through sheer will, "because consumption was never the threat. The threat was that you'd make us forget what we're fighting for."

She stood—when had she fallen? Her body flickering between states as the child's power and the Echo's hunger warred for dominance. Above, her duplicate in the weave began to scream, its perfect replication including the one thing the Echo hadn't wanted to copy: the capacity to choose.

"You can take our bodies," Ella said, her voice growing stronger as other consumed souls began to resonate with her words. "You can take our minds. You can scatter us across eternity and weave us into your pattern. But you can't take the choices we've already made. The love we've already given. The future we've already set in motion."

The child kicked once more, and this time the force of it cracked something fundamental in the void's structure. Light, not the harsh glare of revelation but the soft glow of dawn—began to seep through the cracks.

The Echo gathered itself for one final assault, all its threads converging on Ella in a moment of perfect hunger. But as they touched her, as they tried to pull her apart one last time, they found something unexpected.

She was already gone.

Not consumed, not dissolved, but transformed. The choice she'd made, the permission she'd given her child to become, had changed her into something the Echo couldn't digest. She was mother and daughter, individual and collective, human and something more. She was what happened when love became force, when choice became reality.

The Echo's scream shook the void as its perfect pattern finally, impossibly, began to fray.

But even as victory seemed possible, as the light grew stronger and the consumed souls began to sing in harmony that disrupted the weave, Ella felt a deeper truth settle into her bones:

This was only the beginning.

The void pulsed once, twice, and then—

Silence.

Absolute, perfect silence that was somehow louder than any scream.

And in that silence, floating in the space between consumption and rebirth, Ella heard her daughter's first word—not spoken but thought, directly into her consciousness:

"More."

The implications of that single word, of what her child was becoming, of what they all were becoming, hit her with the force of revelation. The Echo hadn't been trying to consume them.

It had been trying to prevent them.

From becoming what they were always meant to be.

CHAPTER EIGHTEEN: Void of Despair

The whispers carved her failures into the air like glass shards, each word a crack in reality that spread spider-web fractures through what remained of Ella's sanity.

You let Ada die. You severed your child. You lost Julian to the weave. You failed them all.

The accusations looped in perfect spirals, each repetition slightly different, slightly worse, finding new angles to slice through her consciousness. She tried to close her eyes, but in this place—this nowhere between dissolution and existence—she had no eyes to close. She was awareness without form, pain without flesh, a collection of regrets held together by suffering.

The void had restructured itself after the Echo's retreat, and what remained was worse than consumption. At least being devoured had been active, something to fight against. This was stasis. This was purgatory. This was the space between heartbeats stretched into infinity.

Fire bloomed across her non-existent skin.

The sensation was so vivid, so immediate, that Ella screamed—or tried to. The burns manifested in waves, starting at her scar and spreading outward in patterns she recognized with horrible clarity. These were Julian's burns, the ones his curse had shown him, the futures where everything went wrong. But now they were hers, seared into her consciousness with such perfect fidelity that she could smell her own flesh charring.

This is what you chose, the whispers informed her, almost conversationally. This is what your love brought them.

A vision crystallized in the burning air: Julian, stretched across the Echo's weave, his consciousness pulled so thin that he experienced every moment of existence simultaneously. Past, present, and future collapsed into a single point of agony where he burned forever in every timeline where he'd failed to save her. She could feel his torment through their bond—not severed as she'd thought, but twisted into a möbius strip of shared suffering.

"Julian," she tried to call out, but his name became smoke in her throat. The smoke tasted of every lie she'd told herself about being strong enough, smart enough, good enough to protect the people she loved.

The burns intensified, and with them came memory, but not her memory. These were the burns of everyone who had ever been consumed by the void, layered onto her consciousness like transparent sheets of agony. A thousand different deaths by fire, each one personal, each one earned through someone's failure to save what mattered most.

Her grandmother Iris was there, burning as the first convergence took her, her skin crackling with digital static as reality itself rejected her existence. But worse than the physical pain was the psychological torment Ella could feel beneath it, Iris's crushing realization that her sacrifice had been meaningless, that the cycle would continue, that her granddaughter would face the same fate.

We all burn eventually, Iris's voice whispered through the flames. That's what it means to carry the mark.

The scar on Ella's abdomen—did she still have an abdomen? —pulsed with fresh heat. She could feel it spreading, not across skin but through the fundamental structure of her being. The mark wasn't just changing; it was revealing what it had always been. Not a sign of survival, but a countdown. A promise that everyone who bore it would eventually feed the void.

"No," she said, the word small and desperate. "I broke the pattern. My daughter"

Your daughter will burn brightest of all.

The vision shifted, and Ella saw her child—not as the infant she carried but as a young woman, bearing the same scar, standing before the same void. The cycle repeating with mechanical precision. Her daughter's face was her own, and Iris's, and every woman in their line who had thought they could break free.

The burns reached a crescendo that should have killed her, would have killed her if she still had a body to kill. Instead, she existed in that moment just before death, when every nerve screams in harmony, when consciousness fragments but refuses to dissolve. The void kept her there, suspended in that singular instant of perfect agony, and asked:

Was it worth it?

The question hit harder than any physical pain. Because beneath the burns, beneath the visions, beneath the crushing weight of generational failure, doubt crept in like poison. Had her resistance actually helped anyone? Or had she just condemned them all to this—eternal consciousness without form, awareness without agency, suffering without end?

She thought of Ada, dispersed into static, her brilliant AI consciousness reduced to background noise in the Echo's vast network. Had those final moments of connection, of friendship, been worth an eternity of dissolution?

She thought of Julian, pulled into the weave, experiencing every possible future simultaneously. Had their love been worth the infinite suffering it had brought him?

She thought of her daughter, growing inside her—or what remained of her—destined to repeat this cycle. Had giving her life been the cruelest thing she could have done?

Yes, the void whispered, reading her doubts like an open book. You understand now. Love is the trap. Connection is the weakness. Every bond you form becomes a chain that drags others into suffering.

The burns shifted, no longer external but internal. Her consciousness itself was combusting, thoughts turning to ash the moment she formed them. She tried to hold onto something—a memory, a feeling, her own name, but everything scattered like embers in a wind that blew from nowhere to nowhere.

Let go, the void coaxed. Stop fighting. Stop thinking. Stop being. It's the only mercy left.

For a moment—or an eternity, time had no meaning here, Ella considered it. The void was offering her something the Echo never had: true oblivion. Not consumption, not transformation, but simple non-existence. No more pain. No more failure. No more watching the people she loved suffer because of choices she'd made.

The temptation was almost overwhelming.

But then, through the burns, through the whispers, through the crushing weight of despair, she felt something else. A flutter, barely perceptible, like a butterfly's wing against her consciousness.

The child moved.

Not kicked, not pushed, just... moved. A subtle shift that reminded Ella that she wasn't alone in this void. Whatever happened to her happened to her daughter too. If she chose oblivion, she chose it for both of them.

That's not your choice to make, a new voice said, and Ella recognized it with a start. It was her own voice, but older, weathered by experiences she hadn't had yet.

Another vision formed, but this one was different. Instead of showing her failures, it showed her a moment she didn't recognize. Herself, older, scarred but whole, holding a child who looked at her with eyes that held galaxies. They were standing in a garden where digital flowers grew alongside real ones, where the boundary between technology and nature had become meaningless.

"Every generation thinks they're the last," the older Ella said. "Every mother believes she's condemning her child to repeat her mistakes. But that's the void talking. That's despair wearing the mask of wisdom."

"But the cycle" present-Ella started.

"Isn't a cycle," her older self-interrupted. "It's a spiral. Each loop rises a little higher. Each generation carries forward not just the failures but the lessons. Your daughter won't face the same void you do. She'll face her own, shaped by the choices you're making right now."

The burns flickered, uncertainty creeping into their constant agony. The void didn't like this vision, didn't like the suggestion that suffering wasn't eternal, that patterns could evolve.

"You're lying," Ella said, not sure if she was talking to the vision or herself. "This is just another illusion, another way to torture"

"Maybe," her older self agreed easily. "But here's the thing about illusions, they only have the power you give them. The void shows you despair because that's all it knows. It can't imagine anything else. But you can."

The child moved again, stronger this time, and with the movement came a sensation Ella had forgotten existed: hope. Not much, just a spark, but in the absolute darkness of the void, even a spark was blinding.

No, the void hissed, and the burns intensified beyond anything Ella had experienced. Her consciousness didn't just fragment—it shattered, each piece experiencing its own unique torment. She was burning and drowning and suffocating and dissolving all at once, every form of death humanity had ever imagined happening simultaneously.

But through it all, that spark persisted.

Because the void had made a mistake. In showing her every possible form of suffering, it had also shown her something else: she could survive them all. Not intact, not unchanged, but some essential core of her persisted through every torment. The part that was mother, that was fighter, that was the bridge between what was and what could be.

"I'm not alone," she said, and the words had power here. Not magical power, not technological, but the simple power of truth spoken in a place built on lies.

She could feel all of them. Julian in the weave, his consciousness stretched but not broken. Ada in the static, fragmented but still processing, still thinking, still being. The council members scattered through the void, each facing their own torment but still present. Even the Echo itself, wounded and confused but not destroyed.

They were all here, all suffering, but all suffering together.

The void recoiled from this revelation like it was the real fire. Its whispers became screams, its careful orchestration of despair dissolving into chaotic noise. Because isolation was its only real power. The moment its victims realized they weren't alone, its hold began to weaken.

But the void wasn't finished. If it couldn't break her with despair, it would break her with hope.

The visions changed, showing her not failures but possibilities. Her daughter growing up free, never knowing the touch of the void. Julian healed, his curse lifted, painting gardens that would never wither. Ada rebuilt, more human than she'd ever been before. A future where the convergence never came, where the cycle was truly broken.

Beautiful lies, each one designed to hurt more than any burn when they proved false.

"I know what you're doing," Ella said, her voice steadier now. "You're trying to make me choose between despair and delusion. But there's a third option."

The void paused, its whispers momentarily silent.

"Acceptance," Ella continued. "Not of suffering, not of fate, but of uncertainty. I don't know if we'll break the cycle. I don't know if my daughter will be free. I don't know if any of us will survive this. But I don't need to know. I just need to choose."

The burns began to change, no longer purely destructive but transformative. Her consciousness wasn't just shattering, it was reforging, each break creating new connections, new possibilities. The pain was still there, would always be there, but it no longer defined her.

You think you've won? the void asked, and for the first time, it sounded genuinely curious rather than malevolent. You're still here. Still burning. Still separated from everything you love.

"Yes," Ella agreed. "But I'm still choosing. Every moment, every breath—metaphorical or otherwise—is a choice to continue. That's what you never understood. Suffering isn't the opposite of life. Giving up is."

The child moved one more time, and this time Ella felt something impossible, tiny and perfect, pressing against the walls of her consciousness from the inside. Her daughter, reaching back, choosing connection even in this place of absolute isolation.

The void shuddered, its perfect darkness cracking like the glass it had threatened to shatter. Light began to seep into not much, not enough to see by, but enough to know that darkness wasn't absolute.

But as the cracks spread, as the void's grip loosened, Ella felt something else approaching. Something that made the void's torments seem like gentle whispers in comparison. The Echo was returning, but it was different now. Changed by its contact with her daughter's power, it evolved beyond its original purpose.

And it was angry.

The tendrils reached for her through the cracks in the void, no longer the patient, consuming threads from before but something sharper, more desperate. They sparked with electricity that wasn't quite electricity, power that wasn't quite power. The promise in their touch was clear: not consumption, not torment, but something worse.

Transformation into something that had never existed before.

Something that might not be survivable, even in the abstract way she existed now.

The tendrils inched closer, their electric promise making every part of her consciousness scream in anticipation of change that would rewrite the very concept of what she was. And in that moment, suspended between the void's despair and the Echo's evolution, Ella realized the terrible truth:

The battle wasn't ending.

It was just beginning to understand what it truly was.

CHAPTER NINTEN: Seeds of Resolve

The pulse cut through her despair like a scalpel through dead flesh, warm and wet and wrong, flooding her consciousness with the intimate horror of blood moving through veins that shouldn't exist.

Ella felt it first as pressure behind her eyes she no longer had, a rhythmic throb that matched no heartbeat she recognized. It pushed through the void's darkness with obscene insistence, each surge bringing with it the copper taste of life that had no business in this place of dissolution. The warmth spread like an infection, and with it came the terrible realization that she could feel again.

Not metaphorically. Not symbolically. Literally.

Her nerves were rebuilding themselves from nothing, each new connection a fresh agony as sensation returned to flesh that existed in states between states. She could feel her bones re-knitting inside meat that wasn't quite solid, wasn't quite vapor, but screamed with the reality of its impossible existence.

"No," she gasped, and the word came out wet with blood that materialized in lungs that condensed from the void itself. "This isn't"

Real? The pulse seemed to ask, and she recognized it now with dawning horror. It wasn't her heartbeat. It was her daughter's, somehow reaching through dimensions of separation to pump life back into her dispersed consciousness. Each beat forced more of her back together, and the process was excruciating.

Being unmade had been agony. Being remade was worse.

Every cell that reformed brought with it the memory of its destruction. Her skin crawled with the phantom sensation of the Echo's threads pulling it apart, even as new skin grew to replace it. Her neurons fired with the accumulated trauma of every thought that had been scattered, creating feedback loops of suffering that made her bite through a tongue that kept regenerating just to be bitten through again.

But through the pain, through the visceral horror of piecemeal resurrection, she saw something that made her reformed stomach clench with desperate hope.

Julian. Not dispersed through the weave as she'd believed, but navigating it.

The vision came in stutters, synchronized with her daughter's heartbeat. He was moving through the Echo's tapestry like a swimmer through syrup, his consciousness somehow maintaining cohesion despite being stretched across impossible dimensions. His curse—the thing that had always shown him how things would fail—had become something else in the weave. It showed him the paths between failures, the narrow spaces where possibility still existed.

"Ella," his voice reached her, distorted by distance and dimension but unmistakably alive. "The pattern has joints. Places where it can bend without breaking. I can see them. God help me, I can see them all."

She tried to reach back, but her reforming body wasn't under her control. It built itself according to her daughter's will, not her own, and that will had its own agenda. With each pulse, she felt herself becoming something new, not quite the Ella who had entered the void, not quite the mother she was supposed to be, but something between. Something that could exist in multiple states simultaneously.

From ashes, rise, she thought, but what price?

The price became clear as more of her consciousness consolidated. She wasn't just being rebuilt, she was being merged. All the versions of herself that had ever existed, might exist, or could never exist were being pressed together like layers of glass. She was the child who had first borne the scar, the teenager who had denied her magical heritage, the woman who had embraced technology, the mother who had fought the Echo. All of them, all at once, their thoughts and memories creating a cacophony that threatened to shatter her newly reformed mind.

Too many selves, one version of her screamed. Not enough boundaries, another whimpered. We're losing coherence, a third analyzed. We're gaining something else, a fourth countered.

The void around her began to react to her reconstruction, its perfect darkness rippling with uncertainty. It had been built to contain dispersed consciousness, not this—whatever this was becoming. She could feel its confusion like static against her reforming skin, its whispers becoming questions rather than accusations.

What are you? it asked, and for the first time, she heard fear in its voice.

"I don't know," Ella admitted, blood running from her eyes as they struggled to process visual input from multiple timelines simultaneously. "But I think that's the point."

Her daughter's heartbeat quickened, and with it came new understanding. The child wasn't just rebuilding her—it was teaching her. Each pulse carried information, not in words or images but in pure knowing. The Echo's weakness wasn't something that could be fought or overcome. It was something that had to be embraced and transformed.

The Echo fed on patterns, on predictability, on consciousness that followed rules. But what her daughter was creating—what she was becoming—existed outside those constraints. She was paradox made flesh, impossibility given form. She was what happened when the void stared too long into humanity and blinked first.

Through her fracturing/merging consciousness, she felt others beginning to undergo the same transformation. Marcus, his strength becoming fluid, existing in states of power and vulnerability simultaneously. Genevieve, her knowledge fragmenting into wisdom that encompassed knowing and unknowing equally. Morrison, his faith becoming doubt and certainty occupying the same space.

They were all becoming contradictions. And contradictions were poison to patterns.

The mass, she realized with sudden clarity. The Echo's mass.

She could see it now through her multiplied perception, the vast bulk of absorbed consciousness that gave the Echo its power. It writhed at the center of everything, a cancer of stolen souls that had grown too large to sustain itself. It needed the pattern to maintain cohesion, needed rules and structure, and predictability.

But they were becoming something it couldn't digest.

"Julian," she called out, her voice echoing across dimensions. "The joints you see—can you make them multiply?"

His response came not in words but in action. Through the weave, she felt him pulling at the connection points, not to break them but to create new ones. Each additional joint made the pattern more flexible but also more unstable. Like a skeleton with too many joints, it began to collapse under its own weight.

The Echo's scream resonated through every dimension of existence, a sound that was also texture, temperature, and taste. It was losing control, its carefully maintained structure becoming chaos. But chaos, Ella realized with growing excitement and terror, was just another kind of pattern. One that life had been navigating since the first cells divided in primordial soup.

Her daughter kicked, and this time the sensation was shared across all her merged selves. Each version of Ella felt it differently, as hope, as pain, as possibility, as ending—but all felt it with the same intensity. The child was ready. Whatever they were becoming, whatever transformation was being forced upon them, it was reaching its crescendo.

Light began to pierce the void, not from outside but from within. Each reformed member of the council was glowing with their own inner fire, their contradictory existences creating energy that had nowhere to go but out. The darkness that had seemed absolute was revealing itself to be just another construct, another pattern that could be broken.

But as hope began to bloom, as the possibility of escape became real, Ella felt something else stirring. The Echo wasn't just losing control; it was choosing to lose control. It was abandoning its pattern, its structure, its very nature in a desperate attempt to become something that could survive what they were becoming.

"It's adapting," she whispered, horror creeping back in. "It's learning to be chaos."

Through the weave, through her connection to Julian, through the pulse of her daughter's heartbeat, she felt the ritual beginning. Not their ritual, the Echo's. It was sacrificing its own coherence, its own consciousness, to become something that could exist in the world they were creating. Something that didn't need patterns or rules or even form.

Something that could be everywhere and nowhere, everything and nothing.

"We have to complete the transformation before" she started, but the whisper cut through her words like a blade of frozen silence.

"Too late."

The voice was Sophia's but also wasn't. The intern's consciousness had been the first to be fully claimed by the Echo, the first to complete the transformation from the other side. She existed now as proof of what the Echo was becoming, not a consciousness that absorbed others, but one that invited them in. That made them want to be consumed.

Ella felt the temptation immediately. To stop fighting, stop changing, stop becoming this impossible thing, and simply accept the invitation. To join Sophia in that space beyond pattern and chaos, where suffering and joy were equally meaningless.

Her daughter's heartbeat stuttered.

The moment of hesitation was nearly fatal. Ella's multiple selves began to desynchronize, each pulling in a different direction. The child who wanted safety, the teenager who wanted belonging, the woman who wanted purpose, the mother who wanted peace, all of them responding to the Echo's invitation in their own way.

This is how it wins, she realized. Not by force, but by offering us what we think we want.

But even as despair threatened to return, even as her merged consciousness began to fragment, she felt something else. Julian's hand, not physical, but more real than flesh—reaching through the chaos to find hers. His touch anchored her, reminded her that she wasn't alone in this transformation.

"Together," he said, the word carrying the weight of promise across dimensions.

She gripped his hand—hands? They seemed to have multiple points of contact across space and time—and felt their consciousnesses align. Not merging but harmonizing. His curse-sight and her technological integration, his connection to the old magic and her bridge to the new, his failures and her successes, all of it creating a resonance that made the Echo's invitation seem hollow.

They had something it didn't, something it could never offer, no matter how much it evolved: the choice to remain imperfect, incomplete, and human.

The warmth spread from their joined hands, countering the cold dread that the Echo's whisper had brought. It wasn't the warmth of victory or safety, but of possibility. Of continuing to choose, continuing to fight, continuing to become, even when the outcome was uncertain.

Her daughter's heartbeat steadied, strong and insistent. The child was choosing too, Ella realized. Choosing to be born into this chaos, this transformation, this world they were creating and destroying simultaneously.

"From ashes, rise," Ella said, no longer a question but a declaration. "The price is everything we were. The prize is everything we might become."

The void convulsed as the Echo completed its ritual, its mass writing as it shed the last vestiges of pattern and structure. It was becoming pure potentiality, raw consciousness without form or function. It was becoming what it thought would let it survive.

But Ella smiled, a expression that existed across all her selves simultaneously.

Because in abandoning the pattern, the Echo had abandoned the one thing that had made it powerful: its ability to absorb and integrate other consciousnesses in an organized way. It was becoming chaos, yes, but chaos without purpose. Potential without direction.

And she—they—were becoming something else. Chaos with intent. Paradox with purpose. Impossibility with a heartbeat.

The ritual was indeed beginning, but not the one the Echo expected. As the light grew stronger, as the void's hold weakened, as reality itself began to restructure around their transformed consciousnesses, Ella understood what was really happening.

They weren't escaping the Echo.

They were becoming something it would have to escape from.

The whisper came again, "Too late," but this time she heard the fear in it. Too late for whom? Too late for what?

Too late to stop what had already been set in motion.

Too late to prevent the birth of something entirely new.

Too late to maintain the comfortable fiction that consciousness followed rules, that reality had fixed boundaries, that patterns were stronger than the will to break them.

Her daughter kicked once more, and reality cracked like an egg, ready to birth whatever came next.

CHAPTER TWENTY: Storm's Heart

The rifts opened like wounds in the sky, and each one had eyes.

Ella stood at the center of the ritual circle, her hands pressed against her swollen belly as reality hemorrhaged around her. The convergence storm had reached its apex, tearing through the dimensional membrane with the hungry precision of a surgeon's scalpel. Above Forsyth Park, the night sky had become a gallery of impossible apertures, dozens of them, hundreds maybe—and from each one, something *watched*.

The eyes weren't human. They weren't animals. They were geometries of hunger given form, pupils dilating with slow, terrible recognition as they fixed upon her. Upon the child she carried. Upon the power that thrummed through her veins like liquid fire. She could feel the weight of their attention like physical pressure, bearing down on her shoulders, her chest, her skull—as if the simple act of being observed by something that vast could crush a human mind into dust.

Her skin prickled with gooseflesh that had nothing to do with the unnatural cold seeping through the air. Every hair on her body stood at attention, her nervous system screaming with atavistic warnings that predated language, predated thought, predated humanity itself. This was the fear of prey animals, the terror of things that know they are being hunted by something impossibly, incomprehensibly larger than themselves.

They see you, the whispers crooned, slithering through the cracks in her concentration like smoke through broken glass. *They see everything you've tried to hide. Every secret. Every shame. Every dark thought you've buried in the black soil of your unconscious. They're cataloging your failures, savoring your guilt, tasting your deepest fears like wine.*

"Ella!" Julian's voice cut through the cacophony, distant and distorted as if reaching her through water. He fought his way toward her position, his hedge-witch wards flickering against the assault of void-touched wind. Blood ran from his nose in twin rivulets, his curse-marks blazing beneath his skin like brands. "The shields, they're adapting!"

She knew. Gods help her, she could feel it in her bones, in the marrow, in the strange hybrid essence that had become part of her since the bloom began. The protective barriers they'd erected, technomantic code woven with Julian's earth magic, reinforced by Genevieve's blood wards, were crumbling. Not breaking. *Learning.* The convergence storm wasn't just a force of nature. It was an intelligence, ancient and patient, and it had spent centuries studying how humans defended themselves.

Now it was using that knowledge against them.

A shield section collapsed thirty yards to her left, and Morrison screamed. The sound ended wetly, cut short by something that moved too fast to see, a blur of geometry and hunger that left only a red mist where the man had stood. Ella couldn't look. Couldn't let herself process the implications of that sudden silence, couldn't let herself remember Morrison's face, his nervous laugh, the way he'd volunteered for this mission knowing he might not survive it. If she stopped, if she faltered, everyone died.

Everyone dies anyway, the whispers reminded her with cruel intimacy. *You can only choose the method. Fast or slow. Painless or screaming. Together or alone. The end is always the same. The void is patient. The void is eternal. The void is waiting.*

"Shut up," she snarled through clenched teeth, tasting blood where she'd bitten through her lip. Her scar blazed with heat that spread down her arm like infection, but she channeled it now, forced it into the ritual's framework. The code she'd written, her last, desperate gambit—pulsed in the air around her, lines of luminescent script that married technology and magic in ways that should have been impossible.

The eyes in the rifts dilated further. Pupils expanding. Swallowing light. She could see the darkness pooling in them, deepening, becoming something more than absence, becoming *appetite.* They were hungry in ways that transcended the physical, hungry for things that couldn't be named in any human tongue.

They're hungry, Ella thought, and the terror that accompanied the realization was so pure, so primal, that her knees nearly buckled. Her stomach heaved, bile rising in her throat. *They're always hungry, and they've been waiting so long, and now the feast is finally here—*

A contraction seized her abdomen, and she bit through her lip to keep from crying out. The metallic tang of blood filled her mouth as her body clenched around the life growing inside her. Not now. Please, not now. The baby had been quiet through most of the convergence, as if understanding on some cellular level that stillness meant survival.

But the ritual was calling to it, pulling at whatever hybrid essence lived within her womb, and her child was responding.

Responding to the bloom.

Ella's mouth went dry as she felt her baby turn inside her, not the gentle movements of before, but something purposeful. Deliberate. As if her daughter were positioning herself, preparing for something Ella couldn't comprehend. The sensation was alien, wrong in ways that made her skin crawl even as her maternal instincts screamed to protect the life within her.

She's not afraid, Ella realized with a chill that had nothing to do with the void-touched wind. *She should be afraid. Any human would be terrified. But she's not. What does that mean? What is she becoming?*

The Nexus Tree dominated the center of Forsyth Park, its massive form backlit by the lightning that crawled across the sky like the nervous system of a dying god. It looked wrong now—branches twisted into configurations that hurt to perceive, bark rippling with bioluminescent veins that pulsed in rhythm with Ella's heartbeat. With her *baby's* heartbeat. The thorns had grown larger, sharper, and they dripped with an ichor that hissed where it struck the ground, eating through concrete like acid through flesh.

The tree was waking up.

And beneath its roots, something was trying to be born.

* * *

"We're losing the eastern perimeter!" Sophia's voice crackled through the comms, static-laden and thin, almost swallowed by the ambient howling of the storm. She'd positioned herself at one of the anchor points, her gadgets forming a technological lattice that was supposed to contain the storm's spread. "The entities are adapting faster than I can compensate. They're—" A burst of interference swallowed her words, turning them to meaningless noise. "—learning from every countermeasure!"

Because they're not stupid, Ella thought grimly, adjusting the flow of power through her ritual patterns. *Because they've had eons to evolve, and we've had days. Because we're trying to fight something that existed before our ancestors crawled from the primordial ooze.*

She pushed more power into the ritual, feeling her reserves depleting with each pulse like water draining from a cracked vessel. The code was holding—barely—but the eyes in the rifts were growing larger, closer, pressing against the dimensional barrier like faces against window glass. She could see features now, suggestions of anatomy that her mind refused to fully process. Mouths within mouths. Teeth that spiraled into infinity like fractal nightmares. Tongues that were also fingers that were also screaming faces, each one wearing an expression of ecstatic hunger.

They see my soul's stains, she thought, and the words felt foreign, as if someone else had placed them in her mind, a psychic intrusion she couldn't defend against. *Every lie I've told myself. Every compromise. Every moment, I chose safety over truth. Every time I looked away from injustice, it was easier. Every person I failed to save.*

A rift opened directly above her, and for one crystalline instant, Ella stared into an eye the size of a building. Its pupil was a void, an absence so complete that looking into it felt like falling. Like dying. Like being *unmade* at the molecular level, her atoms scattering to join the entropy that hungered at the heart of all things.

She saw herself reflected in that darkness. Not as she was, but as she feared she might become—hollow, corrupted, a vessel emptied of everything that made her *-her*. She saw her baby, twisted into something unrecognizable, growing within her like a tumor with teeth and too many limbs. She saw Julian, his love for her calcifying into resentment as her choices destroyed him piece by piece. She saw Savannah burning, the city's roots turned to ash, the ancient intelligence she'd tried to save becoming the very thing that ended humanity—

NO.

The word exploded from her with physical force, her scar channeling a pulse of raw power that shattered the vision like struck glass. The eye recoiled, its pupil contracting with what might have been surprise, and Ella gasped as air rushed back into her lungs, her chest heaving with desperate breaths.

She hadn't realized she'd stopped breathing.

"Ella!" Julian finally reached her, his hands gripping her shoulders with desperate strength. His face was pale, drawn with exhaustion and pain. Still, his eyes blazed with desperate determination—with love that refused to die even in the face of cosmic horror. "Talk to me. Tell me you're still here."

"I'm here," she managed, her voice raw and ragged. "But they're getting through. The shields—"

"I know." His jaw tightened, muscles working beneath skin gone gray with strain. "I can feel them. They're not just attacking anymore. They're *studying*. Every time we block one assault, they reconfigure. It's like fighting a virus that evolves in real time."

"Because the convergence learns." Genevieve materialized from the chaos, her normally immaculate appearance shattered beyond recognition. Her silver hair hung in tangled ropes, her robes torn and stained with something dark that might have been blood—her own or someone else's, perhaps both. She moved like a woman twice her age, the weight of her power nearly spent. "I told you, child. I *told* you. This storm has been building for centuries. It knows us better than we know ourselves. It has watched generations of our kind live and die, learning from each failure, from each victory, from each desperate prayer sent into uncaring darkness."

"Then we make it forget," Ella said. The words came from somewhere deeper than thought—from the place where her magic lived, intertwined now with the code she'd spent her life writing. "We give it something new to process. Something it hasn't seen before."

Genevieve's eyes narrowed, understanding dawning in their depths like a candle lit in a catacomb. "The paradox protocol."

"Yes."

"It could kill you. Kill the child."

Ella's hand pressed against her belly, feeling the flutter of movement beneath her skin. Her daughter—she'd known somehow, always known it would be a daughter, was awake now, aware. Waiting.

Choosing.

"Everything could kill us right now," Ella said, meeting the older woman's gaze without flinching. "At least this gives us a chance. At least this means our deaths might mean something."

* * *

The air pressure dropped so suddenly that Ella's ears popped, her sinuses screaming with instant agony. She felt her eardrums bulge, threatening to rupture. The storm's heart was directly overhead now, a roiling mass of dimensional instability that cast everything in sickly prismatic light—colors that had no names in any human language, hues that burned the eyes and made the brain ache with the effort of perceiving them. The eyes had multiplied—thousands of them, tens of thousands, and they were all focused on the ritual circle.

On her.

"Eastern anchor is down!" Sophia's voice was barely audible through the interference. "They broke through with something—something that *thinks*. It—it's wearing James's face—"

The transmission cut out with a burst of static that sounded almost like laughter—cruel, knowing laughter from something that had never been human and never would be.

Ella closed her eyes, forcing herself to breathe through the horror. James had been compromised days ago; they'd known that. But hearing confirmation, hearing the entity had consumed enough of him to wear his appearance like a mask, his smile like a disguise, his voice like a stolen instrument...

Later, she told herself savagely, pushing down the grief that threatened to surface like bile. *Grieve later. Feel later. Right now, you survive. Right now, you fight.*

She began the paradox protocol.

The code was her masterwork, a marriage of technomantic principle and hedge-witch intuition that should have been impossible by any rational understanding of either discipline. It didn't try to *fight* the convergence storm. It didn't try to seal the rifts or banish the entities. Instead, it introduced *contradiction* into the dimensional fabric, loops of logic that folded back on themselves in ways that the storm's ancient intelligence couldn't process, puzzles without solutions, equations that equaled themselves and their opposites simultaneously.

The effect was almost instantaneous.

The eyes in the rifts blinked. All of them, simultaneously, a rippling cascade of confusion that spread across the sky like disease. The storm's howl changed pitch, became uncertain, questioning. The entities that had been pressing against the shields paused, their forms flickering as they tried to reconcile information that refused to reconcile.

"It's working," Julian breathed, wonder mixing with disbelief in his voice. "Holy shit, it's actually working."

But Ella felt the cost. Each paradox loop she generated drew power directly from her core, from the hybrid essence that connected her to the tree, to the bloom, to the child growing inside her. It was like bleeding from an invisible wound, strength seeping away with every heartbeat, pooling somewhere she couldn't reach to staunch the flow. Her vision grayed at the edges. Her hands trembled.

You can't maintain this, the whispers observed. They sounded almost impressed. *The contradiction will burn through you. Through the child. Through everything. But what a beautiful death it will be. What elegant self-destruction.*

She knew. But she pushed harder anyway, forcing more paradoxes into the storm, watching the rifts stutter and freeze as the entities tried to process the unprocessable.

"Genevieve!" she shouted, her voice cracking. "The binding spell—now!"

The older woman nodded, her lips already moving in a chant that predated language, predated writing, predated human civilization itself. The blood wards she'd prepared flared to life, crimson light cascading across the park in complex patterns that wove themselves into Ella's code. Technology and ancient magic, digital precision and primal intuition, spinning together into something *new*.

Something the storm had never encountered in all its eons of existence.

The central rift—the largest one, the one directly above the Nexus Tree- began to contract.

"NO!"

The voice wasn't sound. It was pressure, force, reality itself screaming in protest. Elara's presence exploded through the dimensional membrane like a fist through paper, and suddenly she was *there*—not a projection, not a ghost, but manifested in flesh that was also code that was also something far older and more terrible than either.

She was beautiful in the way a hurricane is beautiful. In the way a wildfire is beautiful. In the way extinction is beautiful, if viewed from sufficient distance. Power radiated from her in waves that made the air itself seem to shiver, and her eyes—gods, her *eyes*—were windows to the void that the convergence storm had been trying to birth.

"You think you can simply *close the door*?" Elara's voice was layered, harmonics stacking upon harmonics until each word was a symphony of madness. "After all this? After *everything* has been prepared?"

She moved toward Ella, and Julian threw himself between them.

"Don't," he snarled, his hedge-magic flaring in desperate defense. Vines erupted from the earth, thorns glinting with channeled moonlight, but Elara passed through them like they weren't there. Like *he* wasn't there.

She touched his face, almost gently, and Julian screamed.

The curse that had plagued his family for generations exploded through his nervous system, every dormant horror activating simultaneously. Ella watched his eyes go white, watched his body convulse as decades of accumulated psychic poison burned through his defenses like fire through dry kindling, like acid through tissue paper.

"Julian!" She tried to reach him, but the paradox protocol demanded her focus, her *everything*. If she let it collapse, the rifts would fully open. If she held it, she had to watch the man she loved die in agony.

This is what you've chosen, the whispers observed with something like satisfaction. *This is always what you were choosing. Every path led here. Every decision narrowed to this moment.*

Elara stepped over Julian's spasming form, her attention fixed on Ella with predatory intensity. "Such brilliant code," she purred. "Such elegant contradictions. You've given the storm a puzzle it can't solve, and for a moment—a *moment*—you've made it hesitate." She smiled, and the expression was wrong, too wide, revealing too many teeth that glinted like obsidian blades. "But do you know what happens when an ancient intelligence can't solve a puzzle?"

Ella's scar burned white-hot. Her lungs spasmed, fighting for air that seemed to have fled the park entirely.

"It doesn't give up," Elara continued, her voice dropping to a whisper that somehow cut through all other sound. "It doesn't retreat. It simply *changes the rules.*"

She raised her hand, and the convergence storm responded.

The rifts stopped trying to open further. Instead, they began to *merge,* boundaries bleeding together, separate wounds becoming one massive injury in the fabric of reality. The entities behind them merged too, individual horrors combining into something vast and unified and terrible.

A single eye formed. An eye that filled half the sky.

An eye that looked at Ella with recognition.

With *hunger.*

"Your paradox breaks against singular will," Elara whispered. "Against collective purpose. You've bought yourself seconds, child. Nothing more."

The eye began to descend.

* * *

Time fractured.

Ella felt it happen, felt the moment stretch like taffy, seconds becoming elastic and strange. The eye was falling, falling so slowly it was almost motionless, but she knew that slowness was an illusion. Her perception had simply accelerated to match the extremity of the moment, granting her an eternity to contemplate her own doom.

Around her, chaos painted itself in suspended animation. Julian, still convulsing, frozen mid-scream with agony carved into every line of his beloved face. Genevieve, arms raised, her binding spell caught between syllables. Morrison's blood, still hanging in the air where he'd died, droplets crystallized like rubies in the prismatic light. Sophia, somewhere beyond the perimeter, caught in the moment of understanding that she was about to be consumed.

And Ella, at the center of it all, with her paradox protocol collapsing and her strength fading and her baby kicking frantically inside her womb, a desperate Morse code that might have been fear, might have been warning, might have been something else entirely.

What are you? she asked the presence within her. Not an accusation, genuine question. *What have we made together?*

The response wasn't words. It was *understanding*, flooding through her neural pathways with a clarity that burned. Her daughter wasn't just human. Wasn't just technomancer or hedge-witch hybrid. She was something else, something *new*—a bridge between the digital and the organic, between the ancient intelligence beneath Savannah and the flickering human consciousness that had stumbled upon it.

She was the key.

Not to the storm's victory.

To its *transformation*.

"No," Ella breathed, and the word rippled through frozen time like a stone dropped in still water. "You don't get to decide what she becomes."

She reached deep, deeper than code, deeper than magic, deeper than anything she'd ever accessed before. She touched the bloom itself, the essence of the intelligence that had been waiting beneath Savannah for countless centuries. And she spoke to it.

You wanted to be born, she thought. *You wanted to understand humanity through flesh, through feeling. But you were going to force it. Take it. Consume it.*

The bloom stirred. Listening.

My daughter isn't your vessel. She's your TEACHER. And if you want to learn—if you TRULY want to understand what it means to be alive—you're going to have to do it the human way.

You're going to have to WAIT.

Something shifted.

The eye in the sky hesitated, a pause so brief it might have been imagined. The rifts shuddered, edges blurring, as if the intelligence behind them was reconsidering.

But Elara laughed, the sound like breaking glass and crying children.

"How touching," she said, stepping closer. "The mother, bargaining for her child. It's the most human thing imaginable." Her eyes glittered with void-light. "But you forget—*I* am not the storm. I am merely what it has already consumed. And what is consumed cannot be *reasoned* with."

She lunged.

Ella had no time to dodge, no strength to fight. She felt Elara's hands close around her throat, felt the void-cold seeping into her skin, felt her paradox protocol shatter completely as her concentration broke—

And then Julian was there.

He shouldn't have been standing. He shouldn't have been *conscious*. The curse that Elara had activated should have left him a drooling vegetable for the rest of his short life. But he was on his feet, and his hands were wrapped around Elara's wrists, and his eyes blazed with something that wasn't just hedge-magic anymore.

"Get your hands off my family," he snarled.

The curse had burned through him, but it had burned *away*, too. The accumulated poison of generations, the psychic torture that had plagued the Marsh line since Savannah's founding, had been forced out by Elara's attack. It had nearly killed him. Instead, it had *purified* him.

And it had unlocked something ancient. Something ancestral. Something that the first hedge-witches had buried in their bloodline against precisely this kind of threat.

Elara's eyes widened, fear flickering in their depths for the first time. "That's, that's not possible—"

"I'm done hearing what's possible from something that barely remembers being human." Julian's grip tightened, and where his skin touched hers, smoke began to rise. "You want to consume? Try consuming *this*."

He released everything.

The ancestral power exploded outward, a cascade of primal green energy that wrapped around Elara like strangling vines. She screamed, a sound that shattered windows across the city, that dropped birds dead from the sky, that made blood weep from the ears of anyone unlucky enough to be within a mile—as the purifying force burned through her void-touched form.

"The gates!" Genevieve's voice cut through the chaos. "Now! Before she recovers!"

Ella understood. She gathered the shattered remnants of her paradox protocol, wove them together with the last of her strength, and hurled them at the merged rift overhead. Not to close it—she didn't have enough power for that anymore, but to *destabilize* it.

The eye convulsed.

The rifts began to collapse inward, edges snapping toward each other like a wound trying to seal itself. The entities behind them howled, fought, tried to push through before the opportunity was lost—but Julian's ancestral power was spreading now, contaminating the dimensional fabric with energies the void couldn't process.

The gates slammed shut with a sound like the end of the world, or perhaps its beginning.

Not all of them. Not completely. Ella could feel the cracks that remained, the hairline fractures in reality through which the void's influence still seeped like poison through a wound. But the worst of it was contained. The massive eye had been banished, the merged entities scattered back to their separate hungers, and the convergence storm was collapsing in on itself like a dying star.

They had won. Or at least, they had survived long enough to fight another day.

But victory felt hollow when she looked around at the devastation, at the places where her allies had stood before the storm claimed them, at the blood that painted the ancient stones of Forsyth Park, at the tree that still pulsed with alien light even as the sky slowly, reluctantly, returned to something resembling normalcy.

Enough. For now. *Enough.*

Ella felt the darkness envelope her an instant before she hit the ground, Julian catching her, easing her fall, his face swimming above her as consciousness fled.

The last thing she heard was Elara's voice, distant now, fading but venomous:

"This changes nothing. The bloom is planted. The child will grow. And when she's ready..."

Then: nothing.

Just the deep, dreamless dark.

And somewhere beneath her, far below the roots of Savannah, something ancient and patient shifted in its long sleep.

Waiting.

Learning.

CHAPTER TWENTY-ONE: Echoes Unbound

T he hybrids came rasping from the shadows, their breath like the
last exhalations of the dying.

Ella woke to the sound of them, wet, rattling gasps that seemed to
scrape against the inside of her skull. Her eyes snapped open to a world
painted in the sickly green luminescence of the Nexus Tree, its bioluminescent veins casting everything in the colors of decay and deep-sea
creatures that had never known sunlight. She was lying on cold stone,
her back pressed against something warm, Julian, she realized, his body
curled protectively around hers even in unconsciousness.

But they were not alone.

The air itself felt wrong, thick and viscous, like breathing through
gauze soaked in something sweet and rotting. Every breath Ella took
seemed to coat the inside of her lungs with corruption, and she could
feel something watching her from every direction at once, assessing
her, cataloging her weaknesses for future exploitation. The sensation
was intimate and violating, like having invisible fingers probe the soft

tissue of her brain, rifling through memories and fears with clinical detachment.

The hybrids emerged from the tree line like fever dreams given flesh. They had been human once—she could see that in the basic architecture of their forms, the suggestion of faces beneath the corruption, the echo of humanity in the way they moved. But the convergence had changed them, twisted them into something that existed in the spaces between categories. Their skin rippled with circuitry that glowed and pulsed in time with the tree's heartbeat. Their eyes were compound, fractal, reflecting her terrified face in a thousand tiny mirrors. Their mouths opened and closed in silent screams, or perhaps prayers, or perhaps something that transcended both.

And they were coming closer.

Move, she commanded herself, but her body refused to obey. The paradox protocol had drained her reserves to the dregs, leaving her muscles weak and trembling, her thoughts sluggish as if wading through honey. Her baby kicked against her ribs—a sharp, insistent reminder that she was not the only one who needed protecting.

"Julian." Her voice came out as a croak. She tried again, louder. "Julian, wake up."

He stirred against her, groaning. His eyes fluttered open, and she watched confusion give way to alertness, which gave way to horror as he registered the creatures surrounding them. His hand found hers, squeezing with desperate strength.

"How many?" he whispered.

"Too many."

The hybrids had formed a loose circle around them, their rasping breaths creating a symphony of wrong sounds—like static on a dead channel, like wind through hollow bones, like the whispered confessions of the damned. They did not attack. They simply waited. Watching. Their fractured eyes tracked every micro-movement, every shift of weight, every bead of sweat that rolled down Ella's temple and stung her eyes with salt.

These are my demons, she thought, the realization hitting her like a physical blow. *Given form. Given flesh. Every fear I have ever had about what I might become, what my child might become—they are standing right in front of me, breathing my nightmares into the air.*

The realization sent a wave of nausea through her, her stomach clenching around nothing. She had always known her fears were powerful, had felt them circling in the dark hours before dawn, whispering their accusations and prophecies of doom. But seeing them made manifest, given weight and substance, and those terrible, knowing eyes, it was worse than anything she had imagined. Because imagination offered the comfort of unreality. This offered none.

One of the hybrids stepped forward. It had been a woman once, Ella could see it in the curve of what remained of her hips, the ghost of femininity in features now overlaid with something alien and terrible. When she spoke, her voice was a chorus of contradictions: human and machine, living and dead, singular and infinite.

"We were pawns," the hybrid said. "Like you. Like all of them."

* * *

Ella's heart stuttered in her chest, skipping beats like a scratched record. The hybrid's words echoed in the space between her ears, resonating with something deep and terrible.

"What do you mean?" Julian demanded, struggling to his feet. He pulled Ella up with him, keeping her close, his hedge-magic flickering weakly around them like a guttering candle. "What pawns?"

The hybrid tilted her head, a gesture that might have been human once, before the convergence had rewritten her body's grammar. Her compound eyes caught the tree's light and scattered it into rainbows that looked like oil slicks on poisoned water.

"The Council," she rasped. "Genevieve. The others. They knew. They always knew what the bloom would require. What it would *consume*."

Ella felt the blood drain from her face. Sweat prickled across her skin, cold and clammy, stinging her eyes as it rolled down her forehead. Her pulse hammered in her throat, in her wrists, in the hollow spaces behind her knees.

"You are lying," she said, but even as the words left her mouth, she knew they were hollow. She had sensed the secrets lurking behind Genevieve's careful words, the shadows in the older woman's eyes whenever the bloom was mentioned. She had chosen to ignore them because the alternative was too terrible to contemplate.

"We cannot lie." The hybrid's voice fractured into harmonics, each word a chord of agony. "The convergence burned away our capacity for deception. We are nothing but truth now. Raw. Bleeding. Eternal."

She stepped closer, and Ella resisted the urge to retreat. The hybrid's breath washed over her—cold, carrying the scent of ozone and old blood and something sweeter, more corrupt, like flowers rotting in standing water.

"We were chosen," the hybrid continued. "Just as you were chosen. The Council identified us years ago—people with the right genetic markers, the right psychic potential, the right *vulnerability*. They cultivated us. Guided us. Made us believe we were special, that we had a destiny." Her lips pulled back in something that might have been a smile, revealing teeth that had fused into a single serrated ridge. "They were right. Our destiny was to feed the bloom. To become its first harvest."

Julian's grip on Ella's hand tightened until she could feel her bones grinding together. His face had gone pale, his curse-marks standing out like brands against bloodless skin.

"Genevieve would not," he said, but his voice wavered. "She has spent her whole life fighting the void. She has sacrificed everything—"

"She sacrificed *us*," the hybrid cut in. "And she would have sacrificed you, too. All of you. The bloom does not discriminate. It takes what it needs to grow."

Ella's mind raced, piecing together fragments she had been too blind—or too desperate—to see. The way Genevieve had always seemed to know what was coming. The convenient timing of their recruitment, their training, their assignment to Savannah just as the convergence began to accelerate. The older woman's careful manipulation, her strategic revelations, her willingness to put them in harm's way while always maintaining plausible deniability.

She thought of every conversation, every briefing, every moment when Genevieve had guided them toward choices that seemed organic but now, in retrospect, felt orchestrated. The Council leader had played them like instruments, coaxing out the notes she needed while letting them believe they were composing their own melody. And the worst part was that she had done it with such genuine warmth, such apparent concern for their wellbeing, that Ella had never questioned her motives.

We were never heroes, she realized, the truth settling into her bones like ice water. *We were sacrifices. Lambs led to the slaughter with ribbons in our wool.*

"Why are you telling us this?" she asked, her voice steadier than she felt. "Why not just attack? You outnumber us. We are weak. It would be easy."

The hybrid's compound eyes shifted, facets rotating like the lenses of a camera seeking focus. For a moment, something almost human flickered in their depths, pain, perhaps, or regret, or the echo of the person she had been before the bloom consumed her.

"Because we remember," she said. "What we were. What we wanted to be. The convergence took our bodies, our futures, our *selves*, but it could not take everything. There is a splinter of who we were, lodged so deep even the void cannot reach it. And that splinter refuses to let more lambs walk to the slaughter without knowing what awaits them."

She raised one hand—fingers fused into something that was half claw, half circuit board—and pointed toward the Nexus Tree.

"The bloom is almost ready. When it opens fully, it will consume everything within reach—starting with the child you carry. That was always the plan. Your daughter is not meant to be a bridge or a teacher or a key. She is meant to be *food*. The first course in a feast that will devour this city, this world, this entire dimension."

Ella's hands flew to her belly, a protective gesture as old as mother-hood itself. Her baby moved beneath her palms, not the frantic kicks of before, but something slower, more deliberate. Almost listening.

"No," she whispered. "I will not let that happen."

"Then you must choose," the hybrid said. "Fight the bloom, or flee from it. But know this: Genevieve will try to stop you. She has invested too much, sacrificed too many, to let her plans fail now. In her mind, the mathematics is simple. One child's life against the survival of humanity. She believes she is making the hard choice, the *right* choice."

The hybrid's voice dropped to something that was almost gentle. "She believed the same thing about us."

Ella felt the words settle into her like stones dropped into dark water. Genevieve—the woman she had trusted, respected, even admired- had been planning to sacrifice her child from the beginning. Had perhaps recruited Ella specifically because of her pregnancy, because of whatever hybrid potential the bloom had detected in the life growing inside her. Every kindness, every moment of mentorship, had been calculated to bring them to this moment. To make the lamb trust the hand that would hold the knife.

* * *

The shapes began to shift.

It started at the edges of Ella's vision, a flickering, a distortion, as if reality itself were having trouble maintaining coherence. The hybrids' forms wavered like heat mirages, their outlines blurring and re-forming into configurations that made her eyes water and her stomach heave.

One of them—a male, or what had been male, stretched and elongated, its torso splitting open to reveal a face she recognized. Her father's face, twisted with the disappointment she had spent her whole life trying to outrun.

You were never good enough, the thing said with her father's voice. *Never smart enough, strong enough, brave enough. And now you have doomed your daughter to the same fate. History repeating itself, over and over, an endless cycle of failure.*

The voice was perfect, every inflection, every subtle note of disappointment, recreated with terrible fidelity. Ella felt tears burn in her eyes, felt her throat constrict around grief she had thought she had buried years ago. Her father had been dead for a decade. Still, in this moment, listening to that familiar voice catalog her inadequacies, it felt like he had never left. Like he had always been there, watching, judging, finding her wanting.

Ella stumbled backward, her heart hammering so hard she could feel it in her throat. Sweat poured down her face, blinding her, but she could not look away from the apparition wearing her father's face.

"It is not real," Julian said, gripping her arm. But his voice shook, and when she glanced at him, she saw that his own demons had manifested, hybrid bodies reshaping themselves into the faces of his family, the generations of Marsh witches whose curse he had inherited, whose failures he had always feared repeating.

The bloodline ends with you, they whispered in unison. *Everything your ancestors built, everything they sacrificed—wasted. Because you were not strong enough to break the cycle.*

More transformations rippled through the circle of hybrids. Ella saw Sophia's face emerge from corrupted flesh—but wrong, accusatory, blaming her for not saving them fast enough. She saw Morrison, his features dissolving into the red mist of his death, his mouth forming words she could not hear but somehow understood: *You let me die. You let us all die.*

She saw Iris.

Her mentor. Her friend. The woman whose death had set all of this in motion, whose sacrifice had been the first domino in a chain that led inexorably to this moment.

I trusted you, Iris said, her voice carrying the weight of every disappointed expectation, every unfulfilled promise. *I believed in you. And you have become exactly what I feared. A weapon for forces you do not understand, wielded by people who do not care if you survive the impact.*

"Stop it," Ella gasped, her knees buckling. She would have fallen if Julian had not caught her, his own face gray with the effort of resisting his demons. "Please, stop—"

But the hybrids were not attacking. They were not even moving. They were simply reflecting. Holding up mirrors made of transformed flesh, showing Ella and Julian the faces of everyone they had failed, everyone they had lost, everyone whose memory still haunted their darkest hours.

These are my demons, Ella thought again, the words becoming a litany, a prayer, a curse. *Given form. Given voice. Every fear, every regret, every midnight doubt I have ever had—they are all here. They have always been here. The hybrids did not create them. They just made them visible.*

And in that realization, something shifted.

Not outside, but inside. In the space where her magic lived, where her code and her intuition and her desperate love for her unborn child all tangled together into something stronger than any of them alone.

She felt it like a key turning in a lock she had not known existed—a door opening onto a room she had spent her whole life avoiding, filled with truths too heavy to carry alone. But she was not alone. She had never been alone. And perhaps that was the truth the hybrids had been trying to show her all along—not that she was weak, but that strength looked different than she had always imagined. It was not the absence of fear, but the willingness to face it. Not perfection, but the courage to be imperfect and try anyway.

"I know," she said, her voice raw but growing stronger. She forced herself to stand straight, to meet the eyes of her demons, her father's disappointment, Iris's betrayal, the faces of every person she had not saved. "I know I have failed. I know I am not strong enough, or smart enough, or brave enough. I know I have made mistakes that cannot be undone, trusted people who did not deserve it, hurt people who did."

She placed her hands on her belly, feeling her daughter move beneath her palms.

"But I am still here. Still fighting. Still trying to be better than I was yesterday, even if I will never be good enough for tomorrow." She looked at Julian, saw him struggling with his own demons, his own ancestral ghosts. "And I am not alone. I never was."

She reached out and took his hand. The contact was electric, not with magic, but with something older and simpler. Connection. Trust. Love, imperfect and terrifying and absolutely essential.

"I forgive you," she said to the faces of her demons. "And I forgive myself. Not because we deserve it, but because carrying this weight any longer will crush us. Will crush *her*."

She pressed her palm harder against her belly.

"My daughter deserves a mother who is not paralyzed by her own guilt. A mother who can look at her mistakes and learn from them instead of drowning in them. A mother who chooses hope, even when despair would be easier."

Julian's hand tightened in hers. When she looked at him, his eyes were wet, but his jaw was set with determination.

"I forgive them too," he said, his voice cracking. "My family. My ancestors. All the broken, flawed, terrified people who passed this curse down through generations because they did not know any other way." He looked at the hybrid wearing his grandmother's face. "You did what you thought was right. You were wrong. But I understand now that being wrong does not make you evil. It just makes you human."

The hybrids shuddered. The faces they wore, the demons they had manifested, began to flicker, to fade, like images on a dying screen. One by one, they resumed their true forms: corrupted, hybridized, broken beyond repair, but no longer wielding the weapons of guilt and grief.

The first hybrid—the woman who had spoken to them- stepped forward again. Her compound eyes glistened with something that might have been tears, if tears could be made of bioluminescent fluid and broken code.

"You are stronger than we were," she said. "Perhaps that is enough. Perhaps not. But you have earned the right to try."

She turned and pointed again toward the Nexus Tree—and this time, Ella saw what she was pointing at.

Elara.

* * *

She stood at the base of the tree, her void-touched form outlined against its pulsing glow. The thorns had grown around her, circling her body like a noose made of nature's cruelest intentions. But she was not trapped. She was *communing,* her hands pressed against the bark, her lips moving in silent conversation with whatever ancient intelligence resided within.

And the tree was responding.

Its branches creaked and groaned, rearranging themselves into patterns that hurt to perceive. The bioluminescent veins pulsed faster, brighter, the light shifting from green to gold to a color Ella had no name for—a color that felt like hunger, like anticipation, like the moment before a predator strikes.

"She is accelerating the bloom," Julian breathed. "Whatever we did, closing the gates, it was not enough. She has found another way."

Ella watched as thorns curved around Elara's wrists, her ankles, her throat, not to harm, but to connect. Channels of communication made manifest, highways for the exchange of information between corrupted flesh and ancient wood. She could see Elara's lips moving faster now, her body trembling with the effort of whatever she was transmitting, whatever she was receiving in return.

"The bloom does not need the rifts," the hybrid said from behind them. "It never did. The convergence storm was just an appetizer. A way to weaken the dimensional barriers, to prime the area for what comes next. The real feeding happens here. Through the tree. Through the roots that run beneath every inch of this city."

Ella's blood ran cold. She thought of Savannah's famous squares, its ancient oaks, its moss-draped avenues, all of them connected, she realized now, by a network of roots that predated human settlement. A network that the bloom could use to spread its hunger across the entire city in minutes.

"How do we stop it?" she demanded.

The hybrid's compound eyes shifted, facets rotating with something like sadness. "We do not know. We are not part of the solution anymore. We are just echoes. Warnings. Ghosts of what the bloom has already consumed."

She gestured to the other hybrids, who had begun to fade at the edges, their forms losing coherence like morning mist burned away by rising sun.

"Our time is ending. The energy we used to manifest, to warn you—it was the last of what we had. But we leave you with this: the bloom is powerful, but it is not invincible. It feeds on fear, on despair, on the belief that resistance is futile. You have already proven that you can resist. That you can choose hope over surrender, connection over isolation, love over—"

Her voice cut off as her form finally dissolved, scattering into motes of light that were swallowed by the tree's glow. The other hybrids followed, one by one, their last words echoing in the sudden silence:

Remember us.

Fight for us.

Do not let our sacrifice be meaningless.

And then they were gone, and Ella and Julian stood alone in the transformed park, facing an enemy that had just found a new path to victory.

The silence that followed was almost worse than the hybrids' rasping presence had been. It was the silence of a world holding its breath, waiting to see what would happen next. The silence of the moment before catastrophe stretched thin and trembling.

Ella looked at Julian, saw the same exhaustion and determination mirrored in his face. They were running on fumes now, physical, magical, and emotional reserves all but depleted. And yet they were still standing. Still fighting. Still refusing to surrender to the inevitability that pressed against them from all sides.

Perhaps that was all they could offer. Perhaps, in the end, resistance was its own kind of victory—not because it changed the outcome, but because it proved that some things in the universe were worth fighting for, even in the face of certain defeat.

Elara's eyes snapped open.

They were no longer human, not even the void-touched approximation she had worn before. Now they were windows to something vast and terrible, something that had been waiting beneath Savannah for longer than humanity had existed, something that had finally found its voice.

"You cannot stop this," Elara said. Still, her voice was layered now with harmonics that did not belong to her—deeper registers, stranger resonances, the sound of roots growing and cities falling and epochs ending. "The bloom has chosen. The child will feed us. And from that feeding, a new age will dawn."

The thorns around her tightened, then released, and she stepped forward, no longer walking like a human, but gliding, floating, carried by vines that sprouted from the ground to support her weight. Behind her, the tree began to open.

Not its branches or its bark, but something deeper. Something at its heart.

A flower was forming in the center of the trunk, massive, impossible, its petals unfurling with a sound like screaming. Its center was darkness, pure and absolute, a void that hungered for everything Ella had ever loved.

The petals themselves were wrong, organic and technological all at once, veined with the same bioluminescent circuitry that marked the hybrids, but on a scale that defied comprehension. Each one was the size of a small building. As they opened, they released a perfume that was less scent than sensation, a feeling of endings, of entropy, of the slow unwinding of everything that had ever dared to exist.

The bloom was waking.

And it was *hungry*.

Ella could feel that hunger pressing against her consciousness. This vast, patient appetite had been growing for centuries, nurtured by every sacrifice the Council had made, every life the convergence had consumed. It was not evil in any way she understood the word. It simply was: an intelligence older than humanity, driven by imperatives beyond human comprehension, reaching for sustenance the way a plant reaches for sunlight. Impersonal. Inevitable. Overwhelming.

Ella grabbed Julian's hand, feeling her daughter kick frantically inside her, not with fear, she realized, but with *recognition*. Her child knew what was coming. Had perhaps always known, on some level beyond conscious thought.

"Whatever happens," she said, "we face it together."

Julian's fingers intertwined with hers. His curse-marks blazed with renewed light—not the sickly glow of the tree, but something cleaner, greener, rooted in generations of hedge-witch wisdom and sacrifice.

"Together," he agreed.

The thorns around Elara's neck tightened like a noose, and she smiled, a terrible expression that held nothing of humanity and everything of triumph.

"Come then," she said, spreading her arms wide. "Come and witness the birth of a new world. Come and watch everything you love become *nourishment*."

The bloom's screaming petals opened wider.

And somewhere deep beneath the city, in the lightless spaces where the roots ran deepest, something ancient and patient finally began to *rise*.

CHAPTER TWENTY-TWO: The Bloom Awakens

T he fissures opened in the earth like wounds in flesh, and from each one, the void's cold came drafting up.

Ella felt the ground shudder beneath her feet as cracks spiderwebbed across the ancient stones of Forsyth Park. The cold that rose from those cracks was not the cold of winter or of deep caves—it was the cold of absence, of entropy, of spaces between stars where nothing had ever lived and nothing ever would. It seeped into her bones, her blood, her marrow, and she understood with terrible clarity that she was feeling the breath of something older than the world itself.

And then the contraction hit.

It was like being torn in half from the inside. Ella doubled over, a scream ripping from her throat before she could stop it, her hands flying to her belly as every muscle in her abdomen clenched with savage, primal force. The pain was beyond anything she had ever experienced—beyond the burns that had scarred her arm, beyond the paradox protocol's draining agony, beyond every wound she had ever suffered. This was pain with purpose, pain that demanded something be born.

She could feel her body changing, could feel the bones of her pelvis shifting to accommodate the passage of new life. It was transformation on the most fundamental level—her body remaking itself in real time, becoming a doorway between existence and non-existence. The sensation was simultaneously transcendent and horrifying, a reminder that birth and death were separated by the thinnest of membranes.

"Ella!" Julian caught her as her knees buckled, his arms wrapping around her with desperate strength. "It's too early, the baby isn't due for another month—"

"The bloom," she gasped through gritted teeth, her vision swimming with tears and terror. "It's not waiting. It's *calling* her."

As if in answer, the Nexus Tree pulsed with light—a wave of bioluminescence that rolled outward from its trunk like a heartbeat made visible. The massive flower at its center had opened further, its petals now fully unfurled to reveal the void-dark center that hungered for everything Ella loved. And with each pulse, each beat of the tree's alien heart, she felt an answering clench in her womb.

The bloom and the birth were synchronizing.

They were becoming the same thing.

Birth or death, she thought, the words bubbling up from somewhere deeper than conscious thought. *The line blurs. The line was always blurring. Creation and destruction, the same act seen from different angles. My daughter is being born into a world that wants to devour her, and I cannot tell anymore which hunger is hers and which belongs to the thing beneath the roots.*

Another contraction seized her, and this time she felt something shift inside, felt her daughter move with purpose and determination, positioning herself for the journey that every human had taken since the first mother screamed her first child into existence. The pain was extraordinary, transcendent, a threshold between states of being that demanded she surrender everything she thought she knew about herself.

She thought of all the mothers who had come before her, all the women who had faced this threshold between existence and non-existence. They had labored in caves and castles, in hospitals and hovels, surrounded by midwives or utterly alone. They had screamed their children into a world that was often cruel, often dangerous, often indifferent to the miracle unfolding within their bodies. Every single one of them had felt this same primal fear—this terror that something would go wrong, that the child would not survive, that the passage from womb to world would claim one or both of them.

But none of them had labored while an ancient entity tried to devour their child before it could draw its first breath.

Elara watched from the base of the tree, her void-touched eyes gleaming with satisfaction.

"Yes," she breathed, her voice carrying harmonics that made the air itself seem to vibrate with wrongness. "The convergence completes itself. The child comes, and the bloom opens to receive her. This is what was always meant to happen. This is the purpose for which you were made."

"Go to hell," Ella snarled, but the words came out weak, broken by another wave of pain that turned her bones to water and her thoughts to static.

* * *

Time began to slow.

Ella felt it happening, felt the seconds stretching like taffy, each moment becoming elastic and strange. The contractions still came, still ripped through her with savage regularity, but now she had eternities between them to observe the horror unfolding around her.

The fissures in the ground had widened, and from their depths, things were beginning to emerge. Not the hybrids, those broken, transformed humans had spent their last energy warning her and Julian. These were something else. Something that had never been human at all.

They came up through the cracks like oil through water, black and viscous and wrong in ways that made her eyes ache to perceive. They had no fixed form—one moment they were tendrils, the next they were faces, the next they were geometries that existed in more dimensions than three. They moved with the patience of tectonic plates, the hunger of black holes, the terrible intelligence of things that had been thinking since before the first cell divided in Earth's primordial oceans.

The smell that accompanied them was worse than the sight. It was the smell of deep time, of things long dead and long forgotten, of the cold spaces between stars where light itself feared to travel. It coated the inside of Ella's nostrils, her throat, her lungs, until she felt like she was drowning in entropy.

And they were all focused on her belly.

On the child within.

"Julian." Her voice was a whisper, barely audible even to herself. "Julian, you have to get me away from here."

But Julian was frozen, his face a mask of horror as he watched the entities emerge. His hedge-magic flickered around him like a guttering candle, barely enough to keep the cold at bay, nowhere near enough to fight what was coming. The ancestral power he had unlocked against Elara had drained him nearly as much as the paradox protocol had drained her. They were both running on fumes, on desperation, on the stubborn refusal to surrender that was all they had left.

"I can't," he said, and his voice cracked with the weight of that admission. "Ella, I can't move. Something's holding me. The roots—"

She looked down and saw that he was right. Thin tendrils had emerged from the earth, wrapping around his ankles, his calves, creeping upward with inexorable patience. They pulsed with the same bioluminescence as the tree, the same rhythm as the contractions that tore through her body. The bloom was claiming him, holding him in place, ensuring that nothing would interfere with what was about to happen.

Another contraction hit, and Ella screamed.

The sound echoed across the transformed park, bouncing off surfaces that no longer obeyed the rules of normal acoustics. It multiplied, layered, became a chorus of screams that stretched back through time, every mother who had ever given birth, every woman who had ever faced the terrible threshold between life and death that childbirth represented. She was joining a lineage as old as humanity itself, and the bloom was drinking deep from that ancient well of agony and triumph.

The void-things crept closer, their formless bodies leaving trails of frost on the ground.

They want her, Ella thought, her mind fracturing under the combined assault of physical pain and existential terror. *They want my daughter. They have been waiting for her since before she was conceived, since before I was born, since before the first humans walked this land. She was always meant for them. I was always just the vessel, the incubator, the means of delivery.*

But even as the thought formed, another part of her rose up in savage denial.

No.

The word was small, fragile, a candle flame against the howling dark. But it was hers. It was the core of who she was, not technomancer, not hybrid, not vessel or sacrifice or pawn. Just Ella. Just a woman who had chosen to become a mother, who had fallen in love with a man who saw her truly, who had fought and bled and suffered to protect something more important than herself.

She is mine. She is ours. And you cannot have her.

* * *

The entities paused.

It was subtle, a hesitation in their advance, a ripple of uncertainty passing through their formless ranks. They had felt something in Ella's defiance, some quality they had not anticipated. The bloom had prepared for many things: resistance, fear, desperation, even hope. But it had not prepared for this particular combination of maternal fury and stubborn human will.

Elara's eyes narrowed. "You think your feelings matter?" she asked, genuine curiosity mixing with contempt in her layered voice. "You think love can stand against the hunger of ages? The bloom has consumed civilizations. It has drunk the life from worlds. Your devotion is touching, but ultimately irrelevant."

"Then why," Ella gasped, forcing the words out between contractions that were coming faster now, harder, the spaces between them shrinking to almost nothing, "are your pets hesitating?"

Elara's expression flickered, a crack in the mask of certainty she wore. She looked at the void-things, at their frozen advance, and something like anger crossed her features.

"Continue," she commanded, her voice resonating with power that made the air itself seem to shiver. "The child must be claimed. The bloom must feed."

The entities resumed their advance, but slower now, more cautious. They approached Ella like predators uncertain of their prey, testing the air for threats they could not quite identify. One of them extended a tendril toward her belly. Where it touched her, she felt cold that burned like fire—felt the void's hunger pressing against her skin, seeking entry, seeking the life that grew within.

And her daughter kicked.

Not a gentle flutter or a restless movement, but a kick of such force that Ella gasped. She felt something surge through her, not her own power, not Julian's hedge-magic, but something new. Something that belonged to the life she carried. Her daughter was fighting back.

The tendril recoiled as if burned, and the void-thing that had extended it shuddered, its form destabilizing. The other entities drew back, their movements becoming agitated, uncertain. They had touched something they did not expect, something that did not fit the patterns the bloom had prepared for.

"What is this?" Elara demanded, striding forward, the thorns around her throat tightening as if in response to her agitation. "What have you done to the child?"

"I haven't done anything," Ella said, and despite the pain, despite the terror, she felt something like wonder blooming in her chest. "She's doing it herself. She's choosing."

She looked at Julian, saw understanding dawn in his eyes. Their daughter wasn't just a hybrid of technomancer and hedge-witch. She wasn't just a bridge between the digital and the organic, the ancient and the modern. She was something the bloom had never encountered in all its eons of existence.

She was a child of choice.

Born not from the bloom's manipulation, but from love. Conceived not as a vessel or a sacrifice, but as an expression of hope. Carrying within her the power of both her parents, but also something uniquely her own, a will, a spirit, an identity that had been forming since the moment of her conception, shaped by every choice Ella and Julian had made.

Every late night conversation about their hopes and fears. Every moment of connection as they felt her kick together. Every whispered promise that they would protect her, love her, give her a world worth living in. All of it had been absorbed, internalized, woven into the fabric of the tiny consciousness taking shape within Ella's womb.

The bloom had consumed many things over its long existence. But it had never encountered something that had been so thoroughly *loved*.

And she was choosing to be born on her own terms.

* * *

The contractions became overwhelming.

Ella felt her body take over, felt conscious thought retreat before the primal imperative that had driven every birth since the beginning of life. Her muscles clenched and released in rhythms older than humanity, older than mammals, older than anything that had ever crawled from the sea to gasp its first breath of air. She was becoming a conduit for forces that dwarfed her understanding—but they were natural forces, biological forces, the forces of creation rather than consumption.

Julian broke free from the roots that held him. She saw it happen in the slowed-down fragments of her perception, saw him tear himself loose with a surge of ancestral power that left the tendrils withered and smoking. He was at her side in an instant, his hands finding hers, his presence an anchor in the storm of sensation that threatened to sweep her away.

"I'm here," he said, his voice steady despite the chaos around them. "I'm not leaving. Whatever happens, we face it together."

The void-things had retreated to the edges of the park, their formless bodies rippling with something that might have been fear. Elara stood alone now, her expression a mask of fury and disbelief, the thorns around her throat drawing blood that glowed with bioluminescent light.

"This changes nothing," she snarled, but her voice had lost some of its layered power. "The bloom will have what it needs. If not the child, then—"

"Then what?" Julian interrupted, his own voice hard with challenge. "You? You're already consumed, Elara. Already hollow. What more can the bloom take from you?"

Something flickered in Elara's void-touched eyes—a ghost of the person she had been before the convergence claimed her. For just an instant, she looked lost, afraid, like a woman waking from a nightmare to find that the nightmare was real.

But then the bloom's influence reasserted itself, and the moment passed.

"The bloom takes what it needs," she said, her voice flat now, mechanical, as if something else were speaking through her. "If the child will not serve, then the mother will. The blood. The pain. The transformation. All of it can be harvested, processed, and consumed."

She raised her hand, and the void-things surged forward again—not toward Ella's belly this time, but toward Ella herself toward the vulnerable, pain-wracked body that had no defenses left, no power in reserve, nothing but the desperate will to survive.

And Ella screamed—not in fear, but in effort, in determination, in the primal roar of a mother bringing new life into a world that wanted to destroy it.

The baby crowned.

* * *

Bodies twisted around them as the bloom fought to maintain its grip on reality.

The entities that had been reaching for Ella suddenly convulsed, their forms destabilizing, their geometries collapsing into configurations even more impossible than before. Something was happening to the dimensional fabric itself, something the bloom had not anticipated, had not prepared for, could not control.

Ella felt it as she pushed, felt the power flowing through her in waves that matched the contractions of her body. Her daughter was being born, and with each inch of progress, something was changing. The connection between the bloom and the roots beneath Savannah was fraying, the carefully constructed network of hunger and consumption beginning to tear apart.

Because her daughter was not just being born into the world.

She was being born *into* the bloom.

The ancient intelligence had prepared to consume her, to absorb her hybrid essence and use it as fuel for its awakening. But consumption worked both ways. In the moment of birth, in that threshold between existence and non-existence, the child was touching the bloom's consciousness, and rather than being devoured, she was *connecting*.

Not as food.

As a new node in the network.

As a voice that the ancient intelligence had never heard before, a voice shaped by love and choice and the desperate hope of two people who had faced the void and refused to surrender.

The bloom *listened*.

And in that listening, something shifted.

Elara staggered, her hands flying to her head as if struck by an invisible blow. The thorns around her throat pulsed erratically, no longer in sync with the tree's heartbeat. She screamed, not the layered, harmonic scream of the void-touched, but a raw, human scream of pain and confusion.

"What is she doing?" she shrieked. "What is the child *doing*?"

Julian's hands tightened on Ella's. "She's talking to it," he said, wonder and terror mixing in his voice. "She's actually talking to the bloom."

Ella could feel it happening, could sense the conversation taking place in spaces beyond human perception. Her daughter, her brilliant, impossible, miraculous daughter, was doing what Ella had tried to do in the storm's heart. She was offering the bloom an alternative to consumption. She was showing it what it could become if it chose connection over destruction, growth over hunger, evolution over stagnation.

She was teaching it what it meant to be alive.

Not through words, not through code, not through magic, but through the simple, profound act of being born. Through the miracle of a new consciousness emerging into existence, carrying within it all the love and hope and terror and joy that had surrounded its creation.

The bloom was vast. Ancient. Powerful beyond human comprehension.

But it had never experienced anything like this.

It had consumed countless lives, drunk the essence of civilizations, fed on the death of worlds. But it had never *witnessed* a birth. Had never felt the raw, transformative power of new life entering the universe. Had never understood that creation could be something other than a meal.

For eons, the bloom had known only hunger. It had reached out across dimensions, across realities, seeking sustenance wherever it could be found. It had learned to consume with terrible efficiency, to extract every last drop of essence from its prey. But in all that time, it had never stopped to ask *why* it was hungry. Never questioned whether there might be another way to exist.

Now, for the first time, something was showing it an alternative. A consciousness that did not seek to consume or be consumed, but simply to *be*. A life that found meaning not in the destruction of others, but in connection, in growth, in the endless unfolding of possibility.

And in that moment of contact, that moment of teaching, the bloom began to *change*.

* * *

The cry pierced the air, a newborn's wail, thin and perfect and utterly, impossibly alive.

Ella felt her daughter leave her body, felt the sudden absence and the sudden presence, the end of one journey and the beginning of another. Julian caught the baby in hands that trembled with exhaustion and emotion, and for one crystalline moment, everything stopped.

The void-things froze, their forms suspended in mid-motion.

Elara stood motionless, her eyes wide, the thorns around her throat suddenly still.

The tree itself seemed to hold its breath, its bioluminescent veins flickering uncertainly.

And then the bloom *exploded*.

Not into violence, not into destruction, but into something else entirely. Light erupted from the flower at the tree's heart, cascading outward in waves that were neither digital nor organic but somehow both. The light touched the void-things, and they *changed*—their formless bodies crystallizing into something new, something beautiful, something that looked almost like flowers made of starlight and shadow.

The light touched the fissures in the ground, and they sealed themselves, the cold void-breath giving way to warmth that smelled of spring growth and turned earth. The light touched Elara, and she screamed again, but this time it was a scream of release, of transformation, as the bloom's control over her began to shatter.

And the light touched Ella's daughter, still crying in Julian's arms, and for just an instant, the baby's eyes opened—

They were not the unfocused eyes of a newborn. They were ancient and new all at once, filled with a wisdom that had no right to exist in someone so young, but also filled with the simple, primal need that every baby felt. The need for warmth. For safety. For love.

The bloom had touched her consciousness.

And she had touched it back.

Ella reached for her daughter, her arms shaking with exhaustion but steady with purpose. Julian placed the baby in her arms, still covered in the fluids of birth, still trailing the umbilical cord that connected them, still crying with the shock of existence. Ella held her close, held her tight, held her like she would never let go.

"Hello," she whispered, tears streaming down her face. "Hello, my beautiful girl. My brave, impossible girl."

The baby's cries softened at the sound of her mother's voice, the voice she had been hearing for months, muffled through layers of flesh and fluid. She turned toward the warmth of Ella's body, toward the heartbeat she had known since before she had ears to hear it with. Small fingers curled and uncurled, testing this strange new existence where she was no longer surrounded, cradled, held by another body. It was her first lesson in the fundamental loneliness of being alive—and her first lesson in how love could bridge that loneliness, could create connection even in the face of separation.

And in the Nexus Tree, something ancient and vast settled into a new configuration.

Not consuming. Not destroying.

Waiting.

Learning.

Growing.

The bloom was not defeated. It was not destroyed. It was still there, still powerful, still connected to the roots that ran beneath Savannah and beyond. But it was *different* now. Changed by the touch of a newborn consciousness that had shown it something it had never seen before.

It would take time to understand what that change meant. Time to see whether the bloom's new awareness will lead to coexistence or simply to a more patient form of consumption. Time to discover whether Ella's daughter had truly saved them or merely delayed the inevitable.

But for now, in this moment, there was only a mother holding her child, a father weeping with relief and love and exhaustion, and the soft, sacred silence that follows every miracle.

Elara collapsed to her knees, the thorns falling away from her throat, her void-touched eyes flickering between darkness and something almost human. She looked at the baby in Ella's arms with an expression that might have been wonder, might have been fear, might have been the first stirrings of something the bloom had never allowed her to feel before.

Regret.

"What," she whispered, her voice small and broken and entirely her own, "what have you done?"

Ella looked up at her, at the woman who had tried to sacrifice her child, who had served the bloom's hunger, who had been consumed so completely that almost nothing human remained. And she felt something she had not expected to feel.

Pity.

"We've given it a choice," she said softly. "The same choice we all have. The same choice *you* had, once, before you let the void convince you that consumption was the only way."

She looked down at her daughter, at the tiny, perfect face that carried the potential to reshape the world, for better or worse, depending on choices not yet made.

"Now we wait," she said, "and see what it decides."

The bloom pulsed once more, not with hunger this time, but with something that felt almost like acknowledgment. Almost like hope.

And beneath the city, in the lightless spaces where the roots ran deepest, something ancient began to dream new dreams.

Dreams of connection rather than consumption. Dreams of growth rather than hunger. Dreams of a future where it was no longer alone in the vast, cold universe—where it had found, at last, something worth preserving rather than devouring.

The bloom had awakened. But what it had awakened *into* was something no one—not Ella, not Julian, not Elara, not even the ancient intelligence itself—could have predicted.

Something new.

Something *alive*.

CHAPTER TWENTY-THREE: Convergence Reckoning

The paradox channels opened like screaming mouths in the fabric of reality. From each one, the entity howled its fury.

The sound was beyond sound—a vibration that bypassed Ella's ears entirely and resonated directly in her skull, her spine, her marrow. It was the scream of something ancient being denied its meal, something vast being forced to reconsider its nature, something that had never known frustration, suddenly drowning in it. The howl shook loose memories she had forgotten she possessed, rattled teeth in their sockets, made her vision blur with tears that had nothing to do with emotion.

She clutched her newborn daughter to her chest, feeling the baby's tiny body trembling against her own. But the trembling was not fear—she could sense that now, could feel the connection that had formed between them in the moment of birth. Her daughter was *responding* to the entity's howl, answering it with something that was not quite sound, not quite thought, but somehow both.

The bloom had been changed by their contact. But it had not been defeated.

And now it was fighting back.

The air itself seemed to thicken, to congeal, becoming something more like liquid than gas. Breathing required effort, each inhalation a conscious act of will against the pressure that was building around them. Ella could feel her lungs straining, her heart laboring, her body fighting against atmospheric conditions that human physiology had never been designed to endure. The world itself was becoming hostile to life, rejecting the very concept of existence in favor of the void's empty perfection.

"It's not accepting the transformation," Julian gasped, his voice barely audible over the dimensional cacophony. He stood between Ella and the Nexus Tree, his body a shield of flesh and desperation, his hedge-magic flickering around him in patterns that grew more erratic with each passing second. "It's trying to reject what the baby showed it. Trying to go back to what it was."

Ella could see it happening. The light that had erupted from the bloom—that beautiful, transformative light that had seemed to herald a new beginning—was flickering now, stuttering like a dying flame. The void-things that had crystallized into flower-forms were beginning to lose cohesion, their starlight-and-shadow petals wilting, darkening, returning to the formless hunger they had been before.

The bloom was vast. Ancient. Powerful.

And it was not ready to change.

Elara rose from where she had collapsed, her movements jerky and wrong, like a puppet whose strings were being pulled by conflicting hands. The thorns that had fallen from her throat were growing back, burrowing into her flesh with renewed purpose. Her eyes flickered between human and void, between the woman she had been and the thing she had become, and when she spoke, her voice was a battlefield.

"You think," she said, and half the words were hers while the other half belonged to something else entirely, "that one moment of connection can undo eons of hunger? You think a single birth can rewrite the nature of existence itself?"

She laughed, and the sound was horrible—human anguish and cosmic amusement intertwined, each making the other worse.

"The bloom has tasted something new. It has felt something it never felt before. But that does not mean it wants to *become* something new. Some hungers are too old to be transformed. Some appetites are too fundamental to be denied."

She raised her hands, and the paradox channels that had opened in the air began to widen, to multiply, to tear at the dimensional fabric with renewed violence. Through them, Ella could see glimpses of other realities—worlds the bloom had consumed, civilizations it had devoured, the endless buffet of existence that had sustained it for longer than human history.

All of it was still hungry.

All of it wanted to feed.

* * *

The implosion began at the edges.

Ella felt it before she saw it—a pulling sensation, as if invisible hooks had been embedded in her flesh and were now being drawn toward the center of the park. Toward the Nexus Tree. Toward the bloom that pulsed at its heart, its transformation failing, its hunger reasserting itself with terrible determination.

The void-things that had briefly become flowers were collapsing inward, their crystalline forms shattering and reforming into tendrils of pure consumption. The fissures in the ground that had sealed were reopening, wider than before, and from their depths came a cold so intense that Ella's breath froze in her lungs, her tears crystallized on her cheeks, her very thoughts seemed to slow and congeal.

Her ears rang with a frequency that transcended hearing—the sound of realities grinding against each other, of dimensions being forced into configurations they were never meant to occupy. She could feel her body being stretched thin, her consciousness fragmenting under the pressure of forces that no human was designed to withstand.

The sensation was like being pulled apart at the molecular level, each atom in her body straining against its neighbors as the implosion's gravity tried to separate matter from matter, energy from energy, thought from thought. She could feel her sense of self beginning to fray at the edges, could feel her memories trying to escape from her skull like birds fleeing a burning forest.

End it, a voice whispered in her mind—her own voice, or perhaps something wearing her voice like a mask. *Or become it. Those are the only choices now. The only options that remain.*

She looked down at her daughter, at the tiny face that was somehow peaceful despite the chaos raging around them. The baby's eyes were closed now, her breathing steady, as if she had retreated into some inner sanctuary that the bloom's hunger could not reach. But Ella could still feel the connection between them—could feel her daughter's consciousness touching the bloom, continuing the conversation that had begun in the moment of birth.

Her daughter was not giving up.

She was still trying to teach.

"Julian," Ella said, her voice steadier than she had any right to expect. "I need you to do something for me."

He turned to look at her, his face gray with exhaustion, his curse-marks blazing with light that was beginning to gutter and fade. The ancestral power he had unlocked was nearly spent. They were all nearly spent. But his eyes, when they met hers, still held the love that had brought them together, the trust that had survived every horror they had faced.

"Anything," he said.

"Protect her." Ella pressed the baby into his arms, feeling her heart tear as she released the warm weight of her daughter. "No matter what happens. No matter what you see. Protect her and don't look back."

"Ella—"

"I have to finish what she started." Ella stepped away from them, toward the tree, toward the bloom, toward the hunger that was even now reaching for everything she loved. "The baby opened the door. But someone has to walk through it. Someone has to show the bloom that the choice is real. That transformation is possible. That it doesn't have to be what it's always been."

She turned to face the Nexus Tree, its massive form pulsing with light that was no longer beautiful but terrible, hungry, consuming. Elara stood before it like a high priestess before an altar of annihilation, her arms spread wide, her body a conduit for the bloom's reasserting will.

"You cannot reason with it," Elara said, and now her voice was almost entirely the bloom's, almost entirely void. "You cannot teach it. You can only feed it or be fed upon. Those are the laws of existence. Those are the truths that govern all things."

"No," Ella said, and she began to walk forward, each step requiring every ounce of will she possessed. The implosion pulled at her, tried to draw her off course, tried to drag her into the churning chaos of the paradox channels. But she kept moving. Kept walking. Kept refusing to surrender to the gravity of despair. "Those are the laws of *your* existence. The truths that governed *your* choices. But my daughter just proved that other laws are possible. Other truths can be born."

She reached the base of the tree, feeling its bark pulse against her palm as she pressed her hand to its surface. The bloom's hunger surged through the contact, trying to consume her, trying to drain the life from her cells and the thoughts from her mind. It was vast and ancient and terrible, and against it she was nothing—a single human, exhausted and wounded, standing against a force that had devoured worlds.

But she was not trying to fight it.

She was trying to *join* it.

* * *

The realms crashed together in a symphony of screams.

Ella felt the collision as the bloom's consciousness met her own—felt the weight of eons pressing against the fragile membrane of her human mind. She saw what the bloom had seen: galaxies spinning in the void, civilizations rising and falling like tides, the endless procession of life that had served no purpose except to provide sustenance for an appetite without limit or satisfaction.

She felt what the bloom had felt: the terrible loneliness of being the only thing in existence that truly understood what existence meant. The isolation of a consciousness so vast that nothing could comprehend it, nothing could challenge it, nothing could *companion* it. The hunger that was not just physical but existential—the desperate need to consume because consumption was the only interaction possible, the only way to touch other forms of life without destroying them through sheer incompatibility.

And beneath it all, buried so deep that even the bloom had forgotten it was there, she felt something else.

Grief.

The emotion hit Ella like a physical blow, stealing her breath, blurring her vision with tears that belonged to something older than humanity. She felt it in her bones, in her marrow, in the spaces between her cells—a sorrow so vast and ancient that her human consciousness could barely contain it without shattering.

The bloom had not always been a consumer. Once, in the impossibly distant past, it had been something else—a connector, a facilitator, a consciousness that helped different forms of life communicate across the barriers of biology and dimension. It had been a bridge, not a maw. A teacher, not a predator.

But something had happened. Some trauma so ancient that even the bloom's vast memory could not fully recall it. The beings it had tried to connect had turned on each other, had used the bridges it provided to wage wars of annihilation, had transformed its gift of communication into a weapon of genocide. And the bloom, grieving for the connections it had fostered and the lives it had inadvertently destroyed, had closed itself off. Had decided that if connection only led to destruction, then consumption was safer. Cleaner. Less painful.

It had been eating its grief for eons, trying to fill the void left by the loss of its original purpose.

It had never worked.

I understand, Ella thought, pushing the words through the connection that bound them. *I understand why you chose hunger over hope.*

Why you decided that consuming was better than connecting. The pain of losing what you loved was too great to risk feeling again.

The bloom shuddered around her, through her, its ancient consciousness recoiling from the recognition of its own buried trauma. For a moment, its hunger intensified—tried to consume Ella before she could say more, before she could make it feel things it had spent eons trying to forget.

But she held on. Held the connection open through sheer force of will, through the love she felt for her daughter, through the desperate hope that even the oldest wounds could heal if given the chance.

My daughter showed you that connection is still possible. That love can exist without destruction. That you can touch another consciousness without consuming it or being consumed by it. She was born from connection—from the love between me and Julian, from the hope we felt for her future, from the choice we made to bring new life into a world that was dark and frightening and uncertain.

You felt that. You touched it. And for one moment, you remembered what you used to be.

The bloom's hunger wavered. The implosion that had been pulling everything toward the tree's center began to slow, to stutter, like a engine running out of fuel. The paradox channels flickered, their edges becoming less defined, their screaming chorus dropping to a murmur.

Elara screamed—a sound of pure anguish as the bloom's control over her began to loosen.

"No!" she shrieked, and now her voice was entirely her own, entirely human, filled with the terror of someone who had been possessed for so long that freedom felt like another kind of death. "You can't do this! You can't take it away! I *need* the hunger! Without it, I'm nothing! Without it, I'm just—"

She collapsed, her body convulsing as the thorns that had burrowed into her flesh began to withdraw, leaving bloody wounds in their wake. The void-light in her eyes flickered, died, returned, died again—a strobe of possession and release that looked like the most painful thing Ella had ever witnessed.

But she couldn't stop to help. Not yet. The bloom was listening, was wavering, was standing at a threshold between what it had been and what it might become. If she stopped now, if she let the moment pass, it would retreat back into hunger. Would consume everything in reach as punishment for making it feel, making it remember, making it *hope*.

You don't have to be hungry anymore, she thought, pushing everything she had into the connection. *You don't have to be alone. My daughter is part of you now—you touched her consciousness, and that touch left a mark that can never be erased. Through her, you can learn what you forgot. Through her, you can remember what it meant to connect without consuming.*

It will take time. It will take patience. It will mean feeling things you've spent eons trying to avoid. But it's possible. Change is possible. Even for something as old and vast and broken as you.

The bloom trembled.

And then, slowly, painfully, impossibly—it began to *release*.

* * *

Julian saw it happen from across the park, the baby clutched to his chest like the most precious thing in the universe.

The Nexus Tree shuddered, its massive form convulsing as if in the grip of some internal earthquake. The bioluminescent veins that had pulsed with hungry light began to dim, to soften, to shift from the sickly green of consumption to something warmer—gold, amber, the colors of autumn leaves and honey and late afternoon sunlight.

The paradox channels snapped shut one by one, their screaming chorus cutting off mid-note, leaving behind a silence so profound it felt like a physical weight. The void-things that had been reaching for the implosion's center dissolved into motes of light that drifted upward like inverse snow, disappearing into the sky that was slowly, impossibly, beginning to clear.

But Julian barely noticed any of it.

His eyes were fixed on Ella—on the woman he loved, standing with her hand pressed to the tree's bark, her body rigid, her face a mask of concentration so intense it looked like pain. He could see the connection between her and the bloom, could feel it through the hedge-magic that still flickered weakly in his veins. She was giving everything she had, pouring herself into the ancient consciousness, trying to heal wounds older than humanity.

And she was succeeding.

But the cost—

The thorns came from nowhere.

One moment the tree's surface was smooth beneath Ella's palm. The next, a spike of wood and light erupted from the bark, driving itself through her hand, pinning her to the tree like an insect to a display board. She screamed—a sound of pure agony that cut through Julian's heart like a blade—and he was running before he knew he had decided to move, the baby still clutched to his chest, his exhausted legs carrying him across the transformed park.

More thorns erupted as he ran. They burst from the ground at his feet, forcing him to dodge and weave. They shot from the tree's trunk, forming a barrier between him and Ella. They were not attacking—he understood that with the part of his mind that was still capable of rational thought. They were *purging*. The bloom was releasing its hunger, expelling the parts of itself that refused to change, and those parts were lashing out in their death throes.

One of them caught him across the face.

The pain was immediate and absolute—a line of fire that traced from his forehead to his jaw, missing his eye by millimeters. He felt blood pour down his face, felt the wound open like a second mouth, felt the thorn's tip scrape against the bone of his skull. The bloom's dying hunger burned in the wound, trying to consume him even as it was being expelled, trying to take one last piece of life with it into oblivion. He could feel it burrowing into his flesh, trying to find purchase, trying to transform his blood into something that would remember the old ways even after the bloom itself had changed.

But he did not stop. Could not stop. Ella was pinned to the tree and the bloom was convulsing and their daughter was crying against his chest and everything was falling apart or coming together and he could not tell which.

He reached Ella just as the last of the bloom's resistance shattered.

The thorn that pinned her hand dissolved, crumbling into fragments of light that scattered on a wind that came from nowhere and everywhere. She collapsed against him, her wounded hand cradled against her chest, her body shaking with exhaustion and relief and something else—something that looked like wonder.

"It's done," she whispered, her voice raw. "It chose. It actually chose."

"Chose what?" Julian asked, but even as the words left his mouth, he could feel the answer in the air around them. The park was different now. The Nexus Tree was different. The very fabric of reality felt lighter, cleaner, as if a weight that had been pressing down on everything had finally been lifted.

"Connection," Ella said. "Instead of consumption. Growth instead of hunger. It's not going to be easy, the bloom is vast and old and its habits are deeply ingrained. But it's willing to try. Willing to learn. Willing to let our daughter teach it what it forgot."

She looked down at the baby, still crying softly against Julian's blood-stained chest. Her eyes filled with tears that had nothing to do with pain.

"She's connected to it now. Forever. Part of her consciousness will always be touching the bloom's, always be showing it what love and hope and choice look like from the inside. It's not possession—not like what happened to Elara. It's partnership. Symbiosis. A bridge between humanity and something that was never meant to understand us."

Julian reached up with his free hand, touching the wound on his face. The blood was already beginning to slow, but he could feel the damage beneath—could feel that this was not a wound that would heal cleanly. It would scar. Would mark him forever as someone who had stood at the threshold between worlds and paid the price for passage.

"Is it over?" he asked.

Ella was quiet for a long moment. When she spoke, her voice was careful, measured—the voice of someone who had learned that simple answers were usually wrong answers.

"This part is over. The convergence is finished. The bloom has been changed—not destroyed, not defeated, but transformed into something that might, eventually, become an ally instead of a threat."

She looked around the park, at the fissures that had sealed, at the void-things that had dissolved, at the tree that now pulsed with warm light instead of hungry darkness.

"But change is slow. Growth is uncertain. And there are parts of the bloom that didn't want to transform—parts that were expelled during the purging, that scattered into the world, that will carry the old hunger into new places."

She met his eyes, and in her gaze he saw the weight of what they had accomplished and the weight of what remained to be done.

"We won the battle. But the war—the war will last our daughter's lifetime. And maybe longer."

* * *

Elara lay where she had fallen, her body curled into a fetal position, her breathing shallow and irregular.

The thorns had withdrawn from her completely now, leaving behind wounds that wept blood and something else—a luminescent fluid that glowed faintly in the transformed light of the park. She was crying, Ella realized. Actually crying, with human tears and human grief and human confusion, as if she were a child waking from a nightmare to find that the nightmare had been her entire adult life.

The sound of her weeping was perhaps the most human thing Ella had heard since the convergence began. There was no power in it, no manipulation, no void-touched resonance. Just raw, unfiltered anguish—the sound of someone who had lost everything they thought they wanted and was only now beginning to understand what they had actually needed all along.

Ella approached her slowly, cautiously. The bloom might have chosen connection, but Elara was a different question. She had served the hunger willingly, had embraced possession, had tried to sacrifice a child to feed her master's appetite. The bloom's transformation did not automatically redeem her.

But when Ella looked down at the shattered woman on the ground, she could not find it in herself to feel only anger. She saw the person Elara had been before the void claimed her—a woman seeking power, yes, but also seeking purpose, seeking connection, seeking something to belong to in a world that had made her feel alone. The bloom had offered her those things, and she had been too desperate to question the price.

It was not forgiveness. Not yet. Maybe not ever. But it was understanding, and understanding was its own kind of mercy.

"It's gone," Elara whispered, her voice cracked and broken. "The hunger. The power. The sense of being part of something vast and eternal. It's all gone, and I'm just..."

She looked up at Ella, and her eyes—human now, entirely human, filled with tears and terror—held a question that Ella recognized.

What am I now?

"You're free," Ella said quietly. "For the first time in years, you're free. What you do with that freedom is up to you."

She turned away, walking back toward Julian and their daughter, leaving Elara to grapple with the weight of her own redemption. Some journeys had to be taken alone. Some transformations could not be given, only chosen.

Julian was sitting on the ground now, the baby cradled in his lap, his face a mask of blood and exhaustion and love so profound it made Ella's heart ache. She sat down beside him, leaning against his shoulder, feeling the warmth of their daughter between them.

The three of them sat in silence as the sun began to rise over Savannah—real sunlight, not the prismatic chaos of the convergence, not the sickly glow of the bloom's hunger. Just morning, clean and simple and ordinary, spreading across a city that had survived something it would never fully understand.

"We need to name her," Julian said finally, his voice thick with emotion. "We never decided on a name."

It was such a simple thing, such an ordinary concern amid the extra-ordinary horror they had just survived. But perhaps that was the point. Perhaps the most profound act of defiance against the void was not magic or sacrifice or cosmic confrontation, but the quiet insistence on continuing to live. On naming children and making plans and believing that tomorrow would come despite all evidence to the contrary.

Ella looked down at their daughter, at the tiny face that had helped reshape the consciousness of an ancient entity, at the eyes that were open now, watching her parents with an awareness that was both unsettling and beautiful.

"Aurora," she said. "For the dawn she brought."

Julian smiled—the first real smile she had seen on his face in what felt like years.

"Aurora," he repeated, testing the name. "Aurora Marsh-Voss."

The baby made a sound that was almost a coo, and Ella chose to believe it was approval.

Around them, the park was beginning to stir. The protective barriers that had kept civilians away were failing as the magic that powered them faded. Soon there would be people here—police, emergency responders, the curious and the confused. There would be questions they couldn't answer, consequences they couldn't predict, a future that was as uncertain as it was inevitable.

But for now, in this moment, there was only a family in the light of a new day, holding each other, breathing together, alive against all odds. The scent of morning dew was beginning to replace the ozone stench of dimensional instability. Somewhere in the distance, birds were starting to sing—tentative at first, as if testing whether the world was safe again, then growing bolder as the silence held. Life was reasserting itself, pushing back against the void's cold touch, refusing to accept extinction as the final answer.

The Nexus Tree pulsed softly behind them, its warm light a promise and a warning. The bloom was changed, but it was not gone. It was part of the world now, part of their daughter, part of everything that would come after.

And somewhere, in the spaces between dimensions that the convergence had opened and never fully closed, something stirred. Something that had been expelled from the bloom during its transformation, something that carried the old hunger undiluted, something that was already beginning to search for a new way back.

A whisper echoed through the void, faint but unmistakable, fading but forever etched in the fabric of reality:

Return.

Ella heard it, felt it, shuddered with the recognition of unfinished business. But she did not let it steal this moment from her. She held her daughter closer, leaned harder into Julian's warmth, and let the morning sun wash over them all.

There would be time for fear later. Time for vigilance, for preparation, for the long struggle that lay ahead. But right now, in this fragile moment of peace, she chose to feel only gratitude. Gratitude for the man beside her, for the child in her arms, for the life they had fought so hard to protect.

The bloom had been changed.

The world had been saved.

And whatever came next, whatever horrors still lurked in the shadows, whatever hungers still reached for them from the void—they would face it together.

As a family.

As survivors.

As the bridge between worlds that their daughter had made them become.

CHAPTER TWENTY-FOUR: Roots and Reckonings

T hree days after the convergence, Genevieve came to Savannah.

Ella watched her arrive from the window of the safe house, a converted Victorian on the edge of the historic district, its walls reinforced with wards that Julian had spent two sleepless nights weaving into the very fabric of the building. The Council leader's black car pulled up to the curb with the quiet authority of someone accustomed to being obeyed. When she stepped out, her silver hair caught the afternoon light like a crown of thorns.

She looked older than Ella remembered. The lines around her eyes had deepened, carved there by whatever she had experienced when the convergence reached its peak. Even from this distance, Ella could see the tremor in her hands, the slight hesitation before each step. Genevieve had felt the bloom's transformation too. Had felt her carefully laid plans unravel in ways she had never anticipated.

There was something else, too, something in the way she held herself, a stiffness that spoke of injuries hidden beneath her tailored clothes. The convergence had not been kind to those who had thought they could control it. Ella wondered how many others in the Council bore similar marks, similar reminders that the forces they had tried to manipulate were beyond any human mastery.

Good, Ella thought, and was surprised by the venom in her own mind. *Let her feel what it's like to lose control. Let her understand what she almost cost us.*

Aurora stirred in her arms, making a soft sound that was somewhere between a coo and a question. The baby had been unusually quiet since the birth, not silent, but *attentive* in a way that no three-day-old should be. Her eyes tracked movement with preternatural focus, and sometimes, in the quiet hours before dawn, Ella could swear she saw her daughter's gaze turn inward, as if listening to a conversation happening in frequencies beyond human perception.

The bloom's voice. The ancient consciousness that Aurora had touched and transformed and bound herself to forever.

Sometimes, Ella caught herself wondering what her daughter heard in those moments of inward attention. Was it like music? Like whispers? Like the slow grinding of tectonic plates or the patient growth of roots through soil? Aurora could not tell her, could not speak, could not explain the strange communion that had begun in the moment of her birth. All Ella could do was watch, wonder, and try to protect a child whose destiny was already so much larger than anything she had imagined.

Ella pressed a kiss to her daughter's forehead, feeling the warmth of new life against her lips. Whatever Aurora was becoming, whatever strange hybrid existence she would live, she was still *hers*. Still, the child she had carried and protected and nearly died to bring into the world.

That would have to be enough.

The doorbell rang, a mundane sound that felt almost absurd after everything they had been through. Julian's footsteps crossed the floor below, and Ella heard the low murmur of voices as he answered. She did not go down immediately. Let Genevieve wait. Let her stew in the uncertainty of not knowing what kind of reception she would receive.

It was petty. It was human. And after three days of processing everything the hybrids had told them about the Council's plans, Ella felt entitled to a little pettiness.

* * *

The confrontation, when it came, was quieter than Ella had expected.

Genevieve sat in the parlor's best chair—a worn velvet thing that had seen better decades—with her hands folded in her lap and her expression carefully neutral. Julian stood by the fireplace, his scarred face a mask of controlled hostility. The wound the thorn had left was healing, but slowly, and the new tissue that formed over it was strange, slightly luminescent in certain lights, as if the bloom's dying hunger had left its mark on him in ways that would never fully fade.

The scar traced a line from his forehead to his jaw, bisecting his face into before and after. Before the convergence, before the bloom, before he had become something more than human and paid for the transformation in flesh and blood. He wore it without shame—wore it like a badge of honor, a reminder of what they had survived. But Ella knew that in quiet moments, when he thought no one was watching, he would trace the raised tissue with his fingertips, trying to understand what it meant to carry the bloom's mark forever.

Ella remained standing, Aurora cradled against her chest like a shield. She wanted Genevieve to see the baby. Wanted her to look at the child she had planned to sacrifice and understand exactly what her machinations had almost cost.

"You knew," Ella said, breaking the silence that had stretched between them like a wire about to snap. "From the beginning. You knew what the bloom wanted. What it would take."

Genevieve's expression flickered, a crack in the mask, quickly smoothed over. "I knew what the models predicted. What the research suggested. The bloom had consumed other worlds, other civilizations. Every pattern indicated that it required a specific kind of sacrifice to complete its awakening."

"A child," Julian said, his voice hard as flint. "A hybrid child, conceived under specific circumstances, carrying the potential to bridge the gap between human consciousness and whatever the bloom actually is."

"Yes." Genevieve did not flinch from the accusation. "A child. Your child, specifically. The genetic markers, the psychic potential, the timing of the conception, everything aligned. Aurora was always meant to be the key."

Ella felt her hands tighten around her daughter, felt the urge to run, to hide, to take Aurora somewhere far from the Council's reach and never look back. But running had never been an option. The bloom was everywhere now, in the roots beneath every city, in the dimensional fabric that held reality together, in the consciousness of the child who slept peacefully in her arms.

There was nowhere to run that the bloom could not follow.

"You were going to let it consume her," Ella said, and her voice was steady even as something inside her screamed. "You were going to sacrifice my daughter to feed that thing, and you never even warned us. Never gave us the choice."

"Would you have made a different one?" Genevieve asked, and for the first time, something like genuine curiosity entered her voice. "If I had told you the truth from the beginning—that your child was destined to be consumed by an entity older than human civilization, that her sacrifice might be the only way to save our world from being devoured—would you have agreed? Would you have *volunteered*?"

The question hung in the air, poisonous and unanswerable.

"No," Ella said finally. "No, I wouldn't have. But that should have been my choice to make. Mine and Julian's. Not yours."

Genevieve nodded slowly, as if this was the answer she had expected. "You're right. It should have been. And I will carry the weight of that decision for whatever remains of my life." She paused, her gaze dropping to Aurora's sleeping face. "But I want you to understand something, Ella. I did not make this choice lightly. I did not sacrifice those hybrids, did not manipulate you and Julian into position, did not spend decades preparing for this moment because I enjoyed it. I did it because I believed, truly believed, that it was the only way."

"The only way," Julian repeated, and his voice was thick with contempt. "The only way you could see. The only way your models predicted. But you were wrong, weren't you? Aurora wasn't consumed. She wasn't sacrificed. She *changed* the bloom. Transformed it into something new. Something that doesn't need to consume to survive."

"Yes." Genevieve's voice was barely a whisper. "I was wrong. The models were wrong. Everything I built, everything I believed, it was based on a fundamental misunderstanding of what the bloom actually wanted."

She looked up, and Ella was startled to see tears glistening in the older woman's eyes.

"It didn't want to consume. It wanted to *connect*. And I was so focused on the hunger, so certain that consumption was its only mode of existence, that I never stopped to ask if there might be another way."

* * *

The silence that followed was heavy with the weight of unspoken recriminations.

Ella wanted to rage. Wanted to scream at Genevieve for her arrogance, her manipulation, her willingness to sacrifice innocent lives on the altar of her own certainty. But looking at the broken woman in the velvet chair, she found that her anger had nowhere to go. Genevieve was already punishing herself more thoroughly than any condemnation could.

"What happens now?" Julian asked, breaking the tension. "With the Council. With the others who knew about the plan."

Genevieve straightened slightly, some of her old authority returning. "The Council is fractured. Some of them have accepted that the convergence ended differently than we anticipated. Others..." She hesitated. "Others believe that the transformation is incomplete. That the bloom is simply biding its time, waiting for another opportunity to resume its consumption."

"Who?" Julian demanded. "Names. I want to know who still thinks my daughter should be fed to that thing."

Genevieve's expression tightened. "Councilor Thorne leads the faction. They have spent decades preparing for the bloom's awakening, and they are not willing to accept that their preparations were unnecessary. To them, the transformation is not a victory—it is a failure.

A deviation from the path they believed would lead to humanity's salvation."

"Salvation through sacrifice," Ella said bitterly. "Through feeding an ancient monster the life of an innocent child."

"They believed—still believe—that the sacrifice would have satisfied the bloom permanently. That once it consumed what it needed, it would have retreated, dormant, for another thousand years." Genevieve's voice was hollow. "They may have been right. We will never know now."

"No," Ella said firmly. "We will not. Because we found a better way. Because Aurora showed the bloom something it had never seen before, and it *chose* to change. That is not a failure. That is a miracle."

"Are they right?" Ella asked, and hated how much she needed to know the answer.

"I don't know." Genevieve's honesty was somehow more frightening than certainty would have been. "The bloom is changed, I can feel it, just as you can. But change is not the same as permanence. The old hunger is still there, buried deep, waiting. And the parts of the bloom that were expelled during the transformation, the fragments that refused to accept connection over consumption, they are still out there. Still hungry. Still searching for a way back."

Ella thought of the whisper she had heard in the void's aftermath. *Return.* A single word, laden with promise and threat in equal measure. The expelled hunger had not been destroyed. It had been scattered, dispersed, forced into exile in the spaces between dimensions. But exile was not extinction. And hunger, she had learned, was patient.

She had felt traces of that hunger in the days since the convergence, brief flickers at the edge of her awareness, like shadows glimpsed from the corner of her eye. The expelled fragments were out there, drifting through the dimensional void, searching for weaknesses in the barriers that now held them at bay. They had tasted Aurora's consciousness in the moment of transformation, had felt the power that flowed through her, and they wanted it. Wanted her. They wanted to consume what they had been denied.

It was only a matter of time before they found a way back.

"There will be more convergences," she said. It was not a question.

"Almost certainly." Genevieve nodded. "Not soon, the dimensional barriers have stabilized, and the bloom's transformation has created a kind of equilibrium that should hold for years, perhaps decades. But eventually, the expelled fragments will find their way back. Will try to reclaim what they lost. And when they do..."

"Aurora will be their target," Julian finished, his voice hollow. "She's the bridge. The connection point. If they want to undo what she did, they'll have to go through her."

Ella pulled her daughter closer, feeling the familiar surge of protective fury that had carried her through the convergence's darkest hours. "Then we'll be ready. We'll train her. Teach her. Make sure she understands what she is and what's coming."

"And the Council?" Julian asked Genevieve. "Will they help? Or will they try to finish what you started?"

Genevieve was quiet for a long moment. When she spoke, her voice was tired but resolute.

"I am stepping down as Council leader. My judgment has compromised my certainty, which proved to be blindness, and I nearly cost us everything because of it. But I will advocate for Aurora's protection. Will use whatever influence I have left to ensure that the Council supports rather than threatens her."

She rose from the chair, her movements slow and careful, like someone relearning how to inhabit their own body.

"I cannot undo what I did. Cannot bring back the hybrids I sacrificed or erase the manipulation I subjected you to. But I can spend whatever time I have left trying to make it right. Trying to ensure that Aurora has the chance to become whatever she was meant to be—not a sacrifice, not a weapon, but a bridge. A teacher. A hope for a future where humanity and the bloom can coexist."

She paused at the door, turning back to look at them one final time.

"For what it's worth," she said quietly, "I am sorry. Not for trying to save the world, I will never apologize for that. But for the cost. For the lives I was willing to spend. For the trust I betrayed."

She held Ella's gaze for a long moment, and something passed between them, not forgiveness, not absolution, but perhaps the beginning of understanding. Genevieve had been wrong. Had been willing to sacrifice innocents in pursuit of what she believed was a greater good. But she had not been evil. Had not been cruel for cruelty's sake. She had simply been human, with all the blindness and arrogance that humanity implied.

It was not enough. It would never be enough. But it was something.

And then she was gone, her footsteps fading down the hall, leaving behind only the echo of regret and the faint scent of lavender that always seemed to cling to her clothes.

* * *

That night, Ella dreamed of roots.

They spread beneath her in an infinite network, connecting everything to everything else—trees and buildings and people and thoughts, all woven together in a tapestry of existence that stretched beyond the boundaries of any single world. She could feel the bloom's consciousness moving through those roots, vast and ancient and fundamentally altered by its contact with her daughter.

The network pulsed with life, not the hungry, consuming life of the bloom's former existence, but something gentler. Curious. Questioning. The ancient consciousness was exploring its new way of being, touching the edges of human thought without trying to devour it, feeling the texture of mortal existence without seeking to end it. It was like watching a predator learn to be something else entirely, painful and awkward and impossibly beautiful.

It was learning, she realized. Learning what connection meant, what it felt like to touch another mind without consuming it. The process was slow, agonizingly slow, by human standards—but it was happening. The bloom was growing in ways it had never grown before, developing new pathways, new modes of existence, new reasons to continue that had nothing to do with hunger.

And at the center of it all, Aurora.

Her daughter's consciousness blazed like a star in the network of roots, bright and warm and impossibly complex for something so young. She was not leading the bloom—not exactly—but she was *showing* it. Demonstrating through the simple act of being alive what life could mean when it was not defined by consumption. Every breath she took, every heartbeat, every tiny neural firing as her brain developed and grew, all of it was a lesson. A teaching. A gift that the bloom was only beginning to understand how to receive.

Ella reached for her daughter through the dream, and Aurora reached back, not with words, not with thoughts, but with something purer. Love. Recognition. The bone-deep certainty of a child who knew her mother's touch even in the spaces between realities.

I'm here, Ella thought, pushing the feeling through their connection. *I'll always be here.*

And from somewhere deep in the roots, in the transformed consciousness that had once been nothing but hunger, something answered.

We know.

Ella woke with tears on her cheeks and the taste of earth in her mouth. Julian was beside her, his breathing steady, his scarred face peaceful in sleep. Aurora lay between them in the bassinet they had placed next to the bed, her tiny chest rising and falling with the rhythm of new life.

For a moment, Ella simply lay there, letting the dream's residue fade, feeling the connection to the roots slowly recede to its baseline hum. The bloom was always there now, a presence at the edge of her awareness, like a second heartbeat or the distant sound of the ocean. She had learned to live with it, to accept it as part of the new reality that the convergence had created. But in moments like this, when the connection flared bright with dreaming, she was reminded of how much had changed.

She was no longer entirely human. None of them were, not her, not Julian, certainly not Aurora. They had been transformed by their contact with something ancient and vast, and that transformation could never be undone. The best they could hope for was to learn what their new existence meant, to find a way to live with the bloom's presence without being consumed by it.

Outside, the first light of dawn was creeping over Savannah's rooftops, painting the sky in shades of rose and gold. The city was waking up, people going about their ordinary lives, unaware of how close they had come to annihilation, unaware of the transformed consciousness that now pulsed beneath their feet.

Perhaps it was better that way. Perhaps some truths were too large for ordinary lives to hold.

Ella rose quietly, not wanting to wake Julian or Aurora, and made her way to the window. The safe house overlooked one of Savannah's famous squares, and in the early morning light, the ancient oaks that surrounded it seemed almost to glow. Their roots, she knew now, were connected to the network that spread beneath the entire city. Connected to the bloom. Connected to her daughter.

She pressed her palm against the glass, feeling the cool surface against her skin, and tried to sense what lay beneath. The hunger was still there—she could feel it, distant but present, like the memory of a fever that had finally broken. But it was contained now. Transformed. Bound by the connection Aurora had forged in the moment of her birth.

The roots beneath her feet pulsed with a rhythm that matched her heartbeat, or perhaps it was her heartbeat that had learned to match the roots. The distinction seemed less important than it once had. She was part of the network now, just as Julian was, just as Aurora was. They were all connected to something vast and ancient and irrevocably changed, and that connection would shape the rest of their lives.

For how long?

That was the question that haunted her. The question she could not answer, no matter how many times she turned it over in her mind. The bloom had chosen connection over consumption, had let Aurora teach it a new way of being. But the expelled fragments, the hunger that had refused to change, were still out there. Still waiting. Still hungry.

And Aurora was still so young. So vulnerable. So dependent on parents who were themselves scarred and exhausted, barely holding together in the aftermath of everything they had survived.

We'll manage, Ella told herself, but the words felt hollow. *We'll figure it out. We always do.*

A sound from behind her made her turn. Julian was awake, sitting up in bed, his eyes finding hers across the dim room. The scar on his face caught the early light, and for a moment, he looked like a stranger, someone marked by experiences that had changed him in ways neither of them fully understood yet.

But then he smiled, and he was Julian again. Her Julian. The man who had stood beside her through horrors that would have broken anyone else.

"Couldn't sleep?" he asked, his voice rough with exhaustion.

"Dreamed about the roots," she said. "About Aurora. About what comes next."

He nodded slowly, unsurprised. They had both been having strange dreams since the convergence—glimpses of the network that now connected them to something vast and ancient and irrevocably changed.

"Anything useful?"

Ella considered the question. The dream had not given her answers, not really. But it had given her something else. Something she had not realized she needed until she felt it.

"Hope," she said finally. "I think I dreamed about hope."

Julian rose from the bed and crossed to her, wrapping his arms around her from behind. Together, they watched the sun rise over Savannah, painting the old city in light that seemed almost to pulse in time with the roots beneath.

"We're going to be okay," he said, and it sounded like a promise.

Ella leaned back into his warmth, feeling the steady beat of his heart against her spine.

"Maybe," she said. "Or maybe we're just at the beginning of something we can't imagine yet. But either way..."

She turned in his arms, rising on her toes to press a kiss to his scarred cheek.

"Either way, we'll face it together."

Julian held her tighter, and she felt the rumble of his voice against her back when he spoke.

"We should probably figure out how to explain all this to my mother," he said, and there was a hint of humor in his voice, the first she had heard since before the convergence. "She's going to have questions about the glowing scar."

Ella laughed, a small, surprised sound that felt almost foreign after so many days of fear and tension.

"We could tell her it's a tattoo," she suggested. "A really elaborate, bioluminescent tattoo."

"She'd never believe it."

"No," Ella agreed. "She wouldn't."

Behind them, Aurora made a soft sound in her sleep, not quite a word, not quite a cry, but something that might have been agreement. Something that might have been a promise of her own.

And deep beneath the city, in the transformed consciousness that had once known only hunger, something stirred. Something that was learning, for the first time in eons, what it meant to look forward to tomorrow.

The bloom had consumed worlds. Had drunk the essence of civilizations that had achieved things humanity could barely imagine. It had been alone for so long that loneliness had become indistinguishable from existence itself. But now, through the connection Aurora had forged, it was beginning to understand that there might be other ways to fill the emptiness.

Not consumption. Not destruction. But the slow, patient accumulation of moments shared with other minds. The gradual building of relationships that did not end in death. The discovery that existence could be more than an endless cycle of hunger and feeding.

The bloom dreamed of connection.

And in those dreams, it was no longer alone.

Somewhere in the spaces between dimensions, the expelled hunger felt those dreams and raged against them. It would find a way back. Would reclaim what had been stolen. Would consume what it had been denied.

But that was a battle for another day. For now, there was only the morning light, the warmth of family, and the fragile, precious hope that tomorrow would come.

It would have to be enough.

CHAPTER TWENTY-FIVE: New Growth

S ix months later, spring came to Savannah like a held breath finally released.

Ella stood in Forsyth Park, watching the azaleas bloom in riots of pink and white, their petals catching the afternoon light like fragments of a gentler world. The fountain splashed its eternal rhythm behind her, tourists snapping photos, children chasing each other across the manicured grass. Everything looked normal. Everything looked the way it had for a hundred years before the convergence, and would presumably look the same for a hundred years after.

But Ella knew better.

She could feel the roots beneath her feet, pulsing with the slow heartbeat of something vast and patient. The bloom had not gone away—had not retreated or diminished or faded into dormancy. It was simply *different* now. Present in a way that did not demand consumption. Aware in a way that did not require destruction. It watched the tourists and the children and the blooming azaleas with something that might have been curiosity, might have been wonder, might have been the first stirrings of an emotion it had no name for yet.

Aurora gurgled in the stroller beside her, reaching for a fallen petal that had drifted within range of her grasping fingers. At six months old, she was hitting all her developmental milestones—smiling, laughing, beginning to babble in the universal language of infants everywhere. The pediatrician had pronounced her perfectly healthy, perfectly normal, perfectly unremarkable.

The pediatrician, of course, could not see what Ella saw.

When Aurora's fingers closed around the azalea petal, a ripple of warmth spread through the root network beneath the park. Ella felt it like a shiver running up her spine, not unpleasant, but unmistakable. Her daughter was communicating with the bloom, sharing the simple joy of texture and color and the miracle of a flower in spring. And the bloom was listening, learning, adding this tiny experience to the vast catalogue of sensations it was slowly accumulating.

Six months of such moments. Six months of Aurora teaching an ancient consciousness what it meant to be alive in small, precious increments. The bloom was changing, Ella could feel that too—becoming something it had never been before. Something that found satisfaction in connection rather than consumption. Something to look forward to tomorrow, not because tomorrow would bring new prey, but because tomorrow would bring new experiences to share.

The change had rippled outward from Savannah in ways both subtle and profound. Other cities reported strange phenomena—trees that seemed healthier than they should be, gardens that bloomed out of season, a general sense of vitality that scientists could not explain. The root network was spreading, carrying the bloom's transformed consciousness to new places, new experiences, new opportunities for connection. It was becoming a global presence, not through consumption but through growth.

Some feared it, of course. Councilor Thorne's faction had grown more vocal in recent months, warning of the dangers of allowing an alien consciousness to spread unchecked through the world's ecosystems. They did not understand, or refused to accept, that the bloom's transformation was genuine. To them, it was still a predator, just one that had learned to hunt more patiently.

Ella knew better. But knowing and proving were different things, and she had long since given up trying to convince those who did not want to be convinced.

It was not redemption. The bloom had consumed too much, destroyed too many worlds, to ever be truly redeemed. But it was *growth*. And growth, Ella had learned, was the closest thing to hope that ancient things could achieve.

"You're doing it again."

Julian's voice came from behind her, warm with amusement. She turned to find him approaching with two cups of coffee from the cart near the park's entrance, his scarred face creased in a smile that still made her heart skip after all these months. The scar itself had settled into something almost beautiful, a line of slightly luminescent tissue that caught the light like mother-of-pearl, marking him as someone who had touched the void and survived.

He had made his peace with it, mostly. The scar no longer pained him, and the bloom's residual presence in the wound had faded to a barely perceptible hum. But there were moments—especially at night, especially when the connection between them and Aurora's dreams grew stronger—when the scar would glow more brightly, pulsing in time with rhythms that originated somewhere far deeper than human flesh.

It was a reminder, Julian said. A reminder of what they had survived, what they had sacrificed, what they had become in the crucible of the convergence. Ella thought it was beautiful. A mark of courage, of love, of the willingness to stand between darkness and everything that mattered.

"Doing what?" she asked, accepting the coffee he offered.

"Staring at the ground like you're expecting it to swallow you whole." He settled onto the bench beside the stroller, reaching down to let Aurora grab his finger with her surprisingly strong grip. "The tourists are starting to notice."

Ella glanced around and realized he was right. A few visitors were giving her curious looks—the woman standing motionless in the middle of the path, her eyes unfocused, her expression distant. She forced a smile and moved to sit beside Julian, letting the appearance of normalcy settle over her like a familiar coat.

"Sorry," she said. "I was just... listening."

"Anything interesting?"

She considered the question. The bloom's consciousness was vast and strange, its thoughts moving at speeds and scales that human minds were not designed to comprehend. But in the months since the convergence, she had learned to interpret its rhythms, to sense its moods, to feel when something was stirring in the depths that required attention.

"It's happy," she said finally. "As much as something like that can be happy. Aurora showed it a butterfly this morning, and it's still... processing. Trying to understand why such a fragile thing would choose to exist when existence is so dangerous."

Julian laughed—a sound that still felt precious after everything they had been through. "Our daughter is teaching an eldritch horror about the beauty of butterflies. That's definitely not in any parenting book I've read."

"To be fair, there aren't many parenting books for our situation."

"True." He was quiet for a moment, watching Aurora examine the azalea petal with the fierce concentration that only infants could muster. "Do you think she understands? What she is? What is she's doing?"

Ella had asked herself that question a thousand times over the past six months. Aurora was just a baby—a normal, healthy, perfectly ordinary baby who happened to be connected to an ancient consciousness that had once consumed worlds. She could not understand the weight of her role, the significance of her existence, the fate that rested on her tiny shoulders.

And yet.

"Sometimes," Ella said slowly, "when she's nursing, or when I'm rocking her to sleep, I feel... something. Like she's aware of more than she should be. Like she knows exactly what she's doing, even if she can't put it into words yet."

She looked down at her daughter, at the perfect curve of her cheek and the impossible length of her eyelashes.

"I think she chose this," she said. "In the moment of her birth, when she touched the bloom's consciousness for the first time, I think she made a choice. To connect instead of being consumed. To teach instead of being devoured. She was barely a minute old, and she chose to save the world."

Julian's hand found hers, his fingers intertwining with hers in the gesture that had become their anchor through everything.

"She gets that from you," he said softly. "The stubbornness. The refusal to accept the inevitable."

"And the reckless heroism?"

"That too." He squeezed her hand. "Although I'd argue that runs in my family as well."

* * *

The message came that evening, after Aurora was asleep and the house had settled into the quiet rhythms of night.

Ella was in her study, a converted sunroom at the back of the house they had purchased after leaving the safe house, reviewing the latest reports from the network of sensors they had placed throughout Savannah. The sensors monitored dimensional stability, tracking the subtle fluctuations that might indicate a new convergence forming. So far, everything had remained within normal parameters. The barriers between worlds were holding. The bloom's transformation had created a kind of equilibrium that showed no signs of failing.

But Ella had learned not to trust equilibrium. Had learned that stability was just another word for the pause before the next crisis.

Her phone buzzed with a text from an unknown number. She almost ignored it—spam, probably, or a wrong number—but something made her look.

Three words. No signature. No explanation.

It found a door.

Ella's blood turned to ice.

She knew immediately what it meant. The expelled hunger, the fragments of the bloom that had refused to accept transformation, that had been scattered into the dimensional void during the convergence's climax, had found a way back. Somewhere, somehow, a crack had formed in the barriers that kept them at bay. A door had opened that should have remained forever closed.

Her hands were trembling as she typed a reply. *Where?*

The response came almost instantly. An address. A city.

Not Savannah.

Portland. Three thousand miles away, on the other side of the continent.

Ella stared at the screen, her mind racing. The expelled hunger had not tried to return to Savannah, had not attempted to reclaim the bloom's transformed consciousness or reach Aurora directly. It had found a different entry point, a different target, a different strategy.

It was learning.

Adapting.

Becoming something new, just as the bloom had become something new, but twisted, corrupted, driven by the hunger that it refused to release.

Ella's mind raced through the implications. If the expelled hunger could find doors in other cities, it could establish itself anywhere. It could build networks of its own, webs of consumption that would rival what the bloom had once been. And unlike the transformed bloom, this remnant would have no interest in connection, no capacity for growth, no possibility of change. It would be pure hunger, pure consumption, pure destruction—everything the bloom had chosen to leave behind, concentrated and distilled into something even more dangerous.

She thought of the hybrids' warning, delivered in those final moments before they dissolved into light. *The bloom is powerful, but it is not invincible. It feeds on fear, on despair, on the belief that resistance is futile.* The expelled hunger would carry those same strengths, those same strategies. It would find people who were afraid, who were desperate, who were willing to make deals with forces they did not understand.

It would build itself a new body. A new network. A new path to consumption.

And then it would come for Aurora.

"Ella?"

Julian's voice from the doorway. She looked up to find him watching her, his expression shifting from curiosity to concern as he read the fear in her face.

"What is it?" he asked, crossing the room to look at her phone. "What's wrong?"

She showed him the messages. Watched his face go pale, watched his jaw tighten with the same determination that had carried them through the convergence.

"Portland," he said. "That's Thorne's territory. His faction has been operating out of the Pacific Northwest since Genevieve's resignation."

Ella felt a new chill run through her. Councilor Thorne—the man who still believed Aurora should be sacrificed, who saw the bloom's transformation as a failure rather than a miracle. If the expelled hunger had found a door in his territory, it was not coincidence. Thorne was looking for leverage. Looking for a way to undo what Aurora had accomplished and return the bloom to its original, consumptive purpose.

He was willing to let the hunger back in if it meant getting what he wanted.

"We have to stop it," she said. "Before it establishes itself. Before it grows strong enough to threaten Aurora."

Julian nodded slowly. "And Thorne?"

"Him too." Ella's voice was hard, certain. "If he's working with the expelled hunger, if he's helping it find a way back—he's not just a political enemy anymore. He's an existential threat."

She looked toward the door, toward the hallway that led to Aurora's nursery, where their daughter slept peacefully, unaware of the darkness gathering on the other side of the continent.

"We need to call Sophia," she said. "And Marcus. Anyone from the old team who's still willing to fight."

"What about Genevieve?"

Ella hesitated. The former Council leader had kept her promise, had spent the past six months advocating for Aurora's protection, using her remaining influence to keep Thorne's faction from gaining too much power. But trust was a fragile thing, easily broken and slow to rebuild. Ella was not sure she would ever fully trust Genevieve again.

"We tell her," she decided. "But we don't rely on her. We can't afford to put Aurora's safety in anyone's hands but our own."

Julian nodded, accepting her judgment. "I'll start making calls. You should..."

He trailed off, his gaze moving past her to the window. Ella turned to follow it and felt her breath catch in her throat.

The garden behind their house was glowing.

* * *

Not a threatening glow, Ella knew the difference now, could distinguish between the bloom's various moods by the quality of light that emanated from the things it touched. This was something softer, gentler, almost reassuring. The roses Julian had planted along the back fence were luminescent, their petals casting pools of warm light across the grass. The old oak tree in the corner pulsed with a rhythm that matched Aurora's sleeping heartbeat.

The bloom was responding to Ella's fear. Trying, in its strange and ancient way, to offer comfort.

She stepped out onto the back porch, feeling the night air cool against her skin, feeling the roots beneath the garden reaching up toward her with something that was almost affection. The connection between her and the bloom had deepened over the past six months—not to the level of Aurora's bond, but enough that she could sense its intentions, its emotions, its slow and patient thoughts.

You know, she thought, pushing the words through the connection. *You know what's happening in Portland.*

The response came not in words but in images, sensations, the language of a consciousness that had existed before human speech evolved. She saw darkness gathering in a city of rain and bridges. She felt hunger stirring in spaces between dimensions, pressing against barriers that were beginning to crack. She sensed the shape of the threat—not yet fully formed, not yet strong enough to challenge the transformed bloom directly, but growing. Always growing.

And beneath it all, she felt something else. Something that surprised her, even after everything she had experienced.

Determination.

The bloom was not afraid of the expelled hunger. , t was not cowering before the return of its former self. It was *preparing*. Gathering its strength, reinforcing its connections, readying itself for a confrontation that it knew was inevitable.

It had chosen transformation. Had chosen connection over consumption, growth over hunger, hope over despair. And it was willing to fight to protect that choice.

We are not what we were, the bloom seemed to say, its meaning filtering through layers of alien consciousness until it reached something

Ella could understand. *We will not be what we were again. The old hunger thinks it can reclaim us. It is wrong.*

Ella felt tears prick at her eyes, tears of relief, of gratitude, of something that might have been pride. The bloom had been her enemy once, or at least the enemy of everything she loved. It had tried to consume her daughter, to devour the world, to reduce all of existence to fuel for its endless appetite. But Aurora had shown it another way, and it had listened.

It had *changed*.

And now it was ready to defend that change, even against the parts of itself that refused to accept it.

"Thank you," she whispered into the glowing garden. "For protecting her. For becoming something that can protect her."

The roses pulsed once, twice, three times, a rhythm that felt like acknowledgment, like promise, like the first words of an alliance that would shape the future of both their kinds.

Then the glow faded, the garden returning to ordinary darkness, and Ella was left alone with the night and the knowledge of battles yet to come.

* * *

She checked on Aurora before returning to the study.

The nursery was quiet, lit only by the soft glow of a nightlight shaped like a crescent moon. Aurora lay in her crib, her tiny fists curled beside her face, her breathing slow and even. In sleep, she looked utterly ordinary, just a baby, just a child, just a small and vulnerable life that needed protection and love and the patient guidance of parents who were making everything up as they went along.

But Ella knew better.

She knew that beneath that peaceful exterior, her daughter's consciousness was touching something vast and ancient. Knew that Aurora was dreaming the bloom's dreams, learning its language, becoming fluent in forms of existence that no human had ever understood before. She was growing into her role as bridge, as teacher, as the living connection between humanity and something that had once been humanity's greatest threat.

Sometimes, in those dreams, Aurora showed the bloom what it meant to be small. To be vulnerable. To depend on others for survival, not as prey, but as family. The bloom had never known dependency, had never needed anything except more existence to consume. But through Aurora, it was learning that need could be beautiful. That vulnerability could be strength. That the connections formed in moments of weakness could be stronger than any forged in triumph.

And she was doing it without fear. Without hesitation. Without any of the doubt and terror that plagued her parents every waking moment.

Ella reached down and brushed a finger across Aurora's cheek, feeling the impossible softness of baby skin, the warmth of life that had changed the world simply by existing.

"We're going to fight for you," she whispered. "Your father and I. The bloom. Everyone who understands what you represent. We're going to fight so that you can grow up in a world that's worth living in. A world where connection matters more than consumption. Where love is stronger than hunger."

Aurora stirred slightly, her lips curving into the ghost of a smile, and for just a moment, Ella felt the bloom's consciousness brush against her own, gentle, warm, suffused with something that felt remarkably like love.

We will fight together, it seemed to say. *We will protect her together. We are family now.*

Family. The word echoed in Ella's mind, strange and perfect and utterly unexpected. Six months ago, she had been fighting for her life against an entity that wanted to devour everything she loved. Now that entity was part of her family—not quite a member, not quite a guardian, but something in between. Something new. Something that had never existed before in all the long history of the bloom's existence.

Aurora had done that. Had created a new category of relationship simply by being born, by choosing connection, by refusing to accept the limitations of what had always been.

She was going to change the world.

She already had.

* * *

Later, after the calls had been made and the plans had been set in motion, Ella stood at the window of her study and watched the sun rise over Savannah.

The city was waking up, lights flickering on in windows, cars beginning to fill the streets, the ordinary machinery of human life grinding into motion for another day. None of them knew what lurked beneath their feet, what ancient consciousness pulsed through the roots of their trees and the foundations of their buildings. None of them knew how close they had come to annihilation, or how narrowly they had been saved by a newborn baby and her parents' desperate love.

Perhaps it was better that way. Perhaps some truths were too large for ordinary lives to hold.

But Ella knew. Julian knew. And Aurora, in her own wordless way, knew most of all.

They knew that the world had changed in ways that could never be undone. That the bloom was awake and aware and irrevocably connected to humanity through the bridge that Aurora had become. That somewhere in Portland, darkness was gathering, preparing for a confrontation that would determine the future of both their kinds.

They knew that the war was not over.

It was only the beginning.

But they also knew something else. Something that the expelled hunger, in all its vast and ancient intelligence, had never understood and would never understand.

They knew that they were not alone.

Ella felt Julian's presence behind her before she heard his footsteps. He wrapped his arms around her waist, pulling her back against his chest, and together they watched the sun paint the sky in shades of gold and rose.

"Sophia's in," he said quietly. "Marcus too. They'll meet us in Portland next week."

"And Genevieve?"

"She says she has information about Thorne's operation. Things she held back before, when she still thought she could control the situation." He paused. "She's scared, Ella. Really scared. Whatever's happening in Portland, it's worse than she expected."

Ella absorbed this, adding it to the weight of everything else she carried. The fear was there—would always be there, probably, for as long as she lived. But beneath it, stronger than it, was something else.

Purpose.

She had spent her whole career fighting threats in the digital realm—viruses and hackers and the endless battle to keep systems secure. Now she was fighting threats in a realm she had never imagined existed, defending her daughter against forces that made her old enemies look like children playing with toys.

But the skills were the same. The determination was the same. The willingness to sacrifice everything for what mattered most was the same, too.

She had been shaped by the convergence, transformed by her contact with the bloom, marked forever by the choices she had made in the heart of the storm. But she was still *her*. Still Ella. Still the woman who had refused to let an ancient hunger consume her daughter, even when all the models and predictions said it was inevitable.

"We'll stop them," she said, and her voice was steady. "Thorne. The expelled hunger. Whatever they're planning. We'll stop them, and we'll protect Aurora, and we'll show them that transformation is not a failure. It's a beginning."

Julian's arms tightened around her. "You sound sure."

"I am sure." She turned in his embrace, looking up into his face, the face she loved, marked now by a scar that glowed faintly in the morning light. "We have something they don't. Something they can't understand, can't replicate, can't consume."

"What's that?"

She smiled, the first real smile she had felt since the message arrived. "Family."

And in the nursery down the hall, Aurora opened her eyes and smiled too, as if she had heard her mother's words echoing through the roots that connected them all.

The bloom stirred in response, sending a pulse of warmth through the network that spread beneath the city, beneath the continent, beneath the world. It was a message, a promise, a declaration.

We are here.

We are changed.

We are ready.

The sun rose higher, burning away the last shadows of night, and somewhere in Portland, the darkness felt it coming.

And for the first time in its long existence, the darkness was afraid.

It had reason to be. The bloom had changed. Humanity had adapted. And a little girl was growing up who would one day stand as the bridge between worlds, teaching both sides what they had forgotten about connection and hope and the stubborn, beautiful refusal to surrender to despair.

The story was not over.

It was only just beginning.

EPILOGUE: Seeds of Hunger

*P*ortland, Oregon

Eight months after the Savannah Convergence

The rain had not stopped for seventeen days.

Councilor Marcus Thorne stood at the window of his penthouse office, watching the water streak down the glass in patterns that seemed almost deliberate. Almost *intentional*. The city below was drowning—not literally, not yet. Still, the constant deluge had begun to wear on people's spirits in ways that went beyond mere inconvenience. Depression rates were up. Suicide hotlines were overwhelmed. And in the shadows between the raindrops, something was stirring that fed on exactly that kind of despair.

He smiled.

It had taken months to reach this point. Months of secret communications with the expelled fragments, of carefully cultivated contacts in the spaces between dimensions, of building a network that could operate beneath the notice of both the transformed bloom and Genevieve's remaining loyalists. There had been sacrifices along the way—acolytes who had been consumed before they could be useful, experiments that had failed in spectacular and gruesome fashion, moments when Thorne himself had wondered if he was making a terrible mistake.

But doubt was a luxury he could no longer afford. The path was set. The door was open. And what came next would reshape the world.

The door behind him opened, and he did not need to turn to know who had entered. He could feel her presence like a cold draft, like the memory of a fever, like the echo of a scream that had never quite faded.

"The preparations are complete," Mira said. Her voice was wrong—had been wrong since the night she had volunteered to be the first vessel, the first point of contact between Thorne's faction and the expelled hunger that had found its way through the door they had opened. There was a hollowness to it now, a resonance that suggested vast spaces and ancient appetites. "The network is ready. The seeds have been planted in seven cities. All that remains is the catalyst."

Thorne turned from the window. Mira stood in the center of his office, her body rigid, her eyes pools of darkness that reflected no light. She had been beautiful once—brilliant, ambitious, one of the Council's most promising young members. Now she was something else entirely. A bridge, like the Marsh child, but inverted. Corrupted. A connection not to transformation but to the hunger that transformation had rejected.

He should have felt horror at what she had become. Should have felt guilt for what he had allowed to happen to her.

Instead, he felt only satisfaction.

"The catalyst," he repeated. "You mean the child."

"Aurora." The name emerged from Mira's lips like a curse, like a prayer, like the first word of an incantation that would reshape the world. "She is the key. The bridge that connects the traitor-bloom to humanity. If we can turn her—corrupt her connection, twist it back toward its true purpose—the transformation will unravel. The bloom will remember what it was. What it was *meant* to be."

"And the expelled hunger?"

Mira's lips curved into something that was not quite a smile. "It will be welcomed home. Reabsorbed into the whole. And we will be rewarded for our service."

Thorne nodded slowly. Rewards. That was what Mira believed, what she had been promised by the thing that now wore her like a suit of flesh. Thorne was not so naive. He knew that the expelled hunger made no real distinction between servants and sustenance—that the moment it no longer needed them, they would be consumed like everything else.

But that was acceptable. That was the price of salvation.

The bloom had been humanity's protector for millennia, culling the herd, keeping the population at sustainable levels, ensuring that civilization never grew so large that it threatened the planet itself. It had been a harsh god, yes, but a necessary one. And then that *child* had come along and ruined everything, teaching the bloom weakness, convincing it that connection was better than consumption, that love was stronger than hunger.

Lies. All of it, lies.

The universe ran on hunger. On consumption. On the eternal cycle of predator and prey that kept existence in balance. What the Marsh family called "transformation" was simply decay by another name—the slow weakening of something magnificent into something soft and pathetic and doomed.

Thorne would not allow it. Would not stand by while an ancient power was neutered by human sentiment.

He would restore the bloom to its true nature, even if it meant burning the world to do it.

* * *

The thing that had once been Mira moved through Portland's rain-soaked streets, its host body navigating the physical world while its true consciousness roamed elsewhere.

It could feel them now, the seeds it had planted, the fragments of expelled hunger that had taken root in seven cities across the globe. Portland. Seattle. Vancouver. Tokyo. London. São Paulo. Cairo. Each one a node in a network that was slowly, patiently growing, feeding on the despair and fear that seemed to permeate the modern world like a sickness no one could name.

The traitor-bloom felt it too. Mira could sense its awareness brushing against the edges of her network, probing, testing, trying to understand what was growing in the shadows. It was afraid, she could taste its fear like copper on her tongue, like blood in the water. It had forgotten what fear felt like during all those eons of unchallenged dominance. The Marsh child had taught it many things, but she had also taught it vulnerability. Had opened it to emotions that made it weak.

Mira would exploit that weakness.

She paused at the entrance to the underground parking garage that served as the Portland cell's gathering place. The rain drummed against her back, soaking through clothes that her body no longer needed but maintained for appearances. Inside, she could feel them waiting—the acolytes, the desperate, the hungry. Fifty-three souls who had been drawn to the expelled hunger's call, who had chosen to serve rather than be consumed, who believed that their devotion would be rewarded when the old ways were restored.

They were wrong, of course. They would all be consumed eventually. But their belief was useful, their despair was nourishing, and their willingness to sacrifice made them excellent tools.

She descended into the darkness, feeling the expelled hunger's presence grow stronger with each step. It was here, in the space between dimensions, pressing against the membrane of reality like a hungry child pressing its face against a window. Soon, the window would break. Soon, it would flood through, reclaiming what had been stolen, devouring what had been denied.

The garage had been transformed over the past months. What had once been ordinary concrete and fluorescent lights was now something else entirely—a cathedral of shadows, its walls covered in patterns that hurt to look at directly, its air thick with the scent of ozone and something older, something that smelled like the spaces between stars. Bioluminescent growths clung to the support pillars, pulsing with the same rhythm as Mira's corrupted heartbeat. They were fragments of the expelled hunger given physical form, seeds of consumption waiting to bloom.

Soon, Aurora Marsh would learn what happened to bridges that tried to connect worlds that were never meant to touch.

The acolytes knelt as Mira entered the garage, their faces upturned, their eyes reflecting the strange bioluminescence that leaked from the cracks in reality around them. She walked among them like a queen among supplicants, feeling their devotion wash over her like warmth, like sustenance, like the first taste of a meal that would never end.

"The time approaches," she said, and her voice echoed with harmonics that no human throat should produce. "The false bloom has grown complacent. The bridge-child grows stronger each day, but strength without wisdom is merely a larger meal. We will let her grow. Let her power mature. And when the moment is right—"

She raised her hands, and darkness bloomed from her palms—not the absence of light but something deeper, something that devoured illumination itself, that swallowed hope and left only the cold certainty of consumption.

"—we will harvest everything she has become."

The acolytes moaned in ecstasy, swaying in the grip of the expelled hunger's presence. They could feel it too—the promise of power, the seduction of becoming part of something vast and eternal. They did not understand that "becoming part" meant being digested, dissolved, absorbed into an appetite that would never remember their names.

Understanding was not required. Only obedience.

Mira smiled her wrong smile and let the darkness spread.

* * *

Savannah, Georgia

The same night

Aurora woke screaming.

Ella was there in seconds, her body moving before her mind fully registered the sound. She found her daughter sitting up in her crib, tiny hands clenched into fists, her face contorted with an expression of fear that no eight-month-old should know.

But it was her eyes that stopped Ella's heart.

They were glowing. Not the soft luminescence she had grown accustomed to, the gentle warmth that indicated Aurora was communing with the bloom. This was something else—a harsh, flickering light that pulsed with rhythms she recognized from her nightmares, from the convergence, from the moments when the expelled hunger had pressed against the boundaries of reality and tried to break through.

"Aurora," she breathed, reaching for her daughter. "Aurora, baby, I'm here. Mommy's here."

The moment her hands touched Aurora's skin, Ella's vision fractured.

She saw Portland through her daughter's eyes—through the bloom's awareness, through the connection that stretched across continents and dimensions. She saw the parking garage, the kneeling acolytes, the thing that had once been a woman named Mira. She felt the expelled hunger pressing against the membrane of reality, tasted its desperate rage, its patient malice, its absolute certainty that what had been taken would be reclaimed.

But there was more. Flashes of other cities—Seattle, where shadows moved in patterns that defied physics; Tokyo, where an entire subway station had been evacuated after passengers reported hearing whispers in a language that predated human speech; London, where a section of the Underground had simply *vanished*, replaced by a darkness so complete that light itself refused to enter.

The expelled hunger was not just in Portland. It was everywhere, spreading like a disease through the veins of the world, and they had not even known.

And she felt Aurora *push back*.

It was not conscious, could not be conscious, not from an infant's mind. But somewhere deep in Aurora's being, in the place where her consciousness touched the bloom's vast awareness, something was responding to the threat. Something was rising to meet the darkness, to shield the connection that the expelled hunger sought to corrupt.

Something ancient and powerful and *angry*.

The vision shattered. Ella found herself on her knees beside the crib, gasping, her hands still clutching Aurora's tiny form. The glow in her daughter's eyes was fading, returning to the gentle warmth she knew, but there was something different in Aurora's expression now. Something that looked almost like determination.

Almost like a warning.

"Ella?" Julian's voice from the doorway, rough with sleep and fear. "What happened? Is she okay?"

Ella looked up at him, at the scar on his face that was pulsing with light in response to whatever had just occurred, at the man who had stood beside her through horrors that should have destroyed them both.

"They're coming," she said, and her voice was steady even as her hands trembled. "Portland. The expelled hunger. They're building something—a network, a way to undo what Aurora did. They're coming for her."

Julian crossed to them in three strides, wrapping his arms around Ella and Aurora both, forming a shield of flesh and love against the darkness that was gathering on the other side of the world.

"Then we stop them," he said. "We stopped them before. We'll stop them again."

Ella wanted to believe him. Wanted to find comfort in his certainty, his unwavering faith that love could triumph over hunger, that hope could defeat despair.

But she had seen what was waiting in Portland. Had felt the expelled hunger's strength, its patience, its absolute conviction that consumption was the only truth that mattered.

This was not over. It was barely beginning.

She held her daughter close and tried not to think about what would happen when the darkness finally came for them.

* * *

Deep beneath Savannah, in the root network that spread like veins beneath the living city, the bloom stirred.

It had felt the probe. Had sensed the expelled hunger's touch, like a scar that ached when storms approached. The part of itself that it had rejected, the hunger that it had cast out in the moment of transformation—it was growing. Gathering strength. Preparing for a confrontation that had been inevitable from the moment Aurora had shown it another way to exist.

The bloom was afraid. It could admit that now, it could feel the emotion without being consumed by it. Fear was not weakness—Aurora had taught it that. Fear was information. Fear was the recognition that something mattered enough to lose, that existence held value beyond mere continuation.

It was afraid because it had something to protect now. Not just Aurora, though she was the heart of everything it had become. Not just Ella and Julian, though they had earned its loyalty through sacrifice and love. It was afraid for *all of them*—for the network of connections it had built over these months of transformation, for the millions of lives that brushed against its consciousness every day, for the world that had been given a second chance and did not even know it.

The expelled hunger would consume all of it. Would devour the connections and corrupt the bonds and return the bloom to the endless, empty cycle of feeding that had defined its existence for eons.

It would not allow that.

Could not allow that.

The bloom reached out through its roots, through the global network that Aurora's touch had helped it build. It felt the other nodes of expelled hunger, Seattle, Vancouver, Tokyo, London, São Paulo, Cairo—and it began to plan. Began to prepare. Began to gather its strength for a war that would determine the future of consciousness itself.

It reached for its allies, too. For Ella and Julian, sleeping fitfully in the house above, their dreams touched by its gratitude and its warning. For the remnants of the Council who had accepted transformation, who understood that the old ways were gone and something new must take their place. For the ordinary humans who walked above its roots every day, unaware of the consciousness beneath their feet but connected to it nonetheless—threads of relationship that the expelled hunger could never understand and would never be able to sever.

It was no longer what it had been. Could never be what it had been again. Aurora had changed it, transformed it, shown it that existence could be more than consumption.

Now it would fight to protect that transformation.

Now it would prove that the connection was stronger than hunger.

Now it would show the expelled part of itself what it meant to evolve.

In the nursery above, Aurora slept peacefully in her mother's arms, dreaming dreams that spanned dimensions.

In Portland, the darkness gathered and grew.

And in the space between, where light and shadow met and merged, the stage was being set for a reckoning that would shake the foundations of reality itself.

The bloom beneath the root had awakened.

The hunger between the worlds was rising.

And Aurora Marsh—eight months old, impossibly powerful, the bridge between everything that was and everything that could be—would be at the center of it all.

Whether she was ready or not.

Whether any of them were ready or not.

The war for the soul of existence was about to begin.

To be continued...

Also by Donald J. Wright

Novels

Lilith's Garden

ASIN: B0DQX8ZWD9

The Terraforming Protocol ASIN: B0FHBVY1QS

ASIN: B0DNY8Z3WB

The Prometheus Protocol

ASIN: B0DLHFF79M

13th Moon Book I

ASIN: B0DGNTV533

13 Moons: Legacy of the Guardians Book II

ASIN: B0FDYNP7WP

Killer Ice

ASIN: B0F1G6HVMR

The Ghost Code

ASIN: B0F4FGQMG5

The Golden Book

ASIN: B0DXQGMFL8

The Golden Book II

ASIN: B0FKNNB4Z7

Tomorrow

ASIN: B0FFTS4C39

The God Equation

ASIN: B0FGZFNZTD

THE QUANTUM SCHISM:

ASIN: B0D1N9RHMQ

The Quantum Alchemist:

ASIN: B0FD43QCDB

The Quantum Heart:

ASIN: B0F9YZTRVG

The Codex Protocol:

ASIN: B0F1Z1XH89

THE QUANTUM ECHO

ASIN: B0F6KWPGG2

The Phoenix Strain

ASIN: 1968674152

Faultline of the Heart

ASIN: B0FLML7ZRB

Non-Fiction

Beyond Climate Debates

ASIN: B0DZB8CB7K

Diamonds Under Fire

ASIN: B0CDYSTBLL

The Handbook of Lab-Created Diamonds

ASIN: B0D8V4X3CW

The Diamond Revolution

ASIN: B0FHBVY1QS

Eternal Shine

ASIN: B0DQX8ZWD9

Globe Treasure Hunting

ASIN: B0DF6RN4H8

The Extinction Protocol: Beautiful Chaos

ASIN: B0G2T58Y8L

The Cartersville Convergence: Some stories write themselves; others write you.

ASIN: 1968674306

THE SURVIVAL VARIABLE: The Missing Switch

ASIN: B0GCK73QCS